the BLACK DOVE

ALSO BY STEVE HOCKENSMITH

Holmes on the Range

On the Wrong Track

the BLACK DOVE

STEVE HOCKENSMITH

ST. MARTIN'S MINOTAUR

NEW YORK

This is a work of fiction. All of the characters, organizations, and events portrayed in this novel are either products of the author's imagination or are used fictitiously.

THE BLACK DOVE. Copyright © 2008 by Steve Hockensmith. All rights reserved. Printed in the United States of America. No part of this book may be used or reproduced in any manner whatsoever without written permission except in the case of brief quotations embodied in critical articles or reviews. For information, address St. Martin's Press, 175 Fifth Avenue, New York, N.Y. 10010.

www.minotaurbooks.com

Library of Congress Cataloging-in-Publication Data

Hockensmith, Steve.
The black dove : a Holmes on the range mystery / Steve Hockensmith.—1st ed.
p.   cm.
ISBN-13: 978-0-312-34782-6
ISBN-10: 0-312-34782-0
1. Cowboys—Fiction. 2. Brothers—Fiction. 3. Private investigators—Fiction. 4. Doyle, Arthur Conan, Sir, 1859–1930—Influence—Fiction. 5. Triads (Gangs)—Fiction. 6. San Francisco (Calif.)—Fiction. I. Title.

PS3608.O29 B63   2008
813'.6—dc22

2007039976

First Edition: February 2008

10 9 8 7 6 5 4 3 2 1

FOR MAR, FOREVER

the BLACK DOVE

PRELUDE

Or, Killing Time

I don't know who first said, "Good things come to those who wait." I just hope it's not in the Bible, as blasphemy's hardly the best way to begin a new book. Still, it must be said: Whoever it was, Ben Franklin or Bill Shakespeare or Moses, he was a god damn dolt.

Which puts me and my brother in good company, actually, for we are god damn dolts ourselves.

"Wait here," we'd been told. So there we waited, though surely we'd seen nothing that day that might suggest good things would be coming *our* way anytime soon. Quite the opposite, in fact.

We were, after all, poking our noses into a murder in what some would consider the most sinister section of the world's wickedest city—Chinatown in San Francisco, California. Why, in hindsight, "god damn dolts" doesn't even do it justice. For stupidity such as we were displaying, there are no fit words in the English language, and the best I can do to sum it up is pause here to spit.

"You really think we're gettin' anywhere with all this?" I asked my brother a few minutes after our host hurried from the room, leaving us alone.

"Even if we ain't, we are," Gustav said—and said no more.

And folks call the *Chinese* inscrutable. When my elder brother's got his mind fixed on a mystery, there's just no scruting the man.

Take what he was doing just then as a for instance—scuttling across the floor on all fours. A person not in the know might've assumed he was succumbing either to some kind of conniption or the sudden, inexplicable conviction that he was, in fact, a cat.

Me, I knew better. What Gustav believed himself to be was a detective—one modeled upon *the* detective. And if the late, great Sherlock Holmes would get to wriggling around on rugs whenever he searched a room, why then, my brother just had to go and do the same.

" 'Even if we ain't, we are?' " I said to him. "Sweet Jesus—your answers are harder to figure than most people's questions."

"Look," Gustav growled as he crawled along, his nose so close to the floor it could almost plow a furrow in the plush red carpet, "we didn't have no choice but to come in here and see what could be seen. If it don't pan out, at least we can check it off the list and get to huntin' for clues elsewheres."

"You got a particular 'elsewheres' in mind?"

Gustav picked up a tiny puff of white fluff, sniffed it, then tossed it over his shoulder and got back to eyeballing the floor.

"Nope. But don't you worry. We'll pick us up a new trail soon enough. We done touched a nerve here."

"Oh, well, then—my faith has been restored. If gettin' on people's nerves is all it'll take to crack this case, then indeed the right man is on the job."

My brother scowled at me over his shoulder, but before he could reply in kind, one of the room's two doors swung open, and a pair of Chinamen came striding in. They were dressed identically in loose-fitting black blouses and trousers, with flat-topped, round-brimmed hats upon their heads.

We'd never laid eyes on either fellow before, but we'd seen their like a lot lately: They were highbinders, hired killers working for Chinatown's "fighting tongs."

"You know," I said under my breath, "if this is that new trail you promised, I don't think I care to follow it."

"Me, neither," Gustav said, pushing himself up off his knees.

There was even less to like a moment later, when the room's other door—the one my brother and I were darting toward at the time—flew open, and two more highbinders stepped inside.

Of course, there's another name for such thugs as we were facing, one you've most likely run across in newspaper or magazine stories: "hatchet men." And if you've ever wondered whether Chinatown outlaws are slapped with that handle for the obvious reason, I can provide an authoritative answer for you based on what happened next.

They are.

1

EXPERIENCE

Or, Gustav and I Are Most Definitely *Not* in the Pink

It wasn't just fear I felt as I faced those highbinders and their hatchets. I was almost as surprised as I was petrified. Not that I was about to die, mind you. It was more the manner of it.

An early death was a possibility—perhaps even a probability—of which I'd been acutely aware almost from birth. As a lad on the family farm in Kansas, I figured it was smallpox, starvation, or Sitting Bull that'd get me. After most of my kin were indeed *got* (by a flood, as it came to pass), I took to drovering with my brother Gustav, thus giving myself ample opportunity to meet my maker via stampede, saddle-dragging, bull's horn, or rustler's bullet. On top of which, my brother had me half-convinced my big mouth was going to get me brained in a saloon brawl sooner or later.

So imagine my dismay upon learning I'd end my days being chopped into chow mein in Chinatown. That one I didn't see coming. Though perhaps I should have, given our luck of late.

Our detour into the peculiar began a full year earlier, in June of 1892, when a fellow puncher passed along a magazine story he thought might amuse us: "The Red-Headed League" by Dr. John Watson. The joke being that Gustav and I could be charter members of any such league ourselves, since we each have hair the crimson of cardinal feathers.

But handing us "The Red-Headed League" turned out to be much more than just a jape. It was like giving lil' Chrissy Columbus his first toy boat, or telling Paul Bunyan he's just not working out as a seamstress and shouldn't he consider a line of work more suiting his size?

It was, in other words, the sort of seemingly meaningless gesture that can change lives (and perhaps end them).

You see, Gustav had long been chafing in the saddle, and not just in the way that leaves you walking bowlegged. A finer cowhand than he you could not chance to meet, yet my brother was feeling ever more thwarted nursing other men's cattle for a dollar a day. Life as a cowboy requires much in the way of skill and grit, but your brains you can leave wrapped up in your war bags. And Gustav—he was itching to unpack his and put them to work.

"The Red-Headed League" showed him how, for at its center was a man who made his way in the world not by the sweat of his brow but by the shrewdness of the mind beneath it. Details and data were his stock in trade, and these are free to all . . . who have the keenness of vision to see them clearly.

The man called himself "a consulting detective," and his name, of course, was Sherlock Holmes. He was dead, we later learned—lost to a waterfall under circumstances most mysterious. But in my brother his spirit found itself a new vessel.

An imperfect one, though, as even Gustav would admit. Sharp of eye though he may be, my brother is also utterly void of learning. The only letters he knows are the ones he's seen on brands, and if they're not burned into cowhide, he can't make head nor tail of them. But that hasn't stopped him (and his tag-along baby brother) from pursuing a career in the detectiving trade—though it does partially explain why said pursuit has largely been in vain.

Take our last visit to an actual detective agency, for example.

"Fill these out," a dapper, slender, profoundly bored-looking fellow told us when we walked in and (after a good three minutes being ignored) caught his eye. He opened a desk drawer and produced a pair of forms bearing his employer's seal: the all-seeing eye of the Pinkerton National Detective Agency.

He tossed a couple stubby pencils atop the sheets of paper, then jerked his head at a bare table in a corner at the back of the room.

"Over there."

"Yessir. We'll have 'em back to you in two shakes," I said with a smile.

The Pinkerton just stared at me silently through droopy-lidded eyes. Two shakes or two million, it clearly made no nevermind to him.

"I'll fill one out for you first," I whispered to my brother as we walked past the filing cabinets and mahogany desks that filled the smallish office. "Then we'll trade sheets, and I'll do one for myself."

We sat down and huddled together over the employment forms.

"Make sure the handwritin' don't look the same," Gustav said softly. "Booger one of 'em up a bit. You know—write it out left-handed or upside down or somethin'."

"Yeah, yeah. Sure."

I got to work on my brother's application.

Name: Gustav Dagobert Amlingmeyer

Aliases: "Old Red," "That Little Quiet Feller"

Address: The Cosmopolitan House (Hotel), 511 Eighth Street, Oakland

Telephone exchange/number: I have no earthly idea

Date of birth: October 22, 1866

Place of birth: Marion County, Kansas

Height: Five feet, six inches (I guessed.)

Weight: 125 pounds (I guessed again.)

Hair: Red

Eyes: Blue

Scars, birth marks, disfigurements, or other notable physical features: Bullet hole on right side below rib cage; old rope burns on hands; various and sundry nicks, cuts, and abrasions; freckles on arms and shoulders; an exceptionally thick mustache; an exceptionally hard head

Education: Enough (I lied.)

Previous occupations: Farmhand, cowhand, freelance genius

Law enforcement/private investigation experience: Oh, shit (I *almost* wrote.)

I leaned closer to Old Red, who was hunched over pretending to scribble on the form before him.

"They're askin' if we ever been lawmen before. Should I mention the S.P.?"

The memory of our brief, disastrous tour of duty as agents of the Southern Pacific Railroad Police puckered up Gustav's puss like a big chomping bite of raw lemon.

"Well, hell," he groaned. "It *is* the only time we had real badges pinned to us."

"But we was fired."

"We quit before we was fired."

"Yeah, but a lot of folks died before we quit."

"Most of 'em woulda died whether we'd been there or not," my brother pointed out halfheartedly.

"How 'bout the train that got blowed up, then? It'd still be haulin' folks up and down the Sierras if we'd never stepped aboard. And if the Pinks check on us with the S.P.—and the Pinks bein' the Pinks, they will—then it'll all come out."

"Fine, then. *Don't* mention the S.P. Just say that . . . ."

Gustav screwed up his face again, silent for a moment as he dictated in his head.

"Say we've made a scientific study of the detectin' and deducifyin' methods of Mr. Sherlock Holmes."

"Got it."

I looked back down at the line about experience.

None, I wrote.

Old Red was watching me, though, so I added a few more words for appearance's sake.

But we're young and eager to learn—and cheap, to boot.

"Alrighty," I said. "Let's trade."

We swapped sheets fast, Gustav hacking out a phony little cough to cover the sound of rustling paper. He needn't have bothered—no one was paying us any mind. The slick-looking Pinkerton was filling out paperwork of his own, while the only other person in the room—a prim, pretty office girl who had so far evaded my every attempt at eye contact—was clacking away on one of those ear-pummeling "type-writing" contraptions.

I licked the tip of my pencil and got back to work.

Name: Otto Albert Amlingmeyer

Aliases: "Big Red" (frequently used by friends and colleagues), "You Handsome Devil You" (frequently used by female acquaintances)

Address: The Cosmopolitan House, Eighth Street, Oakland

Telephone exchange/number: If the Cosmopolitan House has a telephone, it's used about as often thereabouts as a broom, feather duster, or mop—which is to say never.

Date of birth: June 4, 1872

Place of birth: The kitchen table

Height: Six feet, one inch

Weight: 200 pounds, more or less (It was actually *more* at the time—city living does tend to soften a man.)

Hair: Red

Eyes: Blue

Scars, birth marks, disfigurements, or other notable physical features: Damned ugly knees and elbows (from being dragged halfway across Texas by a roped steer); bite marks on foot (from finding a Gila monster in my boot the hard way); Cross J brand on right buttocks (it's a long story)

Education: Six years of formal schooling; a lifetime of informal schooling via newspapers, magazines, books, open ears, open eyes, and an open mind

Previous occupations: Farmboy, granary clerk, cowboy, drifter, yarnspinner

Law enforcement/private investigation experience: I am pleased to report that I remain unmolded clay, unmarred by the fumbling fingers of employment with government authorities or private parties unequal to the exacting standards of the Pinkerton National Detective Agency.

"There," I said, jabbing down the final period. "Done."

Old Red glanced back at the thin Pink, who was listening listlessly to a pair of mumbly men who'd just wandered into the office. "You think we got much of a chance?"

"Sure. That feller wouldn't have asked us to fill out these forms if—"

The Pinkerton opened his desk drawer and pulled out two more applications.

"Fill these out." He jerked his head at the table we were using. "Over there."

"Well, anyway," I muttered. "I'll do my best to sweet-talk him."

We passed our competition on the way to the front of the office. They were of a type we'd seen often since arriving in the San Francisco area a month before: men with shuffling gaits and downcast gazes wearing well-tailored suits that seemed a size too large. The Panic (as the newspapers had taken to calling the latest wave of bank runs) had dumped hundreds of such unfortunates on the streets in recent weeks, and it was remarkable and sad to see how quickly a proud, prosperous businessman could shrivel into a desperate, hungry beggarman.

Still, I couldn't feel too awfully bad for most of them. At least they'd had heights from which to fall. Gustav and I were pretty much born at rock bottom and had somehow managed to sink even lower from there. Now we had nowhere to go but up—or so I hoped.

"Here you are, sir—our 'cur-icky-cullum vetoes,'" I said to the Pinkerton, sliding our applications onto his desk. "I'd just ask you to keep in mind as you look 'em over that me and my brother are men of experience, men of the world. *Men,* to boil it down to its essence. And while the, shall we say, *unconventional* credentials of *men* such as ourselves might be hard to quantify on paper, they have imparted to us the very qualities that Mr. Allan Pinkerton himself would have sought when recruiting—"

"Well, well. Brothers, huh?" the Pink cut in, looking up from the forms to give us each a quick, up-and-down once-over.

We hardly made a matching pair, aside from our scarlet hair. Not only do I have a few inches and more than a few pounds on my brother, I'd citified my look over the last weeks, swapping out my work denims and boots for a secondhand suit and patent leather shoes. I'd even gone so far as to buy myself a bowler. But Old Red had no interest in slicking himself up, and he still dressed as if we might be ordered to hop atop a horse and round up strays any minute.

"Yessir—brothers," I said. "Though I reckon nobody'd mistake us for *twins* . . . thank God."

Gustav rolled his eyes.

"No, twins you're not," the Pinkerton replied, his lips so pursed they bent his feathery little mustache into a gray V. "Funny thing, though. Your *handwriting's* absolutely identical."

My brother shot me a glare hot enough to pop corn by.

"Ho ho—you *are* a detective, ain't you!" I said to the Pink. "You see, we've got ol' Mrs. Wiegand to thank for that. She was our schoolteacher back in Kansas. How that woman fussed about penmanship! Made us write the same sentence over and over till the letters looked exactly—"

"And no experience, huh?" the Pinkerton said, looking back down at the papers on his desk.

"Not of the kind y'all were askin' about on them forms. But experienc*es*, we've had aplenty. Rough and tumble stuff. Just the kind of thing that prepares a man for work as a—"

The Pink started shaking his head, and he didn't stop till I'd stopped talking.

"Forget it," he said. "We can't use you."

"Hold on, now—don't be hasty, mister," I protested. I had only one card left up my sleeve, and I figured it was about as much use as a joker . . . when you're playing dominoes. But I played it anyway. "We might not have on-the-job type detective trainin', but that don't mean we ain't got no know-how. Why, for the last year, we been makin' us a scientific study of the cases of Mr. Sherlock—"

I was silenced by a mighty thud—the sound of the Pinkerton picking up his wastepaper basket and whacking it down on his desk. It was already overflowing with identical sheets of crumpled paper.

"This is *one day's* worth of applications," the Pink said.

He picked up our forms . . . and placed them on the top of the pile.

"Well, dammit," I snapped. "If y'all ain't hirin', why didn't ya just say so in the first place?"

The prim'n'proper office girl finally turned away from her typewriting, but the look she gave me wasn't the come-hither kind I'd hoped for earlier—it was more of the get-the-hell-out-of-here variety.

Her boss-man's gaze went even icier than hers. Slight and spruce though the Pinkerton was, I sensed that he'd had plenty of rough-and-tumble experiences himself—that, in fact, he'd probably done more of the roughing and not so much of the tumbling.

He straightened his back and placed his bony hands side by side on his desk.

"Who says we're not hiring?"

He left the rest unsaid.

We're just not hiring the likes of you.

Ever.

2

THE DUMPS

Or, Gustav Chooses to Wallow in Misery Rather Than Solve a Mystery

You know, mister, I happen to agree with you," I said, holding the Pinkerton's hard gaze. "Not only ain't we experienced enough to be Pinks, we obviously ain't *jackass* enough, neither."

The detective pushed back his chair, the look on his long, narrow face saying, *You* really *don't want to make me stand up.*

Old Red and I turned and sauntered away, both of us trying to salvage some small measure of dignity with stiff spines and slow, even steps.

The Pinkerton office was on the third floor of a moderny "flatiron"-type office building—a huge triangle with an open space in the middle that ran from the lobby all the way to the roof. It had the acoustics of an opera hall, with every sniffle, sneeze, footstep, and fart echoing through the place like thunder. So I waited till we were well on our way down the stairs to give quiet voice to my true take on things.

"Well, that was a real boot-toe to the balls, wasn't it?"

"It sure as hell wasn't a pat on the back," Gustav said.

"So now what? We want another shot at the Pinks, we'll have to hop a train down to Los Angeles. Or a ship up to Portland or Seattle, maybe."

My brother frowned and shook his head. He distrusts any conveyance that isn't hitched to at least one horse, and the mere sight of a man on roller skates is enough to make him ill at ease. Trains make him just plain ill. As do boats, we'd recently discovered during our first (and messiest) ferry ride over from Oakland.

"Naw," he said. "We ain't got money for tickets, anyhow. Hell, a couple more trips across the Bay, and we're pretty much busted."

"Well, this is a big town, right? There's other detective outfits around. We'll just try our luck with the small-fry."

" 'Try our luck with the small-fry'?" Gustav looked over at me like I'd suggested we flap our arms and fly to the moon. "Brother, let me ask you—*what* luck?"

He had a point. Lady Luck never has smiled much on us Amlingmeyers. In fact, she's always been a lot more liable to frown—so much so that my brother and I are the only two of our clan left among the living.

Still, I wasn't about to let "Lady" Luck have the last laugh . . . the bitch.

"Screw luck, then," I said as we stepped outside into the hustle and bustle (and hustling bustles) of Market Street. "Who needs luck when you got brains and guts?"

Old Red gave me another skeptical look. "Who says you've got—?"

"Tut tut, Brother. I've got brains enough to know where you're headed with *that,* so don't bother. Now just follow me, and I'll show you how to take a slap in the face and keep on smilin'."

And off I went down Market toward Fourth Street—and the offices of the Southern Pacific Railroad.

Though S.P.H.Q. was a dozen blocks off, a streetcar ride was out of the question, given Gustav's feelings about locomoting on anything other than horseback. I didn't mind the walk, though. Fact is, I loved it—loved striding past gaudy shop windows and barking street vendors, loved being jostled by fast-strutting dudes wearing flowery waistcoats and silver stickpins, loved tipping my hat to a never-ending stream of girls in skirts so daringly high-hemmed you could not only see their dainty feet but even a hint of ankle.

In short, I loved the city—almost as much as my brother hated it. Give Gustav solitude, silence, and a saddle under his ass, and he's . . . well, not happy, but at ease, at least. Swap those things for crowds, noise, and a paved sidewalk beneath his boots, however, and the man gets to scowling so fierce even the burly, blue-coated policemen hop to clear from his path, and babies in buggies burst into tears as he stomps by.

And he didn't look any happier when we reached Southern Pacific headquarters. During our fleeting period of employment with the railroad, my brother and I were beaten, shot at, hurled more than once from moving train cars and witness to (and unintentionally party to) the fiery destruction of an S.P. engine. All in all, one of the more memorable weekends of my life.

Yet, though our railroad police badges had been snatched back weeks ago, I still had reason to drag Old Red by the Southern Pacific's digs on Fourth from time to time. Two reasons, actually: one business, one pleasure. Neither of which was awaiting us there that day.

"Can I help you, gentlemen?" asked a bony, blonde office girl as my brother and I walked in. She moved over to the gated railing that separated railroad employees from the great unwashed, dropping her voice as I stepped up close. "It's been a week, Otto. Where have you been?"

"Why, didn't you notice our tans, Gladys?" I replied. "We just got off the boat from Tahiti not half an hour ago. Of course, we had to run over to see you first thing. Old Red here, he said those island gals was the prettiest on earth, but I knew how to prove him wrong right quick."

Gladys stifled a grin. Gustav (not entirely successfully) stifled a groan.

"Well, just in case you're wondering, there's still no package for you from New York," the girl said softly. She picked up a brochure for an S.P. special and pretended to entice me with it as one of her coworkers strolled by behind her. "And still no sign of any 'Diana Corvus,' either."

"Thank you, but like I said—we ain't here for none of that." I turned to my brother. "Now admit it, would you? We didn't spy a prettier lass than Gladys in all the South Seas."

"Yeah, right," Old Red mumbled, his gaze drifting down to his toes. The only flirting I've ever seen him do is with death (which he fears considerably less than females), and when I get to pitching woo he usually gets the itch to leave. "If you'll pardon me, miss . . . I feel the need to take the air."

And he shuffled off toward the door.

I didn't make him wait outside long. Between Gustav's cowboy getup and my size (not to mention the flaming red hair we share), we're hardly what you'd call "inconspicuous." I'd been plying Gladys with sweet nothings for more than a month now, and it was only a matter of time before some eagle-eyed supervisor noticed how often we consulted with her on timetables and fares—without ever buying a ticket. Much as I enjoy a good dilly-dally with a like-minded lady, I couldn't risk getting Gladys in trouble.

Not because I'm such an admirably chivalrous gentleman, alas. I just needed a friend inside the Southern Pacific.

For one thing, I'd have mail coming there sooner or later. Just as Gustav had set his sights on Holmesifying, I'd taken to Watsonization, and a book I'd written about our adventures had been sent to *Harper's Weekly* in New York City—with S.P.H.Q. as the return address.

And for another thing, I already *had* a friend in the Southern Pacific. Only she'd disappeared weeks ago, leaving nothing behind her but a hole in my heart no mere Gladys could hope to fill.

"Face it, Brother—you ain't never gonna find Diana Corvus," Old Red said as we trudged back toward Market. "There ain't no such person."

"Well, for someone who don't exist, she sure makes a powerful impression on a man."

I grinned dreamily, reveling for a moment in my memory of the lady. She was a railroad detective, as we'd oh-so-briefly been, but what's more she was a beautiful, smart, funny, beautiful, brave, beautiful, *beautiful* railroad detective. And she was pretty, too. And she didn't just put up with me and my brother—she actually seemed to like us. Which was deeply gratifying for, as I might have neglected to mention, she was rather attractive.

Making her acquaintance had been one of the few good things to come out of our time with the S.P., and I was determined to acquaint myself with her—and her with me—much more. Unfortunately, according to Gladys, there was no Diana Corvus on the S.P. payroll . . . nor had there ever been, my (fond) memories to the contrary notwithstanding.

"You know what I mean," Gustav growled at me. "You may as well be lookin' for Doris McBogus or Delores O'Flimflam or some such."

"Hey, we don't *know* 'Diana Corvus' ain't her real name. I mean, come on. She's a spotter. A spy. She keeps her eye on S.P. employees, not vicie versie. What's the railroad gonna do? Put her name on the sign over the door? Hell, no. The lady works on the Q.T. Us not findin' her just means she's good at her job."

"Good at lyin's what she is."

"She prefers the term 'persuadin',' remember?"

A stream of screaming, weaving schoolboys came careening between us, apparently intent on crashing into as many pedestrians' posteriors as they could on their way to whatever mischief they had planned. Their cheerful roughhousing put another grin on my face, but Old Red looked like he was set to grab for the hickory switch—especially after one of the boys glanced back at him and shouted, "Excuse me, Mr. Hickok!"

"Of course," I said once the thundering herd had passed, "good as the lady may be at hidin' her tracks, I still say you could pick up her trail. If you really wanted to."

"And why *would* I want to?" Gustav shot back.

Oddly enough for a fellow who tended to treat women like quicksand—something to give a wide berth lest you be sucked in and swallowed whole—he'd taken it even harder than me when the lady up and vanished after our little misadventure together. I would say he'd been down in the dumps ever since, but that might suggest that my brother spent time anywhere else. Even on his best days, he's as morose a man as you'll ever see still breathing.

So whatever's down *beneath* the dumps—that's where Old Red had been ever since we'd lost our brass stars and parted with Diana.

"Well, I'll give you one good reason to find her," I told him.

"Yeah?"

"Yeah. Practice. Findin' a needle in a haystack ain't nothin' to you . . . on the range. You know farms, ranches, trails, cattle towns, and such better than anybody. But could you find that needle *here*—in a city? Hell, could you find the damn needle factory if someone gave you the address and pointed you in the right direction? I ain't so sure. It's somethin' to think about, you really wanna detect professional-like."

"I *been* thinkin' about it," Gustav grumbled.

"And?"

"And . . . ." My brother looked away and sighed. "You might just have you a point."

"Well, thank you for concedin' that it's possible, at least."

Old Red plowed on as if I hadn't spoken.

"True, I don't know squat about city things. But I do know The Man's method. And I been wonderin' if that's enough."

Now, I reckon you've read far enough to know who "The Man" was without me telling you. You could put a lot of fancy names to his "method"—and I reckon he and Dr. Watson did just that. But it really boils down to plain old looking and thinking, both of which Gustav can do with the best of them.

Where the best of them would best *him*, though, would be in the *knowing*.

"Detectin' don't mean nothin' if you got no idea what you're even lookin' at," I said. "You can read a footprint, a snapped twig, or a pile of horseshit like a book, but would you know a pawn ticket if you saw one? Or an e-lectric generator? Or a . . . I don't know. Any of a thousand things. A million."

I nodded toward Fourth Street and the telephone wires, streetlamps, awnings, and office buildings that lined it. The sidewalks were aswirl with humanity in all its diversity, with high-born and low-brow, native son and fresh-off-the-boat walking side by side—and all of them moving so fast as to make Old Red and myself seem to be standing still.

"Just look around. This here's a big town. We may've bounced around a bit, you and me, but our world . . . it's always stayed so *small*. You gotta broaden it up some. You gotta learn."

Old Red squinted at me skeptically. "I gotta 'practice.'"

"Exactly."

The squint turned into an eye-roll.

"Look," I said, "you don't wanna listen to me, fine. Put it to the test, then."

"How do you mean?"

"I mean let's set you to deducifyin'. Pick out a stranger, say, and see what you can Holmes out of him on sight. Then we talk to the feller and find out how close you got. You peg him dead-on, fine. The Man's method's all you need. You booger it up, though, you gotta set yourself to learnin' city-style detectin'."

"By trackin' down Diana Corvus, I suppose."

"Why, what a capital notion!" I exclaimed. "That'd be just the thing."

"So, it's a wager you're after."

"No. I'm suggestin' a *test*."

"No. You're *anglin'* for a *bet*. Except you ain't even puttin' anything up on your end."

I shrugged. "What do you want from me?"

"How 'bout a promise to shut up about Diana Corvus once and for all?"

I stopped walking and held out my hand. "Done."

Old Red stopped, too—stopped *still,* making no move to take my hand. We stood there a moment eyeing each other as irritated passersby pushed by us on both sides like crick water flowing around a rock.

"Who picks the feller?" Gustav finally asked.

"Tell you what, Brother—I'll give you the advantage. I pick the street, then you get to pick your man. Anyone who passes by in the span of . . . oh, let's say a minute, is fair game. You tell me what he does for a livin', maybe three or four other things that strike you, and if you're right on all counts, you win."

Old Red gave me the kind of look you'd give a man offering to shake your hand after stepping from a particularly odiferous outhouse—but he didn't say no.

I'd recently tried to buck my brother up a bit with a gift: a beat-up copy of *The Adventures of Sherlock Holmes* I'd spotted in a book peddler's stall. We were already halfway into our third read-through, and Gustav's brain was abrimming with new nuggets of The Man's wisdom. An opportunity to put them to use would be difficult indeed to resist.

That's the way I had it figured, anyway—and for once, I figured right.

"Done," Old Red said.

Our shake didn't last long—we'd only just clasped hands when a quick-stepping swell in a checked suit and a flat-topped boater came barreling between us. But it was enough. The deal was sealed.

"I don't like the looks of that," Old Red said of the grin that snaked across my face.

"Come on."

I led us up to Market and, from there, north up Dupont.

"You're walkin' like you had a particular street in mind all along," Old Red said sourly.

"Not really," I replied. And I wasn't lying . . . much.

It wasn't a street I'd been thinking of. It was a *neighborhood*—one my brother and I had passed through just once before, during an earlier visit to the city.

Gustav smelled it before he saw it. Four blocks south, and already you could catch a whiff of burning punk and hot braziers, strange spices and the rot of poverty.

"Shit," Old Red sighed. "I shoulda guessed."

"You know," I told him, "you really shoulda."

A few minutes later, we reached Chinatown.

3

THE WILD, WILD EAST

Or, My Little Trick Blows Up in My Face . . . Literally

There was no sign to welcome us to Chinatown—not in English, anyway. But there was a welcoming committee of sorts directly across the street.

A white fellow wearing sandwich boards was distributing leaflets and spittle-spewing ravings to any and all passersby whose skin color matched his own. The board across his chest read PROTECT THE WHITE WORKING MAN—CHINESE OUT OF CALIFORNIA!!!

"Remember: If you're going into Chinatown, keep your cash in your pockets!" he barked at my brother and me as we tried to scoot around him. "Every dollar you give a Chink's a dollar you're taking away from a real American!"

"*Was?*" I said, using the thick German accent all my siblings had perfected imitating our dear old *Mutter* and *Vater* back on the family farm in Kansas. "*Schade. Ich spreche kein Englisch.*"

To my surprise, the man just grinned and pressed one of his pamphlets into my hands.

"Have someone translate this for you, friend," he said. "Kraut, Mick, Polack, or Frog—it doesn't matter. Us whites gotta stick together."

"*Danke, Herr Scheisskerl!*" I said, smiling back. "*Ich werde meinen Arsch damit bei der ersten Gelegenheit wischen.*"

The sandwich man waved me a friendly farewell—unaware, of course, that I'd just promised to make use of his little leaflet the next time I took seat in a privy.

"That just more of the same?" Gustav asked, pointing at the pamphlet.

I looked down and read out the title. "'The Yellow Threat, How the Slant-Eyed Hordes Are Destroying America, by the Anti-Coolie League of—'"

"Yeah, yeah," my brother cut me off. "More of the same."

I left the leaflet where our *Mutter* taught us all such hateful things belong: in the gutter. Then Old Red and I crossed Sacramento Street, and it wasn't just the sandwich-man's twaddle we were leaving behind us. It was San Francisco.

With the crossing of a single street, we seemed to have stepped over the entirety of the Pacific Ocean. Mere seconds before, we might have been in the good old U. S. of A. But for all intents and purposes, we were in China now.

Colorful paper lanterns hung from every balcony like enormous, over-ripe fruit. Every other available space was covered with signs and posters, all of them adorned with the blocky, tic-tac-toe calligraphy of the Celestial Empire. The buildings fell into two camps: squat and dingy or tall-peaked and abristle with bright, elaborately curlicued woodwork.

As for the *people,* there was one camp and one camp only. The narrow streets were packed solid with Chinese men in black hats or skullcaps, loose-fitting tunics, and baggy trousers.

And it wasn't just white folks who were scarce. There were hardly any women or kids, either. When we did happen to pass females venturing out of doors, many of the men ogled them openly, even hungrily—particularly if they were pretty and wrapped in vivid silks, as some were.

Gustav and I won our fair share of stares, too, for I was leading us as deep into Chinatown as I could, and it was unlikely the residents there-abouts had many visits from Stetson-bedecked cowpokes like my brother. Heads turned as we went striding past, and shopkeepers lingered in their doorways to gape at us. The few how-do nods I attempted went unacknowledged, though, and only one man bothered speaking to us: When I finally settled on a spot that seemed sufficiently seedy for our deducifying "practice," a surly looking cabbage peddler pushed his cart away muttering something that sounded like "fink why." Whatever it meant, I assumed it wasn't "Make yourselves right at home."

"Alright—here we are," I said, throwing my arms open wide. "Pick your man and let the Sherlockery commence."

Old Red pointed at the cabbage man as he plodded away. "I could tell you what *he* does for a livin' easy enough."

"I suppose so. But what else could you come up with? Betcha ol' Holmes could tell us his age, weight, height, religion, hat size, favorite color, and the last time he trimmed his toe-nails. What do *you* see? Is he married? Does he have children? Does he smoke cigars? Gamble? Pick his nose in bed? What did he have for breakfast? Who irons his underwear? *Is* his underwear ironed? Hell, does he even *wear* underwear? Tell me something. *Anything.*"

"Now just hold on!" Gustav snapped. "I ain't picked that feller for sure. I still got me a minute to choose, don't I?"

"More like thirty seconds, now," I started to say.

I stopped myself, though. I was starting to feel a mite guilty about how sky-high I'd stacked the deck. Yes, I'd meant to befuddle my brother. How could he possibly make head, tail, or anything in between from what he'd see in Chinatown? But I wasn't out to make him feel like a fool. I just wanted to give him a little giddyup—and point him toward Diana Corvus.

"Take *two* minutes," I said.

"That's mighty goddamned generous of you."

Old Red stalked away a few paces, moving his gaze slowly from one end of the block to the other.

The street was paved with cobblestones, as in the rest of the city, but the sidewalks were mere wooden planks—and rotting ones, at that. And that wasn't all that was rotten, for there was garbage and grime everywhere.

The businesses along the block weren't nearly as gawdy-exotic as the fruit stands, butcher shops, restaurants, and stationers lining Dupont and the other big thoroughfares. Here the stores were dingy and dank-looking, and the main stock-in-trade seemed to be shadows and dust.

Most of the men in sight seemed worn out and gray, as well—not to mention utterly unreadable. A smile or a frown or a raised middle finger I know how to interpret. But all we were getting were long, blank-faced looks, neither friendly nor hostile.

Only one fellow out of the bunch could I draw a bead on at all: the cabbage man. There's nothing particularly mysterious about disgust. The peddler quickly disappeared, though, wheeling his cart around the nearest corner.

Old Red's most promising subject was gone, and he knew it.

I could see my brother's growing frustration in his clenched fists, the tense, pinched set of his shoulders, the herky-jerky way he swung his stare from one doorway to the next in search of a man he could study. A man he could *know*.

"God damn," he spat.

Time was running out. His minutes had turned into seconds.

Then he snapped to his full height and said it again: "God *damn*!"

But the words sounded different this time. Not just louder. Brighter. Almost gleeful.

"That feller. There."

Old Red pointed across the street at a man who'd stepped from one of the grungy little stores just a moment before. He was a smallish fellow, but that was about all I could tell, for he turned and scurried away before I could see his face. He was clearly dressed American-style, though, in a dark suit and spats—and with no queue hanging down his back.

Now, a Chinaman without his ponytail's about as common as a horse without hooves, a fish without fins, or a banker with a heart. So it looked like Gustav had found himself a white man. And lickety-split he was Holmesing him up.

"He's a doctor," he said, starting across the street in pursuit. "Respected in his community, well off—until recently. He's had him a run of bad luck that put him in a bind money-wise. Got himself knocked around, too. Bodily, I mean. But he's pickin' himself up again. He might not look like it, but he's one tough little bird."

We reached the other side of the street side by side and began hustling up the rickety sidewalk.

"Alright, I'm impressed—assumin' it ain't pure bullshit," I said. "Now you wanna tell me how you deduced all that?"

"No deducifyin' necessary," Old Red said, and he shot me a cocked eyebrow that was, for him, the same as a cocky grin. "We know him. That's Dr. Gee Woo Chan."

I gaped at my brother. "Doc Chan? From the Pacific Express? It couldn't be."

But it could, I saw when I looked again at the man we were chasing.

He seemed stockier around the shoulders and thicker around the middle than the polished, polite Chinaman we'd met during our one and only train run as Southern Pacific police. The height was right, though, as was the hair: Chan was the only Chinaman I'd ever seen who didn't wear a queue. The man was even limping slightly, and the last we'd heard of Dr. Chan, he'd been bashed over the head and tossed off the express we were supposed to be protecting.

"Well, hell's bells. I do believe it *is* him." I picked up my pace to a near sprint. "Hey, Doc! Stop! *Doc!*"

The fellow didn't even turn around to look at me, and I started thinking Old Red was wrong after all. I kept after the man, though, already savoring the vexation I'd see on my brother's face when "Dr. Chan" turned out to be Dr. O'Grady the dentist or Mr. Stein the encyclopedia salesman.

"Doc? Is that you? Yoo-hoo!"

I was almost close enough to reach out and touch the man now, and he finally stopped and started to turn toward me.

" 'Scuse me, sir," I said. "I was wonderin'—"

I didn't finish my sentence for two reasons.

First off, it *was* Dr. Chan.

And second, I was interrupted—by the derringer in his hand and the blast of gunfire in my face.

4

FEAST AND FAMINE

Or, Chan Tries to Make Amends and Avoid Explanations

*F*ortunately, it was only the literal gun*fire* I felt on my face—the sting of scorched powder in my eyes and a flash of heat upon my forehead. The *bullet* pierced not flesh but felt, tearing through the crown of my bowler and whipping the hat right off my head.

"Shit, Doc!" I shrieked, instinctively crouching down and throwing up my hands. "It ain't our fault you got throwed off that train!"

Chan's eyes bulged behind his round-wired spectacles.

"Big Red?"

Then he looked down, goggling at his smoking derringer as if he had no earthly idea how it came to be in his hand.

He dropped the gun to the sidewalk as my brother came dashing up to join us.

"Old Red?" Chan said. "I . . . I'm so sorry."

"Hey, don't apologize to *him*," I said as I stood up straight again. "I'm the one who almost got his melon drilled."

Gustav swept off his Stetson and started beating me over the head with it.

"What the hell?" I snatched the hat out of his hands. "Why are *you* goin' at me now?"

Old Red pointed at the top of my head. "Your hair's still smokin'."

"Sweet Jesus!"

I slapped my brother's Boss of the Plains over my ears and pulled it down so tight the brim covered my eyes. After a moment, I lifted it back up again.

"Am I out?"

"You're out," Gustav said, grabbing his hat back.

I ran my fingers gingerly through my hair. The clump just over my face felt bristly and warm to the touch, and the skin over my eyes had a tingle that was slowly giving way to an unpleasant throb.

"Now I know how a match feels."

"I'm so sorry," Chan said again, apologizing to the right Amlingmeyer this time.

"Oh, don't worry 'bout it, Doc," I said. "I guess I just have that effect on some people."

"It was an accident, really. I . . ."

Chan spun around and rushed back toward the store we'd seen him leave a minute before—a small, jumble-stuffed affair with Chinese lettering over the door and what looked like a giant, hairy carrot hanging in the window.

"Wait here! Please!" he called over his shoulder.

He pulled out a set of keys, unlocked the door to the shop, and disappeared inside.

"I sure hope he ain't goin' back for a shotgun," I said.

Old Red ambled over to the gutter and retrieved my hat. "Don't worry. He's such a sorry shot, I don't think he could hit you with a *cannon.*"

He handed me the battered bowler. It had landed top-down in an pile of brownish filth, and a few stringy strands of what looked like rotting jerky still clung to the crown.

"I have been havin' the damnedest luck with my lids lately." I brushed the hat off and pushed a pair of fingers through its fresh, ragged holes. "Had two shot off my head in as many months. Maybe I oughta make like Johnny Appleseed and take to wearin' a tin pot."

"Couldn't look any dumber on you than that derby did."

"Awww, you're just old-fashioned."

Off behind my brother, I noticed several merchants still staring at us from in front of their stores.

"Don't rush over to help me all at once, now!" I called to them. "You'll step on each other's toes!"

I turned the other way and found more of the same: shopkeepers and their customers watching us warily, making no move to lend a hand or take to their heels, either one.

I held up the bowler.

"Any of y'all wanna buy a hat?"

I got no takers—or any reaction of any kind, for that matter. Just more stares.

"Quite an assortment of humanitarians they got around here."

"They're used to mindin' their own business, that's all," Gustav said. He knelt down and picked up Chan's discarded derringer. "Ain't that different from some of the cow-towns we been through."

"I suppose . . . only wouldn't the local law have come around by now to see what's what?" I took another look up and down the street and saw nothing but Chinamen, and not a one of them in blue. "I know Frisco's supposed to be a wide-open town, but I wouldn't think you could fire off a gun without bringin' at least *one* copper a-runnin'."

My brother shrugged. "Maybe the po-lease don't hear so good if the shot's comin' from Chinatown."

Chan came bustling out of his shop, a small, silver tin clutched in his hands.

"Here you go, Big Red." He thrust the tin out toward me. "A medicinal balm. It should keep the skin from peeling."

"Skin? Peelin'?" I touched my forehead lightly, my fingertips barely brushing against flesh. The sting was strong enough to make me wince. "Damn. Did my scalp get all scorchy?"

"Well, I don't know if it's 'scorchy,'" Chan said miserably, still holding out his "balm." "But you do have a little . . . *color* up there."

"Looks like someone tried to iron out your skull," Old Red said.

"Oh, that is just dandy."

I eyed Chan's tin suspiciously. In its center was a dollop of waxy, green paste. It looked like tallow mixed with mashed peas.

"You say that'll help it heal up?"

"Oh, yes." Chan scooped out some of the salve and stretched his goop-covered fingers up toward my face. "Please. Allow me."

I let him smear the stuff over my forehead. Almost instantly, the stinging faded. There was a price to pay, though.

"Good god, Doc," I said, giving the air a sour sniff. "What's in that stuff, anyway?"

"Herbs. Ground roots." Chan stepped back and inspected his handiwork—which gave him an excuse not to look me in the eye. "This and that."

"Well, the 'this' stinks and the 'that' reeks." I jammed my ruined derby down over my head. It chafed against my burn, but I was alright with some discomfort if it would stifle the stench. "How do I look?"

"Fine," said Chan.

"Ridiculous," said Gustav.

I sighed.

"Truly . . . I am so very sorry," Chan said.

I waved a hand dismissively. "Oh, it was an accident. No need for more apologies."

"It'd be good to hear a *reason*, though," Old Red said.

For the first time, Chan seemed to be aware that we had an audience. His gaze darted up and down the street, at the other Chinamen out gawping at us like kids watching a circus parade.

"Yes. Certainly. Perhaps we could discuss it over a meal. I was just heading out for lunch, and I'd be honored if you'd join me. As my guests, of course. To make up for what happened."

"Alright," Gustav said with a nod. "Thank you."

"Yeah, sounds good, Doc," I threw in. "Why, if it'll get us a free meal, you can take a potshot at me any time."

Chan smiled weakly and headed back to close up his shop again. I caught a little glimpse of the inside, and it sure didn't seem like any doctor's office I'd ever seen. Bins and baskets lined the walls, all of them full of what appeared to be nuts, berries, and roots. Given that Chan called himself a doctor, I assumed it was a pharmacy . . . though one that looked like it was run by and for squirrels.

When Chan was done locking the door, he led us around the corner to a quiet, dimly lit restaurant—and one of the finest meals I've ever had.

Now, Chinese cooking was nothing new to me and my brother. Every city of any size in the West has its share of chop suey shacks, and Old Red and I track them down whenever we can, for Chinese food sports twin virtues men of our means can ill afford to ignore: It's hot and it's cheap.

But the eatery Chan took us to was a far cry from the drafty lean-tos we'd come to expect when sniffing out our next plate of chicken chow mein. It was clean, for one thing. And fancy, too—brightly colored tapestries hung from the walls, and every last bit of woodwork was festooned with ornate swirls and curlicues. The other customers were a prosperous lot, by the look of them—plump, chatty, and cheerful. A few were even dressed American-style, like Chan.

All stared openly as we took our seats.

Chan did the ordering in his mother tongue, talking to the waiter so long he may as well have saved himself the bother and just said, "One of everything, please." And indeed that's what it looked we were getting when the food started showing up. We were served soup, rice, dumplings, buns, and such a bewildering array of vegetables and meats I quickly lost track of what was what.

Chan whipped up quite the wind as the plates came and went, rattling on about how this or that dish had been prepared, which ingredients were local and which imported, the proper way to hold the "chopsticks" the Chinese did their eating with, and the special healing properties of a good cup of hot tea. Everything, it seemed, except why he'd tried to put a hole in my noggin not a half hour before.

Of course, I was too busy packing on fat for the winter to worry about pinning Chan down. But Gustav's got about half the appetite I do and four times the curiosity. So naturally he was first to finish with the food and dig into the mystery.

"Thank you, Dr. Chan. That was a right tasty meal. I'm just glad my brother could be here to share it with us. You know . . . him almost havin' his head shot off and all."

Chan's shoulders sagged, and it seemed only something taut and unyielding in his gut kept him from slumping face-first into a mound of white rice.

"Yes. That was most unfortunate."

The Chinaman's usually light accent thickened, his voice suddenly sounding strained, labored, as if the words were sticking to his tongue like nut butter.

"I suppose I've been . . . on edge ever since my experience on the Pacific Express."

"I understand entirely, Doc. It's mighty unsettlin' seein' the Reaper take a swing at you." I pointed at the last pork bun. "Anyone got their eye on that?"

Chan shook his head and Old Red rolled his eyes, so I snatched up the fluffy white doughball and tore into it.

"Seems to me you wasn't just 'on edge,' Doc," my brother said. "You was *prepared*. I mean, you didn't have that hideout gun back on the Express, did you? And either you've put on some weight the last month or you're wearin' some kinda paddin' or armor under that suit of yours."

Chan squirmed nervously in his chair, his fidgeting creating strange bulges and ripples in his clothes so obvious even I finally noticed them. The doctor *was* wearing something heavy and stiff under his shirt.

"I see your eye for detail is as sharp as ever," he said. "Yes, I bought a gun. And a chain-mail vest. For protection. Hard times are coming for this country—and that means *very* hard times for the Chinese here. After the last Panic, two thousand members of the Anti-Coolie League marched into Chinatown and tried to burn it to the ground. The League doesn't have that kind of strength again . . . yet. But every day, more of my countrymen are beaten senseless by hoodlums from North Beach and the Barbary Coast. I'm not going to let that happen to *me*."

"Good for you, Doc," I said through a mouthful of pork bun. "Half the time, all you gotta do to rid yourself of bullyin' riff-raff is stand up to 'em."

"And the other half of the time, the riff-raff slits your throat," Gustav snipped at me. Then he turned back to Chan, and his voice softened. "Still, I gotta wonder . . . why would you think them 'hoodlums' would come after *you*?"

"Well, it's not just me, of course. They'll abuse any Chinaman they can get—"

Old Red shook his head, and Chan trailed off into silence.

"Before you popped off your shot at my brother, he shouted to you," Gustav said. "Called you by name more than once. Yet you drew on him anyway. Which says to me you ain't just afraid of bein' roughed up randomlike. You think someone's gunnin' for *you*."

Chan's gaze drifted down to the table. Aside from that, he didn't move—or speak.

"You got money problems, Doc?" my brother asked him. We were at a corner table, with no one else nearby, yet he dropped his voice down whisper-quiet all the same. "Owe somebody, maybe? Somebody *mean?*"

Chan stayed so utterly still it looked like he was in a staring contest with a plate of fried pork.

"Look. Me and Otto, we know why you was on the Pacific Express," Gustav went on gently. "Found out the whole story 'fore the train took that dive over a mountainside. You was bringin' back arty-facts from the Chinese exhibit at the World's Fair in Chicago. Got 'em on loan—and guaranteed their safe return with your own cash, we was told. So when the Express wrecked . . . well, I was just wonderin' if that wrecked *you*. Cuz if it did, maybe we could help out somehow."

Of course, out here in the West, sticking your nose into another fellow's financial affairs is roughly akin to sticking your finger in his eye. So Chan would've been within his rights to upend the nearest plate of delicacies over Old Red's head.

"Thank you," he said instead. He finally tore his gaze from the tabletop and looked at my brother, his expression somber. "You are very kind."

Then his face changed, the lips curling into a wry smile, the flesh around his nose and eyes crinkling.

The eyes themselves, though—they remained just the same.

"But don't worry about me," Chan said. "I haven't been 'wrecked.' Simply derailed temporarily. As the saying goes, I'm poorer but wiser. More poor than wise, perhaps, but I'll even the scales again one day. And that's all there is to it, really."

He picked up his chopsticks and used them to nab himself another morsel of sauce-smeared pork.

"And what of you two? I didn't see you mentioned in any of the newspaper articles about what happened on the Express. Are you still working for the railroad?"

My brother glanced over at me, raising one eyebrow ever so slightly. *That's all there is to it?* he was saying. *I think not.*

I replied with what to most men's eyes would've looked like a simple twitch of the shoulders. Gustav, however, would recognize it for what it was: a resigned shrug.

You can lead a Chinaman to water . . . , I was saying.

"There's a reason you didn't read about us, Doc," I said aloud. "The story they wrote up in the papers is grade-A S.P. bull crap. Here's what *really* happened."

Chan did his best to be a good audience as I filled him in on what he'd missed after getting tossed off the Pacific Express. He popped his eyes and gasped and shook his head in admiring wonderment in all the right places. Yet there was a feeling of play-acting about it—that overexpressive quality you notice too late when you've been boring the pants off somebody.

Not that I thought Chan wasn't interested. My tale simply couldn't compete with whatever was preying on the man's mind.

"That's amazing," Chan said when I was done. "You should take your story to a newspaper or magazine. It would cause a sensation."

"I couldn't agree more, Doc," I replied, about to reveal that those very wheels hadn't just been set in motion, they were spinning full speed: The tale had already been put to paper and sent off to Smythe & Associates, publishers of *Jesse James Library, Billy Steele—Boy Detective*, and perhaps one day *Big Red (and Old Red) Weekly*. If *Harper's* wouldn't give my first book a good home, maybe Smythe & Associates would open its rather shabbier doors to my second.

But before I could tell Chan of my stabs at Watson-style scribing, there was a commotion at the front of the restaurant. After that, there was no use going on, for Chan was so gobsmacked I could've stuffed a string of firecrackers down his pants without winning his attention back.

Five Chinese men had trooped inside together. They didn't move as most such groups would—two by three, maybe, or just jumbled up in a bunch. No, they were in a diamond: one in front, one in back, two to the sides, and one in the middle.

The fellows on the flanks and riding drag were all meaty, tall, black-clad, and (to judge by the stern looks on their broad faces) tough. The man taking point, on the other hand, had the wiry-scrappy-scrawny build of my brother, and his eyes scanned the room with the same all-seeing keenness. His gaze fastened for a moment on Old Red and me—and lingered even longer on Dr. Chan.

Yet Chan ignored the man. He was staring into the heart of the diamond, at a bright-eyed, good-looking Chinaman perhaps thirty years of age. His slender body was draped in silky, gaudy-patterned robes that may as well have been sewn together from ten-dollar bills, they were so showy. And the fellow had a regal bearing to match his finery, striding in with the chin-out, back-straight strut of a man of means who means for folks to know it.

Certainly, the restaurant's owner knew. He grinned and stooped and bowed so low he could've kissed the metaphorical red carpet he was so cravenly rolling out. He led the party to the largest table available, an eight-seater in the middle of the room, but the short, sharp-eyed bodyguard (for bodyguard he plainly was) rejected it with a brusque shake of the head.

Two tables in the corner opposite ours were quickly commandeered, and the patrons already eating there scooped up their bowls and scurried off with nary a complaint.

"Who is that feller?" I asked under my breath as the bigshot settled into his chair and his guards took up positions around him. "Last I heard, Frisco hasn't had an emperor since Norton the First passed away."

"San Francisco may not have an emperor, but Chinatown does," Chan whispered back. "That's Fung Jing Toy."

He paused, waiting for some indication that we felt the full weight of what he'd said. When he didn't see any, he spoke again, his whisper so low this time I wasn't sure if I actually heard the words or merely absorbed their meaning from the movement of his lips and the spooky expression on his face.

"Little Pete."

"Holy shit," I said. "I didn't recognize him without his pitchfork and horns."

Gustav's response was a simple "Well, well."

We'd been hearing about Little Pete almost nonstop for the last month. Nearly every day, I'd read out some new story in the local papers about him. Gambling halls, opium dens, whorehouses, "white slavery," fixed sports of every stripe—Little Pete had a hand in so much sin and corruption he could almost compete with City Hall.

Yet finding ourselves in the presence of a bona fide Napoleon of crime wasn't half as surprising as the look the man gave Chan.

He turned toward our friend the doctor . . . and he *smiled*.

Not as you might do to acknowledge a friendly acquaintance, though. More the way a fox might grin at a hen as he sneaks from the farm with another bloodied chicken a-twitching in his jaws. An "I'll attend to you later" sort of smile. Almost a promise.

Apparently, the most dangerous man in San Francisco didn't just know Dr. Gee Woo Chan. He had unfinished business with him.

5

A GOOD-BYE AND A HEL-LO

Or, Gustav Loses a Bet He Wants to Win and Wins One He Wants to Lose

Less than two minutes after Little Pete's party came in, ours was going out. It wouldn't be altogether fair to characterize Dr. Chan's exit as a "skedaddle," but neither was it a "mosey." He threw down some wrinkled greenbacks without even asking for the tab, then hopped up and announced it was time to get back to work.

Little Pete didn't seem to notice our departure, already being deep in conversation with the wiry Chinaman who'd been at the head of his procession. Yet, though the little henchman nodded and smiled and looked admiring as lackeys must, he never quite met his boss man's gaze. Apparently, just giving the place the once-over wasn't good enough for him—he was now giving it an eighth-over or ninth-over. Gustav and me he watched leave with a mixture of suspicion and smirky scorn, as if he was sizing us up as potential competition . . . and coming to the conclusion he had nothing to worry about.

Chan didn't give Old Red a chance to ask more questions once we got outside, quickly launching into a fast-walking, fast-talking guided tour of the block. Up that way was a Buddhist temple. Down that way was the Presbyterian mission house. Yonder was a market with fish so fresh they were still gasping for breath. Over there one could buy "ghost money" to burn at an ancestor's grave.

36

And here was Chan's apothecary shop again. Good-bye.

An old Chinese man, stoop-shouldered and gray-bearded, was loitering out front of the store, and he drew closer as Chan gave me and my brother hurried farewell handshakes. The old-timer croaked something in Chinese as he shuffled up, his voice as rough as sandpaper on your privates, and Chan whirled on him and snapped a few harsh words in reply.

During our train trip together, I'd watched Chan withstand an onslaught of abuse from whites without once losing his air of kindness and quiet dignity. So what I was witnessing now—disdain on his face, a snarl in his voice—came as a shock. I'd read that the Chinese revere their elders, but there was no reverence here. Only contempt.

The two Chinamen exchanged a few words, the gravel-throated geezer wheedling and resentful, the doctor gruff and dismissive. It looked like Chan was about to brush right past the man into his shop, but something he heard stopped him, and the sneer on his face was swiftly swapped for surprise. After a little more back and forth with the old man, Chan turned to me and my brother again, his expression as pleasant as ever.

"Duty calls, it appears. Good-bye, Big Red. Old Red. I hope you'll come visit me again soon."

"Sure, Doc." I tipped my hat—flashing him the still-tingling powder burn on my forehead. "Only next time, I'd appreciate it if your reception wasn't quite so warm."

Chan tried on a smile, but it didn't fit him very well. "Pleasant" he could still manage. "Amused" was beyond him just then.

"Good luck, Doc," my brother said.

Chan nodded stiffly, then swung back around to the old man and barked out what sounded like a command. They hurried away up the street side by side, but for as long as we stood there watching them, neither one turned to look at or speak to the other.

"There goes a peculiar pair," Gustav said.

"The world's full of 'em." I jerked my head toward the southeast, where the Ferry House awaited us a dozen blocks away. "So . . . shall we retire to our Oakland chateau?"

Old Red gave me what I think of as Long-Suffering Stare Number

Four. That's the one where his eyebrows knit together, his thin lips purse, and the clenched set of his jaw adds a subtle hint of low-simmering anger.

"Don't you wanna know what's troublin' Chan?"

"I am seething with barely restrained curiosity." I shrugged. "And I also heard the man tell us it ain't none of our damn business. Not in so many words, mind you, but it was there in between the lines. Hell, it was outside, under, and over the lines, too. He could've asked us for help. He didn't. There it is. Time to go home."

"And just forget about the doc?"

"Hey, you want a mystery to solve? I got one for you: Where is Diana Corvus?"

Long-Suffering Stare Number Four gave way to Exasperated Glower Number One.

"What? I won that bet."

"You most certainly did not. Everything you said when you first spotted Chan was something we already knew. And here we are, an entire hour later, and all you've really deducified about the man is that there's a lot more yet to deducify. Well, I am not impressed. Now if you think you should get another shot, fine. We'll pick up where we were when Chan happened by. I'd say you had about fifteen seconds left to choose." I stretched out my arms and turned to one side, then another. "Alright—get to it. Pick your man."

Old Red just growled something unintelligible (and no doubt unprintable) and stomped away.

"That's a forfeit, Brother!" I crowed as I started after him. "Ha! Sit tight, Diana—we're comin' to find ya!"

Whether Gustav had indeed conceded was hard to say, for he spoke not a word as we headed for the Ferry House. Even if he'd tried to put up an argument, there's no guarantee I would have heard it. We were cutting across the city on a diagonal through the squalid tangle of groggeries, dancehalls, deadfalls, and whorehouses called the Barbary Coast, and the rough and rowdy neighborhood's riotous din was well-nigh deafening. When one could make out actual words over the manic cacophony of the concert saloons and the general all-around roar of a thousand belligerent drunks all bellowing at once, they nearly always took the same form:

shouted inducements (when approaching) and insults (if not stopping) from the prostitutes flashing their pallid flesh behind the bars of their bagnio "cribs."

These siren songs held no sway over my brother and me, by the way. I wish I could say it was because my high moral fiber doesn't allow for any truck with the flesh trade. Yet that, sadly, would be a lie. My morals are plenty fibrous on most matters, but when it comes to women, they've been known to go as soft as tapioca pudding.

No, the simple, rather unflattering truth of the matter is this: Gustav had ruined whoring for me years before.

"You know what I think about sometimes?" he said to me once in an El Paso saloon.

I'd been eyeing a dark-haired good-time gal all night and had just announced my intention to purchase her services—what would have been my first foray into the lion's den of carnality as commerce.

"What's that?" I muttered in reply, unable to tear my gaze from the beautiful and alluring (in hindsight, worn-out and drunk) woman who'd captured my heart . . . or parts due south, at least.

"What if our sisters was the last of the family left 'stead of you and me?" Old Red said. "It could've happened easy enough. 'Stead of you ridin' out that flood that did everyone in, let's say Ilse and Greta did. I've almost got myself killed a thousand times over droverin'. What if I wasn't alive to come collect 'em afterward, like I done you? The farm gone. All of *us* gone. What's a couple young girls to do? Who looks after 'em? Where do they end up?"

By the time Gustav was done, I was no longer staring lustfully at that soiled dove—I was staring resentfully at *him*.

"You just cannot let me have any fun, can you?"

"Who's stoppin' your fun?" Old Red pulled a silver dollar from his pocket and plonked it onto the table. "There. On me. Have at it . . . Brother."

"Fine. I will."

I scooped up the coin and turned toward the object of my most unbrotherly affection—who suddenly bore an uncanny resemblance to the sisters I'd lost less than a year before.

"Oh, hell. You win," I grumbled. "But I ain't givin' you your damn dollar back."

After that, anytime I fell under the spell of some harlot's charms, all my brother had to say was, "You know what I think about sometimes?"

To which I would grumpily reply, "Yes, I do. And thanks to you, now I think it, too."

And that would be that.

Perhaps because I've been denied the usual outlet for a drover's amorous impulses, I've fallen into the habit of falling in love with inappropriate women. A cattle baron's wife, the mayor's daughter, even an English noblewoman—I'm ever pining away after some lady so high born she can barely see a low-born like me for the clouds that swim through the skies between us.

So it was with Diana Corvus, though I didn't know what line her father was in or how she'd come to be a Southern Pacific agent or whether one could find her (real?) name in the social registry. I did know, however, that the lady had style and grace—the kind that says, *Too good for you, Otto Amlingmeyer* without her even meaning it to. Her very unattainability represented a challenge I intended to accept . . . provided I ever saw her again.

During the ferry ride back to Oakland, Gustav and I passed the time in the company of our friend Sherlock Holmes, courtesy of Dr. Watson's "A Scandal in Bohemia." It was the best way we knew to keep Old Red from turning green. But the second we were back on solid ground, I was back on the subject of Diana Corvus.

"Maybe she can't find us," I said as we walked up Broadway to our ramshackle hotel.

"Fiddle faddle."

"Maybe she's in trouble," I said as we entered the dingy, dimly lit lobby of the Cosmopolitan House.

"Hogwash."

"Maybe she's testin' us," I said as we tromped up the saggy stairs to the second floor.

"Bullshit."

"Maybe she's—"

"Oh, for Christ's sake!" my brother roared as we finally reached our room. "Would you shut up about Diana god damn Corvus? We ain't never gonna lay eyes on that woman again, do you understand that?" He jammed his key in the keyhole and gave it an angry jiggle. "We ain't nothin' to her, and she ain't nothin' to . . . hel-lo."

"What?"

"The door . . . it ain't locked."

Gustav drew his key back out and stuffed it in his pocket. Then he turned the knob and gave the door a gentle push. Rusty hinges let off a high-pitched squeal as the door slowly swung open.

"I hope I haven't come at a bad time," said the woman waiting for us in our room.

It was Diana god damn Corvus.

6

FRIENDLY PERSUASION

Or, Diana Brings Bad News—and Talks Us into Sniffing for More

The lady had *not* come at a good time, of course. Not only must she have heard my brother's rant about her, there I was with bulletholes in my hat and a forehead slathered with burn-balm that smelled worse than a polecat's underpants.

On the other hand, any time was a good time to see Diana again. If I was to get a glimpse of those lively brown eyes, those lovely dark curls, those full, impishly upturned lips, and that long, slender neck even upon my deathbed, I swear my heart would find the strength to skip a beat before it stopped altogether.

Diana was sitting primly upon our tiny room's only chair, and as I rushed in to greet her, she smiled and came to her feet.

"Miss Corvus—what a lovely surprise! And here we were tryin' to figure out how *we'd* find *you*."

"Oh?" She looked at Gustav as he came slinking into the room behind me, and her smile dimmed. Not going cold, mind you—simply softening like the light of a lamp that's been dialed down to a lower glow. "How fortunate that I saved you the trouble of trying."

"Miss," Old Red said, greeting her with a curt nod and a doffed hat. As was his custom in the presence of a lady, he directed his eyes at a spot on the floor about two feet from her toes.

"Please, Miss Corvus. Sit yourself down again and tell us how you come to be here."

I swept off my custom-ventilated bowler and held it out toward the chair. After catching a quick whiff of Chan's malodorous ointment, however, I immediately slapped the hat back atop my head.

"Thank you," Diana said as she sat, shooting my hat an amused glance that added, *If you don't want to tell me, I won't ask.*

"I hope you don't mind my invading your privacy like this," she said aloud. "I thought it better to wait for you up here."

"How is it you got in, anyways?" Old Red asked.

"Oh, I just let myself in," Diana said—and left it at that.

So the lady could pick a lock. Now I *knew* I was in love.

"Well, it's a good thing you took the liberty—loiterin' in the lobby would've been askin' for trouble," I said. "You won't find many low-lifes lower than our neighbors at the Cosmo. But we save us a pretty penny livin' here . . . which is good, cuz a pretty penny's about all we got left."

Diana nodded. "I understand. I heard you lost your jobs with the Southern Pacific."

"We *quit*," Gustav corrected her, almost managing to look her in the eye—his gaze rose as high as her collarbone before faltering and sinking back to the floor.

"We was probably gonna get canned anyhow," I added.

"All the same," Old Red snipped, "we quit."

"Well, I wish I could say the same." Diana's smile turned rueful. "*I* was fired."

"No! You?" I gasped. "How could they?"

"Very easily, actually. You remember Colonel Crowe, of course."

"Why, sure," I said.

The man was pretty hard to forget, really—unless you're one of those folks who bumps into crackpot Lilliputian military men every day. It was Crowe who'd hired Gustav and me to be train guards, which probably goes to show how cracked his little pot truly was.

"The colonel was blamed for what happened on the Pacific Express," Diana said. "He was dismissed first. I was always viewed as a sort of . . . protégé of his, so I was swept out, as well."

"When did all this happen?" Old Red asked, sounding strangely skeptical. He didn't say "supposedly," but I could hear it in his tone.

"Just last week. In a way, I didn't mind being sacked, though. It gave me time to pursue a personal project of mine."

"Which was?" I asked.

The lady gave me the answer I hoped to hear.

"Finding you."

I shot Gustav a "See?" smirk, chastising him for his lack of faith in our friend. He missed it, though, as he was still bashfully inspecting the floorboards.

"You didn't make it easy," Diana went on. "I tracked you as far as a lodging house called the 'Cowboy's Rest,' but after that the trail went cold."

"That's kinda how we wanted it after we left the Rest," I explained. "Dispute with management, you might say."

You might also say the SOBs actually tried to shanghai us. But that's another story—and one the lady didn't get to hear.

"How is it you found us, then?" Gustav asked her.

"Oh, it was simple, really—nothing worthy of your hero Mr. Holmes. Knowing your ambitions as I do, I merely asked an acquaintance to contact me should the two of you ever cross his path. You see, he's—"

"A Pinkerton over in Frisco," Old Red finished for her, sounding annoyed with himself for not deducing it sooner.

"That's right," Diana said. "Maintaining friendly relations with the Pinkertons has come in handy for me on several occasions. Likewise, I've found it helpful to be on good terms with the clerks in the Southern Pacific mailroom. Which is how I came to have this."

She opened her drawstring handbag and pulled out a sealed envelope. "For you."

She offered the letter to me.

I tried to keep my hand steady as I stretched it out toward her. Yet still it got to shaking as soon as I saw where that letter was from.

For Gustav's benefit, I read the return address out loud.

Harper & Bros., Publishers
325 to 337 Pearl Street
Franklin Square

New York, New York

"The *Harper's Weekly* folks?" Old Red asked.

"Yup."

"Sendin' just a letter?"

"Yup."

"You know, if they didn't send your book back, maybe—"

I cut my brother off with another "Yup." I didn't want to hear the words, in case they weren't true. Yet they were echoing in my head all the same.

Maybe you've got yourself a publisher.

I tore open the envelope, pulled out a neatly folded sheet of paper, and started reading silently.

"Dear Sir or Madam," the letter began.

Well, hell, I thought. *That can't be good.*

And I was right.

"Miss Corvus," I sighed once I'd made it through to the end, "would you mind pluggin' your ears for a moment?"

"Not at all," Diana replied gently.

She pressed her hands to the sides of her head.

"*Shit damn Christ son of a bitch piss bastard!*"

I took a deep breath, then gave the lady a grateful nod.

"Thank you."

Diana uncovered her ears. "Any time."

"So . . . they ain't gonna print it," my brother said, face twisted into a prodigious grimace. He'd dug his spurs in me deep to get me to do something with my writing. Now it looked like he'd gotten a taste of the rowels himself.

"Not only ain't they gonna print it, they ain't even gonna mail the thing back 'less I send *them* two bits to cover postage. Sweet Gee-ronimo . . . they're holdin' my book for ransom!"

"Well, there's only two things for you to do," Diana said firmly. "First, you're going to send them that twenty-five cents, get your book back, and try again with another publisher. Right?"

I blinked at her a moment, not sure if I was ready to stop wallowing and get back to *hoping* again so quick.

"Right?" she said again, the word snapping out with all the force of a cavalry officer's "Charge!"

"Right. And the second thing?"

"I would've thought that was obvious." She came to her feet and started for the door. "You're going to have a drink. Come on."

I followed, though I had no earthly idea where the lady might be leading us: There wasn't a respectable drinking house in town that would allow a female to mingle with men at the bar. Yet I knew that mere decorum—or a niggling little inconvenience like the truth—wouldn't stop Diana Corvus.

I'd once told her (completely in a spirit of awestruck appreciation, mind) that she was the most audacious liar I'd ever met. The compliment seemed to please her, but she'd refused to accept it. She was merely uncommonly persuasive, she said.

So in deference to her preference, I won't say that she *lied* us into a private booth at a nearby chophouse. When she told the head waiter she and her "cousins from Albuquerque" needed a little privacy to go over plans for our dearly departed grandmother's funeral, she was merely *persuading* her way to what she wanted.

Which she got.

After ordering our drinks (three brandies seemed like the most appropriately somber choice), we returned to the subject of my literary masterpiece and the New York nincompoops who'd failed to recognize its genius. Diana was of the opinion that I should approach a dime-novel outfit next, so I told her I'd already done just that with another book, this one about our disastrous passage on the Pacific Express.

"Oh?" she said. "I suppose *I* must be in the book then, hmmm?"

"Of course! You're one of the heroes!"

Diana smiled wryly. "I'm honored. It's just too bad the Southern Pacific doesn't agree with you." Her smile drooped on one side, then wilted and died entirely. "In fact, they'll be apoplectic if your book is ever published. The story they fed the newspapers didn't bear much resemblance to what really happened—and powerful men don't like to be contradicted."

"And you think we oughta be worried about that?" Old Red said. "Whether or not the S.P.'s apo-papa-paletic or whatever?"

It was the first thing he'd said since "Sure. Brandy. Fine," ten minutes before.

"I'm not saying you should be *worried*. Just prepared," Diana replied. "Colonel Crowe lost his job over this, and he'd been with the Southern Pacific eight years. You were with the railroad all of three days—and you don't exactly have friends in high places. The last thing you need is *enemies* in high places."

"Well, what would you have us do, then?" Gustav pressed her. "Use the book for kindlin'? Or just change it around so it's in line with the flap-doodle the S.P. put out?"

"I'm not suggesting either. I just wanted to warn you that—"

"*Warn,* huh?" Old Red snapped. "Alright, then. Consider us warned. Not that it's gonna change a danged thing. We don't care to 'maintain friendly relations' with the S.P.—or anyone else who stabs us in the back."

Diana gave Gustav the sort of look you'd give a favorite mutt that's suddenly taken to growling at you instead of wagging its tail.

I offered her a reassuring grin—while giving Old Red a swift kick to the shin.

"You know, I just realized," I said, scooping up my brandy glass, "here we been sharin' our first drink together, and we ain't done a proper toast."

Diana returned my smile (although hers looked considerably strained) and held up her brandy.

After taking a long moment to rub his shin resentfully, Gustav finally lifted his own drink—though he did it so slowly you might've thought it had been poured into a "glass" crafted from solid lead.

"To friendly relations," I said, giving my brother a taste of his own Exasperated Glower Number One.

Don't you dare *booger this up,* I was telling him.

"Friendly relations," he grated out.

"Friendly relations," said Diana.

We clinked and sipped—or Old Red and Diana did, anyway. Me, I clinked and *gulped*.

I needed a change of subject, and I needed it fast. Fortunately, it's hard to keep my tongue tied long, fond of wagging as it is.

"I wish I'd known we'd be havin' this little tea party today," I said. "I would've invited Doc Chan to join us."

"Dr. Chan . . . from the Pacific Express?" Diana asked, taken aback. "You've seen him?"

"Who you think put these holes in my hat? Why, the poor little feller's as jittery as a frostbit Chihuahua."

I proceeded to tell her all about our chance encounter with Gee Woo Chan.

I intended it purely as a diversion, like pointing out the window and saying, "My oh my, ain't *she* a purty one?" before swiping the biscuit of another drover's plate. And it worked, too. Better than I could've hoped for—or *would've* hoped for, considering all it eventually led to.

"Poor Dr. Chan," Diana said when I was through telling the tale. "But how fortunate for him, too. To have run into you two, I mean."

"I suppose so," I said, though truthfully I was in no position to do any such supposing—because I had no idea what she meant.

"Whatever his troubles may be," Diana went on, "they're surely no match for us."

" 'Us'?" Old Red said.

Diana nodded. "You and me and your brother. *Us.* Three unemployed detectives with a friend in need."

Gustav peeked up at the lady warily, his head cocked slightly to one side. "And you think we oughta be friends in deed how, exactly?"

"By learning why Dr. Chan's in fear for his life, of course. And then . . ." She shrugged and took another quick sip of brandy. ". . . doing something about it."

My brother looked over at me. "Some folks'd say it's none of our business."

Diana turned to me, too. "Well, then I would quote the late Mr. Sherlock Holmes to these 'folks': 'It's everyone's business to see justice done.' "

" 'Every *man's* business' is what He said," Old Red harrumphed.

"Which still makes it your business by duty," Diana said. "I make it mine by choice."

"That settles it, then," I announced, hoping by saying it I was making it so. If Diana wanted to jump into the Bay and do the backstroke back to

Frisco, I wasn't going to talk her out of it—so long as I was invited to take the dip with her. "To seein' justice done."

I held my brandy out over the table.

"To seeing justice done," Diana echoed, bringing her glass up against mine.

After a pause of approximately two centuries—or so it seemed to me—Gustav raised his glass, too. He raised his gaze, as well, finally looking at Diana full-on, with no bowed head or blushes.

"To findin' the truth," he said.

And he knocked his drink into ours hard enough to push them apart.

7

NO PLACE FOR A LADY

Or, We Head to Chinatown by Way of Hell

After another round of brandies (and a long stretch of sullen silence from my brother), Diana called it a day. Or called it a dusk, more like, since sundown was setting in by the time we said our farewells.

It wouldn't be good-bye for long this time, though. We planned to meet again the very next morning at the Ferry House in San Francisco. From there, we would proceed to Chinatown, where we would pour our help down Chan's throat like he was a sick boy who wouldn't take his castor oil. There would be no "no."

Gustav had agreed to this plan with no more than the occasional grunt or, when pressed, curt nod. So once Diana was in a hansom clip-clopping off down Broadway, I asked if I should hail a hack for him, too.

"Why the hell would you do that?" Old Red said.

"I just figured you wouldn't be able to walk yourself back to the hotel," I told him. "You know, what with that giant stick up your ass and all."

"Better a stick than my own head."

"Meaning?"

"Meaning, can't you tell when you're bein' used?"

I gazed at Diana's departing cab and sighed wistfully. "A lady like that can use me any ol' way she pleases."

My brother responded with a phrase so foul I wouldn't dare set my pen to writing it lest the paper burst into sulphurous flame. A rough paraphrasing would be, "Oh, you silly man, you."

"Hey, you just tell me this then," I shot back. "If Diana's usin' us, what the heck's she usin' us *for?*"

Old Red kicked at a nonexistent rock on the sidewalk. "I don't know. It just don't sit right, though. First she's tryin' to give us the heebie-jeebies about the S.P., then she's pushin' us back to Chinatown to see Chan again. I look at her, and . . . well, I can't help but remember what The Man said."

" 'Stop bein' so cantankerous, you little coot'?" I suggested. "Oh, wait. That was *me* said that."

" 'Women are naturally secretive,' " Gustav growled, quoting from "A Scandal in Bohemia."

"Well, with all due respect to you and The Man . . . that's horseshit. You may as well say all apples got worms or every bear can ride a bicycle. It just ain't so."

My brother gave me the kind of fierce, deeply lined scowl you usually only see carved into totem poles.

"Look," I said, "even if Diana *is* keepin' secrets, then you oughta be happy as a damn clam—cuz now you got yet another puzzle to play with. And I'll tell you how to solve this one, too: *Coax* some answers out of the lady. Be pleasant. Sly. Smooth. You know . . . not an asshole."

"Try to sweet-talk her, you mean?"

"Oh, hell no!" I hooted. "Leave that to me. All you gotta do is be civil—which I know poses quite the challenge for you, but I think you can pull it off if you truly try. Sooner or later, Diana'll let down her guard, and then you'll get your chance to find out what she's *really* up to."

"Oh, now you're just humorin' me."

"Absolutely. But that don't mean I ain't right."

"Yeah," Old Red sighed. "Could be."

"Alright, then. That's that." I clapped my hands together and gave them an eager rub. "Now if you care to accompany me, I have a few errands to run 'fore we head back to the Cosmo for the night."

"What sorta errands?"

"Well, first, I gotta get me a new hat." I took off my ruined derby and ran my fingers over the bristly tuft of hair atop my head. "Then I wanna see if there's a barber can do something with this barbecued forelock of mine. Might just get myself a shave while I'm at it. And I do believe it's about time I took myself a hot bath. Could probably use me some new cologne to cover up the smell of Doc Chan's liniment, too . . . ."

"Brother," Gustav said, shaking his head, "what you *really* need they don't sell in stores."

With that, he trudged off toward our hotel, leaving me to dandify myself alone. When I returned to our room a few hours later, as slicked up as an otter's ass, I found him asleep on the bed, the newest issue of *Harper's* steepled on his stomach. The magazine featured a new tale from Johnny Watson, "The Resident Patient," and Gustav had drifted off while studying on the illustrations. Apparently, my brother found a mere drawing of Sherlock Holmes to be more inviting company than his own flesh-and-blood brother.

I didn't mind, though. Old Red's hell to duds-shop with—he considers anything fancier than denim work-pants and a checked shirt foppish. And as for hats, nothing but a white Boss of the Plains will do.

But me, I'm more a when-in-Rome sort of fellow. And when in Frisco, men trade in ten-gallon hats for something more on the order of two quarts. Which is why I'd decided to buy my first boater.

When I woke up the next morning, I found my brother holding the flat, disc-ish hat gingerly, balancing it on the tips of his fingers as if it had been woven from poison ivy instead of straw. He was fully dressed, and he had the alert, up-and-at-'em bearing of a man who's had his morning coffee.

"I reckon I oughta congratulate you," he said when he noticed my opened eyes.

"Yeah?" I whispered hoarsely. Before I've had *my* first cup of Arbuckle, that's about as articulate as I get.

"Yeah. I didn't think you could find a lid that'd make you look more nitwitted than that ol' bowler did. But you managed it somehow." He put the straw hat back atop our bureau, where I'd left it the night before, then grabbed his Stetson and plopped it on his head. "Anyways . . . come on. Gotta get a move on or we'll miss our ferry."

"Alright, alright. And here I thought *I'd* be the one draggin' *you* off to—" I pushed myself up to a sit and gave the air a quizzical sniff. "Whoa. Did I spill my . . . ? Oh. Ho ho ho."

"What's there to 'ho' about?"

"You, as a matter of fact. You threw on a splash of my cologne, didn't you?" I leaned toward him, squinting up at a scrape on his cheek due east of his mustache—which was as neatly trimmed as I'd ever seen it. "And I do believe you're freshly shaved. Hmmm. Spit-shined your boots, too, I see. Well well well, how 'bout that? So you decided to ladle on a little charm, after all."

"I ain't aimin' to charm nobody."

"Oh, please, Brother. It's plain as day. The only thing missing's a pink carnation in your lapel . . . which we can buy on the way to the ferry, if you like."

"Now, hold on. It's not that I . . . well . . . a man can't . . . you know . . ."

Old Red snatched up my trousers and threw them into my face.

"Shut up and get yourself dressed, would you?"

Thirty minutes later, we were on our way across the Bay on the nine o'clock ferry. There wasn't much chop to the waves that morning, yet my brother's face quickly went so sweaty and pale you might've thought we were on a raft riding out a typhoon. I helped him keep his spirits up and his gorge down with yet another rereading of "The Resident Patient."

Old Red regained his color, if not his composure, when we got off the boat. As promised, Diana was waiting for us outside the Ferry House, and the mere sight of her brought a blush to his cheeks and a knot to his tongue.

"Good morning, gentlemen," she said as we walked up.

"Good mornin' to you, madame," I replied, tipping my hat with a jaunty flip of the wrist. "If I may say so, you are lookin' truly radiant this morning."

Gustav forewent the flattery, merely brushing a finger over his hat brim and mumbling something that sounded like, "Gmornuh."

"Good morning. And thank you, Otto." Diana looked up at the scorch-mark on my forehead, which had lost most of its scarlet glow. "You're look-ing rather *less* radiant, actually—for which I'm sure you're grateful."

"Very. I don't know what Doc Chan put in that glop of his, but it sure helped me heal up in a hurry. Good thing, too." I flicked the rim of my boater. "These here straw hats may be all the rage, but it feels like I'm wearin' a wicker basket on my head. Like to rub my head raw if that burn was still botherin' me. But I reckon a little discomfort's the price one must sometimes pay for dressin' *à la mode*, am I right?"

Old Red gave his eyes such a roll he probably got a good look at his own brain.

"Why, Otto—I had no idea you were interested in fashion," Diana said.

"Oh, there's more to read in *Harper's* than detective yarns, y' know."

"Well, I applaud you for expanding your horizons. And what's more—" The lady looked up at my straw hat and nodded. "I like it. It makes you look very . . . modern."

"I'm mighty pleased to hear you say that, miss. Cuz some of your less-sophisticated, stick-in-the-mud types ain't got no appreciation for 'mod-ern' finery."

I waggled my eyebrows at my brother.

"I got better things to think about than *hats* just now," he growled.

"Of course," Diana said. "We can catch a streetcar to Chinatown over this way."

She started toward East Street.

My brother and I didn't follow her.

"Uhhh," I said.

Diana stopped. "Gentlemen?" Her gaze slid over to Gustav. "Oh. I'm so sorry. I forgot about your . . . condition. We can walk to Chinatown."

"My 'condition'?" Old Red rumbled, momentarily managing to meet Diana's eyes with a here-and-gone, peek-a-boo glance. "I ain't got no 'condition.' I just don't like ridin' nothin' that ain't got reins I can hold in my own hands. But I'll be god . . ." He spluttered to a stop, gave his head a bitter shake, then started again. "I'll be *goll durned* if I'm gonna make a woman walk a dozen blocks out of her way. Come on."

He marched away toward the street.

Before Diana and I hustled off after him, I noticed the lady's lips slip to one side into a smirk. It was as if my brother had just passed some secret test she'd set for him—or failed it, perhaps.

One cable car after another went trundling away down Market, and if we'd taken one it would've been simplicity itself to hop off at Dupont and shoot north up to Chinatown. But Diana insisted on another route: straight over from East Street on Clay. It was a heck of a lot more direct, and a hell of a lot more scenic—the "scenery" consisting of the unbridled debauchery of the Barbary Coast.

The first time I'd walked through the Coast, I'd heard a conductor shout, "All out for the whorehouse!" as his streetcar slowed to a stop before a particularly grandiose bagnio. Everyone aboard had hooted and guffawed—for they were all men. Diana's presence put the kibosh on any such antics now, however, and all but the most brazen sports who hopped on and off our car did their best to keep their backs to her.

For her part, Diana didn't gaze upon the Coast's drunken sailors, dive saloons, melodeons, macks, and prostitutes with anything that looked like disgust or even curiosity. She remained so unruffled by the iniquity around us, in fact, that her very indifference began to feel like another test. Back on the Pacific Express, before we knew she was an S.P. spy, we'd gone out of our way to shield her from every sight or situation we deemed too frightful for a female. Would we try to play white knight now?

Old Red was certainly white enough for it . . . as in "white as a sheet." He was clinging to the nearest railing so tight it's a wonder the brass didn't break off in his grip. He was in no shape to stand up for propriety, for he hardly seemed capable of standing up at all.

Which left it to me to prove that chivalry wasn't dead—even though I had the feeling Diana would gladly drive a stake through its heart herself.

"Why is it," I asked after we'd traveled a block in awkward silence, "that I feel like you're just sittin' there waitin' for me to say, 'This ain't no place for a lady'?"

"Perhaps because I am," Diana replied. We were sharing a seat, and as she swiveled around to face me fully, her thigh brushed up against mine.

Even through all her soft lady's skirts, I could feel the firm flesh of the woman beneath. "After all, you *have* said it to me before."

"Yup. And you sure didn't like hearin' it. But I reckon it was true enough when I said it. Just like it's true now."

"Oh?"

Diana arched an eyebrow and tilted her head, the look warning me like the clitterclatter of a rattlesnake's tail: Watch your step. She'd been posing as a suffragette when we'd first come across her, and I wondered now how much of a pose that had really been.

"What *is* the place for a lady, then?" she asked me. "The drawing room, the kitchen, the nursery—and nowhere else?"

"I ain't sayin' that. But ladies, you know . . . they just belong . . . somewheres decent."

Diana turned toward the street again just as we rolled by what was obviously a bordello, since the girls leaning out the windows to taunt passersby were already (un)dressed for work.

"Well, there's not much decent around here, I'll grant you. Yet I see lots of ladies."

"You know them gals ain't ladies."

"They're women. They're here." Diana looked at me again, a low-burning fire in her eyes that I realized now was always there, just waiting for someone or something to stoke it up white-hot. "If you don't think a 'lady' has the strength to even pass through a place like this, how is it *they* have the strength to survive it?"

Old Red had been riding alone in a seat on the other side of ours, saying nothing and seemingly seeing nothing, just hanging on for dear life. I'd almost forgotten he was there at all until he swiveled around to speak to us.

"They *don't* always survive it."

And he quickly turned away again.

Whatever reply the lady might have made was cut off by the sound of catcalls from the sidewalk. A throng of jeering men—plainly a gang of the young street toughs the local papers had dubbed "hoodlums" for no reason anyone could adequately explain—had encircled a lone Chinaman. They'd already upended the basket of washing he'd been carrying, and now they were pushing him this way and that, sending him flying from man to man like the pigskin in a football game.

On the Chinaman's face was a look of hopeless terror. No one would come to his aid, he knew, and his only hope was that the "hoods" would tire of abusing him before his brains were beat out.

He and his tormentors slid past us like the scene from a diorama—a hellish vision close and real, yet untouchable, too.

"Well," my brother muttered glumly, "we must be gettin' close now."

And indeed we were. Less than a minute later, we were back in Chinatown—and once the streetcar went cling-clanging away, we were almost the only whites in sight.

What few of us were around, the Anti-Coolie League's sandwich man was trying to scare away, for he was once again out ranting about "the heathen Chinee." When he spotted me across the street, he grinned and waved a pamphlet over his head like a little flag.

"Hey, friend! You read this yet?"

I smiled and nodded.

"*Gehen Sie sich bumsen!*" I called to him cheerfully.

Diana gave a little mock gasp. "Otto—such language!"

I blushed so fiercely it felt like someone had wrapped a hot towel around my face. "Don't tell me you *sprechen* the *Deutsch*."

"No. But I'm fluent in obscenity."

Old Red turned and gave the lady the most level gaze he'd yet directed her way.

"Would you like me to demonstrate?" she said to him.

"Naw . . . that ain't necessary," my brother mumbled, spinning away quick.

Diana narrowed her eyes ever so slightly, and I couldn't quite decide if she was looking upon Old Red with wry fondness or noting with satisfaction the effect she could have on him.

"This way," Gustav said, hustling north up throng-choked Dupont toward the relatively deserted side street that was home to Chan's shop.

Only when we got there this day, Chan's street wasn't deserted at all. A milling, murmuring crowd was clustered in a clump about halfway down the block.

"Awww, hell," Old Red groaned.

"Is that—?" Diana began.

I didn't hear the rest. I was already sprinting ahead, making a beeline for something I hadn't once seen in Chinatown till just then: a policeman. I pushed through the mob to get up close.

"Hey! What's goin' on here?"

The copper gave me a long, sleepy-eyed sizing up before deigning to reply.

"Some Chink killed himself, that's all," he said in a voice that sounded like a yawn. "The quack who ran this place."

And he jerked his blue-helmeted head at the shop behind him—Dr. Chan's pharmacy.

8

CHAN

Or, We Nose Around for Answers and Don't Like What We Sniff Out

I took a step toward the door.

The policeman sidestepped to block me.

"Where do you think you're going?"

"Inside," I said.

I started to move around him.

The copper moved, too.

"No, you're not."

"Yeah, I am."

I tried to get around him again. He was a big fellow, tall as me and almost as broad, but he could move fast. We bumped together this time, the big brass buttons of his frock coat gouging into my chest.

"Look, I know Dr. Chan," I said. "He's a—"

I almost made the mistake of saying "friend of mine," which would've *guaranteed* we'd never get through that door. Fortunately, Diana closed my mouth before I could put my foot in it.

"Officer," she said, snaking through the crowd with Gustav behind her, "we need to speak with whoever's in charge here."

She plunged a hand into her drawstring purse, fished out a smallish, golden-brown doodad, and pushed it up under the copper's bulbous nose.

His eyes bulged.

Old Red's eyes bulged.

My eyes bulged.

The doohickey was a Southern Pacific Railroad Police badge.

"We're here to consult with Dr. Chan on important S.P. business," Diana said. "If something's wrong, we need to know what. Our superiors will expect a full explanation."

The big copper's eyelids went droopy with disdain. "Oh, they will, will they? And they'd be expecting it from *you*, little missy?"

"Indeed, they would."

The policeman shook his head and snorted out a grunt of a laugh.

His condescension was all for show, though. In California, the Southern Pacific gets what the Southern Pacific wants, from the governor's mansion all the way down to the harness bull in Chinatown.

"Hey, Sarge!" the cop shouted over his shoulder. When he didn't get a response, he took a step backward into Chan's shop and tried again at twice the volume. "*Sarge!*"

Toward the back of the store was a narrow, doorless pass-through, and the sound of footsteps thumped out from somewhere beyond it.

"What?"

A head poked out—bald, blocky, sharp-edged. Paint it red and it could've passed for a stack of bricks.

"Got some S.P. pussyfooters out here, Sarge. Say they had business with the Chink. Now they wanna see *you*."

"Sarge" craned his thick neck to peer at us around the bull's bulk. The sight of Diana, so fetching in her white summer dress, and Old Red, so outlandish in his white Boss of the Plains, slapped surprise across the man's slab of a face. He recovered quick, though.

"Let 'em through."

And he disappeared with another *clomp-clomp-clomp*.

The big copper stepped from our path and waved us past.

"S.P. or not, hayseed," he hissed as I followed Diana and Gustav inside, "next time, you *ask*."

"*Hayseed?*" I thought. *But I'm wearing a boater.*

As we hurried up the center aisle of the store past bins and baskets of roots, pods, and mysterious blobs, Old Red glanced back at me. He gave his head a little jerk forward, toward Diana, his eyebrows up high.

See? he was saying.

I replied with a coy shrug.

See what?

My brother shook his head and looked away.

I knew exactly what he was "talking" about, though. If the Southern Pacific had canned Diana, why was she still running around with an S.P. badge?

It was a question I preferred to put off . . . partially because I wasn't sure I'd like the answer.

As we neared the back of the store, I noticed a pungent odor—a reek that, at first, I assumed was the product of the foulest flatulence my brother had ever unleashed when not on the cattle trail. (Feed a fellow nothing but beans for a few weeks, and eventually he gets to out-odoring the cows.) Yet as the smell grew stronger, I realized that even with a belly-ful of beans, beer, and jalapeño peppers, no mere man could produce such a smell.

Not alive, anyway.

Beyond the pass-through was a box-packed storage room and, to the right, a narrow, steep stairwell leading to the second floor.

"Come on up . . . if you really want," Sarge said, leaning out around the corner at the top of the stairs. "I'm warning you, though. It stinks even worse up here."

Then he was gone.

Of course, this warning didn't slow Diana and Gustav. And it didn't slow me, either. It was the *stench* that did that.

With each step I took up the stairs, the putrid aroma grew more po-tent. It was one of those scents you can taste as much as smell . . . which was mighty unfortunate, since it smelled like a bucketful of buttermilk and hard-boiled eggs left out all day under an August sun.

"What *is* that, anyway?" I coughed out.

"Ain't quite right for a bloated-up body," Gustav said. "But it's close."

"It's gas from the pipes, actually," Diana said without looking back at us. "It has no smell in its natural state, so the gas company adds chemicals to give it an easily detectable odor."

"Oh, that's easy to detect, alright." I swiped off my straw hat and gave it a wave under my nose. "Any easier and I'd pass out."

My brother's only response was a vexed grunt—and I figured I knew why. The buildings he knows best are lit with oil lamps, candles, or the simple glow of a fire, not gas. If Diana hadn't been there to set us straight, he might have "deduced" that somebody upstairs had been breeding skunks. The stink of that gas was just the kind of thing I'd been riding him about the day before: a city clue . . . the kind he couldn't catch.

Old Red stomped to the top of the stairs with such booming clops I almost feared he'd splinter the steps.

Up on the second floor was a small, dimly lit flat through which the noxious vapors swirled so heavy I could practically feel them flowing around me like water. That wasn't what stopped me dead in my tracks, though. The bed in the corner did that. Or the man stretched out atop it, anyway.

It was Dr. Chan, alright—though not the same Dr. Chan we'd talked to just the day before. His clothes, normally so neat and sleek, were rumpled, and his round-rimmed spectacles were gone. He was lying on his back, eyes half-lidded, mouth half-open. *All* dead. And all grayish-blue, too, to judge by the darkened tinge to his hands and face.

I'd seen skin that color before—when I'd buried the last of my family, aside from Gustav. Like my kin back in Kansas, Chan had died for the simplest reason there is: He couldn't breathe anymore. The only difference being their lungs had filled with floodwater and his had filled with gas.

I grabbed a sheet bunched up at the foot of the bed and pulled it over the body.

"There's a lady present, case you hadn't noticed."

"Sorry," Sarge said with all the sincerity of a cat apologizing to the mouse it was about to stuff in its mouth. "I hope the *lady*'s not upset."

I turned and got my first good look at the man in his entirety. He was stocky, thick-necked, and clad not in a bull's blue frock but a businessman's brown tweed.

And he wasn't alone. Behind him was a tubby Chinaman sporting such a jutting gut he could make even a bulky fellow like myself feel like Jack Sprat. A neatly trimmed mustache and chin whiskers adorned his jowly face, and he dressed himself American fashion, though not in the starchy formal attire Chan had favored. Instead, he was wearing a white seersucker suit with matching hat. If not for the man's Oriental features, he could've passed for a Southern gentlemen on his way to the veranda for a sip of mint julep.

"You needn't worry about me," Diana said to Sarge, her voice hushed but remarkably calm. "I probably saw more dead men before I was four than you've seen in your entire life, Sergeant . . . ?"

Sarge gave the lady a smirky half-smile, unimpressed by her bravado. "Mahoney," he said. "Cathal Mahoney."

"Ahhhhh." Diana nodded. " 'The Coolietown Crusader' himself."

Mahoney waved off the nickname with a swipe of his paw—though I could see he was pleased the lady knew it.

"Oh, that's just newspaper bunk. I'm only doing my job."

"Which is?" I asked.

"Sergeant Mahoney recently took over the police department's China-town Squad," Diana explained. "He's become a great favorite of the *Morning Call*."

"Oh," I said. "I see."

The *Call* was one of the local papers Old Red and I didn't bother with, as it tended to run stuff that made the sandwich man's rants against the Chinese sound like the Sermon on the Mount. If Cathal Mahoney was a favorite of theirs, he'd likely be no favorite of ours.

I peeked over at the big Chinaman, wondering what his take on all this might be. But it was hard to tell if he was even awake to have one. His heavy-lidded eyes were closed to mere slits, and his face was utterly blank.

Diana turned toward him, too.

"And this is . . . ?"

Mahoney answered before the Chinaman could.

"Wong Woon. He's a sort of dick for hire. Like you, I guess."

Woon woke up enough to bow his head ever so slightly.

"A colleague, hmmm?" Diana said, her eyes still on the Chinaman. "Working for whom?"

"Excuse me," Mahoney cut in, "but I still don't know who *you* are, exactly."

"Oh, for god's sake, haven't we had enough how-do's?" Gustav shook a pointed a finger at the bed. "There's a dead feller under that sheet, and we're standin' around gabbin' like we was at an ice-cream social!"

"The Coolietown Crusader" gave my brother a glare that said his next crusade might be against loud-mouthed cowboys—and it could start any second.

"I apologize if we seem a tad overanxious, Sergeant," Diana said soothingly. "But you must understand—we'd become rather fond of Dr. Chan. You see, he recently met with some misfortune while traveling on a Southern Pacific special, and we've been in communication with him about the appropriate level of compensation. Finding out Chan's dead . . . well, it's quite a shock. As for who we are . . ."

The lady gestured to each of us in turn, introducing us as "Gustav Amlingmeyer, Otto Amlingmeyer, and Diana Corvus of the Southern Pacific Railroad."

Which had at least some truth to it. Old Red and I were definitely *of* the S.P.'s past. As for Diana . . . I didn't know what the truth was.

"Alright," my brother grumbled, "now that we're all acquainted-like, why doesn't somebody tell me what the heck supposedly happened here."

"There's no 'supposedly' to it, Tex," Mahoney scoffed. "Chan killed himself."

"Well, why don't you lay it all out for us, *Frisco*," Old Red said, "and then we'll just see what supposin' needs to be done."

"Please," Diana threw in—and good thing, too, since Mahoney looked like he was thinking of throwing *us* out.

"Fine," Mahoney growled. "Here's the story. One of Chan's neighbors was passing by this morning and smelled gas. He came inside to investigate, but Chan was nowhere in sight. So he came up here and found Chan laid out like that, with the gas line for the lights opened up. Everyone in Chinatown knows Chan had money troubles. Obviously, the man gassed himself." He shrugged. "To them, it's the honorable thing to do."

Gustav listened intently to Mahoney's report—while not sparing the man so much as a glance as he made it. In fact, my brother's eyes were on everything *but* Mahoney.

He was making a methodical study of Chan's digs, inspecting everything from the floorboards to the ceiling and back again.

The flat was narrow and gloomy—it could've been a sharecropper's shotgun shack but for the smudged-up light fixtures jutting from the walls here and there. The only other adornments to the place were a birdcage hanging from a brass stand in one corner and what looked like a gaudily decorated shelf, almost like a miniature theater stage, on the floor in another. Lining the walls were pasteboard boxes and small crates in tidy rows.

At the far end of the room was a door, ajar. It led to what appeared to be a dingy kitchenette. It, too, was chock-a-block with neatly stacked boxes. Over the grime-grayed sink, ragged yellow "curtains"—they looked more like old dishrags—swayed slightly in the listless breeze that blew in through an open window.

When Mahoney was done, Old Red drifted over to the birdcage and peeked inside. Then he moved on to the little stagelike affair on the floor in the opposite corner. It was painted light red, with large Chinese letters running down the back in gold. Resting atop it were bundles of paper that looked like play money, a plate with an orange on it, and a cup filled with dark, thin twig-looking things.

"So you think it's obvious, huh?" Gustav squatted and picked up one of the brownish-black sticks. "Well, let me tell you something, Sarge . . ." And he launched into a line from "The Boscombe Valley Mystery": " 'There is nothing more deceptive than an obvious fact.' "

Mahoney wrinkled his nose as if my brother's words had just doubled the room's already impressive stench. "That's the dumbest thing I ever heard."

Old Red gave the little stick in his fingers a whiff, too distracted to take offense.

"You've found a clue," Diana said, sounding both excited and strangely amused.

"I don't know if you could go so far as to call it that. But it shoots any notion of suicide clean out of the saddle as far as *I'm* concerned." My brother held up the stick and looked over his shoulder at Woon. "What are these things, anyhow?"

"Joss sticks. Incense. That's an altar," Mahoney said before the Chinaman could so much as part his lips. "Now what are you talking about? Why couldn't Chan have committed suicide?"

"An altar, huh?" Gustav dropped the "joss stick" back into its cup. "Well, looks like somebody nicked whatever god it is Doc Chan used to pray to."

"What do you mean?" Diana asked.

"Well, it's plain enough this thing used to sit in the sunshine—you can see by the way the paint's faded here and there." Old Red pointed at a spot in the center of the altar. "But not there."

The rest of us leaned in closer, like puppets pulled by the same invisible strings.

My brother was right. There was an oval-ish spot where the paint was noticeably darker—rich red as opposed to sun-bleached pink.

Mahoney straightened up first.

"That's your proof Chan didn't kill himself?"

"Nope. That's just extry data." Gustav rose up and walked to Chan's bed—and body. "Ain't the real nub of it at all."

Then he stopped and stood silently before the bed like a mourner paying his last respects.

"Yeah?" Mahoney prodded him. "And the 'nub' is . . . ?"

"There's a dead canary in that birdcage yonder," Old Red said.

And he reached down, whipped off the sheet, and rolled Chan over.

"Hey!" Mahoney squawked. "Get your paws off that body!"

Gustav ignored him, going down on one knee and brushing his fingers gently over the back of Chan's head.

"Don't look like any of you supposed pro-fessionals even bothered to . . . hel-lo."

He tugged at Chan's pants and took a peep at the dead man's keister.

That, at last, was too much for Mahoney. He charged forward and grabbed Old Red by the collar.

Before he could yank my brother to his feet, though, the cop felt hands on *his* collar. Mine.

"*Don't,*" I said. "He knows what he's doin'."

Even if I *don't,* I chose not to add.

Mahoney let go of Gustav and twisted free of my grip.

"Let me give you yokels some advice," he snapped, jabbing a finger into my chest like I was a balloon he was trying to pop with a pin. "This isn't some pissant cow town. It's San Francisco. And around here, men who lay hands on a cop get their heads busted no matter who they work for."

"Sergeant, I'm sorry—but just hear Mr. Amlingmeyer out," Diana pleaded. "There's method to his madness, I promise you."

"Ain't madness at all. Just method," Old Red said. Despite the jostling he'd received, he was still hunched over Chan's body, his hands now snaking into the dead man's pockets. " 'Madness' wouldn't get you this, now would it?"

He turned around holding up a folded slip of paper. Out of force of habit, perhaps, he handed it to his usual translator: me.

"Gimme that," Mahoney snarled, snatching the paper from my fingers. He unfolded it with an angry snap of the wrist.

"Oh." He handed the little note to Woon. "It's in Chinese."

The Chinaman appeared utterly unruffled by our little tussle, and he peered down at the paper as coolly as a man looking over a menu.

When he finally spoke, it was in a surprisingly lilting, sing-song voice—though his words sure struck a sour note.

"Suicide note," he said.

"Bull-*shit,*" said my brother.

9

BODY OF EVIDENCE

Or, Gustav Makes a Few Deductions and a Few New Enemies

Excuse me?" Mahoney said, hacking out an incredulous laugh.

"You heard me." Old Red pointed at the slip of paper in Woon's hand. "If that's a 'suicide note,' I'm the Queen of Sheba."

"I'll tell you what you are, you little—"

"Why don't you read the note for us, Mr. Woon?" Diana said, shifting everyone's attention to the chubby Chinaman—and away from the brawl that was about to break out. "So we can judge for ourselves."

Woon peered at her a moment . . . then refolded the note and slid it into one of the voluminous pockets of his seersucker suit.

"No," Woon said, his heavily accented voice still silky-soft. "Is private message. For certain gentleman only. I see he receive it."

He looked over at Mahoney, seemingly sending *him* a private message, as well.

"And that's good enough for you?" my brother snapped at the cop.

Mahoney's eyes flicked from Woon's now-empty hand to his round, placid face. "Chan wrote that? Saying he was gonna kill himself?"

Woon nodded once, the slow down-up of his head pressing then stretching the folds of flesh hanging from his chin like the bellows of a squeezebox.

"Suicide note."

"Alright, then," Mahoney said. "That settles it."

Just from the way my brother drew in his breath, I knew what was coming next: a retort so pointed it'd draw blood. Diana must've seen it coming, too.

"Putting aside the note, for the moment," she said before Gustav could cut the copper to the quick—and get himself beat to a pulp. "My colleague here said he had reason to doubt suicide. Something about . . . a dead canary?"

"That's right." Old Red jerked a thumb at the birdcage, his eyes never leaving Mahoney. "The little feller in there."

"Uh-huh." Mahoney drew the sounds out slowly, as if he was agreeing with some foamy-mouthed lunatic's pronouncement that water is wet. "Soooooo . . . what? You think the suicide note was really for the *bird*?"

"Oh, for Christ's sake," Gustav spat. "The canary would've died before Chan did—died noisy, too. Why do you think they take 'em down in coal mines? For the tunes?"

Mahoney threw up his hands. "*So?*"

"*So* Chan would've knowed his pet was dyin'. His last moments on earth, he would've been listenin' to its pitiful little death rattle." My brother shook his head. "No. Not the Chan I knew. He was a healer. *Maybe* he'd kill himself, but *never* would he have killed that little bird. He would've set it free first."

"That's your proof?"

The cop shot Woon a "Can you believe this shit?" grimace. Whether Woon believed or not, one couldn't say—he merely stared at my brother through heavy, half-lidded eyes, so expressionless a cigar store Indian would've looked like Sarah Bernhardt by comparison.

"The man was suicidal," Mahoney said. "He wasn't going to stop to worry about his canary."

"That ain't enough to get you thinkin', then how's about this?" Old Red persisted. "You say some neighbor found Chan's body after smellin' gas outside. But we didn't get a whiff of nothing till we was practically at the foot of the stairs. Well . . . how is it that feller could know it was gettin' gassy up here?"

Mahoney curled his lips into a sneer. "He'd know because the front door was wide open and gas was blowing right out onto the sidewalk. By the time you three got here, the gas had been off an hour and the downstairs had aired out."

"Excuse *me?* A feller goes to gas himself . . . and he leaves the front door open?" Gustav looked like a man trying to teach long division to a chicken. "And that don't give your brain a little tickle?"

"Look," Mahoney said, "Chan wasn't thinking straight. Everyone in Chinatown knew he was broke . . . thanks to your railroad, I might add. He was about to kill himself. You can't expect everything he did to make sense."

"Well, that's an awful convenient way of lookin' at things, ain't it?" Old Red said. "Cuz then you don't have to wonder why Chan would rub gravel on his head and pull his shirttails outta his britches before climbin' into bed to die."

Woon finally seemed to wake up, his droopy eyes at last popping fully open.

"You say 'gravel'?"

My brother nodded. "In Chan's—"

"Don't bother," Mahoney cut in. "Like I said before, I can already explain everything: *Chan was nuts.* And so are you, Tex."

"But, Sergeant," Diana said, "wouldn't it behoove you to—?"

Mahoney silenced her with a mighty stomp to the floorboards. "Thompson!" He pounded his foot down two more times. "*Thompson!* Get your fat ass up here!"

"Coming, Sarge!" a muffled voice called from below us.

A sudden, surprising chuckle bubbled up from deep in Mahoney's gut. The cop looked relieved, newly unburdened, like a man who's just stepped from the privy five pounds lighter.

"You know what?" he said cheerfully. "Screw the Southern Pacific. Screw *you*." He pointed his smile at Diana, and it turned so wolfish it practically howled at the moon. "All of you."

As Mahoney spoke, a squeaking and shaking grew steadily louder, the clamor of it rising to such a pitch I almost thought I was about to experience my first California "earth-quake." But it wasn't the earth a-quaking— it was just the big bull from downstairs lumbering up the steps to join us.

"Yeah, Sarge?" he panted, red-faced, upon reaching the top of the stairs.

"Show these people the door," Mahoney told him. "And if they don't remember what it's for, throw them through it."

"With pleasure," Thompson said, locking eyes on me.

I held his gaze even as I threw a question at Old Red.

"We goin' peacefully, Brother?"

"Of course we are," Diana answered for Gustav, already headed for the stairwell. "Good day, Sergeant. I expect your superiors will be hearing from ours very soon now."

"And I expect my superiors won't give a damn," Mahoney scoffed. "This is Chinatown, lady. *Nobody* gives a damn."

"I do," Gustav said.

He hadn't taken a step toward the stairs.

Mahoney heaved a heavy sigh. "Look, Tex, let me give you a little more friendly advice." Then he dropped his voice to a hissing whisper that somehow seemed louder than a shout. "Get your ass out of Chinatown. Because the next time I spot you in my district, I'm gonna take that worthless S.P. star of yours and—"

The copper proceeded to conjure up an image that was, for "friendly advice," mighty unfriendly indeed.

"Come on," I said, laying a hand on my brother's shoulder. "Ain't nothin' more we can do here now."

Gustav let me steer him from the room, though he moved slow, peering back first at Mahoney, then at Chan. This was to be our good-by to the good doctor, I realized, and I paused to give him a farewell salute myself.

Thompson got me moving again with a prod from his truncheon.

"Well, gentlemen, I have to admit I'm impressed," Diana said as we were herded to the first floor. "Not on the case half an hour, and already you've made a bitter enemy of the police officer in charge."

"Mahoney wasn't exactly down on one knee offerin' *you* posies," I pointed out.

Ahead of me, Old Red twisted around again for a last, long stare up the steps. A moth flying into the flame couldn't have looked more single-mindedly mesmerized, and I almost expected him to spin on his heel and start climbing right over me and the big cop at my back.

"That idjit Mahoney's just the beginning," he said. "By god, I ain't through makin' enemies 'round here."

His words somehow sounded like both kinds of oath at once—the kind that's a vow and the kind that's a curse.

As it turned out, it was to be one other thing, too: a prophecy.

10

THE ALLEY

Or, We Double Back—and Find Our Troubles Doubled, Too

As Thompson (and his truncheon) ushered us from the shop, we passed two other policemen carrying not billy clubs but a stretcher. Their police ambulance was parked out front.

Chan would be leaving soon after we did, it seemed. His destination: the morgue.

The instant Thompson sent us out onto the sidewalk (with a farewell baton-prod to the kidneys for me), my brother started pushing his way through the still milling crowd of neck-craning Chinamen. He was in too much of a hurry to offer explanations to me and Diana, so all we could do was share a shrug and follow in his wake.

Gustav turned left at the first corner, then left again to take us down an alley—the one running behind Chan's shop, I quickly realized. I would say it was the darkest, dankest, dismalest back street I've ever had the displeasure to find myself in . . . but the day was yet young.

"So we ain't takin' Mahoney's advice?" I said when I caught up to Old Red.

"What? Leave Chinatown?" My brother snorted. "Sure, I'll leave . . . once I know what happened to Doc Chan."

Diana hustled up between us.

"You're going to sneak back in and search Chan's flat?"

73

"Yup. Soon as those lawmen clear out, that is exactly what *I'm* gonna do." Gustav shot the lady a sidelong glance. "'Course, *you* need to clear out, too."

"Oh, I'm not leaving," Diana replied, her tone so matter of fact she might have been telling her hostess she didn't care for another crumpet at an afternoon tea party.

"I'm sorry, miss . . . but I gotta agree with my brother," I said. "And it's not just cuz this ain't no place for a lady. A man's dead, and for all we know Little Pete himself ordered it done. If so, this business ain't for ladies *or* gentlemen—not the ones that plan on keepin' their throats unslit."

"Then why are *you* involving yourselves?" Diana asked me.

"Well . . . cuz we gotta."

I looked around her at Old Red, and he gave me a grim nod. For once, we were in complete agreement. "Cuz we gotta"—that said it all.

And apparently Diana felt the same way.

"I knew Dr. Chan as well as you two did," she said. "So if you 'gotta,' then I gotta, too. And, to put it bluntly, you need me. Neither of you has my knowledge of the city—not to mention my gift for persuasion."

"Ain't so hard to *persuade* when you got yourself a badge to flash," Old Red said, slamming to a sudden stop. As Diana and I reined up beside him, he turned and looked the lady in the eye full-on—no squirming, no blinking, no blushing. "How is it you still got your star, Miss Corvus? You said the S.P. took it back after Colonel Crowe got hisself canned."

Diana smiled in her sly way that seemed to put you in on some joke with her—even though she wouldn't come out and tell it to you.

"The colonel had a drawer full of Southern Pacific badges. So I borrowed one. For a rainy day. And lucky for you I did, or you never would've made it up to Chan's room in the first place."

"I don't know if I'd call your bein' here 'luck,'" Old Red grumbled.

"Gustav," Diana said gently, like she was calming a spooked horse, "I can help."

Hearing his Christian name slipping so tenderly from the lady's lips brought a blush to my brother's face, and his gaze wavered.

"Yeah, well, maybe you could. But—"

Before he could get any further, the clatter and clop of a heavy wagon turned us all around to face the street again.

The police ambulance was pulling past the alleyway.

"Mahoney and Woon might be leaving, too," Diana said.

"Could be," my brother grunted.

"Well, why don't we find out?"

And Diana marched away, moving deeper into the alley. As she went, Old Red stared daggers at her back as if she'd just planted a knife in his.

"Look," I said, "the lady's tied herself to us, and there's no cuttin' her loose if she don't wanna be cut. Not now, anyways. In the meantime, we may as well face facts: She *can* help us. So what say we just get to deducifyin', huh?"

"What do you think I been doin'?" Gustav grumbled, and he set off after Diana.

A moment later, the three of us were together outside one of the shabby back doors lining the alley. It hadn't been hard to figure whose place it belonged to: The windows around and above it were all cracked open, and the putrid smell of gas still swirled outside.

We got ourselves a real snootful, too, for Old Red led us straight to the nearest window and crouched down beside it. Through the smudged, sooty glass, we could see the cluttered storage room at the back of Chan's shop.

"Best hold off a spell 'fore tryin' anything," Gustav whispered. "If Mahoney was to catch any of us in there . . ."

He didn't need to say any more than that. I could still hear the copper telling us what he'd do with our badges should we cross his path again. And given the man's temperament, I couldn't even be sure he was speaking metaphorically.

Old Red hunkered down on one side of the window. Diana and I squatted on the other.

My brother and Diana spent the next minute with ears cocked for noises inside—while I fought to keep my eyes from straying to the lady's décolletage.

"It's awfully quiet in there," Diana finally said.

Gustav's forefinger shot to his lips. "*Hush.* I think I hear . . . shit."

Then I heard it, too. Not shit, of course. An ever-growing grinding sound. And beneath it, something else.

Footsteps.

Behind us.

I murmured another word ladies are never supposed to hear. Funny thing, though—I could've sworn I heard Diana mutter something even worse.

I turned back toward the alleyway expecting to find Mahoney and Woon coming at us, handcuffs at the ready.

What I saw instead was a sour-faced Chinaman wearing a stained apron over his ratty tunic and trousers. Behind him was the source of the rumbling we'd heard: his pushcart.

To my surprise, I realized I knew the man, after a fashion. It was the cabbage peddler Old Red and I had so disgusted the day before.

He said something to us in Chinese, most of it gibberish to me, of course. But I did catch one phrase I could recognize, if not understand. It was the same thing he'd spat at me and my brother the day before—"fink why."

Gustav swept off his Stetson and waved it at the man like he was shooing away a fly. "Move along. Go on. Get."

The Chinaman did none of the above. In fact, he kept coming closer.

Diana stuffed her hand in her purse and pulled out her badge. "It's alright, sir. We're here on official business. No need to concern yourself."

The man squinted at Diana's badge, squinted at us . . . and then smiled. He had a round face and a sickly yellow-green complexion, and his big gap-toothed grin made him look like a jack-o'-lantern carved from one of his own cabbages.

"You no po-lee!" he cackled.

"Thank god," Old Red said. "He speaks English."

"Sort of," I said.

"You're right. We're not police," Diana told the Chinaman. "Nevertheless, we do have the authority to—"

"You no po-lee," the peddler said again. "You want hok gup, yeah?"

"We want *what?*" I said.

"Hok gup," the cabbage man said. "Black . . ." Words failed him—English ones, anyway—so he tried pantomime instead, pushing his hands together and flapping his fingers.

"Black . . . bunny?" Gustav guessed.

"Bunny?" I said. "How in the world do you get 'bunny' outta that?"

"Well, he's doin' floppy ears, ain't he?"

"Naw. It's more like he's diggin' or something." I turned back to the Chinaman. "Black gopher?"

The peddler shook his head in frustration and brought his still-fluttering hands up over his head.

"Black *bird*," Diana said.

The Chinaman nodded, shooting me a glare as he dropped his hands.

"Sorry," I said. "Usually I'm pretty good at this game."

"Hold on," Old Red said. "This feller's tryin' to sell us a *crow?*"

Diana ignored him. "Why do you think we want the hok gup—the black bird?" she asked the cabbage man.

He pointed at the building behind us. "With Gee Woo Chan. But now . . ."

He spread his hands out and shrugged, and there was no mistaking what his gesture meant this time.

Who can say where it's gone?

And his widening smile provided the answer.

I can.

"So . . . what is it *you* want, mister?" Gustav asked.

The peddler walked back to his cart and inspected his wares. After a moment's consideration, he picked up the limpest, brownest, wormiest-looking cabbage and waved it over his head.

"You buy!"

"Well, there's a stroke of luck, at least," Diana said. "As extortionists go, he's pretty cheap."

"Brother," Old Red said, "go buy us a cabbage—and whatever else we can get."

"Right."

I straightened up and went striding toward the man, digging a hand into my pocket as I went. When we were toe to toe, I offered him a nice shiny dime.

"There you are. You can keep the change—and the cabbage, too. Just tell me . . . what?"

The Chinaman was shaking his head, and he brought up his free hand and spread three fingers wide.

"Thirty cents?" I groaned. "Oh, come on. That moldy thing ain't worth a plug nickel."

The cabbage man shook the fingers at my face.

"No!" he barked. "Three *dollah*!"

"What? You can't be serious!"

"Shut up, the both of you," Old Red snapped in that hoarse, whispery way that cuts through you quicker than a holler—because you know folks only use it when trouble's coming.

And trouble *was* coming, clomping down the stairs inside wearing brown brogans and tweed trousers. And a badge, too, I knew, though I couldn't yet see anything above the knee.

I didn't have to—I recognized those big, clunky shoes. They were the ones the Coolietown Crusader had been so tempted to plant up our behinds not half an hour before.

It was looking like they might get there yet.

11

HIDE AND PEEK

Or, Old Red Spots a Double Cross of Note

The cabbage man did us the favor of dropping his voice—though not his price—as Sgt. Mahoney came down the stairs inside.

"*Five* dollah."

It was a whole new haggle now. The Chinaman wasn't just peddling information (or a crappy old cabbage) anymore. He was selling silence, and it was most definitely a seller's market.

Through the window, I could see Mahoney—or his feet, anyway—stomp down a couple more steps, then stop.

"Move it, would ya?" the copper said, twisting around to face someone at the top of the stairs. "We don't get outside soon, I'll never get this stink off of my suit."

I turned back to the cabbage man, jammed my hands in my pockets, and pulled out every coin and crumpled greenback I had. It wouldn't add up to five bucks, I knew, but I was hoping the sheer size of the wad would be too tempting to pass up.

"Here. Take it all. Just get to talkin' quick—and quiet."

The peddler took my money with one hand. The other he used to jab the cabbage into my stomach.

"You look fat choy," the Chinaman said.

Then he left me holding the cabbage.

79

"That's it?" I spluttered as he started pushing his cart away. "I look 'fat choy'?"

The Chinaman nodded. "You look fat choy."

"Well, you look like a thievin' bastard to me," I spat back.

There was no time to demand a refund, though. I just spun on my heel and went diving for cover with the cabbage still clutched against my gut. I landed under the open window between Old Red and Diana.

The cabbage man shambled off grinning like the cat who ate the canary—and then had the goldfish for desert.

"You're wasting your time up there," I heard Mahoney say. "You know as well as I do—hatchet men don't work like this. Not even Scientific. If Little Pete finally had Chan done in, he wouldn't be *subtle* about it. He'd have him hacked to death in the middle of Dupont." The cop's heavy footfalls started up again. "Chan killed himself, and that's all there is to it."

"May-be," someone replied. "May-be not."

The words were heavily accented, the voice lilting—and familiar. It was Woon.

The thud-squeak-thud of footsteps on the stairs doubled, grew louder, then shifted to quieter shuffles. The two detectives were in the storage room, mere feet away from us.

"Hey," Diana whispered. "What if they come out this way instead of out the front?"

The back door was so close, it'd smack my brother in the butt if it swung open now.

"Then we're in a hell of a lot of trouble," Old Red whispered back.

"Woon, *listen*," Mahoney said.

His footsteps stopped.

I got set to start up my own—in a hurry.

"I know Chan was a Six Companies man," Mahoney went on, and Diana, Gustav, and I each let out a quiet sigh of relief. "You've got Chun Ti Chu to answer to. Fine. Just spend the next couple days banging your favorite sing-song girl, then tell him you couldn't dig anything up. Believe me, that'll be a better use of your time than asking a bunch of stupid questions. Chan wasn't murdered . . . no matter what Bullshit Bill Cody said."

I glanced over at the man I assumed was "Bullshit Bill." He wasn't just keeping an ear to the window anymore—he'd leaned out far enough to get a peek inside.

I gave his leg an "Are you crazy?" swat.

He replied with a "Go away" flap of the hand.

"You right," Woon said. "Probably."

"Pra-bah-ree?" Mahoney sneered, mocking the Chinaman's accent. "Jesus, Woon—you said yourself there was a suicide note. Speaking of which . . . you *were* gonna give that back to me, right?"

There was a brief silence before Woon answered.

"Of course."

Then it went quiet again—so quiet I could hear the whisper that slipped from Old Red's lips even though he didn't put a puff of wind behind it.

"Hel-lo."

I tried to poke up for a peep at whatever he'd seen, but Gustav laid his hand flat against the top of my boater and pushed me back down.

"Gee . . . thanks, Woon," Mahoney said, his snide tone smearing the words like mud he was wiping on the other man's shoes. "Now why don't you do us both a favor? Don't you ever—*ever*—try to slip anything past me again. Cuz the next time I catch you playing one of your little Chink games, I'll break your fat neck. Sabe?"

Apparently, Woon nodded to show he had indeed sabed (whatever that meant) for Mahoney said, "*Good.* Now come on. I've wasted enough time here already."

I braced again to make a break for it, maybe lob the only weapon I had—my cabbage—at Mahoney's head. But the sound of footsteps that followed faded away quickly. Woon and Mahoney were headed out through the front of Chan's shop, not the back.

Old Red finally let me stand up now, and I took a look in through the window. The storeroom was empty but for the boxes, bins, and crates stacked up here and there.

"Well, 'Bill'—whadaya make of all that?" I said.

"Ain't got enough data for theorizin'," my brother muttered.

"Perhaps. But we do have *some* data," Diana said. "Whatever it was you saw in there, for instance."

She pivoted to peer into the storeroom, the move bringing her shoulder to shoulder with me. For the next few seconds, my shoulder was very happy indeed.

"Yeah, Brother," I said. "What was you hel-loin'?"

Gustav's gaze went faraway, fuzzy. For a man who said he wasn't ready to theorize, he sure seemed to be doing some awful deep thinking.

"Woon. He didn't give that phony 'suicide note' back to Mahoney," he said slowly.

"Sure as heck sounded like he did."

Old Red shook his head slowly. "He gave Mahoney *something*, but it wasn't the same paper I found on Chan. It was smaller. Didn't have no fold to it, neither."

"And Mahoney didn't notice the difference?" I asked.

My brother hacked out his usual little cough of contempt—"Feh!"

"Woon could've handed over a slice of ham and that fathead wouldn't have noticed the difference," he said. "Still, he had Woon pegged on at least one thing: The man's workin' his own side of the fence. Got something to do with that 'Shun Tea-Chew' and 'Six Companies' Mahoney was yappin' about, most like."

Gustav cleared his throat and looked at his toes—a sure sign that his next words were directed at Diana.

"Seems like I've heard of 'em both somewheres, too, but I can't quite recollect how . . . ."

Diana smiled primly, looking like a schoolmarm savoring the opportunity to remind her pupils who has all the answers.

"If you've heard of one, you've heard of the other," she said. "The Six Companies is an association of Chinese businessmen that acts as a sort of local government. Around here, the president of the Six Companies may as well be the mayor—and the current president's name is Chun Ti Chu."

"Sure. I remember now," I said. "Chu pops up in the papers sometimes. Law and order type. Tong fighter. The only Chinaman powerful enough to stand up to Little Pete." I shook my head. "Poor Doc Chan. If he got caught up in some kinda feud between this Chu feller and the tongs—"

"Don't kick that pony up to a gallop just yet," Old Red cut in. "We ain't even got the bridle on."

I whistled and gave Gustav an admiring nod. "That's a good one, Brother. Real quotable-like. How long you been waitin' to spring it on me?"

Old Red gave me a glare so sharp you could shave with it.

"I'm gonna go make me a reconnoiter," he growled. "You just stay here. And stay *quiet* . . . if that's something you're capable of."

He pushed the window up higher, then swung up a leg and slipped over the sill. Diana and I watched side by side as he crept through the clutter to the pass-through separating the storage room from the rest of the shop.

"Thank you for standing up for me a few minutes ago," Diana half-whispered to me. "With your brother, I mean."

Awww, let her stay—we can't get rid of her anyway. That's all I'd really said to Old Red. It didn't strike me as much of a stand. It barely amounted to a crouch.

Still, who was I to turn away the lady's gratitude?

"You're welcome," I whispered back. "Usually, Gustav takes what I say with a grain of salt the size of a Conestoga wagon. I'm pleased he listened for once."

Inside, Old Red peeped around the pass-through into the rest of the store. When he'd satisfied himself that Mahoney and Woon were gone, he turned and tiptoed toward the stairs without so much as a glance over at us.

"You can be honest with me, Otto," Diana said. "Why does my presence put your brother on edge so?"

I snorted out a chuckle as Gustav disappeared up into the stairwell.

"Miss, that man wakes up on edge. Goes to bed on edge, too. *Dreams* on edge, for all I know. You shouldn't take it personal."

"There you go again," Diana sighed theatrically, mock-exasperated. "Trying to protect my delicate female sensibilities—when I don't have any. Your brother doesn't like me, that's obvious. I'm simply curious as to why."

I turned away from the window and leaned back against the building. The cheap, rotten wood seemed to sag under my weight, and I straightened up again for fear I'd crash right through the wall.

"It ain't that he don't like you," I said (or maybe lied—I wasn't sure myself). "It's just that he's got his head so filled up fulla mysteries and murder and whatnot it makes him a mite mistrustful. And your bein' a gal don't make it any easier for him to let down his guard."

"Why's that?"

"Oh, now *you're* the one bein' coy," I chided her. "It's hard for Gustav cuz he's a man and you're a woman. He ain't spent much time around lady-folk the last few years. Gals . . . they jangle him up a bit, that's all."

"Well, I suppose that's something else your brother has in common with his hero," Diana said. "Though Mr. Holmes wasn't so much 'jangled' by women as disdainful of them. In fact, there were always rumors that his lack of interest in the fair sex extended to . . . well . . ."

Diana didn't come right out and say it, of course, but she gave me the kind of look that puts the word in your head.

Sex.

"Whoa, there! You sayin' Sherlock Holmes was . . . ?"

I squinted one eye and waggled one hand.

Diana shrugged. "People will gossip . . . ."

"Well, it ain't nothin' like that for Gustav," I insisted a little too loudly for a fellow who was still supposed to be laying low. "Like I said, he's just skirt-shy. Bein' around a pretty woman—especially one with a little culture to her. It's kinda embarrassin' for him. On account of he's . . . y' know . . . ."

"Illiterate" seemed like such a harsh brand to burn onto a man as sharp-witted as my brother, and I groped around for a better word. But the only substitutes I could think of were "uneducated" or "ignorant," neither of which struck me as much of an improvement.

I settled on "got his limits."

Diana arched an eyebrow at me. "I've met many a man with 'limits,' Otto. Believe me—most of them don't let it scare them away from women."

"Oh, I know the type," I said, tempted (as a man of limitations and little fear of females) to dare a wink. Somehow, I managed to restrain myself. "But that just ain't Gustav's way. He's always been bashful . . . and mopey . . . and cantankerous. Ol' Casanova himself wouldn't have got so much as a peck on the cheek if he'd been saddled with all that."

"So Old Red's never even had a sweetheart?"

I pushed my boater up high and gave my head a scratch. "You know, miss . . . you sure are askin' a lot of questions about my brother."

Diana chuckled softly. "Once a detective, always a detective, I suppose. I'm sorry if I seem nosy."

"Oh, don't apologize." I flashed her my most dazzling grin—the one designed to blind women to all the faults they'd otherwise see in me. "I'd just like it a lot better if you was askin' questions about *me*."

Before the lady could either slap me or laugh, Gustav came tromping down the stairs and walked to the window.

"Alright—it's clear. You may as well get in here."

"Ladies first," I said to Diana.

"Oh, no," she replied. "Vegetables first."

And I finally remembered I still had a rotten cabbage tucked under one arm.

"Why, thank you," I said, and I opened the window wider (to accommodate my broader backside) and clambered inside with as much grace and dignity as I could muster. Which wasn't much.

"Why are you still luggin' around that damn cabbage?" Gustav asked.

"Cuz it cost me every cent I had, that's why. I ain't just throwin' it away." I held the cabbage up as if admiring its wilted splendor. "He could be our mascot. We'll call him . . . Old Green."

My brother just shook his head and walked away, leaving it to me and Old Green to help Diana through the window. By the time I had the lady settled both feet on the floor, Old Red was already halfway up the stairs again.

Diana and I set off after him through a chest-high maze of boxes and crates. The Chan I'd known had been exceptionally tidy, ever neat and proper in dress and deportment. So it struck me as strange that he'd keep his storeroom in such a state. It made me wonder if the man's outward orderliness had been mere facade—a cover for a messier, murkier soul lurking within.

We found the body gone when we got upstairs, of course. What's more, the blanket that had been beneath it was gone, as well. It was as if the police had simply wrapped Chan up like a Mexican burrito rather than bother with a sheet or shroud.

Gustav pawed over the bed a moment, then dropped to all fours and began searching the floor in Holmes's hound-dog style—nose down, ass up. It made for quite a sight, but Diana didn't waste more than a second's worth of smirk on it. Instead, she commenced her own search, moving to the corrugated paperboard boxes pushed against the wall.

"These are stacked neatly enough," she said. "Not like that mess downstairs."

"Already noted," Old Red said gruffly.

Diana started flipping the boxes open. In the first were stacks of carefully folded socks and underwear. The next contained similarly trim piles of shirts. The next, suit clothes.

"Chan only moved here recently," Diana said. "He didn't even have time to unpack."

"Already noted," Old Red said.

"His old place must've been a heck of a lot bigger—even boxed, his stuff fills this dump up." I looked over at my brother, who was crawling around Chan's bed, eyes down. "And just so's you know, I wasn't *notin'* that for *you*. It was for myself."

"Noted," Gustav said.

Bent over as he was, his backside presented an awfully tempting target for my boot-toe. So I removed myself from temptation by drifting off to the kitchenette adjoining the main room.

Tucked around the corner was a luxury I hadn't expected to find in such dilapidated digs as this: a water closet complete with commode and sink. It wasn't just a surprise—it was a blessing, for I'd begun to hear the call of nature so loud it was a wonder it didn't deafen me. I left Old Green on a countertop and slipped inside.

I couldn't close the door behind me, though. If I had, the tiny privy would've gone blinding black, leaving me nothing to aim by. And for all I knew, there was still enough free-floating gas in the place to barbecue the lot of us should I fire up a light. So I had to ask Diana to plug her ears for a moment while I saw a man about a dog.

"Don't worry, Otto," she called back from the other room. "I grew up around men, most of whom weren't nearly as gentlemanly as you. Believe me, I've overheard a *lot* of conversations about dogs. I won't be offended. In fact, from now on, both of you should feel free to piss, cuss, belch, fart, or pick your nose whenever the urge arises. You don't have to keep apologizing."

"Uhhh . . . is there anything we're *not* allowed to do?" I managed to ask despite a jaw that had practically dropped into the commode.

"You two don't chew tobacco, do you?"

"No, miss," I heard my brother answer, his voice so low I half-suspected he'd crawled under the bed to quietly die of embarrassment.

"Good. Now *that's* a disgusting habit."

Despite Diana's dispensation to be as crude as I pleased, I gave the toilet-chain a yank before taking leave of my morning coffee. As I stood there staring down, I noticed a wastebasket shoved into the gray shadows beneath the sink beside the john. A crumpled-up newspaper lay atop it in a way that seemed altogether too . . . something. Once my bladder was totally tapped, I buttoned myself up and bent myself down.

The newspaper had been wadded, but only enough so as to fit snugly across the top of the ash can. When I plucked the paper out, I saw what it was meant to cover: jagged pieces of painted porcelain and, curling out from beneath the largest shard, what looked from above like a small length of dark rubber or rope. I reached down and pinched the coiled whatever-it-was betwixt my forefinger and thumb.

It felt surprisingly brittle, and as I drew it out into the murky light, I saw that there was something large and blobby attached to the other end. I had it halfway to my face before I realized what it was.

I don't know what a man with the proverbial tiger by the tail is supposed to do. But I can sure tell you what a fellow with a *scorpion* by the tail does, whether he wants to or not.

He screams.

12

THE CRITTER

Or, Chan's Flat Yields Yet Another Stiff

W hat? *What?*" Old Red shouted as he dashed into the kitchenette.

"That! *That!*" I shouted as I dashed *out* of the WC.

I spun around and pointed at the privy floor.

"Hel-lo! Is that a—?"

"It sure as hell is!"

Diana crowded into the cramped room behind my brother.

"Don't get too close, miss," I said to her between panting, panicked breaths. "That there's a—"

"I know what it is." The lady leaned forward, squinting at the floor. "Only that one looks dead."

Indeed, the scorpion was laying just where I'd dropped it.

Perfectly still. On its back.

My brother bent over and crept up cautiously until he was crouched down over top of it.

"Yup. Dead." Gustav glanced back at a me. "You probably scared the poor thing to death with your shriekin'."

"Be fair enough if I did. That ugly SOB like to scare *me* to death first."

Old Red reached down, picked the critter up by one of its big pincers, and brought it to eyeball level. If scorpions know how to play possum, this one had just tricked its way close enough to my brother's face to give him a sting on the nose.

It was no trick, though. In fact, the scorpion remained so unnaturally stiff, I started to wonder if it had ever been alive in the first place.

Up till then, all the scorpions I'd run across (and from) had been a mustardy yellow—the better to blend in with sand and desert rock. But the one Gustav was holding now wasn't just twice as large as any I'd ever laid eyes on, it was a dozen times darker. The only place this fat black bastard would blend in was a nightmare.

"That thing even real?" I asked.

"Yup," Old Red said. "Been dried out, though. Ain't much more than husk now." He held said husk out to me. "Wanna see for yourself?"

"I *been* seein'. It's touchin' I ain't so keen on."

"May I?"

Diana stepped forward and plucked the critter from Gustav's fingers without waiting for an answer.

"Doesn't look like any scorpion I've ever seen," she said, holding it straight up by its tail like it was a candied apple on a stick.

"And just how many *have* you seen?" my brother asked her.

"A few. There was a time I had to check my shoes for them every time I got dressed." She handed the scorpion back to him. "What do you think it means?"

"Maybe somebody was tryin' to sic it on Chan," I suggested. "Only the gas killed it first."

Old Red shook his head. "This thing ain't just dead. It's leathered. Gas wouldn't do that."

"Then maybe it's the 'hok gup' that peddler feller spoke of. Could be he wasn't talkin' about a black bird at all. He was talkin' about a black scorpion."

Diana put her hands together and fluttered the fingers over her head, just as the cabbage man had down in the alley. "Scorpion?"

"Alright—that don't wash, neither," I conceded. "So let's try this on for size. It's like them five orange pips from the Holmes tale. You remember, Brother. What was that one called?"

"You mean 'The Five Orange Pips'?" Gustav sighed.

"Yeah, right, anyway—maybe that's the kinda thing we're lookin' at here. It's a threat. Only not from the Ku Klux Klan, like in the story. From the tongs."

It was my best theory yet, I thought, but Old Red just waved it away like it was more stink from the gas pipes.

"I'll tell you exactly what this means," he said, giving the scorpion a little shake. "It means Chan had a dead scorpion in his jakes. And that's *it* until we round us up more data. Now . . . where was it you found this? I assume it wasn't just sittin' on the crapper readin' the paper." He threw a little sidelong peep in the general direction of Diana's knees. "By your request, I ain't apologizin' for that remark."

"Noted," Diana said.

I stepped closer to the privy and pointed at the wastebasket under the sink.

"It was in there. Looked like someone tried to cover over the top, so I got to scroungin' around to see what I could see. Found Blackie under some busted-up pottery or somesuch."

"Busted-up pottery?"

My brother pushed his way past me, knelt down next to the ash can, and took a look at the jagged pieces of brightly colored porcelain inside. They didn't come from any plate, that was for sure—there were too many bulges and ripples to them.

Gustav began rooting around amongst the shards with his free hand, seeming particularly interested in the smaller bits and dust that had sifted to the bottom of the basket.

"Don't look like no 'pottery' I ever seen. Seems more like . . . hel-lo."

He lifted out a grooved disc about the size of a silver dollar. It was mostly a ghostly pure white, though there were splotches of red, green, and black here and there.

Red lips. Green eyes. Black eyebrows.

It was a woman's face.

"A doll?" Diana asked, leaning in for a peek over Old Red's shoulder.

"Looks thataway."

Gustav slipped the shard into one of his coat pockets, then stood and gently lowered the scorpion into another.

"But Chan didn't have no kids—least not that we ever heard of," I pointed out. "Why would he keep a china doll lyin' around?"

"And why would anyone want to destroy it?" Diana added.

My brother shuffled back toward the bedroom listlessly, lost in thought. "When y'all have you some *answers,* would you let me know? Cuz Lord knows I don't need no more questions."

"Not even 'What next?'" I said as Diana and I trailed him.

"Whadaya mean, 'What next?'" Old Red went down on his hands and knees and got back to playing bloodhound. "We keep huntin' for clues, that's what."

"Any *particular* clues?" Diana asked. "I mean, if I can avoid wasting time determining Dr. Chan's shoe size or examining the droppings in his birdcage, that might be to our advantage, don't you think?"

I expected Gustav to snip back something like, "Can't be particular about what I ain't seen." Instead, he gave the lady something he so often withholds from me: a straight answer.

"We're lookin' for a chain-mail vest, a derringer, spectacles, bits of broken china, bloodstains, a black bird, and anything else that looks cluey-like to you."

A look of supreme satisfaction spread across Diana's face.

"Thank you."

My brother just kept sweeping the floorboards with his mustache.

"Now, let's see," Diana mused, tapping a slender finger against her lower lip. "The spectacles are obvious: When we saw the body, Chan's glasses were missing. You're wondering why anyone would take them. The same with Chan's chain mail and derringer. Why aren't they here? Unless . . . may I venture a deduction?"

"Would it stop you if I said no?" Old Red mumbled, momentarily distracted by a small, mysterious object that turned out to be a dead roach.

"Probably not."

Gustav tossed the little bug husk aside. "Well, then don't bother askin' next time."

"Alright, then. I think perhaps the killer took the vest and the gun because he wanted to hide the fact that Chan was in fear for his life."

"I can't imagine that was much of a secret 'round Chinatown." I took off my boater and ran a hand through my hair. "You know . . . what with the doc creasin' folks' scalps and all."

"Of course." Diana slumped, looking chagrined. "But the other things . . . the broken porcelain, the blood . . ." She took in a deep breath and straightened her spine. "I'm going to try again."

Gustav heaved an exasperated sigh—and swiveled around so he could sit facing her Indian-fashion. "I obviously can't stop you."

"That's right," Diana said. "So. You said we should be looking for bits of china. Which means you think that doll might have been broken out here. Which reminds me of the 'gravel' you told Mahoney you'd found in Chan's hair. Which means maybe that wasn't gravel at all—maybe it was shattered porcelain. Which would explain the blood you told us to look for, too."

"Which makes me go, 'Huh? ' " I said.

"She's deducifyin' that the killer used the doll to clobber the doc," Old Red explained.

"Which would account for Chan's shirttails," Diana added. "When you inspected the body, you said they'd come untucked." She stretched her arms up over her head. "Because Chan was *dragged* to his bed."

"And the spectacles?" Gustav said, looking the lady square in the eye.

Her lips curled just enough to suggest a smile without actually putting one on. "Knocked from Chan's face when he was hit in the back of the head. If they broke, the killer would have to hide them, too. So no one would suspect violence had been done to the doctor."

"Now just hold on a second, you two," I cut in. "You're sayin' Doc Chan was murdered *with a china doll*?"

Diana shook her head. "No. He was knocked unconscious with the doll. He was killed by the gas."

"Well, congratulations, Miss Corvus," Old Red said, a hint of actual admiration shining through his sarcasm. "You now know just about everything I do. Which ain't much when you stack it up against . . ."

His voice trailed off. His eyes went glassy.

"Gustav? *Gustav?*" Diana turned to me. "Is he alright?"

"Oh, yeah. This happens all the time. We just have to remember to water him every so often and eventually he'll—"

Old Red flapped a hand at us angrily. "*Shhhhhh.*"

So Diana and I just stood there, letting him cogitate, I assumed.

But it wasn't a sudden thought that had struck my brother dumb. It was a sound. After a couple seconds of what I thought was absolute silence, I finally heard it, too.

Footsteps. Downstairs.

We weren't alone any longer.

13

A TIGHT SPOT

Or, We Find Our Backs Against the Wall—and Each Other

Gustav, Diana, and I stampeded tippy-toe style into the kitchenette. From there, there was only one other place to go—which is how the three of us came to be jammed into a john that had already been a tight squeeze when I had but a scorpion in a trash can to share it with.

I wouldn't have minded the close quarters so much if the seating arrangements had worked out more in my favor. I was standing, my back pressed against the door, while Old Red ended up on the commode—with Diana on his lap. It was black as night in there with the door closed, yet I still fancied I could see a faint, blush-pink glow coming from the general direction of my brother's face.

"Do you think Mahoney and Woon came back?" Diana said.

I leaned toward the sound of her quiet voice till I was so close I could feel her breath on my cheek.

"If they did," I whispered, "I just pray it ain't cuz one of 'em has to take a leak."

Gustav shushed me.

"I'm just sayin', all they'd need to see is . . . *shit*."

"What?" Diana said.

"I left Old Green out on the counter."

My brother shushed me again—with a punch. I assume he was aiming for my arm, but what with the lack of light and me bent over as I was, he caught me right atop the shoulder instead, his knuckles rapping against big, hard bone.

"Ow," we said in chorus.

Diana shushed *us* this time.

"Betrayed by a goddamn cabbage," Old Red grumbled.

And then we were all shushed once again—and it took hold now, for the shushing was being done by the creak of a floorboard.

It was followed by another, then another, and another, and so on, growing closer each time. I tried to listen the way Holmes and my brother look, using not just my senses but my common sense (whatever I may have of it).

There was no rumble of footsteps atop each other, just a slow, steady step . . . step . . . step. So it was one man, alone. He was treading light, too, not clomping around like he owned the place. Which meant it wasn't Mahoney or Woon or some other copper. The man sounded altogether too small and sneaky for that. Whoever he was, he didn't belong there any more than we did, I figured.

And I soon knew I'd figured right, for our fellow prowler finally spoke.

"Hok gup," croaked a gruff, phlegmy voice.

A gruff, phlegmy, *familiar* voice.

It was the bearded, gravel-throated geezer we'd seen Dr. Chan squabbling with the day before. He had more to say, too, but it was Greek (or, to be more accurate, Chinese) to me. The only words I recognized were "hok gup."

"Black bird *something something* black bird *something*," that's all I could make of it.

The voice grew louder, the footsteps closer, until the floorboards right outside the WC were squealing. There was no lock on the door, so I did the only thing I could to keep the old man out—snake my hands behind my back and clamp down on the knob with all my might.

I didn't have hold of the thing two seconds before I felt it give a jiggle.

"Hok gup *yak yak*," the old goat said. "*Yak yak yak yak?*"

He tried the door again.

It's probably not much to be proud of, but it's something: Set a young cowpoke against an arthritic old Chinaman in a grip-off, and the drover'll win every time. The knob didn't budge.

"*Yak yak yak* hok gup *yak*?"

Naturally, we didn't answer. And after a long silence, the old man apparently concluded there was no one there *to* answer. He moved away as slow and silent as a snail.

"Miss," Old Red whispered hoarsely, "you need to stand up now."

"Why?" Diana asked.

"Umm . . . uhhh . . . my legs is fallin' asleep."

"Well, there's not enough room for me to stand. Can't you wait another . . . *oh*!"

With a sudden rustling of skirts, Diana was on her feet—and on *me*, too, for there wasn't room for her to stand without pressing her body against mine.

"Sorry, miss," my brother mumbled miserably.

At first, I was almost grateful to Gustav for letting his limbs go all a-tingle on him. But as I stood there with the lady squeezing me tight as long johns two sizes too small, I realized that Old Red's legs hadn't fallen asleep at all. A different part of my brother had finally started waking up. And this I knew because I was experiencing the same awakening myself no matter how hard I struggled against it.

Most folks imagine hell to be a vast, cavernous place home to a million screaming souls. But I tell you this: It can be as small as a water closet barely big enough for three.

I began to pray for the old man to pick up his pace and clear out— which he did just as I'd resorted to biting my tongue, pinching my earlobes, and thinking of my dear departed *Mutter*.

"He's on the stairs," Gustav said.

The sound of footsteps grew ever fainter outside.

"He's leavin'. He's leavin'. He's . . . *gone*."

"Thank you, Jesus," I sighed, and I opened the door and made my escape.

Diana stepped out after me.

"Well," she said, "that was—"

"No time for gibber-jabber," Old Red said, slipping past her. "We gotta follow that feller. This might be our only chance to find out who the hell he is."

Of course, it was also our chance to put that WC (and what had happened inside it) behind us. And we took it.

The three of us crept to the top of the stairs, waiting there only a moment before we heard a grunt from down below—the old man hoisting his stiff bones over the windowsill. Gustav gave him a few seconds to get a little further up the alleyway, then led the charge downstairs and out the window.

Our quarry turned out to be surprisingly spry: The old man moved at a teeter-tottering gallop, and by the time we were all outside on his trail, he was already a good fifty feet ahead of us.

"So, Brother," I said as we followed him around the corner onto Stockton Street, "whadaya Holmes off the old buzzard?"

"Not much," Old Red answered without looking at me. Like just about every other street in Chinatown, Stockton is lined with shops and restaurants. Take our eyes off the old man for three seconds, and he could slip through any one of a dozen doors.

"He's poor but tries not to show it—them's nice, silky duds he's wearin', but it's the same outfit he had on yesterday. Stitchin's frayed and the buttons is mismatched, I noticed at the time. He ain't no laborin' man, though. Hands is in too good a shape for that. Gnarled up a bit, but from age, not work. Folks seem to know him, too. Don't respect him, though. Lookee how the fellers up ahead clear outta his way . . . snickerin' all the while? He ain't no big fish, but he ain't exactly small fry, neither."

Diana gazed at Gustav looking equal parts tickled and awestruck. "That's 'not much'?"

My brother just grunted and shrugged.

"Well, who is that man, anyway?" Diana asked. "You say you saw him yesterday?"

"Last time we saw Doc Chan alive, he was walkin' off with that feller," I said, and I told her what there was to tell as we followed the old fart's zigzagging trek across Chinatown.

He was cutting his way to the northeast, turning off onto a new street at almost every corner. Any other Chinaman we might've lost in the swirling sidewalk herds along Washington and Dupont, but the old fogey's snow-white hair, stump-shouldered stoop, and swift, swaying gait we could pick out from half a block back.

And half a block back we stayed, for if we could recognize the coot, *he* could surely recognize *us*. We didn't exactly blend into the crowd. In fact, we were about as inconspicuous as a Fourth of July parade. Fortunately, the old-timer never looked back . . . or at least if he did, we didn't notice.

As the old man's waddling march took us closer to Chinatown's northeast corner—and the Barbary Coast just beyond it—the streets grew ever seedier. And the same could be said of the folks *on* those streets.

Icy-eyed men loitered before slablike iron doors and steps down into black basement pits, every one seeming to watch us with a mixture of cold curiosity and downright frigid contempt. Before, I'd thought Dr. Chan's shop was on a seamy street, but what I was seeing now had more seam to it than a rag quilt.

Then the old man turned down a narrow, filth-strewn street but one block long, and things got *really* bad.

Up until then, I hadn't seen more than a dozen women in all of Chinatown. But once we hit that little lane, I nearly doubled my tally before my first blink. There were women leaning in dilapidated doorways, peering out through cracked windows, watching us stone-faced from rickety-looking second-story balconies that appeared to be little more than old crates propped up with two-by-fours.

And these gals weren't just taking the air. They were advertising.

Drawing some trade, too. There was a steady stream of both Chinamen and wobbly-walking whites moving in and out of what I'll call the *establishments* lining the block. (A phrase like "bawdy house" seems altogether too jolly for such tawdry little vice-dens as these.) Adding to the general air of gloom and doom was a Salvation Army band bleating out a dirge-ish version of "When I Survey the Wondrous Cross" while the ranking officer harassed each and every passerby with the question, "Have you seen Jesus?"

I gave the obvious answer as we hustled past: "Not around here, I ain't."

The street emptied out onto a bigger, busier thoroughfare running at a slant—Columbus, most likely. Which put us a stone's throw from the corner of the Coast called "The Devil's Acre." You'd have plenty of reason to throw stones there, too, for you could hardly take two steps without someone trying to rob you, kidnap you, or just kill you for a giggle. It was the kind of place even the police wouldn't go without a rifle squad and a priest at the ready.

"He ain't leavin' Chinatown, is he?" I said.

Old Red shook his head. "Can't be. A Chinaman wouldn't last five minutes up thataway."

Diana nodded at one of the last buildings on the north side of the block. "Perhaps he's going there."

"That's what I'm afraid of," Gustav said.

Compared to its brethren thereabouts, the building—a cozy-looking two-story house—was remarkably free of grime, with large (though shade-drawn) windows; bright, neatly painted trim; and a fresh-swept stoop sporting a pair of oversized flowerpots.

It also sported a pair of big lugs out front—slouching Chinamen with black hats, loose tunics, and the indolent air of men conserving their strength for the seemingly inevitable moment when they'd be ordered to break every bone in your body. It was obvious who they were because they *wanted* it obvious.

The newspapers would've labeled them "highbinders" or "hatchet men." In less colorful language, they were hired guns for the tongs. Or, to be even plainer still, killers.

The old man breezed right between them without so much as a nod in their direction, scuttling up the steps they were guarding and disappearing through the door beyond.

14

OUTSIDE

Or, I Use My Powers of Persuasion to Talk Us *into* Trouble

The highbinders across the street didn't seem to spot us trailing the old-timer. They just stood there on either side of their stoop like a couple pillars with nothing to hold up.

All the same, it wouldn't do to dawdle around gawking at them. So Gustav, Diana, and I turned and moseyed back the way we'd just come. The leader of the Salvation Army band watched warily as we drew closer, and he didn't bother asking if we'd seen Jesus this time.

"Sorry, maestro—still no sign of Him," I said as we ambled past. "Looks like you might need to get up a search party."

"Otto, *please*," Diana chided me. "If He is around here somewhere, we'll need His help."

"You're right about that," Old Red said sourly. "We can't learn nothin' out here. We gotta get inside."

"You mean into the house?" Diana asked. "If the old man sees you two, there'll be a lot of explaining to do."

"We got no choice. Grandpa's the only trail to follow, so . . . we follow it."

My brother looked over at Diana. He and she were almost exactly the same height, and the gaze they shared now was as even and steely-steady as the iron girders of a modern metal bridge.

"Just me and Otto," Gustav said. "You know what sorta place that most likely is."

"A whorehouse, you mean?"

My brother flushed. Yet for just a fleeting flash, a gone-in-a-wink instant, he didn't look embarrassed by the lady's language. He looked *hurt*.

He snapped the expression away with a curt nod, like shaking out a tablecloth to clear it of crumbs.

"Yup. That's what I mean. If it is a cathouse, they're used to fellers like us tryin' to get inside. But you try to go in there with us . . . ? Uh-uh. Even in a town like Frisco, that's gonna turn heads."

" 'No place for a lady,' huh?" Diana said.

"Now, look, miss . . . ," I began.

"Don't bother, Otto. This time, I'm inclined to agree." Diana sighed. "So . . . what shall I do in the meantime? Darn your socks? Bake a cake?"

"You could go home," Old Red said.

Diana smiled grimly. "Other than that."

"Maybe you could do a little shoppin'," I suggested.

The lady gave me an "I *hope* you're joking" glower.

"I got the feelin' you'll be needin' a mournin' dress pretty soon now," I explained.

"Ah." She reached over and gave my arm three light little pats. "You two know how to take care of yourselves. You'll be fine, Otto. I'm sure of it."

"Miss, I've said it before and I'll say it again—you are the best liar I ever met." I took the liberty of gently placing *my* hand on *her* arm for a moment. "And it's much appreciated."

"Alright, alright," Gustav grumbled. "Enough gum flappin'."

"Get yourself somewhere safe," I told Diana as my brother and I turned to go.

"You can count on me," she said.

Old Red and I were already a dozen strides away before it struck me what a cryptic response this had really been.

"I wonder . . ."

"Don't try to figure her out," Gustav said. "You'll just sprain something."

"Maybe you oughta take your own advice. After all, back at Chan's place, it was *you* who got all—"

"Oh, for God's sake, Brother," Old Red snapped. "We got more important things to worry about just now."

He was looking up ahead, at two of those "more important things": the hatchet men on either side of the door we had to get through . . . somehow.

As we drew closer, we once again passed that hymn-blasting brass band, now solemnly oompah-ing the life out of "What a Friend We Have in Jesus." This time, the bandleader gave me a glare that told me he had it on good authority I was going to hell. Which wasn't news to me. Gustav and I were practically there already.

"Let me do the talkin'," I said as we stepped around a puddle that seemed to be blood garnished with a liberal sprinkling of teeth.

"What kinda play you gonna make?"

"Damned if I know."

The highbinders finally took notice of us as we started across the street, monitoring our approach with apathetic, slack-jawed, sidelong glances. Whatever we might prove to be, they clearly had no doubt they could handle it.

"Don't worry, though, Brother," I said under my breath. "I still got a whole five or six seconds to come up with something."

Five or six seconds later, we were a mere five or six steps from the highbinders and I *still* didn't have a plan. So my mouth just took matters into its own (figurative) hands.

"Ooooo, yessir!" I heard myself hoot. "This must be the place!"

I gave Gustav a boisterous slap on the back and tried to go breezing between those guards just as the geezer had a few minutes before.

The highbinders stepped together like gates slamming shut in front of us.

Old Red and I skidded to a stop.

"Pardon me, gents. But this is a"—I winked and let out a loud *mee-oww*—"ain't it?"

The smaller of the two highbinders—a young, round-faced fellow working so hard to look tough he should've been chewing nails—just said one word. It was the kind of thing that wouldn't usually roll trippingly off a foreigner's tongue, but he seemed to have had plenty of practice with it.

"Exclusive."

"Exclusive?" I grinned. "Well, of course it is! We wanted to rub shoulders with the riffraff, we'd take our trade to the competition."

"*Exclusive*," the highbinder said again.

"Believe me—I don't doubt it," I replied. "Like I said, that's why we're here. You see . . . this place come recommended."

I gave the guards a moment to ask me by whom, but they didn't bother. Which was fine, actually, as it gave me time to reach around and pull a name out of my ass.

"Cathal Mahoney told us to come here. That's *Sergeant* Mahoney to the likes of you. He said we'd be treated right. I'd sure hate to have to tell him otherwise."

The highbinders' eyes widened. I suspect my brother's did, too, but fortunately the guards weren't paying him any mind just then.

"You wait," said the talker of the two, and he turned and went inside.

The other highbinder took a slight step to his left, the better to block us now that his compadre was gone. He made for quite an effective fence standing there, arms and legs akimbo, fearsome scowl freshly replastered over his surprise.

"Lovely weather we're havin', ain't it?" I said to him.

He didn't so much as blink . . . *for a full minute*. Really. Old Red and I couldn't do much in the way of speaking with the hatchet man there in hearing (and hacking, stabbing, and shooting) range, so we had nothing to do but stand there timing him.

Now, certain folks are heartbreakers, some break promises, and others are ever breaking wind. Me, I'm an incorrigible breaker of silences.

"You know, them outfits y'all wear look mighty comfy," I said to the highbinder, pointing at his slack black tunic. "They come in any other colors?"

The Chinaman didn't deign to answer.

"Cuz I wouldn't mind gettin' me some duds like that," I went on. "For lollygaggin' around of a Sunday afternoon. You know. Like a proper

English gentleman." I waggled my eyebrows at my brother. "Know what I mean?"

Gustav most certainly did—I'd ribbed him more than once about Holmes's habit of lounging about in his "dressing gown."

"I'm sure our friend here don't care how you dress yourself any more than I do," he snipped at me.

Translation: *Don't annoy the man, ya idjit.*

As you've no doubt noted already, there's something else I like breaking whenever possible: my brother's balls. It's a compulsion I can't always control, like the urge some fellows feel to drink or gamble or run around pretending they're a "consulting detective."

So I turned back to our "friend" and said, "I like the man's look is all I'm sayin'. Only I'd wouldn't want my jim-jams quite so drab. No offense intended."

But offense finally taken, it seemed. The Chinaman reached behind his back to grab for something tucked away under his tunic.

Old Red and I stepped backwards off the stoop, sliding away together like the tide going out. If there was to be gunplay, we'd have to sit it out—on the shooting end, anyway. Being shot we could do just fine.

We'd lost our Peacemakers back on the Pacific Express, you see, and never got around to replacing them.

I suddenly regretted the time and money I'd spent the night before to buy myself a new *hat*.

But the hatchet man never even noticed how spooked he had us. He was too busy pulling out a small pouch—from which he produced a pile of business cards.

As he rifled through the cards, my brother and I slid forward again, gaping at each other all the while.

When the highbinder found the card he wanted, he held it out to me. The writing on it was mostly Chinese, but there was an address printed in English.

"My cousin, Wing Sing. Tailor. Show this, he give good price."

"Thank you, friend," I said, pocketing the card. "I'll look him up once we've—"

The door behind Wing Sing's cousin swung open, and the other hatchet man rejoined us on the stoop.

"Inside."

He jerked his head back at the door. Beyond it was a hallway so murky-dark it could have been the mouth of a cave.

"Inside?" I said to my brother.

Outside had suddenly struck me as the safer (not to mention saner) place to be.

Gustav eyed the hallway unhappily. Yet he nodded all the same.

"Inside," he said.

So in I went.

Just as I crossed the threshold, the brass band up the street broke into a wheezing, heaving rendition of "Wretched, Helpless, and Distrest," without a doubt the most dismal dirge ever to blacken the pages of a hymnal. Preachers like to talk about "the good news," but there's precious little cheer in that song. All it speaks of is doom.

I had to wonder if the bandleader knew something we didn't. Like maybe we'd be seeing Jesus pretty soon now, after all.

Or St. Peter, anyway.

15

INSIDE

Or, A Soiled Dove Gives Us the Bird

There was no need for the highbinders to lead the way. There was but one way to go—straight ahead.

Inside, we found no foyer, no stairs, no adjoining rooms. Just a narrow, shadowy corridor leading to another door a short distance away. Crimson-tinged light bled through into the darkness from the door's every edge, giving the end of the passageway an eerie reddish glow.

The hatchet men let me and Gustav start toward it, then pulled the door to the stoop closed, and rode drag on us, tight. Their presence at our heels seemed to cut us off from our each previous step and cancel out everything that lay behind us, so that the steps ahead were all that remained of our world.

That world was shrinking fast. When there were but a few steps left to it, the door at the end of the hall swung open, and light flooded into the corridor.

For a moment, I could see only the outline of a woman before us. It was quite the outline, too: short in stature but long on curves. The woman's hair was done up in a big bun, adding one more bulge to her already shapely form—an onion atop the hourglass.

"Welcome, gentlemen. I am Madam Fong."

My vision unblurred, and I found myself face to lovely face with a Chinese woman dressed in a flowery blouse and silky-black pantaloons. To call her beautiful would do her a disservice. She was a goddess, albeit one who was enough the mortal to age. There was the slightest sagging to her smooth crescent chin; the beginnings of a droop to her puckered, painted lips; lines around her almond eyes even the most skillfully applied talcum couldn't quite hide.

You could see her years *in* her eyes, too. Not that they were cloudy or crossed or bloodshot. They just seemed dulled somehow, as if from over-use. They were eyes that had seen too much.

She stepped back and swept out an arm, ushering us into a perfumed parlor room that was one-third Xanadu, one-third Sears & Roebuck, and one-third dirty postcard. There were low-slung divans piled high with embroidered pillows, wicker armchairs with cushions that looked so soft a man might sink into them like quicksand, and everywhere—*everywhere*—ashtrays, picture frames, figurines, and other assorted trifles crafted from teakwood, bamboo, or porcelain. (No obsidian-black birds, though, I noted.)

Plush red carpet covered the floor, pink paisleyed paper was plastered to the walls, and nailed up willy-nilly was "art" that . . . well, suffice it to say, the pictures alternated between nature scenes and scenes of a nature that would make a sailor blush.

But perhaps the room's most notable—and fortuitous—feature was what *wasn't* there: the old-timer.

"Please. Make yourselves comfortable," the madam said as Gustav and I shuffled into the room. Her accent wasn't as thick as some we'd heard that day, yet her words came out clipped and curt, as if she had to spit them out one letter at a time.

"I can't imagine anybody bein' *uncomfortable* in here if they tried," I said, stretching myself out on a settee.

Madam Fong chuckled, the sound of her amusement light and musical—and no doubt well practiced, given her line of work. She nodded at her black-clad doormen, who disappeared the way we'd just come, closing the door behind them.

There was only one other door, on the opposite side of the room, and no windows at all. Despite what I'd said about the coziness of the place, it was starting to feel like a velvet-lined cage.

"You want a drink?" Madam Fong asked, moving toward a cart upon which sat several sparkling cut-glass decanters.

Old Red perched himself stiffly on the edge of an easy chair, looking anything but easy. "No, thanks, ma'am. We ain't thirsty."

He shot me a glare that warned me not to contradict him.

"Leastways, not for liquor," I said, and I gave our host a lewd wink.

"Here we can quench any thirst," Madam Fong replied dryly. "Yours can be taken care of. Any friend of Sergeant Mahoney is a friend of ours . . . if they *are* a friend of ours. Because Sergeant Mahoney is no friend to us."

"Exactly," I said with a nod and a smile—though I didn't know what the hell she was talking about.

"So . . . what is it you offer?"

"Plenty, ma'am. Plen-*ty*." My mind raced to come up with *anything* beyond cocky grins and blarney. "Ol' Cathal, he can be a tough nut. But we know how to handle him."

The madam went gliding away from the liquor cart, looking thoughtful. And when I say "went gliding," that's not just a fancy way of saying "walked." The woman's steps were small but her gait amazingly smooth, and she moved as if she was floating on the wind like a wing-spread bird.

A hawk, maybe. Or a vulture.

"Other men 'handle' Mahoney already," she said.

"But not to suit you, am I right?" I shrugged. "So why not let us take a crack at it?"

Madam Fong smiled again, and I could tell this time she really meant it—because her grin was just the sort of grim, sneering thing she could never show a paying customer. I'd pegged her as thirtyish before, but now I saw a whole other bitter decade etched into the carefully concealed lines of her powdered face.

"I look at you, I do not see rich men. Why would Mahoney listen to you?"

"Cuz money ain't everything," I replied with a breeziness that was all hot air. I looked over at my brother. "You wanna spell it out, or shall I?"

"Oh . . . well . . . you go ahead," Old Red said. "You're the talker."

"Alrighty."

I turned back toward Madam Fong as slow as I thought I could get away with, stretching the moment to the snapping point while I scoured my brain for inspiration. I wasn't even sure I'd found any even as my mouth opened up and an answer popped out.

"You see . . . he's our cousin."

I swept my boater off my head and let my carrot-top do the talking for a second. (Thanks to our flaming red hair, Gustav and I have been taken for Irish so many times I once proposed that we change our names to O'Amlingmeyer.)

"Paddy and Seamus Mahoney, at your service. Our cousin—'Cal,' we've always called him—he sent word to us down in Texas a while back. Said he could slip us onto the po-lease payroll now that he was runnin' the show with the Chinatown Squad. And Paddy and me, we're gonna take Cal up on it. Only we ain't sure we can get by up here in Frisco on a lawman's pay. So we're lookin' to supplement our income a mite."

"I see," the madam said in that cool, reserved way of a person sniffing for a whiff of bullshit. "So you and your brother could help us by . . . ?"

"Just stayin' friendly is all. Droppin' by to chat from time to time. You know, like whenever Cal's plannin' on gettin' his face in the papers with a big *raid*."

Madam Fong gave me a brooding nod. I seemed to be making sense to her . . . so far.

"But why come to us? Here?" she asked. "Why not Little Pete? Or even Chun Ti Chu? They would like Mahoney 'handled,' too."

"Well, first off, Paddy and me don't know who the hell 'Little Pete' or 'Chunky Chew' is. We're new in town. Don't know the lay of the land yet. Second off, we thought we oughta start small. Take our time, work our way up to the big boys. And third off, Cal just happened to mention that this was where they kept the purtiest whores in Chinatown . . . so of course we had to come here first! Right, Brother?"

I yelped out a *yeee-haaa* of the sort people seem to expect from Texans. Old Red tried to join in, for appearance's sake, but he couldn't put much oomph into it. He never has been one for huzzahs, unless it's to get a herd moving.

The madam endured our howlings with the sort of pained/amused look I assume one sees on missionaries attending tribal dances in the deepest Congo. On the surface, there's a smile. Underneath, they're thinking, "Savages."

"What about your cousin's friends?" she asked. "Won't they expect you to work for them, too?"

"Well, that's the beautiful part of it. They probably will . . . which'll give us the perfect perch for keeping an eye on *everybody*."

I tried my best to look smug—and my best is pretty damned good, to hear Gustav tell it.

"Now, we don't deny we're still in the dark on a lot of things," I went on. "The longer we're around, though, the brighter the sun shall shine. You take care of us, we'll throw whatever light we can your way."

The madam was on the move again as I spoke, doing her glide-walk toward the door on the far side of the room. "We will need time to think about it. But for now I can offer—"

"'Scuse me, ma'am," Old Red broke in.

The woman stopped and turned to look at him. "Yes?"

"I can't help noticin' how you keep sayin' 'we' and 'us.' We come to you to talk one-on-one. If we're dealin' with another party here, I'd like to know it."

Madam Fong tilted her head ever so slightly to one side, like a crow eyeing something shiny.

"This is Chinatown, Mr. Mahoney. There is always a 'we.'"

She picked up a little mallet on a table by the door and struck a brass gong the size of a dinner plate. It didn't make much of a sound—more of a *clink* than a *bong*—but it did the job.

The door opened, and a dozen girls scurried into the room with small, quick steps. Their eyes were downcast, their slender bodies wrapped in colorful silks or sheer chemises.

The madam had summoned her harem.

The girls took up positions against the far wall, arranging themselves at slight angles to us so as to maximize our view of the merchandise. Some stood, some knelt. Nary a one looked us in the eye. When they were all in place, they went motionless, almost lifeless—we could've been looking at the "Slave Girls of the Orient" exhibit in one of the tawdrier wax museums.

"A gift—or a down payment, maybe," Madam Fong said. "From 'us' to you. Choose what suits you and . . . enjoy."

I turned to my brother wondering just how far we'd take this charade. The answer made itself plain pretty quick, at least to my eyes: not very.

Old Red looked worse than he had coming over on the ferry that morning. And the thing that was seasicking his stomach now, I saw when I followed his hollow gaze, was one of the fallen women before us.

Or "fallen girl," I should say. She was a ghostly pale, wispy-thin thing with no womanly curve to her anywhere. And for good reason. She couldn't have been any older than twelve.

Gustav wiped the revulsion off his face fast—but not fast enough to fool a sharp-eyed man-reader like the madam.

"Something wrong?" she asked.

Old Red shrugged and looked down at his boots and put on an *aww-shucks* shit-eating grin, the very picture of the unpolished bumpkin flum-moxed by big-city sin. My brother's no William Gillette, but he's not a half-bad actor when he cares to make the effort.

"It's just that I . . . well . . . I had my heart set on a certain gal, and I don't see her here. Not if my cousin described her right, anyhow."

"Oh? You know her name?"

Gustav nodded eagerly. "Oh, yeah. It ain't exactly what we white folks'd think of as purty, but I hear the little lady's enough the looker to make up for it a hundred times over."

He leaned so far forward in his chair it barely seemed he could have enough cheek on cushion to keep himself from falling off.

" 'Hok Gup.' That's what Cal called her."

It took all the acting skill *I* have to hide my surprise. It hadn't even occurred to me that "Hok Gup" might be somebody's name. Yet when I thought back on how that old coot kept repeating the words over and over while creeping around Chan's place, it seemed obvious he'd been search-ing for a who not a what. If someone steals your boots, you don't wander around calling for them.

And I wasn't the only one to get a jolt from my brother's words. A few of the chippies peeked up at him wide-eyed. The little urchiny girl dared the longest stare—though she looked down quick when she noticed *I'd* noticed.

As for the madam herself, she just nodded slowly and said, "You want the Black Dove. I should have known. So many men do."

She gave the gong another clang, and her girls scampered from the room. Most of them seemed relieved to be going. But the waif dragged her feet, one ear so obviously cocked to catch whatever should be said next her head practically spun on her neck like a lazy Susan. She was the last one out, by her own design, and as she left she began to shut the door.

The madam slid over quick and caught it before it closed.

"Wait here," she said to us.

And then she slipped away, pulling the door of the velvet cage closed behind her.

16

THE WORST

Or, Our Hosts Decide to Bury the Hatchet—in Us

So," I said after giving Madam Fong a few seconds to float off into the shadows on the other side of the door, "Hok Gup is a gal."

"Looks thataway."

Gustav stood and started making a slow circuit of the room, inspecting the madam's bric-a-brac like a judge sizing up the pies at a county fair.

"Well, hurrah for us—we've actually learned something," I said. "Only I don't see how it gets us any closer to whoever killed Doc Chan."

"The old man was huntin' for the girl over at Chan's place." Old Red turned around just long enough to offer me a shrug. "She must tie in somehow."

"Yeah, maybe. Only why was Grandpa lookin' for her over there if she was here all along? I mean, he didn't have no trouble gettin' in here—unlike us. Oh, and thanks for the thanks for that, by the by."

"Thanks," Gustav mumbled, distant and dreamy, as if talking in his sleep.

"Don't mention it," I said. "So anyway, if ol' Methuselah was tryin' to find the girl, why didn't he check with Madam Fong first? And where'd he go after he did finally come in here?"

"Well," Old Red said, his tone turning sour, "could be he's with the Black Dove this very moment."

"Ooooooo," I groaned, my mind conjuring up a picture too frightful to describe. "That is one deduction I could've lived without."

Gustav stopped before a small, platformlike structure sticking out of the far wall. "Well, don't dwell on it too much. It ain't very likely the old man would . . . hel-lo."

"Hel-lo what?"

"Didja notice this thing here?"

My brother stepped aside to give me a clear view of the wall-mounted whatever-it-was he'd been eyeing. It reminded me of a crèche, except with one big figurine—a stern-looking Chinaman with a long black beard—instead of a bunch of small ones.

"No, I hadn't noticed it," I said. "In case *you* hadn't noticed, there's a lot *to* notice 'round here. Any particular reason I should have set my sights on that thing?"

"There's a whole bundle of reasons right there."

Old Red pointed at the little scowling Chinaman's besandaled feet. Around it were several small, brass bowls filled with "joss sticks"—just like the ones on the altar in Chan's bedroom.

"Yeah, alright. I see what you're gettin' at," I said. "So now I guess we've learned *two* things: 'Hok Gup' is a Chinese floozy, and Doc Chan and Madam Fong have the same taste in home decoratin'."

Gustav went into such a smolder it's a wonder he didn't set those incense sticks to smoking.

"Feh," he spat. "You can lead a horse's ass to water, but you can't make him *think*."

I sat up straight and gave him a round of applause. "Bra-vo, Brother. Nicely turned. Almost witty, even. Keep practicin', and one of these days maybe you'll actually be funny."

"I ain't tryin' to be funny."

"That works out well for you, then."

"Feh," Old Red said again, and he turned away and sank to his hands and knees.

He spent the next few minutes crawling around taking in a dog's-eye-view of the room while I watched (and carped) from the comfort of my settee. We'd found a new trail to follow, my brother tried to assure me, but I wasn't so sure it was headed toward *Chan's* killer. It seemed more likely to lead to our own.

Which brings us back to where you stepped in, dear reader—and where a gaggle of hatchet men stepped in, too.

The first two came in via the door Madam Fong had gone gliding out through. They were black clad, broad shouldered, and cold eyed, but I wasn't ready to assume the worst just yet. When the worst finally comes—and it frequently does for me and my brother—there's no need for assumptions. It makes itself damned plain.

"Well, hello there," I said to the highbinders.

"," they replied. Which is to say, they said nothing. They just closed the door and took up positions before it, blocking the exit off with such definitive finality it may as well have not been there at all.

One of the tong men was taller than the other—was, in fact, taller than any Chinaman I'd ever laid eyes on. He was older than the other, too, with the dark features and deeply lined face of an Indian chief. Though the highbinders didn't say a word, it was somehow obvious that, of the two, the big man was the boss.

"Don't mind my brother there," I said to him, jerking a thumb down at Gustav. "He's just lookin' for loose change."

"," the Chief said.

"," his friend added.

"Hok Gup on her way, then?"

" "

" "

"Or are one of *you* the Black Dove?"

" "

" "

"No offense, but if that's the case, we're gonna have to pass on our freebie—neither one of us rides sidesaddle, if you catch my meanin'."

" "

" "

"That was a joke."

" "

" "

" "
.
" "
.

"Alright, look. If y'all are tryin' to put the fear on us . . . well, it's workin'. Why don't you say something? Introduce yourselves. I'm Paddy. This here's Seamus."

Shit . . . I'm *Seamus*, I remembered a second too late. Not that it made any difference.

"," the highbinders said.

"Brother," Old Red growled.

I nodded. "I do believe you're right."

Gustav's tone had said it all: *Time to go*.

I got up off the couch.

"You know, if this is that new trail you promised, I don't think I care to follow it."

"Me, neither," Gustav said.

He was on his feet now, too, though he remained bent over in a crouch, scuttling sideways like an arthritic crab.

We were both headed for the other door.

The hatchet men headed for *us*.

Now I was ready to assume the worst. And just in time, too: The door we were dashing toward opened before we could reach it, and our two pals from the front stoop stepped into the room.

Old Red and I started backing the other way, but there wasn't much of anywhere to back *to*. We ended up behind a loveseat and the liquor cart—and up against a wall.

"Four on two, huh?" I said. "Alright. That makes one for my brother and three for me. Hell, that's almost fair."

The Chief reached behind his back, and at his signal his compadres did likewise. Somehow, I had the feeling they were *not* about to present their calling cards . . . though, in a way, I suppose that's exactly what they did.

One of the highbinders from out front drew a knife. The other produced a slung shot—a metal ball hung from a two-foot-long whip. And the Chief and his chum both came up with short-handled hatchets, which they proceeded to raise up like tomahawks as they drew within a few feet of us.

"Well," I whispered hoarsely, "that tilts things a tad, don't it?"

"Toes," Gustav said, and he snatched one of the decanters off the liquor cart and hurled it baseball-style at the Chief.

The big Chinaman ducked.

The others charged.

The one with the knife reached me first, jumping around the loveseat with his blade back, ready to stab. I caught him off guard by hopping up close instead of flinching back or freezing, and before he could make a jab at me, I took my brother's advice—by stomping my heel down on the highbinder's foot as hard as I could.

Like his pals, he was wearing slipper-shoes that looked as soft-topped as moccasins, and my heavy, hard-soled brogans came down atop his toes with a satisfying *crunch*. The man dropped his knife and raised up a howl I ended quick with a roundhouse punch to the nose.

Would-be assassin number one slumped to the floor.

I turned to take on two through four.

Of course, the rest of the gang hadn't just been lounging around waiting their turn. There was a crackling sound, and a dark shape whipped past just inches from my face. White shards rained down from atop my head.

It took me a couple startled seconds to realize it wasn't my skull that had just been splintered—it was my lid. The fellow with the slung shot had made a fling at me over the loveseat, but instead of smashing my head down into my boots, he'd merely snapped off the brim of my boater.

What *does* the good Lord have against my hats?

The highbinder's swipe had left him off balance, the heavy black ball at the end of his melon-cracker hanging down behind the back of the seat. Before he could straighten up, I grabbed the leather strap of his slung shot with my left hand and jerked it—and him—forward. As he lurched toward me, I grabbed the back of his head with my right hand and shoved it downward while my left knee came swinging up.

Kneecap met face. Teeth left mouth. Would-be assassin number two sank out of sight.

It was time to deal with three and four—the hatchet men.

The only reason they hadn't already split my head like a rail was Old

Red. He might not have had himself a gun, yet he'd found plenty of use-able ammunition nevertheless, whipping gewgaws and baubles wildly across the room like a cyclone ripping through a pawn shop. Glasses, plates, lamps, vases, spittoons, doodads, thingamajigs, and whatchamacallits—all went flying at the highbinders. The Chief and the other hatchet man were doing a decent job bobbing and weaving, but whenever either of them actually took a step toward us, Gustav drove the man back with a hailstorm of knickknacks.

I joined in, sending a cast-iron match holder shaped like a priest did-dling a nun arcing through the air at the Chief. It moved slow, though, and he dodged aside easily. I looked around for something lighter to pitch at him, but my brother had already snatched up everything within easy reach.

And then I remembered it: the perfect projectile.

I spun around and reached up toward the little altar Old Red had been so interested in a few minutes before. Its statue centerpiece—the fierce, bearded man—was porcelain. Light but solid.

The china Chinaman glowered at me hatefully as I snatched him down. He seemed to be a warrior of some kind—he was wearing armor, and his hands were gripping what looked like a sword tied to the end of a fishing pole—so I hoped he'd understand. All's fair in love, war, and brawls in brothels.

I turned and chucked that statue at the Chief as hard as I could.

It was a good throw: The figurine caught the highbinder square in the back just as he pirouetted out of the path of a cigar box thrown by my brother.

The Chief *oof*ed and crumpled.

The statue hit the floor beside him and shattered in a spray of white shards.

"See there!" Gustav said.

"See where?"

"There!"

My brother pointed at the jagged pieces of porcelain scattered across the carpet.

"Yeah? What am I supposed to—?" I shook my head like a man trying to buck off a bad dream he can't quite wake from. "Look, shouldn't we be *runnin' away* or something?"

"Runnin' where?"

The knife man had crawled off to the door Madam Fong and her gals had left through. He sat slumped against it, face in his hands, blood pouring through his fingers. The slung-shot man stood beside him, panting heavily through split lips. He glared at me murderously, obviously anxious for another round of David and Goliath.

As for the Chief, he was soon back on his feet, and with a grunt and a wave of his big, pawlike hand he sent his fellow hatchet man to block off the other exit. Then he shook a pointed finger at me and snarled out something I can only assume meant, "The big handsome one's *mine.*"

He raised his axe again and stepped toward me, moving slow.

"*Yak yak yak* fan kwei *yak yak*," the Chief said. And he smiled.

Before, he just wanted to kill us. Now it looked like he meant to *enjoy* it.

My brother and I snatched up the only "weapons" left in grabbing range: a fistful of obscene stereopticon slides for Old Red, an embroidered pillow for me.

As the Chief moved in on us, his friends stayed back, spectators now—and, to judge by the eager grins on their faces, ones who were expecting a mighty good show. Even the man whose mouth I'd mangled was wearing a smile. I swear, if the Chief had given those fellows time to run out for popcorn, they would've.

"You got any last words, Brother?" I said. "Cuz I reckon you got about five seconds to say 'em."

"Hush."

I shook my head. "Typical. Well, *I* ain't afraid to speak from the heart. Gustav, I want you to know that—"

"*Shut up.*"

The Chief was less than ten feet away—and to my surprise, he stayed there, freezing midstep, his eyes darting this way and that.

Then I finally heard it, too. Music, growing louder—impossibly loud. And with it, the sound of . . . marching?

The door to the outer hallway flew open, and a man playing a tuba came stomping in. On his heels were half a dozen more musicians, all of them blasting "Bringing in the Sheaves" loud enough to topple the walls of Jericho.

Some folks in need of rescuing get the cavalry. We got the Salvation Army.

The band's new conductor was the last one to squeeze into the room.

"Gentlemen!" she shouted at us over the deafening din. "Have you seen Jesus?"

"Close enough, Miss Corvus!" I hollered back. "Close enough!"

17

AH GUM

Or, A Fallen Woman Gets a Rise Out of Old Red

The concert didn't last long.

The wrecked, debris-strewn parlor; the cowboy holding up a fist-ful of stereopticon slides like a shield; the tall, relieved-looking fellow wearing a boater with no brim; the bruised, bloodied, and extremely confused Chinamen standing around *holding hatchets*—even over the top of a trombone, such sights are hard to miss.

Within seconds, "Bringing in the Sheaves" gave way to "Dropping of the Jaws" and, after that, an impromptu rendition of "Running for Your Life." My brother and I mixed in with the herd and bolted for the door.

"I don't think I've . . . ever been so happy to . . . hear a hymn," I panted once we were safely outside. The musicians kept up their stampede right on out of Chinatown, but Diana, Gustav, and I stopped to catch our breath across the street from Madam Fong's.

We kept a wary watch on the cathouse, but no highbinders followed us out. Apparently, even the most fearsome tong has to think twice before hacking up an entire brass band in broad daylight.

"Thank you for arrangin' the serenade," I said to Diana.

"Yeah . . . thanks," Gustav muttered. He tilted his head and squinted at the lady as if he half-suspected she was some kind of mirage. "How'd you know we were in a fix in the first place?"

"I would say 'woman's intuition,' but I don't believe in it," Diana said. "It was really just a hunch. I saw a woman come out of the alley behind the house and talk to the guards out front. She was Chinese, quite beautiful, well dressed, and she seemed to be in charge."

"That'd be Madam Fong, the proprietress," I said. "Must've slipped out a back door when she was supposedly fetchin' Hok Gup for us."

" 'Fetching Hok Gup'?" Diana asked.

I told her what we'd learned inside—that Hok Gup, the Black Dove, was a girl. My report was interrupted only once, by a pair of staggering sailors who got the giggles when they saw what was left of my battered hat still atop my head. As they were so amused by it, I gave it to them.

"Alright, alright—back to you," Old Red prompted the lady once I was done. "What else did you see from out here?"

"Well, the men went in through the front door, leaving it unguarded, while the woman—Madam Fong—headed around the corner, back into the alley. It struck me as . . . ominous. You two had been gone quite a while by then. So I decided to check on you."

"By havin' a parade?" I asked.

"Why not? I wouldn't be much help on my own. Causing a scene seemed like the best way to disrupt whatever might be going on inside. Fortunately, Captain Crider and his men were more than happy to help . . . once I'd explained that we're actually secret investigators for the Christian Anti-Vice League."

"And 'Captain Crider' believed you?" I marveled. "Even after all that guyin' I gave him?"

"I explained that you were simply establishing your bona fides as a crass, un-Christian lout." Diana smiled. "And doing it quite well, I might add."

I gave the lady a bow. "Why, thank you, miss. The role is a specialty of mine. Sarah Bernhardt has Juliet, and me—I've got 'crass, un-Christian lout.' "

"Hold on, now," my brother said to Diana. "You can't tell me you spent the last half hour just standin' around *here*"—he waved a hand at the filthy, trash-strewn sidewalk and the leering inebriates weaving their way along it—"without gettin' yourself noticed."

Diana nodded. "Oh, yes. I *was* noticed. Frequently. So I did what I had to do to blend in."

Old Red's eyebrows shot up so high they disappeared beneath the brim of his Stetson. "Which was?"

"Haggle. Over my rates. I had my own bona fides to establish, you see." Diana shrugged casually. "Of course, my services were priced well beyond the reach of the average passerby."

Gustav and I glanced at each other, the wonderment upon my brother's face no doubt mirrored on my own.

Was there anything this woman wasn't willing to do? Any lie she wouldn't tell?

Old Red managed to shake off his look of stupefaction first.

"Well . . . we best get ourselves gone 'fore Madam Fong's boys can—"

Diana reached out and grabbed his arm as he turned to go.

"Gustav, wait."

My brother turned toward the lady so stiffly one might've thought he'd just thrown out his back.

Diana nodded at something across the street.

"Friend of yours?" she said.

Her fingers slid away from his sleeve.

Old Red blinked, first at Diana, then over at Madam Fong's. Then his eyes went wide.

I followed his gaze, but it took me a second to spot what had surprised him so. She was easy enough to overlook—just a slip of a thing peeking out from the alleyway beside the bawdy house.

It was the little waif we'd seen lined up with the madam's chippies. She beckoned to us with one of her spindly arms.

"Could be a trap," I said.

"Yup. Sure could."

Gustav started across the street.

The girl ducked away into the alley.

"I don't suppose it'd do any good if I was to ask you to stay here," I said to Diana.

"None at all."

"Fine. I won't bother then."

We caught up to Old Red just as he rounded the corner into the alley. Part of me expected to find the Chief standing there, his cleaver wisely swapped for a forty-five. But there were neither hatchet men nor gun men awaiting us. Just one tiny girl, all alone.

"No time! Talk fast!" she said, her words coming out high and sharp, like the yippy bark of a small dog. She scurried up so close to my brother her little slipper-covered feet practically butted against his boot-toes. "You look for Hok Gup?"

"That's right," Gustav said.

The girl's jaw jutted, her eyes tightened to slits.

"*Why?*"

It was a narrow alley, with looming buildings blocking out the sun on each side. Yet still there was more light than in Madam Fong's cavelike parlor, and I could see now that the girl was older than I'd at first reckoned. She might have been all of sixteen, even. Her slightly oversized blouse, her unpainted face, the way her dark hair had been braided into twin pigtails—it was all designed to make what was pure scrawniness look like unblossomed youth.

Scrawny or not, though, she didn't seem to be afraid of us.

"Huh?" she grunted when Old Red didn't answer quick enough to suit her. "*Why* you want Hok Gup?"

"She got mixed up with a pal of ours somehow—Dr. Gee Woo Chan," my brother explained. "And now he's dead."

"Chan . . . dead?" the girl gasped.

Gustav nodded. "Murdered. And certain folks seem to think Hok Gup was over to his place 'round the time it happened."

The girl shook her head, but it wasn't meant as any kind of answer. It was a denial, a "no" to something she didn't want to be true. Her head sank, her dark eyes glimmering though no tears flowed. She looked like she wanted to cry but had forgotten how.

"Hok Gup's your friend?" Old Red said softly.

The girl looked up and gave him a reluctant nod.

"You're worried about her?"

"Yes," she said, her voice hushed.

"Darlin' . . . you got every reason to be."

And Old Red reached out and placed a hand on her shoulder. It was just a brush of a touch, over in a heartbeat. But for my brother, that was a bear hug.

A shattered doll in a dead man's flat? Rather odd.

A petrified scorpion? A touch peculiar.

Gustav Amlingmeyer tenderly comforting a young prostitute? *Utterly goddamn mystifying.*

"What's your name?" Old Red asked the girl, his voice still whisper-gentle.

"Ah Gum," she said firmly, wiping at her eyes and unslumping her shoulders. The sound of her own name seemed to give her new strength.

Gustav straightened up, too, and when he spoke again his words came out harder and faster.

"Well, Miss Gum, it's like you said before. There ain't much time—for us nor your friend nor you. So you'd best answer me quick as you can: Why was Hok Gup at Chan's place?"

"Because he buy her," Ah Gum said.

"'scuse me? *Bought* her? Like, you mean . . ." I started counting out invisible greenbacks. ". . . with money?"

"No. With catfish." Ah Gum rolled her eyes exactly as my brother so often does. She sure had snapped back fast. "Yes, with money! What you think 'buy' is?"

"Now, just hold on a second," I said. "This ain't Dixie and it ain't 1860. Folks don't get put on auction blocks no more. Not in America, they don't."

"Every day girls on auction block in Chinatown!" the girl spat at me. "Why you think I here? Like this?" She grabbed a fistful of her silk shirt and yanked hard at it, as if she meant to tear it right off her back. "Madam Fong—she buy me!"

"Offa *who*?" Old Red asked sharply, indignant.

"My family send me here," Ah Gum told him. "Woman come to village. She say she look for *mui tsai*—servant girls—for Gold Mountain men. Wives, too."

"Gold Mountain?" I asked.

"Here," Diana said. "That's what the Chinese call California."

The girl nodded. "Everyone rich here, we think. Coming to Gold Mountain—this is luck! I can send back money, later maybe family come. So I go with the woman. Other girls, too. Then we get here and—"

She spread her thin arms wide.

As you see . . . .

"And Hok Gup?" Gustav said. "She was one of the other gals from your village?"

"No. She special. She—"

Ah Gum curled her fingers into claws and grabbed at the air.

"Was take," she said. "Steal."

"Kidnapped?" Diana suggested.

The girl repeated the word, saying it slowly, as if for someone writing it down. "Yes. A year ago, from south islands. Some girls there worth lots money. Long, black hair. Dark eyes. Special pretty."

"The Black Dove," Old Red mused, gaze going glassy.

"When is it Dr. Chan bought your friend?" Diana asked Ah Gum.

"This morning. But he first come see her yesterday. With Yee Lock. Old man who check our—"

She fluttered her fingers down around the region where, unfortunately, she was forced to conduct most of her business.

"Feller with a white beard?" Gustav bent over and put his hand to his back. "Walks with a stoop? Froggy voice?"

"Yes. That Yee Lock."

"That broke-down ol' goat's some kinda *doctor*?" I said.

Ah Gum nodded, though she threw in another eye-roll while she was at it. "Kwong Ducks pay him look after sing-song girls. Keep them not sick, to work . . . long as they pretty. Once they old—" She shrugged. "No one care."

"I'm awfully sorry, miss. I must've misheard you," I said. "The geezer. He works for some . . . ducks?"

The girl gave me a half-lidded glare that told me my intelligence had dropped even lower in her estimation. Whereas before I'd been a half-wit, now I was closer to a quarter- or even eighth-wit.

"Kwong Duck *Tong*. Own Madam Fong's."

"Oh ho." I turned to Gustav. "There's that 'we' you and the madam talked about."

My brother grunted and stroked his mustache absentmindedly for a moment.

"*So*," he said, eyes refocusing on Ah Gum, "Doc Chan and Yee Lock come here yesterday. Then what?"

"They go in with Hok Gup. Later, Chan come out and talk to Madam Fong. He want Hok Gup. He say two hundred dollar—and Madam Fong just laugh. So he come back today with two *thousand*."

"Whoa whoa whoa whoa whoa!" Old Red said, throwing up his hands. "Chan gave Madam Fong two thousand dollars *cash*?"

"Yes. After that, Hok Gup gather her things, and we all cry, we so happy." On cue, the girl's eyes began watering again. "We think she go be *gamsaanpo*—wife of Gold Mountain man. We think she be free."

"She may be yet, Miss Gum," Gustav said, and it didn't sound like mere rote reassurance. It almost seemed like a promise. "Tell me: Is there anybody who *wouldn't* be happy to see your friend stop . . . you know . . . ?" My brother blushed and cleared his throat, the bashful old Gustav Amlingmeyer finally peeking out from behind this charlatan's shining armor. ". . . offerin' her services on the open market? Maybe a steady customer who—?"

"*Ah Gum*," someone said behind us.

We turned to find Wong Woon waddling up the alley fast, his tub gut practically bouncing down to the cobblestones and back with each wobbling trot. As he approached, he kept up a stream of chatter in Chinese, all of it aimed past us at the girl. The only bit I could make out was her name—and interesting that he should know it, I noted.

Ah Gum sassed the big detective back a bit, but it was obvious her heart wasn't in it.

"What are you sayin' to her?" Old Red snapped at Woon.

"I tell her she foolish. Talk to you instead of run to Jesus men at Mission House. Maybe they hide her, help her. But now—"

He jutted his quivering chins at something further up the alley.

The back door of the nearest building had opened up, and Madam Fong was stepping outside. Her powdered face appeared all the more pallid and masklike in the sunlight, contrasting grotesquely with her bright silken clothes. She looked like fresh flowers on an old grave.

When she spotted us, she barked something back into the house, and a moment later the Chief and his fellow hatchet man were marching out the door and toward us. Neither of them was carrying anything more dangerous than a grudge—in plain sight, anyway. Yet by force of habit I started scanning the garbage thereabouts for something heavy to throw.

As the highbinders drew closer, the madam snarled something at Ah Gum, and the chippy went into a broken droop that took half a foot off her height. Suddenly, she was a little girl again, a chastised child.

"Miss Gum, you don't have to—," Gustav whispered to her, his voice strangled.

"Like I say, cow-boy. You come back, I make you forget all about Hok Gup," the girl cut in. Her tone was both lewd and loud, and her eyes darted back and forth between my brother and the person she was really speaking to—Madam Fong. "You don't find better than Ah Gum anywhere."

And she went up on her tiptoes and planted a peck on Old Red's left cheek.

Predictably, Gustav was red-faced as she whirled away and hurried back toward the brothel. But it wasn't Ah Gum's kiss that had brought on the new blush. It was rage. Never mind "if looks could kill." The glare Gustav was giving Madam Fong should've skinned her, skewered her, and roasted her over a barbecue pit.

The Chief had come to a stop perhaps twenty yards away, the other highbinder just behind him. As Ah Gum scurried past them, the Chief spat a few words our way in a gruff, husky voice. I only recognized one phrase: *fan kwei*, which had been thrown our way enough the past day to give me some idea as to its meaning. (My money was on "white assholes.")

"He tell you to leave," Woon said.

"Gee, thanks for the translation," I told him. "I thought he was invitin' us in for tea."

Ah Gum had reached the back door by now, and she tried to scoot past Madam Fong, eyes on her toes.

The older woman caught her by the arm and gave her face a slap loud as a thunderclap. Then she spun the girl around, shoved her into the house, and followed her inside.

"Goddamn pimpin' *bitch*," Gustav muttered.

He took a step toward the door.

The Chief took a step toward *him.*

With surprising speed, Woon maneuvered his bulky body between Old Red and the highbinders.

"You just make it worse for her," he said to Gustav. "Plus, you die." He shook his head gravely. "Very awkward for everybody."

"You need to tell them that," Diana said, nodding at the tong men.

"Yeah," I threw in. "Them sons of bitches was choppin' at us like we was cordwood not ten minutes ago."

Woon shrugged. "You still in Chinatown ten minutes from now, they try again. Better you leave."

"Better for who?" Old Red growled.

For a moment, Woon just gave him a baffled squint, as if my brother had asked him a riddle he couldn't even understand, let alone solve.

"A thousand Chinamen die building railroad, no one notice," he said. "Then one Chinaman die after riding train . . . and the Southern Pacific must know why?"

"We're trying to change our image," Diana said.

"That's right." I held up my hands and spread them wide as if reading something off a banner. " 'The Southern Pacific: The Railroad That Cares.' "

Gustav just stared back at Woon, offering no explanations—his stony silence saying Woon didn't deserve any.

The Chinaman gave his head a jowl-shimmering shake that seemed both bewildered and truly rueful. Then he turned away and headed toward the Chief.

"Better you leave," he said again, not bothering to look back. "You have no business here."

He said something in Chinese to the hatchet men, and the three of them ambled off together.

"What's *your* business here, Mr. Woon?" Diana called out as they reached the bordello's back door.

Woon glanced back at us now—glanced at *me,* actually. And for the first time, I saw what looked like a smile tightening the saggy skin of the man's fat face.

"You forget your cabbage," he said.

Then he followed the highbinders inside.

18

KISS AND TELL

Or, Old Red Reveals a Hot Clue and an Even Hotter Temper

The second the back door to the bagnio swung shut, Gustav was swinging on me.

"You . . . harebrained . . . *idjit*," he spat.

"Hey, I'm sorry Old Green gave us away like that," I said. "I swear—that is the last time I bring along a cabbage when we're doin' any burglin'."

"We *all* forgot about the cabbage, Gustav," Diana pointed out.

Old Red swiveled his glare between her and me like a snake that can't make up its mind which ankle to bite.

"And actually, 'Old Green' did us a favor," the lady went on. "Now we know Woon went back to Chan's flat—which means he's not letting Mahoney chase him off the case any more than we are."

As she spoke, the fire in Gustav's eyes died down to a smolder.

"Yeah, yeah . . . noted," he sighed. "Woon must've talked to that vegetable peddler, too. That's the only way he'd know which of us was chuckle-head enough to bring that cabbage inside." He shot me a halfhearted scowl. "Though seein' as he's met you, maybe he *didn't* need anyone to tell him."

"Well, in my defense, let me say this—"

And I leaned over and blew a raspberry right in my brother's face.

"Could we set the cabbage issue aside, please?" Diana said. "The real question is, what next?"

"Ain't no question," Old Red replied, wiping the spittle from his cheeks with angry little swipes. "We find Fat Choy."

I gaped, surprised.

The lady smirked, amused.

Which probably says things about our respective powers of observation and deduction it would do my pride no good to dwell upon.

So I won't.

"Who the hell is Fat Choy?" I said.

"I assume that's the name Ah Gum whispered in your brother's ear when she kissed him," Diana said to me.

Gustav nodded. " 'Find Fat Choy'—that's what the gal said."

Diana's smirk wilted, her expression turning thoughtful. "But we know nothing about this Fat Choy . . . except that he has some kind of connection to the 'Black Dove.' "

"That ain't all we know," Old Red said. "He ain't some nobody. Folks 'round Chinatown know who he is and that he's tied in with Hok Gup and Doc Chan somehow." He looked over at me. "Remember what the cabbage man said to you: 'You look Fat Choy.' "

I shook my head, chagrined. "I just figured it was some kinda insult."

"Yeah . . . for you, that'd usually be a safe enough assumption," Gustav said.

I puckered my lips and stuck out my tongue, but Diana cut in before I could "defend" myself again.

"Where do we start looking?"

"Chan's place," Old Red said. "If Fat Choy or Hok Gup's been there, either one, they'll have been seen. We need to talk to the neighbors."

"Let's get to it, then." I started back toward the street. "Hangin' around here's just askin' for another bushwhackin'."

Diana followed, but Gustav lingered in the alley. When I turned back to see what was keeping him, he was just standing there staring at the back of Madam Fong's bawdy house. I knew what he was brooding on, or thought I did, anyway: the brave girl who'd risked so much to help a friend . . . and was now most likely paying the price for it.

When Old Red finally turned to leave, the blaze was back in his eyes so red hot smoke should've been puffing up out of his head. He moved fast, arms swinging, hurtling out of the alleyway and up the street like a locomotive at full steam. It was all Diana and I could do to keep up.

The Old Red Express had to slow once we reached Dupont, though. The busy street's plank sidewalks were choked with milling Chinamen, and suddenly the fastest we could manage was a shamble.

"Ain't nobody 'round here heard of 'elbow room'?" Gustav grumbled as we shuffled through the throng.

"They've sure as hell heard of *elbows,*" I replied, for my ribs were sore from the pokings and proddings of more aggressive sidewalkers than we.

We were inching past a meat market at the time, and on display out front was a disconcerting sight: a big, mud-brown fish laid out on ice . . . still breathing. He wasn't flopping and squirming as you might expect. Instead, he just lay there gasping, his round eyes giving him a look of stunned befuddlement.

"I know just how you feel," I said to him as we plodded past.

"Otto, Gustav—look," Diana said. "Up ahead."

I followed the lady's gaze.

A dark cloud was drifting toward us—a pack of young Chinamen dressed highbinder style. The sidewalk mob parted to flow around them on either side, no one daring to so much as brush against a black sleeve.

"Retreat?" Diana said.

I glanced over my shoulder. The boardwalk behind us was packed so snug it would make a sardine can seem positively spacious, and the shops we were passing were jammed just as tight.

"It'd be easier to retreat into a brick wall." I looked ahead again—and found the highbinders no more than thirty yards away. "Look . . . we don't know they're comin' for *us.* Chinatown's crawlin' with tongs, after all. Maybe them boys are Kwong Ducks, maybe they're Kwong Geese or Kwong Hogs or Kwong Who Knows What. I say we just try to blend in and scoot by."

"I don't know about the blending, but I'm all for the scooting," Diana said.

Old Red said nothing. He just glared at the tong men like they were something sticky, stinky, and brown on the bottom of his boot.

And the hatchet men were watching *him* by now. Me and Diana, too. But though I saw curiosity and contempt in their cocky gazes, there was no sense of purpose behind it. No "A-ha! *There's* those crazy white folks we're supposed to cut into cube steak!"

We moved aside, along with the rest of the crowd, and the highbinders seemed to find it particularly amusing that a white lady had to step into the street—the gutter—to let them by. Diana kept her eyes pointed straight ahead, staring past their sneers, while I did my best to ignore the bumps the young toughs gave me as they strutted past.

Gustav's best wasn't quite good enough, though. The three of us had squeezed up single file, with Old Red in the rear, so I didn't see what kicked up the ruckus—but there was no missing it once it started.

One of the hatchet men went careening into his compadres like a skittle ball bowling into the pins, and in a cluster the highbinders spun on my brother shouting in Chinese. Though I knew next to nothing of their lingo, the basic message was easy enough to grasp: These were men you dared not jostle on the streets of Chinatown, even when wearing the armor of white skin.

"Yeah, yap yap yap!" Old Red barked back at them. "Why don't you sons of bitches go beat on a slave girl or something? You know you ain't got the balls to fight a man in broad daylight."

There was a flutter of movement at the back of the pack—a couple of the highbinders seemed set on proving my brother wrong. They were reaching up under the floppy tails of their baggy blouses, and if they were pulling out flowers and chocolates, I was about to be very surprised indeed.

"A thousand pardons, gentlemen! A *million* pardons!" I slapped my hands hard over Gustav's shoulders and gave him a rough shake. "My brother here ain't got the manners God gave a pile of manure. Nor the looks, you might've noticed—and I'll admit you could say the same of me. Yessir! Rude, ugly . . . and did I mention stupid? Woo-hoo! We *are* a couple of dumb bastards! Then again, what would you expect from a pair of fool cowboy *fan kwei*, huh?"

My performance was met, at first, with bewildered stares, but the glowers soon gave way to smiles and chortles, and the mention of "*fan kwei*" got a big laugh. Turns out I spoke more Chinese than I thought.

"We are so sorry," I said, giving the men a bow—and pushing down on Old Red's shoulders to force him to do the same. "Y'all have a wonderful day now. *Fan kwei*."

I began moving away slowly, bowing a few more times as I pulled my brother along with me. Diana was backing away beside us, and she threw in a couple curtsies for good measure.

"So long, boys—we know you got folks to rob and kill and such, so we won't keep you any longer," I said. "Good-bye! *Fan kwei!* Dumb-ass goddamn *fan kwei!*"

The highbinders gave one last guffaw, waved a farewell, then went walking off chattering happily amongst themselves.

"You know," I said to Gustav, finally letting him go, "if I had me any dignity, I'd be mighty pissed at you for makin' me throw it away like that."

"You didn't have to play the buffoon," Old Red harrumphed, stomping away up the sidewalk.

"That's right, Gustav," Diana said as we started after him. "He could have just let those tong men *hack you to death*."

"Oh, no, miss—I couldn't have done that. Then I'd never know why he'd been dumb enough to rile 'em up in the first place." I caught up to Old Red and matched my stride to his. "I mean . . . damn, Brother. That was the kind of fool, mule-headed thing *I'm* supposed to do, not you."

"Hey, somebody had to put them smug ass—" My brother cut himself off with a quick, jerking shake of the head. "Oh, hell. You're right. That *was* a fool thing to do. It's just . . ." He shot a bitter glance over at Diana. "I ain't thinkin' straight."

"That's entirely understandable," Diana said. "You're not your idol— you have a heart. A friend's been killed and his . . . wife may be in danger. Of course you're on edge."

Gustav grimaced like she'd just ground her heel down on his corns.

" 'Wife' is stretchin' things. We don't know what Hok Gup was to Chan."

"Would you prefer the term 'concubine'?" Diana replied coolly.

"I don't know—cuz I don't know the why of it all yet," Old Red shot back.

"The how tells us why," Diana said. "The old doctor we followed, Yee Lock, inspects prostitutes for the Kwong Duck tong, and after he fetched Chan to come look at one, Chan *bought* her." She shrugged. "It's obvious, isn't it? Yee Lock knew Chan was in the market for a wife—a *clean* wife—so he found him one."

" 'In the market' now? Right when he's gone flat-busted broke?" Gustav turned his head to the side and spat in the gutter. "Speakin' of which, where'd he get all that cash? You think about that?"

"Maybe he was workin' for one of them religious mission houses," I suggested. "Rescue-the-fallen do-gooder types."

Old Red nodded. "There you go. For all we know, he was about to set the gal free."

"It'd be nice to think that, wouldn't it?" Diana's full lips puckered into a smile so tight and tart it looked like she'd just taken a big bite out of lemon. "Saving a beautiful young girl from a life of vice. It would make all this seem so much more noble than it is."

"There is such a thing as noble, you know," Gustav grated out through clenched teeth. "Some folks just wouldn't recognize it . . . cuz they'd never stick their neck out 'less they had their own secret reasons."

"Alright, look," I said, "whatever Doc Chan bought Hok Gup for, he's dead and she's missin'. And if the girl's not already dead herself, there's a fair chance she will be before long. So—"

"*So* what are we doin' takin' this goddamn Sunday stroll?"

We'd finally come to a quiet cross street, and my brother shoved his way from the throng and headed west, toward Chan's.

"I'm sorry," I said to Diana as he hustled off. "Gustav ain't usually such a hothead. A cranky little crab, yes, but not a hothead."

"It's alright. I think I'm beginning to understand him, actually." She gazed after my brother in a way that seemed almost wistful. "He's a man of deep feeling."

"I suppose . . . if you consider 'tetchy' deep," I said.

Yet I knew something deep—and dark—had indeed been stirred in my brother that morning. Something beyond the death of a "friend" we barely even knew. Just what it was, though, I couldn't say . . . and neither would Gustav, it seemed, so long as the lady was around.

"Come on." Diana gathered up her skirts for a run. "Like the man said: Stroll's over."

We raced after Old Red together.

19

ANSWERED PRAYERS

Or, Chan's Neighbors Don't Listen to Us—but the Man Upstairs Does

Being encumbered by a bustle and petticoats and shoes designed more to please the eye than support the feet, Diana couldn't move any quicker than a sort of skipping lope. Ever the gentleman, I hung back to keep her company (and enjoy the occasional glimpse of stockinged calf flying out from beneath her bunched-up skirts).

We lost sight of my brother within a minute.

We knew where he was headed, though, and after a few more zigzags across Chinatown, we were back where it all began: the block where Dr. Chan kept shop. Up ahead, we spotted Old Red walking into one of the stores next to Chan's pharmacy . . . and walking out again less than thirty seconds later. We reached his heels just as he headed into the place next door.

Thirty seconds after that, we were back on the sidewalk. The conversation inside had gone something like this:

OLD RED: Excuse me—

SHOPKEEPER: No sabe Englee!

OLD RED: I just need to—

SHOPKEEPER: No sabe Englee!

OLD RED: Look, we're friends of—

SHOPKEEPER: No sabe Englee!

OLD RED: Well, shit.

SHOPKEEPER: No sabe Englee!

ME: Yeah, we kinda figured that out!

And so it went in the next store and the next all the way to the end of the block.

"You can't tell me *nobody* 'round here speaks English," Gustav groused as he stomped out of a butcher's shop where the proprietor at least spared us another "No sabe Englee" . . . by pretending to be deaf.

"They probably all do," I said. "They just don't wanna speak it to *us*."

"Perhaps we should try a new approach," Diana suggested. "Something less intimidating."

"I ain't intimidatin' nobody," Old Red said sourly.

"Not intentionally. But these people have little reason to trust a white man. I think a more . . . genteel front might serve us better."

"Like a white *woman*?" I said.

Diana nodded. "If I were to go in alone, I think we'd see better results. White, black, or Chinese, men accommodate a lady in ways they'd never help another man."

"Especially a lady as *persuasive* as yourself, huh?" Gustav pushed back the brim of his Stetson and rubbed his forehead. "Well . . . it's plain we ain't gettin' nowhere with me doin' the talkin'. So fine. Next place, you give it a go. We'll be right outside, though."

Whether my brother was assuring her that protection would be close at hand or warning her not to get up to any trickery, I didn't know. Nor could I tell what the lady made of the remark—she just nodded again, then crossed the street and strolled alone into a corner market.

"How much you wanna bet she walks outta there with Fat Choy's home address and telephone number?" I said.

My brother shook his head. "I wouldn't take that bet."

We headed across the street and made a painful stab at nonchalance while lingering just outside the market door. Gustav fished out his pipe and began sucking on it unlit, while I knelt down to tie my already firmly tied shoes.

"So," I said, "you admit she's good at detectivin'?"

"Admit it?" Old Red scoffed, practically spitting his pipe out like a watermelon seed. "I ain't never denied it. Hell, she's so good, I can't believe the Southern Pacific would toss her out with the bathwater the way she says."

"Yeah, it's stupid alright. I can see the S.P. firin' Colonel Crowe—after all, the man was crazy enough to hire *us*, right? But why Miss Corvus would have to . . . *what?*"

Gustav was giving me that hard, appraising/disappointed stare he shoots me sometimes—the one that seems to be searching for a head on my shoulders but finds only empty air.

"I didn't say her gettin' the sack was stupid. I said I can't believe it."

I was still parsing this pronouncement when Diana joined us outside.

"So?" Old Red said.

She shook her head brusquely and, without a word, swept up the street and into the next store.

The pace picked up after that: Once again we were hopscotching our way down the block, with Diana spending less than a minute in any one shop. While she was inside utterly failing to work her womanly wiles, my brother and I continued our conversation stop-start style outside.

"You sayin' she still works for the S.P.?"

"I'm sayin' she might. It'd explain why she went to the trouble of trackin' us down—and why she's taken an interest in Chan's murder."

"How's that?"

And on to the next store.

"Could be the S.P.'s keepin' tabs on us. After all, we know what really happened on the Pacific Express. And Doc Chan, he knew a little of the real story, too."

"You think the Southern Pacific Railroad would give a big enough shit about nobodies like us to 'keep tabs on us'?"

And on to the next store.

"Don't forget, Brother—the lady warned us the S.P. wouldn't like it if your book about the Express ever came out."

"Oh, that wasn't a threat-warnin', remember? It was a friendly advice warnin'."

"Jee-zus Key- . . ."

And on to the next store.

". . . -rist. I know you have a hard time thinkin' straight under the best of circumstances, but put you around a pretty gal and your brain twists up like a pretzel."

"Oh, yeah? Well, I seem to recall a certain pretty gal gettin' a *rise* out of you a little earlier, if you know what I mean."

"She was sittin' on my damn lap!"

"Think that'd buffalo ol' Holmes? No, sir. Anyhow, it ain't only that. It's how you been all day. There's a big damn burr under your saddle, Brother, and it ain't just Doc Chan gettin' done for. What the hell is eatin' at—?"

And then we were done.

"Gentlemen," Diana said, stepping out of the dingy shop she'd walked into so very shortly before, "I beg your pardon."

"For what?" Old Red asked.

"*Shit*," she hissed. "That. I hope you're not offended."

"Oh, don't worry about us," I said. "No sabe Englee."

"You've got plenty of company around here, then," Diana said. "Or so they'd have us think. I tried everything . . . even the truth. Nothing worked. These people won't talk to us."

"That's gonna make it a mite difficult to dig us up any new data," I said to my brother.

He nodded, glassy eyed, as he slipped his pipe back into his pocket. "Noted."

"As things sit now, we could stroll right past Fat Choy or Hok Gup both and not even know it was them," I went on. "One's tubby and one's a dark-haired looker—that's all we got to go on."

Gustav gave me another nod with the same blank stare. Wheels were turning—but they didn't seem to be getting anywhere.

"Noted."

"It's startin' to feel like we're up the crick without a paddle," I said.

"Or a boat," Diana added.

"Or a crick."

Old Red blinked his way from his stupor. "You know, when I say 'noted,' that means I am well aware of whatever it is you're pointin' out. Which means you can *stop* pointin' it out."

"Which means 'shut up,'" I translated for Diana.

"I sabe," she said.

Old Red sighed.

"You know, I wish them Salvation Army fellers was still around," I said. "Seems to me the only thing left for us to do now is huddle up and pray for divine intervention."

"Only miracle we're gonna get's the kind we think up ourselves," Gustav said. "We gotta lay into it with some deducifyin'. Figure out what Mr. Holmes would do if . . ."

His gaze drifted away, settling on something beyond the both of us.

"Hel-lo," he said.

"You thunk something up already?"

"Nope." Old Red stretched out a hand and pointed up the street. "I'm just wonderin' what *he* wants."

Diana and I turned to see a slender young Chinaman hustling toward us. He was dressed in saggy, baggy, gray clothes that looked like they'd been tailored for a man twice his size, while atop his head was an equally shapeless—and very American—flat cap. He didn't look like any of the tong crowd we'd tangled with, that was for sure, but I braced for a tussle all the same, clenching my fists and putting myself between the stranger and Diana.

"That's not necessary," she said.

"We'll see about that."

Gustav solemnly held up a hand as the Chinaman slowed to a stop a few feet away. "Hello. Sabe Englee?"

The Chinaman put up a hand of his own—then gave it a dismissive swipe. "Please. I don't just 'sabe' English. I speak it."

"Oh," my brother said.

The man had no accent whatsoever. Had I been blind, he could've been introduced to me as "Joe Smith" and I'd have been none the wiser.

Diana stepped out from behind me. "Can we help you?"

"I'm not the one who needs help," the Chinaman said. "I can't even believe I found you in time. I thought some *boo how doy* would've given you the chop by now for sure."

Old Red squinted at the man as if he suspected his almond-shaped eyes and jet-black hair were merely makeup and a wig. "Do we know you?"

"You do now . . . and not a second too soon." The man held out his hand. "I'm Chinatown Charlie—the guy who can keep you alive long enough to find Gee Woo Chan's killer."

"Well, well," I said as Charlie and my brother exchanged a handshake. "Hallelujah!"

20

GOOD LUCK

Or, We Buy a Stool Pigeon and Get a Bead on a Kwong Duck

There were introductions all around, and when it came time for me to pump Chinatown Charlie's hand, I nodded at his tweed cap.

"You don't happen to have a halo tucked up under there, do you?"

Charlie smiled. "I'm no angel. Just a businessman."

"Your business being what, exactly?" Diana asked. "Protection?"

"Do I look like a bodyguard?"

The Chinaman held out his long, thin arms. He was about Gustav's age—in the neighborhood of twenty-seven—yet he still had the gangly frame and gawky bearing of a boy of half as many years.

"I'd be more what you might call a native guide. Someone who can translate, tell you the wheres, whys, and whos, scout around—"

"Keep us alive," Old Red said.

Charlie nodded. "Like I said before, that's part of the package. But only in a 'Run for your life!' kind of way." He shook a bony finger at us. "I'm not gonna take on any hatchet men for you. I have a hard enough time keeping myself alive around here. What I *can* do is steer you clear of the tongs—and maybe help you find the Black Dove while I'm at it."

Gustav's eyes popped so wide I could've sold them to the corner greengrocer as goose eggs.

"You certainly know a lot about what we've been up to today," Diana said.

"Hey, someone leads a marching band into a Kwong Duck parlor house, it tends to draw attention. Especially when the band ends up running down Pacific Avenue screaming their lungs out."

Charlie chuckled, savoring the image in a way that suggested it wasn't just hearsay for him—it was a memory.

"Not that there wasn't plenty of talk already," he went on. "Three Southern Pacific detectives show up at Gee Woo Chan's . . . and one's a woman and another's a *cowboy*? Believe me—you were noticed. And watched. There's only one person in Chinatown who doesn't know you snuck back into Chan's place after Mahoney left, and that's Mahoney."

"Well, well, well." I turned to my brother. "I do believe you owe Old Green an apology. Sounds like it don't matter one whit that he was—"

"So," Gustav said, talkin' over top of me, "with folks 'round here doin' all this lip-flappin', anybody let slip what really happened to Doc Chan? Cuz this suicide business Mahoney's tryin' to peddle is pure eyewash."

"Half of Chinatown agrees with you," Charlie said. "And even the half that doesn't thinks Gee Woo Chan was *pushed* to kill himself."

" 'Pushed'?" Diana said. "What do you mean by that?"

Charlie gave his head a quick shake. "Sorry, lady. We haven't agreed on terms yet."

"We ain't got time to dither, mister," Old Red snapped. "Case you haven't noticed, there's a man dead and a girl probably good as, 'less we find her quick."

"Yeah, I noticed," Charlie shot back. "And could be *I'm* good as dead just for standing here letting you bark at me. Look around. We're not exactly meeting in secret here, are we?"

He spread his arms out again, this time swiveling back and forth, sweeping his gaze up and down the block. Every doorway and window seemed to have someone in it pretending (not particularly well) that they weren't watching us.

"The Kwong Ducks knew I was talking to you ten seconds after I walked up and opened my mouth. So you want my mouth to *stay* open, you better make it worth it to me. And if you need any help making up your mind, just remember how cooperative the good citizens of Chinatown have been today. No one else is gonna stick his neck out to help a bunch of *fan kwei* stir up trouble with the tongs. No one."

"What makes *you* such an upstanding citizen, then?" Diana asked. "It can't just be greed."

"It could be . . . but for once it's not. The truth is, my neck's already stuck out even further than yours."

As Charlie himself had just pointed out, he'd been far from sneaky about speaking to us. Yet now he leaned in close and dropped his voice down low.

In Chinatown, it seemed, certain things are said in whispers no matter what the circumstances.

"I crossed Little Pete. It was an accident . . . but that's all it takes. He could put up red paper on me any minute. And if he does—"

Charlie sliced one finger across his thin neck and made a *sheee* sound that, while not English, needed no translation.

"We should hire you cuz the biggest badman in Frisco wants you dead?" I said. "I hate to tell a feller how to go about his business, but that ain't exactly what I'd call an enticement."

"How's this for an enticement, then: I speak Hoisanese and Mandarin, and you don't. Simple enough for you?"

"Not really," I said. "What we need is someone who speaks Chinese."

"Otto . . ." From the look on Diana's face, I knew I'd just said something extra-special stupid, even for me. "Hoisanese and Mandarin are both Chinese dialects."

"Oh."

"Look," Charlie said, "you need help, and I need running money. And I need an answer." He locked eyes with Old Red, perhaps sensing—correctly—that my brother was the most likely to make things difficult. "*Now*."

He didn't get his *now*, though. Gustav made him wait while he sized him up, eyes narrowed, mouth pressed into a small, tight line.

"Well, hell," Old Red finally sighed. He peeked over at Diana. "You're the one with the greenbacks. I reckon it's really up to you."

"Right."

Diana opened her handbag and pulled out a roll of cash.

"I'll give you fifty now and fifty if we find Hok Gup," she said, peeling off five bills and holding them up in the air.

Charlie opened his mouth and shook his head.

"And then there's the tip," Diana cut in before he could commence to bitching. "Five hundred more, wired to you anytime, anywhere."

Charlie closed his mouth and nodded.

Stiffly, bit by bit, Diana brought down the hand with the cash in it like her arm was a drawbridge slowly being lowered. When the money was within reach, Charlie snatched it up and stashed it beneath his loose gray blouse.

My brother's gaze remained fixed on the lady, though. And he didn't look particularly grateful, either. In fact, he was eyeing her as he'd just eyed Charlie—and he seemed wary of what he saw.

"You wanna find Hok Gup, you need to find Fat Choy," Charlie said. "You wanna find Fat Choy . . . come with me."

And he started off as Gustav so often does, moving fast, not looking back, simply assuming you're hitched up behind him. Old Red didn't look happy to be on the other end of the harness for once, but that didn't stop him—or me and Diana—from following.

As we hurried after Charlie, I noticed something I hadn't seen when the Chinaman was facing us: Like Chan, he wore no ponytail "queue."

"Just who *is* Fat Choy, anyway?" Diana asked as we caught up to him.

"Another *boo how doy*. A hatchet man. For the Kwong Ducks," Charlie said. "He got his start over at Madam Fong's, guarding the door." He glanced over at me and my brother. "You know the type."

"Oh, absolutely," I said. "Big. Chatty. Homicidal."

"That's Fat Choy—especially the last part." Charlie swung left at the corner, taking us north up Stockton Street. "In fact, that's how he got his name.'"

"'Choy' means 'killer'?" I asked.

Charlie coughed up a scoffing chuckle. "No. And 'Fat' doesn't mean fat, if that's what you've been thinking. 'Fat Choy' means 'good luck.' They call him that because meeting him usually *isn't*. Get it?"

I nodded. "Oh, sure. Like if folks got to callin' my brother 'Mr. Sunshine.' "

"*So*," Old Red piped up from behind us, "Fat Choy worked at the cathouse. *And* . . . ?"

"And he fell in love with one of the sing-song girls. I assume professional detectives like you can figure out which one."

Charlie gave us a few seconds to do our figuring—not that we needed it.

Still, the break in the chatter was good for something beyond dramatic effect: It gave me a moment to notice all the looks we were getting . . . and how they'd changed.

Before, Chinatown folk had felt free to gape at us openly, brazenly. But now it was more like they were peeking, stealing little glimpses before looking away—or even ignoring us altogether in that stiff-necked, staring-at-nothing way that can be every bit as obvious as a pop-eyed gawk.

It gave me the uneasy feeling there was something all those Chinamen didn't want to see. Something that might happen at any moment.

"Fat Choy tried to buy the girl himself a while back," Charlie said, picking up his tale again. "Couldn't afford her. The Black Dove's a big draw for Madam Fong. Her best earner. A smart mack like the Madam doesn't give that up easily. But it looks like Fat Choy wasn't ready to give up, either."

Old Red stared at Charlie so hard he would've walked smack into a streetlamp had one appeared in his path.

"Meanin' what, exactly?"

"Gee Woo Chan was seen bringing Hok Gup home with him this morning," Charlie said. "And Fat Choy was seen storming into Chan's place less than half an hour later."

"And who was doing all this seeing?" Diana asked.

Charlie shrugged. "Everybody."

"And nobody'd tell us that?" my brother fumed. "Nobody'd even tell the damned po-lease?"

"Nobody around here trusts the damned po-lease."

Charlie veered right, steering us into what felt like the fiftieth dark, dank alleyway we'd entered that day.

"Anyway, everybody saw Fat Choy go in, but nobody saw him come out. The front door was wide open, so after a while, one of the neighbors went in to check on Chan. You know what he found upstairs: the gas on, Chan dead. The back door was left open, too, so it looks like Fat Choy took the girl out that way. But that's just a guess. No one's seen them since this morning."

Charlie finally came to a stop.

"And here we are."

"Here" was a mere hole in the ground—a pit dug out beside a dilapidated, grime-blackened tenement house. It was on an incline, ramp-style, and one could walk down into it and keep on going right under the building itself.

This was no storm cellar, though. There were no stairs, no doors, no frame, no indication of structure of any kind. It was like the entrance to a huge dugout or den—the home, perhaps, of the world's most colossal gopher.

At the end of the pit was . . . nothing. *Black* nothing.

Oh, there was more, that we could tell from the sour smells that came seeping out from beneath the building. There were voices, too—muffled grunts that could have been words or groans, either or. But it was as if these were the scents and sounds of the blackness itself, for it was hard to believe there could be anything down in that pit but oblivion.

And in a way, that's all there really was.

"Fat Choy took it hard when he couldn't buy Hok Gup," Charlie said. "He tried to dull the pain with—"

"*Opium.*"

Diana was staring down into the hole. For the first time since I'd met her, I saw something on her face that looked a little like fear.

"That's an opium den?" I asked.

"The worst in Chinatown. Which makes it just about the worst anywhere. A man wants to disappear"—Charlie nodded down into the darkness—"that's the perfect place to do it. You really want Fat Choy, this is where to look first."

I think Charlie was expecting a moment of tremulous reflection, a little pause while the white folks fussed and fretted and reappraised their commitment to their little crusade.

And I would've given him all that, too, if it had been up to me. But, as is so often the case when my brother's around, it wasn't.

"Well, what are we waitin' for?" Old Red said, and he marched straight into that ditch and disappeared into the shadows.

"Someone to talk us out of it?" I called after him.

Our squabblings aside, I've always said I'd follow my brother to hell and back. Now it looked like that was being put to the test . . . literally.

I dropped into the pit and walked into the abyss.

21

CURTAINS

Or, A Tourist Trap Lives Up to the Name

One surprising thing about hell: There's not nearly so much headroom as you'd expect.

The trench I'd hopped down into quickly turned into a tunnel, and before my eyes could adjust to the dark, I scraped my already-tender scalp against the slats of rotting wood that were either the ceiling or the ground floor of the building above. The little yelp I let out didn't slow Gustav, though. The tunnel jogged off to the left, and he jogged with it.

A dull orange-yellow light was leaking out around the corner Old Red rounded, and I moved toward it stoop-shouldered and sore-headed.

As I came around the curve, I found my brother stopped before a small, long-whiskered Chinaman who was even more bent-backed than me. I would've thought he was trying to touch his toes if he hadn't been glaring up at Gustav, his head cocked at such an extreme angle it almost seemed to be fitted to him backwards. The man jabbered at us in Chinese, then twisted his neck even further to eye something behind us.

"Give him five dollars," Chinatown Charlie said. Diana was beside him. "That's his usual fee when I bring people down here."

"You've done this before?" I asked.

"Oh, only about eighty or ninety times."

"Hold on," Old Red said. "You mean to say you're a . . . a . . . a . . ."

"Tour guide?" I offered.

My brother snapped his fingers. "Yeah, that's it. You're a tour guide?"

Charlie shrugged. "Among other things. What did you think I was? A streetcar conductor?"

"And you actually get *tourists* who want to see a place like this?" I asked.

"Every day. The only place they enjoy more is the slave market under St. Louis Alley."

I waited for a smirk that never came. If Charlie was joking, he was doing it with a face as straight as a razor.

"Go on." He nodded at our hunchbacked host. "Pay the man."

Diana looked at Gustav, and he gave her a sharp nod. As she fished out her bankroll, the hunchback scuttled toward her, clearing the way for my first good look at a genuine opium den.

I'd read of such things in magazine stories, of course—one of them being "The Man with the Twisted Lip" by Sherlock Holmes's pal Dr. Watson. And though the good doctor had been writing about a "vile murder-trap" in faraway London, most of his description fit our new surroundings snug enough.

The den he'd depicted was "a long, low room, thick and heavy with the brown opium smoke, and terraced with wooden berths, like the forecastle of an emigrant ship." Ours was just as tubelike and smoky, lit only by two low-burning lanterns and the orange-red coals of a small brazier. But there were no "berths," just tattered canvas cots, and it felt less like the hold of a ship than a coal mine converted into a flophouse. Or a peanut mine, perhaps—opium smoke, it turns out, smells almost exactly like burnt goobers.

The far end of the room was cordoned off by a series of dingy-gray curtains, for the purpose, I assumed, of affording the classier clientele a little privacy. The other customers got none whatsoever—nor did they seem to care.

While Watson wrote of "bodies lying in strange fantastic poses, bowed shoulders, bent knees, heads thrown back," I just saw a dozen logy-looking Chinamen. The sudden appearance of a Stetson-topped cowpoke and a red-haired giant who had to bend at the knee just to keep from scalping himself on the ceiling seemed to make as much of an impression on them as a beautiful sunset makes on your average cowpie. They had eyes only for the long-stemmed pipes they occasionally rousted themselves from their cots to pack with gooey gray paste and light up, fingers all afumble. A few seconds sucking up the acrid fumes from the gurgling pipe, and they had no need for eyes at all—their bodies went slack, their faces vacant as they beheld wondrous visions invisible to all but themselves.

"I've seen that look before," I said.

Gustav was walking slowly between the opium eaters' bunks, headed for the back of the room. "Yeah?"

"Sure. On your face. Every time you get to cogitatin'."

I dropped my jaw and went cross-eyed.

"These fellers here ain't tryin' to think," Old Red muttered. "They're tryin' *not* to."

"Like Holmes with his cocaine?" Diana asked, taking a cautious step deeper into the den.

Gustav threw a scowl back at her.

We'd only learned of the great detective's not-so-great habits recently, from the stories in *The Adventures of Sherlock Holmes*. At first, the revelation that his hero had been a hophead bothered my brother, but he'd shrugged it off soon enough.

"A brain like that, a man's gonna get bored from time to time—crazy bored," he'd said. "That stuff with the needle . . . it probably kept him sane."

"You got yourself a big ol' brain, yet *you* don't feel the need to pickle it when there's nothing to set it to," I told him.

"I got my distractions," he'd said—and he jerked his head at his copy of *The Adventures*, from which I'd been reading aloud.

"This ain't nothing like what Mr. Holmes done," he said to Diana now. "Holmes, he was occupyin' his mind however he could. But them . . ."

He looked around at the opium fiends—most of them skeleton-thin men in dark, baggy clothes as shapeless as shrouds.

"They wanna forget they got minds at all."

"I'm guessing these men have a *lot* they'd like to forget," Diana said. Her large, brown eyes picked up the light of the brazier, and for a moment they seemed to glow like twin coals. Some of the hoppies even tore their gaze away from paradise or Xanadu or Wallawalla or wherever so as to look upon an even more unworldly beauty instead—her. "You can't sympathize with that?"

"Miss," Gustav said, staring straight into the fire of her eyes, "a man shouldn't ever forget. Not *nothing*." Then he looked past her, at Charlie, and waggled his thumb at the nearest cot. "So any of these gents Fat Choy?"

Charlie shook his head.

"Alright, then. Just one more place to look."

Old Red turned and took hold of the curtains that walled off the back of the room.

"Wait!" Charlie barked before my brother could pull the gray drapes apart.

Gustav froze. "Yeah?"

Charlie looked back at the hunchback, and the two Chinamen had a "conversation" that consisted of two words, a shake of the head and a grunt.

The words were "*fan kwei*."

"Alright," Charlie told Old Red. "Go ahead."

Gustav opened the curtains. There was nothing behind them but two more cots and a smoke-smudged wall.

"What goes on back there?" Diana asked.

"The same thing as out here," Charlie replied. "It's just that some of the more . . . *discriminating* customers expect separate accommodations."

"You mean the white customers, don't you?" Old Red said.

"Yeah—the *fan kwei*," I threw in. "Seems like I been hearin' that phrase all day. What's it mean exactly, anyway?"

Charlie laughed—the hunchback, too.

"Foreign devil," Charlie snickered.

"Oh, is that all?" Diana said. "I assumed it was something much harsher than that."

"Me, too. Still, it's a mite pot-callin'-the-kettle-black, ain't it?" I turned back to Charlie. "You're the foreigners."

Charlie's chortling choked off.

"I was born in San Francisco," he said.

"Oh, you know what I mean. You Chinese. This here's *our* country, and yet you—"

"Otto," Diana said before the rest of my leg could follow my foot up into my mouth, "I think you need to stop talking now."

I clamped my lips and nodded.

"Well, I'll be damned," Gustav marveled. "If I'd known that's all it took to shut him up, I would've tried it a long—"

The hunchback called out something in Chinese, and as we swiveled around to face him he went lurching away into the tunnel—smiling and waving at someone we couldn't see.

Charlie spread out his spindly arms and started shooing us back like a farmboy trying to get a gaggle of geese into their pen.

"Move. *Now.*"

We hustled behind the curtains, and Charlie pulled them closed quick but quiet.

"What is it?" Diana whispered.

Charlie peeled back the drapes just enough to peek out. "Trouble."

This, of course, I had already guessed. I leaned in over Charlie's shoulder to see what kind. Not wanting to be left out, Old Red pushed his way in, too, squatting down to peer out from a height roughly even with Charlie's belly button.

Fortunately, Diana was content to leave the peeping to us, for there was no room for her at the curtain unless she clambered up onto my back or went down on her hands and knees.

This is the sight she missed seeing: the hunchback returning to the room with a husky Chinaman dressed entirely in black.

We were being joined by Madam Fong's head hatchet man. The Chief.

"Charlie?" I whispered.

"Yeah?"

"How do you say, 'Oh, shit,' in Chinese?"

22

HAIL TO THE CHIEF

Or, Madam Fong's Right-Hand Hatchet Man Gets Another Swing at Us

We were unarmed, opium dens don't have back doors, and Diana was all out of brass bands. So there was simply no getting around it: We were buggered six ways to Sunday. Maybe even seven.

Hell, a million.

The Chief and the hunchback had stopped at the front of the room to talk, and after a moment another Chinaman stepped out of the shadowy passageway to join them—the other hatchet man from Madam Fong's. His right cheek was still puffy and red from taking a bowl of peppermints to the puss during our little bric-a-brac barrage, and as is so often the case with men who've just had their teeth loosened, he did not look happy.

"Otto," my brother whispered, "when the time comes, you just get Miss Corvus outta here, understand?"

"I most certainly do not," I whispered back. "I'm 'Big Red,' remember? You should be the one hustlin' the lady out, '*Old*.' I'll take care of them tong boys."

"And how do you reckon you'll do that? By bluntin' their hatchets with all the rocks in your head?"

"Well, what're *you* aimin' to do? Bore the poor bastards to death with your—"

My collar suddenly went choking tight, and I was jerked away from the curtain by a hard yank on my shirt.

"*Shut . . . up,*" a voice hissed in my ear.

And not just *my* ear—Gustav's, too. Diana was giving my brother the same scruff-of-the-neck tug.

"Yes'm," I wheezed out.

All Old Red could manage was a nod.

Diana let us go. I would've complimented her on the strength of her grip, but I was afraid she'd just give me another demonstration.

My brother and I leaned in next to Chinatown Charlie again and peeked back out through the drapes—wordlessly, this time.

The Chief and his pal had begun walking slowly past the cots, pausing over each to inspect the bleary-eyed wretch stretched out upon it. The hunchback was chattering at their backs, but they seemed to be ignoring him now: The only response he got was a couple grunts from the Chief that seemed to be the Chinese equivalent of what Diana had just said to me and Gustav.

For their part, the hopheads just lay there, still sucking on their pipes even as the hatchet men passed over them like the Angel of Death. I almost envied them their calm, and if one of their pipes had been passed to me just then, who knows? Maybe I would've tried a puff. I sure as hell wouldn't have said no to a shot of whiskey.

The two highbinders were just five cots from the back of the room.

Then four.

Then three.

Old Red and I moved away from the curtains again and readied the only weapons we had at hand: our fists. Charlie took a couple extra steps backwards, putting himself behind us, with Diana. I couldn't blame him—he'd said he wouldn't fight for us. I just hoped he *would* fight for the lady.

I drew back my right arm, readying it for a roundhouse.

The hatchet men were close enough now for me to hear their footsteps, the rustle of their clothes, their breathing. I could go ahead and throw that punch, and it would probably connect. The Chief was mere feet away . . . inches, more like.

The footsteps stopped. The curtains rustled.

A man spoke.

"*Yak yak Fat Choy yak yak?*"

The words came out raspy, parched. It sounded like the kind of voice a pile of sawdust might have.

More *yak yaks* followed, deeper but less hoarse—the Chief's voice. The first man replied, and after some back and forth, the footsteps started up again.

Heading *away* from us.

After a last exchange of *yak*s between the Chief and the hunchback, the place grew quiet but for the low burbling of the opium pipes. Gabriel could come down there a-blowing his horn, it seemed, and those hoppies wouldn't miss a single puff.

Charlie crept up to the crack in the curtains and took a look out.

"They're gone," he announced, and he threw the drapes open wide.

"What was all that talkin' about?" Old Red asked him.

"Saving your skins."

Charlie stepped out of our nook and squatted down next to the nearest bunk. The man lying on it grinned up at him toothlessly. He was either a well-preserved sixty or a prematurely decayed thirty, it was impossible to tell which.

The two chatted a moment, then Charlie stood up again.

"You owe this man ten dollars." He jerked his head at the hunchback. "But you can give it straight to *him*. That's where it's going anyway."

Diana dug into her handbag once again. "Lucky for us I brought my pin money with me today."

"You already laid out a lot more than pin money . . .' less your pins is solid gold," Gustav said. "How's a railroad spotter come to have so much ready cash, anyways?"

The lady's only response was a smile that splatted up against Old Red's suspicious glower like an egg hurled at a brick wall.

"So," my brother said sourly, turning back to Charlie, "this feller put them tong boys off the scent, did he?"

Charlie nodded. "They weren't looking for you, anyway. They're trying to find Fat Choy."

Gustav's eyes popped wide, then immediately narrowed back to a wary squint. "Oh, yeah?"

"Yeah. Still, it was pretty obvious we didn't want any *boo how doy* finding *us*." He waggled a thumb at the gummy-mouthed opium eater. "So Ah Chu there said he'd seen Fat Choy in one of the other opium dens."

"Which was a lie?" Old Red asked.

Charlie nodded again. "A lie."

"How nice of your friend to help us 'foreign devils,'" Diana said dryly.

"Not 'nice of,'" Charlie said. "'Profitable for.'"

"Hold on a tick." I pointed at the hophead who'd saved us. "What'd you say this feller's name was?"

"Ah Chu," Charlie replied with a roll of the eyes. "And please don't bother saying, 'Gesundheit.'"

"I wouldn't dream of it," I said . . . as I pulled out a handkerchief and held it out to him.

Charlie didn't take the hankie. "Sure, go ahead—laugh. Just be glad you don't know what 'Big Red' means in Mandarin."

"Alright, enough flapdoodle," my brother said. "Charlie, I assume this ain't the only opium den in Chinatown."

"Just the only one on this block."

"Well, then, let's get our asses over to the others. We can shilly-shally around givin' each other the giggles when this is over and done with."

And off he and Charlie went. Once the hunchback got his share of Diana's "pin money," she and I set off after them.

"It's actually lucky for us we ran into Big Queue," Charlie said as we staggered out of the pit into eye-searing sunshine.

I tried to blink away the purplish ink-splotches that blinded me, yet for the next few seconds Charlie and the others still looked like nothing so much as giant talking prunes.

"Ran into *who*?" I said.

"'Big Queue.' You know him. The Kwong Duck hatchet man. He's, you know—"

"Big," Old Red said.

"Very."

So the Chief had a name—sort of.

"Seeing him means we're on the right track," Charlie said.

I squinted over at him. "I'm too blind to tell . . . are you jokin'? Cuz I kinda thought 'the right track' would be the one that *doesn't* leave us with meat cleavers stickin' outta our skulls."

Blinded or not, my brother wasn't wasting any more time—he started off again, heading out of the alley fast.

"The right track's whatever leads us to Fat Choy and Hok Gup."

"Exactly." Charlie galloped past Old Red to take the lead. "Remember, Fat Choy's a Kwong Duck himself. So if the Ducks are looking for him, that means he's not holed up in one of their safe houses or fan tan parlors. And there's the good luck for us, because those places are like fortresses. Even I couldn't get you in."

"We ain't just learned where Fat Choy's not," Old Red said as Charlie swerved left onto Jackson Street and the rest of us stumbled after him like a string of baby ducks. "We can do some deducifyin' on *why* he's not there."

"And what do you deduct?" I asked.

"That them Kwong Ducks got a beef with Fat Choy. Or, more like, they want something from him."

"The Black Dove," Diana said.

Old Red nodded. "Charlie said Madam Fong wouldn't give that gal up cheap. Maybe she never meant to give her up at all."

"So the madam sics Fat Choy on Doc Chan," I said slowly, "only 'stead of bringin' Hok Gup back to the cathouse, he tries to keep her for his-self?"

"Could be," Gustav said. "If we wanna know the real truth of it, I tell you this much for sure—we gotta find that gal 'fore the hatchet men do."

"But it's not *just* about knowing 'the real truth' about Chan, is it?" Diana asked. "Not anymore."

Old Red moved his head sideways, gazing out over his left shoulder, as if he meant to look back but stopped himself just in time.

"That's right," he said, looking ahead again. "The last thing the Doc did on earth was take that gal outta that whorehouse." He clenched his fists—and picked up his pace. "If she goes back in, it'll be over *my* dead body, too."

"Madam Fong and her boys would probably prefer it that way, don't you think?" I said.

If Gustav grunted or growled or gave any kind of response at all, I didn't catch it. He was weaving his way through the usual sidewalk swarm at an almost frantic pace, and the closer he rode Charlie, the faster the Chinaman went. It was hard to keep up—and impossible to keep up a conversation. Which seemed to be the point, at least in part.

Old Red was trying to win a race to the Black Dove, true, but it almost seemed like he was running *from* something, too.

Whatever it was, I got the feeling it was gaining on him.

23

A CHINAMAN'S CHANCE

Or, We Learn How Charlie Lost His Ticket Out of Chinatown

Over the next hour, we descended into five more opium holes. Each was a slight step up from the last, until the final one seemed almost like something fit for human beings rather than just roaches or voles or the spirits of the damned.

Two things remained consistent, though (beyond the smell of charred peanuts and the cadaver-eyed stares of the opium denizens): Nowhere did we find Fat Choy or any word of his whereabouts, and everywhere we were a step behind the Kwong Ducks. Only half a step at one place, for we spotted Big Queue and his chum leaving just as we got set to go inside. We saved our skins by ducking into a butcher's shop where what looked like a bobcat was in the process of losing his.

Yet in the end, our tour of Chinatown's "hop joints" produced nothing beyond throbbing headaches for the lot of us.

"Well, thank you for the sightseein' tour, Charlie, but that ain't what you're gettin' paid for," Gustav grumbled as we stumbled from the last of the opium dens. "You'd best have a stronger card up your sleeve."

"Don't worry—there's lots more up here," Charlie said, giving one of his sleeves a tug. "But first we need to see what the word on the street is."

"The word on the street," as it turned out, wasn't just an expression. Charlie whisked us up and down more alleys and side streets until we were facing a brick wall near the corner of Dupont and Clay. The wall was plastered from the ground to a height of nine or ten feet with broadsheets chock full of Chinese writing. Here were words aplenty—for those who knew how to read them.

We'd passed other such bulletin boards in our various scamperings around Chinatown, but this was by far the busiest. A steady stream of men shuffled past, pausing here and there before what I assumed to be the freshest and most gossip-worthy postings.

Charlie stopped us a discrete distance away.

"Wait here," he said, and he hustled across the street and elbowed his way into the crowd.

Several of his fellow Chinamen slinked off silently, eyes down, upon noticing him in their midst. But one old graybeard had the opposite reaction: He stepped up to Charlie, waved a finger in his face and tore into a rant—which our guide studiously ignored as he perused the newer posters.

"Nothing," Charlie said when he rejoined us a moment later.

"What woulda been *something*?" Old Red asked.

"Yeah," I said. "What's on all them broadsides over there, anyway?"

"A few are newspapers, but they're mostly announcements."

"Like, 'For sale—one slave girl, slightly used'?"

Gustav glared at me.

"That's just a for instance," I said.

"And not a funny one," my brother growled.

"Actually, I've seen some that come pretty close to that." Charlie pointed at a large red handbill, then another, then another. "But that's what I was really looking for. *Chun hung*. Proclamations from the tongs."

"Proclaiming what, exactly?" Diana asked.

"Pretty much the same thing every time. Something like, 'The House of Far-Reaching Virtue'—that's the Kwong Ducks—'offers $300 for the killing of So-and-So for . . .' And then they'll put in some kind of justification. As if it matters."

"So around here the *outlaws* post the bounties?" I said. "Sweet Jesus. And I thought Texas was wild."

"You didn't see no bounty out for Fat Choy, did you?" Old Red asked Charlie.

"Or *us?*" I added.

Charlie shook his head. "No. Not yet."

"You know," I said, "you coulda just stopped at 'no' and left me feelin' a hell of a lot better."

Charlie offered me a halfhearted shrug. "Sorry."

"The authorities allow the tongs to openly post death warrants?" Diana asked.

"Which authorities are you talking about?" Charlie replied, drizzling so much acid over the word "authorities" I could practically hear it sizzling.

"How about the police?" Diana said. "The Chinatown Squad."

Charlie scoffed. "The police don't have much 'authority' around here. And even if they did, Mahoney wouldn't do anything about the *chun hung*. He'd love it if we *all* hacked each other to death."

"Well, what about the Six Companies, then?" Diana persisted. "Chun Ti Chu's supposed to be a powerful man. Why doesn't he put his foot down?"

"Chun Ti Chu *is* powerful . . . but no more so than Little Pete." Charlie curled the fingers of each hand into hooks, then locked them together tight. "The Six Companies and the tongs, they're like yin and yang."

"Who and what?" I said.

"Opposing forces in perfect balance—always at odds yet equal and inseparable." Charlie's mouth slid sideways into a smirk. "Kind of like you and your brother."

Now it was my turn to scoff. "Opposite, I'd buy. But equal? Not the way I get treated."

"*Anyway,*" Gustav said, "that geezer that was givin' you an earful . . . what had him so riled up?"

Charlie sighed. "Me."

"What about you?" Diana asked.

"Everything about me. But mainly this." Charlie swept off his cap and ran a hand through his thick, dark hair. "I'm *juk sing* and *ki di* to boot—I was born here, not in China, and I don't wear a queue."

"Folks 'round here care that much about your haircut?" I said.

"Yeah, they do, actually. The queue's not just 'a haircut.' Back in China, you have to wear one. It's the law. Not having one . . . it's like spitting in the emperor's face."

"Is that what you're doing?" Diana asked.

"Not really. He's not *my* emperor. I wouldn't go out of my way to spit in his face or kiss his fat . . ." Charlie eyed Diana uncomfortably. ". . . ring."

"Cuz you think of yourself as an American," I said.

"Because I *am* an American, no matter what some people say."

Charlie nodded at the men across the street. Only one was looking our way: the crotchety old-timer. Everyone else seemed to be taking special care to keep their backs to us.

"You know what they call themselves? 'Sojourners.' Meaning they're just visitors here. Temporary. They come over, scrounge up as much money as they can, then go back to Kwangtung or wherever, take a pretty wife, and lord it over everybody in the village—the bigshot Gold Mountain man."

Charlie snorted.

"Not for me. *This* is my home. And not just Chinatown—San Francisco. From the time I was six years old, I was a houseboy in Pacific Heights. A 'faithful.' Fourteen years with the same household. I was practically a member of the family. They were even going to send me to college."

"That explains it," I said. "I been thinkin' you talk the lingo pretty danged good for a Chinaman."

"And I've been thinking you speak English pretty poorly for a white man."

"Excuse me?"

Charlie smiled, indicating that this was just a little joke he liked to spring on the tourists every now and again. No hard feelings, ha ha.

Yet there *was* a hardness to it. An edge—and a sharp one.

"What happened to your patrons?" Diana asked.

"The Panic. They had all their money tied up in silver." Charlie shook his head but couldn't quite shake the look of bitterness from his face. "They may as well have invested in mud."

"So that's how you come to be 'Chinatown Charlie,' Frisco's foremost opium den tour guide," I said.

Charlie nodded, suddenly too glum for more sparring with me.

"Whatever chance I had to get out of here, move up . . . it's gone. The way the Anti-Coolie League's been whipping people into a lather about 'the heathen Chinee' lately, there's no way I can get on with another family. The society crowd's only hiring Irish or Mexicans these days. So since the one real skill I've got's pleasing *fan kwei* . . ." He threw out his long arms and slapped a broad, minstrely grin across his face. "Here I am!"

"But there's more to it than that, ain't there?" Gustav said. "You said earlier you got Little Pete peeved at you. How'd you manage that?"

Charlie seemed to shrink in on himself, his grin shriveling, arms wrapping around his sides.

"He asked me to do something for him, and I said no." He managed a slight, tight-shouldered shrug. "A person like me's not supposed to say no to a person like him."

"What exactly did you said no *to*?" Diana asked.

"If I was the kind of person who'd talk about that, I wouldn't have been allowed to live as long as I have."

"Suffice it to say, Little Pete wasn't askin' if you could pick up his laundry or loan him five bucks till payday," I said.

Charlie nodded. "Yeah. That suffices."

"Well, how about Doc Chan, then?" Old Red said. "Seems like Little Pete was mad at him, too. Word ever get around as to the why of *that*?"

Charlie stared at my brother as if he'd just accused Little Bo Peep of killing Chan.

"I don't know what you're talking about. And anyway, Little Pete leads the Som Yop tong. Fat Choy's a Kwong Duck, and he's the one who killed Chan . . . right?"

"I grant you it looks thataway." Old Red slid a hand into one of his coat pockets. "But just take a gander at this."

Out came the scorpion we'd found in Chan's flat. Or most of it, anyway. Both the pincers had broken off, as had a couple legs. The brittle little critter was coming apart.

Charlie leaned in close to peer at it—and he wasn't the only one. The

Chinamen thereabouts had been anxious to ignore us before, but a cow-boy showing off a scorpion on a street corner's a mite hard to overlook, even when you're trying.

But though we got curious stares aplenty from passersby, I saw nothing in those gaping faces that looked like recognition or fear. Just curiosity and disgust aimed at the scorpion and us in equal measure.

Charlie whispered what I assumed was Chinese for "Jeez Louise," followed by "a scorpion" in English.

"That's right," Gustav said. "Whadaya make of it?"

Charlie grimaced as he stepped back again. "Ewww."

There was a long pause, during which one could actually watch the hope slide off Old Red's face like trickles of rain down a window pane.

"That's it?" he finally said. " 'Ewww'?"

Charlie shrugged. "Ewww . . . *yuck*?"

"I think my brother was hopin' you'd recognize that thing," I explained.

"Oh." Charlie bent forward to give the scorpion another once-over. "Well, I'll be. I *do* recognize it!"

"Yeah?" Old Red said.

"Sure." Charlie straightened up. "Her name's Fanny. She's a dancer over at the Bella Union. Didn't recognize her without her tights on."

My brother stuffed the scorpion back in his pocket. "*Two* wiseasses I gotta put up with now . . . ."

"So that means absolutely nothing to you?" Diana said to Charlie. "Even as a symbol?"

"Sorry. No. Where'd you get it, anyway?"

"Oh, that don't . . . hel-lo." Gustav pointed across the street, his expression brightening a bit, going all the way from suicidal to merely woebegone. "Looks like another of them 'fun chunks' is goin' up."

"*Chun hung*," Charlie corrected. He swiveled around to peer at the Chinese workman who was pasting up a fresh poster on the news-wall. "And they're always on *red* paper."

The new handbill was white. But it caused quite the stir all the same, with nattering, gesticulating men pushing in all around. Some even dared glances our way.

165

"I'd better check it out," Charlie said, and he hustled across the street again. The crowd around the poster parted for him, giving him a little leeway on both sides, as if the Chinamen thought being a *juk sing* or *ki di* might be contagious.

Charlie spent all of ten seconds reading the flyer then whirled around and hurried back to rejoin us.

"It's a reward notice: one thousand dollars for information leading to the Black Dove and Fat Choy."

I whistled. "A thousand bucks? Them Ducks are gettin' desperate."

Charlie shook his head. "That's the strange thing about it. It's not the Kwong Ducks offering the reward."

"Oh?" Gustav's ears pricked up so quick it's a wonder they didn't knock off his hat. "Who is it, then?"

"The Six Companies." Charlie waggled a thumb over his shoulder. "That comes from Chun Ti Chu himself."

"Chu?" I said. "I thought he was supposed to be your respectable, pillar of the community type. Why would he be stickin' his clean nose into a low-down dirty mess like this?"

It was Charlie I was asking—and my brother who did the answering.

"I been ponderin' on that quite a spell already," he said. "And I reckon it's about time we up and asked him."

24

YIN

Or, We Try to Pull a Fast One and End Up Looking None Too Swift

About time we up and asked him'?" I said to my brother. "Just like that? We simply waltz in and grill the most powerful man in China-town?"

Charlie clasped his hands together again yin-yang style. "Don't forget Little Pete."

"Right, right," I said. "One of the *two* most powerful men in China-town."

Charlie nodded his approval.

"Why not?" Old Red said. "Chun Ti Chu's obviously got some of his own head mixed up in this here herd. 'Chan was a Six Companies man.' That come right outta Mahoney's mouth when we was eavesdroppin' on him and Woon, remember? And the way Mahoney talked, it sounded like Woon was a 'Six Companies man' hisself."

"If you're talking about Wong Woon, you're right," Charlie said. "He's a 'Chinatown special'—a private detective on the Six Companies payroll."

"Really?" I said. "He sure seemed awful cozy with the Ducks when we seen him at Madam Fong's a while back. Birds of a feather, looked like to me."

"Naw." Gustav shook his head. "That wasn't cozy so much as

courtesy—the kind yink might show yank whenever the two ain't tryin' to tear each other apart."

"Well, what was he doin' there, then?"

"Lookin' for Hok Gup, of course. Why do you think that re-ward poster just went up? Woon's been tryin' to track her down for Chu, only he ain't had any better luck than us."

"So Chu wants the girl . . . because she'd know who killed Chan?" Diana said.

My brother shrugged. "Maybe. But I'm startin' to think this crick runs a mite deeper than that."

"I'm startin' to think this crick's the Mississippi," I said. "Or maybe just Shit Crick, pardon my French."

"That would be '*Merde* Crick,'" Diana corrected.

Charlie gave us what I assume was his "oh, those inscrutable white folks" look.

"So," he said, "you plan to just march into Six Companies headquarters and demand that Chun Ti Chu tell you why he wants the Black Dove?"

"Nope. We'd best go about it more sneakylike than that." Gustav sighed. "'Course, 'sneakylike' ain't exactly my line . . . ."

He turned to Diana and said no more. He didn't need to.

He was handing her the reins. And she took them, too—as well as his Stetson, which she plucked right off his head.

"Alright, boys. I'll show you how to do sneaky." She turned to Charlie and snatched away his cap with her other hand. "But first—let's go shopping."

Fifteen minutes later, we were marching into the offices of the Chinese Consolidated Benevolent Association, a.k.a. the Six Companies. "We" didn't include Charlie, though. Being a known (and obviously less than beloved) character thereabouts, he was waiting for us a couple blocks away . . . wearing my brother's white Boss of the Plains.

And another thing about that "we"—it's not Otto Amlingmeyer, Gustav Amlingmeyer, and Diana Corvus it refers to. No, it was three newspaper reporters who came barging into Six Companies H.Q. that afternoon: John Lestrade of the *Chronicle*, Jabez Holmes of the *Examiner*, and Hatty Adler of the *Evening Post*.

These newshounds were foaming at the mouth over a tip they had (supposedly) just received. Dr. Gee Woo Chan, prominent Chinese physician and survivor of the infamous Pacific Express disaster, had been found murdered that morning. The reporters requested—nay *demanded*—that Chun Ti Chu himself comment on this heinous crime and the bloody smear it left on Chinatown's already rather soiled reputation.

Most of the talking was done by "Miss Adler." The slight, carrot-topped "Holmes" and the strapping, dashing "Lestrade" (who kept his own hair underneath a tweed cap pulled down almost over his ears) limited themselves to ejaculations of the "Yeah!" and "You tell 'em!" variety (it having been determined by the lady that they spoke with too much "twang" to be believable as big-city reporters).

The first obstacle we faced—a pop-eyed, middle-aged, clerk-ish fellow seated at a desk in the building's smallish lobby—slowed us about as much as a tumbleweed slows a stampede. Diana had barely launched into her harangue before he hopped up and scurried away, the silk of his loose trousers *shush-shush-shush*ing as he hustled through a nearby doorway.

An eerie silence fell over the place akin to the quiet of a church come any day but Sunday. With its mixture of ornate woodwork, stained glass, desks, and filing cabinets, the Six Companies office came off as both exotic and mundane—half-temple, half-shipping office. The clerk we'd encountered could've returned carrying lit incense for the altar or forms for us to fill out in triplicate, and either way it would've fit.

As it was, he returned with neither. *Shush-shush-shush* and there he was again, a younger, mustachioed Chinaman at his side.

"Hello," the young man said. "I understand that you—"

"You're not Chun Ti Chu," Diana snapped.

"No. I'm—"

And that was as far as he got. Diana tore into him about the power of the press and the precarious position of the Chinese community and the manifest folly of denying us an interview with Chun Ti Chu (since we'd just make up our own quotes if we didn't get to talk to the man face to face).

The new fellow lasted longer than his predecessor. Maybe all of ten seconds, even. Then he, too, turned and *shush-shush*ed away—though at least he had the courtesy to say, "A moment, please," before he left.

"He fetchin' Chu?" I asked our other host, who watched us nervously from the doorway as if afraid we might make off with his fountain pens or paperclips.

"No sabe Englee," he said with a little apologetic bow.

"Oh, yeah? Then I guess you won't mind if I call you a lyin' son of a bitch, will you?"

I eagle-eyed the Chinaman for any sign he understood, but all he did was offer me a miserable shrug.

"I think this one actually means it," my brother said.

"Good." I turned to Diana and went on in a whisper. "Seems to me these Chinese fellers wouldn't know a 'twang' from a stutter from the strummin' of a banjo, seein' as half of 'em don't even speak the lingo. So how is it they're gonna pick out our accents? And no offense, but I don't think they're gonna pay us much mind with a woman doin' the talkin'. Now if *I* was to start doin' the jawin'—"

"We stick to the plan," Old Red cut in, his voice quiet but firm. "We're just here to help prime the pump, Brother. Don't you worry about the lady. She can get what we need without givin' nothing away. Just remember what The Man said."

"The Man said a lot of things," I pointed out.

Gustav jerked his head at Diana. "About . . . you know."

"Oh." I rolled my eyes. "That."

"Let me guess," Diana whispered. "You're referring to Mr. Holmes's belief that women are 'naturally secretive'?"

Old Red gaped at her. "Well, I'll be . . . ."

"And I will be, too . . . ." I muttered once I'd picked my jaw up off my chest.

"I brushed up on my Watson before coming to see you yesterday," the lady explained. "You can understand why that line stuck in my head, I'm sure. It's so patently ludicrous. Men keep just as many secrets as women . . . wouldn't you say, Gustav?"

"Well, miss," my brother drawled, "I'd say that depends on the man and depends on the woman. Take yourself, for—"

Before he could finish, the younger Chinaman returned.

"Follow me, please."

Diana flashed me a triumphant smirk, and I conceded with a bow and an arm outstretched toward the doorway.

"Ladies first."

"And sometimes best," Diana said.

She sauntered off after the Chinaman.

The young man ushered us back to an oaken office door so dark and heavy-looking I imagined it would take a team of Clydesdales to pull it open. It was the kind of door that told you not just anybody was allowed to walk through it—though that's precisely what we did.

Chun Ti Chu smiled at us pleasantly as we walked in. Half the man's grin was hidden, though—he was pressing some kind of silver doohickey against the side of his head. It almost looked like he was trying to iron his round face flat.

After a couple blinks, I recognized the thingamabob as the business-end of a telephone. Chu said a few words into it in his native tongue, then returned it to its cradle on a desk so large it would need but a little scaffolding and a rope to make do as a gallows. He nodded at the young man, who backed out of the room quickly, closing the door as he went.

"Ahhh," Chu began, pushing back from his desk and coming to his feet. He wasn't tall, but the straightness of his spine created the illusion of a height he didn't have. He was broad-chested, too, but not big or fat. Overall, he seemed exceptionally *solid,* as if beneath the shiny, soft silk of his tunic he was pure granite. He was wearing a brimless, beanielike black cap, and the close-cropped hair around it was granite-gray, too.

It was no wonder Chu had come to be yin to the tong's yang. He was like one of those town-square local-hero statues come to life.

"Dr. Gee Woo Chan is dead," Diana shot at him before he could bow or hold out his hand or offer us cigars or kick us in the shin or whatever it was he customarily did when greeting reporters. "Any comment?"

All three of us whipped up our notebooks and pencils (freshly purchased from a stationer's around the corner) and held them at the ready. We probably looked like a firing squad lined up before Chu as we were, but the man wasn't any more fazed than that statue would've been.

"Gee Woo Chan was a good man," he said, speaking slowly. He had a strong accent, but the words came out with just enough space in between to let you decipher one before he moved on to the next. "An important member of the community. His passing brings much sorrow."

"And what of the rumors that he was murdered?"

Chu pressed his lips together and tilted his head ever so slightly to one side, giving Diana the exact same look of weary disappointment my dear old *Mutter* used to throw my way whenever I slacked off on my chores.

"There are always rumors," he said.

We dutifully scribbled this down (even Old Red, who truly was just scribbling). Then we stared at Chu over our notebooks, waiting for more—which didn't come.

"So you're satisfied it was suicide?" Diana pressed.

"Gee Woo Chan recently suffered a great loss of *mien tzu*," Chu replied. "He 'lost face,' as we Chinese say. He borrowed certain valuables that he could not return—"

"The Chinese antiquities he took to Chicago for the Columbian Exposition," Diana said. "The ones that were destroyed when the Pacific Express crashed."

Chu nodded. "That is right. It was in the newspapers, wasn't it?" The nod abruptly gave way to a doleful shake. "That only added to Gee Woo Chan's shame. He had guaranteed the items' safe return with his own money. He was forced to forfeit everything he had built over the last nine years."

Old Red cleared his throat—his prearranged signal to Diana to follow up on what had just been said. Of course, Chu had just said plenty, so the lady had to do a little guesswork as to what had caught my brother's ear.

"The last nine years?" she ventured.

Gustav pretended to jot something down in his notebook—another signal. Diana had guessed right.

"Yes," Chu said. "Gee Woo Chan first came to America in 1884, part of a commission dispatched by the emperor himself to survey the World's Fair in New Orleans. When the time came to leave, Gee Woo Chan refused to go. He had fallen in love with this country, and he sacrificed much to remain here, but he worked hard and invested wisely and did well."

Chu took a thoughtful pause. When he continued, he spoke with the tone certain men get when talking about missionaries, reformers, suffragettes, or the merely cheerful—folks they consider unrealistic fools.

"That is why the Exposition in Chicago meant so much to him . . . why he made such efforts to make the Chinese exhibition a success. Anti-Chinese feeling is on the rise again. Gee Woo Chan thought he could help Americans learn to respect our culture and traditions as much as he respected theirs."

Chu offered us a tight-lipped smile that seemed more rueful than amused. Thinking you could convince people to shed their prejudices might be a joke, but it's surely not a funny one.

"The artifacts Dr. Chan took to Chicago—who did he get them from?" Diana asked.

Chu's smile, small to begin with, vanished fast. "A local collector."

My brother hacked out another signal-cough.

"Would you like a glass of water?" Chu asked him. "Or some tea, perhaps?"

Old Red shook his head and waved off the offer with a flustered grunt.

"And this collector's name would be . . . ?" Diana said.

Gustav put pencil to paper for more bogus note-taking.

"Fung Jing Toy," Chu said.

The name rang a bell, but one so far off and muffled I couldn't tell where the sound was coming from. To be honest, what with "Gee Woo Chan," "Chun Ti Chu," "Hok Gup," "Fat Choy," "Ah Gum," and "Wong Woon" to keep straight—not to mention *fan kwei*," "*boo how doy*," "*chun hung*," etc.—I'd just about reached my limit for sing-song foreign names and phrases. I would've been a lot happier if that "local collector" had been named Bill Jones.

"This Mr. Toy must be quite a cold-blooded man to ruin Dr. Chan the way he did," Diana said.

Chu shrugged. "He is a businessman."

"And this was just business—so you did nothing?" Diana replied sharply. "We've heard Chan was a friend of yours . . . or the Six Companies, anyway. Why didn't you help him?"

Chu's eyes narrowed, the lids dropping like blinds he was drawing down on something he didn't want seen.

"He *was* a friend, and he *was* helped—but he could only be helped so much. Not everyone agreed that borrowing such valuable items from Fung Jing Toy was wise. Gee Woo Chan undertook that himself. It was his decision. His responsibility."

Before Diana could fire off another question/accusation, Chu turned to me and Old Red.

"Gentlemen? There is nothing *you* would like to ask?"

It was hard to imagine your average news hawk responding to such an invitation with a silent shrug. And as you've no doubt noticed—and my brother is partial to pointing out—I lack "the grand gift of silence" for which Sherlock Holmes once praised Dr. Watson.

No, my grand gift is a big mouth, and I used it.

"Were . . . you . . . and . . . Chan . . . still . . . on . . . good . . . terms?" I said, trying to squelch any trace of twang by speaking as slowly and carefully as Chu himself. "He . . . must . . . have . . . been . . . dis- . . . a- . . . ppointed . . . that . . . you . . . could . . . not . . . help . . . him . . . out . . . more . . . hmmm?"

Chu glowered at me as if I'd just announced myself to be the China-town correspondent of the *Daily Imbecile*—which perhaps I had.

"Gee Woo Chan understood his obligations—and mine. He bore no bitterness toward me or the Six Companies. In fact, I spoke to him just yesterday here in my office."

Old Red didn't say it, but I swear I could hear him think it.

Hel-lo.

Another cough, though, and Chu would be slapping my brother on the back and offering him a lozenge. So Gustav finally dared to speak—though he managed to squeeze his question into one small but infinitely evocative word.

"Oh?"

Chu took on the tense, sheepish look of a fellow trying to take back a bad bet.

"It was purely a social visit. We discussed nothing of importance."

"So . . . Chan . . . just . . . dropped . . . by . . . to . . . chit . . . chat?" I asked, still struggling to keep the cowpoke out of my voice. (To judge by the look Chu gave me, however, I only managed to put in a big bunch of cretin instead.) "Not . . . to . . . ask . . . you . . . for . . . money . . . again?"

It was the cash Chan had laid out for the Black Dove I was thinking of—and Old Red must have been thinking of it, too, for he gave my question his approval with another quick scribble.

"As I indicated, Gee Woo Chan's visit was personal—and private." Chu walked slowly around to the front of his desk, looking like he was going to lean back against it. "And now *I* have a question for *you*."

I would say Chu's hand whipped out quick as lightning, but that wouldn't be doing the man justice. He grabbed Gustav's little notebook with such swiftness it made your average lightning flash look about as fast as a slug oozing through mud.

"How is it," he said, "you can begin writing what I say before I say it?"

"Hey!" Old Red protested. "Give that back!"

Chu frowned down at the notepad, then held it up to give us all a look at my brother's "notes."

"English is not my first language, but I can read it. This, on the other hand . . . what is it?"

It was meaningless chickenscratch—random lines and squiggles scrawled hither-yon across the page.

Gustav flushed so fiercely it looked like someone had smeared a fistful of raspberries across his face.

"It's shorthand, of course," Diana said, and she took a quick step forward and snatched away the notebook with almost as much speed as Chu.

She was so close to the Chinaman he'd head-butt her if he was to take a bow, and still she moved in closer, crowding him, her body mere inches from his.

He didn't back up. He didn't move at all. He was a statue again.

"What do you want with the Black Dove?" Diana spat at him.

She was trying to shock an answer out of the man—and she failed. Chu merely stared back at her, content to stand there silent and still till vines twined up his legs and birds took to nesting on his head.

Before any of that could happen, though, the door behind us opened, and I turned to see what he'd *really* been waiting for.

"Ahhh . . . at last," Chu said as Wong Woon came waddling into the room. "What took you so long?"

25

HAT TRICK

Or, Our Ruse Comes to Naught While Someone Else's Comes to a Head

Well, hey there, Wong," I said as the portly detective trudged toward us. "Would ya believe we got new jobs since you last seen us?"

Woon stopped just a couple steps inside Chu's office. Iron bars couldn't have blocked our exit any better.

"New names, too?" he asked.

"Why, sure. 'Numb de plums' they're called in the writin' business. Everybody gets 'em one. Just look at Mark Twain and . . . uhhhh . . . Mark Twain."

"Brother, please," Gustav said with a sigh—which was about the nicest way he's ever told me to shut up. He turned to Chu. "It was Woon you was talkin' to on the telly-phone when we come in, wasn't it?"

"Yes. You see, I already spoke to reporters from the *Chronicle* and the *Examiner* earlier today. As with Woon, on that." He nodded at the telephone on his desk. "I also rang the offices of the Southern Pacific and spoke to a Mr. Powless of the Railroad Police. He was most displeased to hear you've been presenting yourselves as agents of his organization. He says he recently dismissed all three of you himself."

"Oh, he did, did he?"

I threw a little up-down up-down eyebrow waggle at my brother.

He didn't catch it. He was looking over at Diana, his own auburn brows knit together in befuddlement, as if the strangest thing he'd encountered that day was the possibility she might be telling the truth.

"Look, Mr. Chu," Gustav said, slowly peeling his gaze away from the lady, "Doc Chan was a friend of ours. As I see it, that gives us as much right as any badge to hunt down the man who murdered him. More even."

Chu shook his head slowly. "There has been no murder. Gee Woo Chan killed himself."

"Oh, yeah, right. I forgot. There was a 'suicide note.'" Old Red scowled at Woon. "You still got it in your pocket?"

Woon stared back so blankly I almost expected him to try trotting out a "No sabe Englee."

"I saw that flimflam you pulled on Mahoney," my brother snapped, his words lashing out like a whip at a mule's ass. "I don't know what you handed him back at Chan's place, but it sure as hell wasn't the note I found in the Doc's pocket. Which means we still ain't got no proof that was a suicide note at all."

"My word is not proof?" Woon said, his voice soft yet with a hard edge just beneath the surface—a pillow wrapped around a crowbar.

"No," Gustav said, his own tone nothing *but* iron, no padding to it. "It ain't."

Chu held up his hands. "Please. If you truly were Gee Woo Chan's friends, if you have any respect for his memory, you will drop this matter. You do him no honor by prying further."

"What about Hok Gup?" Diana asked.

The lady was still standing so close to Chu they could just about share slippers. But at the mention of the Black Dove's name, the Chinaman backed off, his gaze dropping to the carpet as he shuffled around his desk.

"That girl's not just a memory," Diana went on. "She's still alive . . . or so we hope. If we don't find Fat Choy soon, though—"

"Yeah," Old Red threw in. "Seems to me if you really gave a crap about findin' Hok Gup, you wouldn't turn away our help."

"*Help?* This is not help."

Chu slumped into the plush chair behind his desk. Before, he'd struck me as a statue—solid, stern, dignified. Now I was starting to see the cracks in the marble. The tilt to the pedestal. The pigeon shit on the shoulders.

"This is meddling," Chu said wearily. "And it ends now."

His next words were to Woon in Chinese. When he spoke to us in English again, his tone was regretful, sympathetic—even if his words weren't.

"I have instructed Wong Woon to take you to the police substation at Waverly Place. As his prisoners. You should consider yourselves under arrest."

"Under arrest?" I said. "For what? Last I heard, tryin' to pass yourself off as a reporter ain't illegal. Stupid, maybe, but not illegal."

Chu shrugged. "Wong Woon will find something suitable. Unfortunately, in Chinatown, there are always many unsolved crimes to choose from."

"Yeah," Gustav growled. "And I'm beginnin' to see why."

"Whatever you try to charge us with, it won't stand up in court," Diana said.

Chu shrugged again. "It doesn't have to. *Good-bye.*"

He picked up a sheet of paper from his desk and began reading it as if we were already gone.

Just in case we didn't get the point, Woon stepped aside and waved us through the door.

"*Go.*"

Diana walked out first, then me. Old Red lingered in the doorway, though.

"Just one thing before I go," he said. "Look me in the eye, Mr. Chu, and you promise me: If you get to that gal first, you ain't sendin' her back to the whorehouse."

I couldn't see Chu any longer, but I heard the rustling of the paper in his hand and the squeaking of springs as he shifted in his seat. And then I heard his voice.

"I give you my word. Hok Gup will not go back to Madam Fong's."

Gustav jerked his chin down in a single, brusque nod. Then he stepped out of the room and turned toward me and Diana.

"Alright. Let's go."

As we paraded through the lobby single file, Woon in the rear, we passed the quivery clerk who'd stymied us with his "No sabe Englee" on our way in.

"*You* lying son of beech!" he spat at me from behind his desk.

So he understood English after all—including the phrase I'd used when trying to test him.

"No," I snapped back as we past him, "*you* lying son of bitch!"

"No, *you* lying son of beech!"

"No, *you* lying son of bitch!"

"No, *you*—!"

And then we were out the front door and on the sidewalk, and the great debate ended in a draw.

"That way," Woon said, pointing to the left.

We dutifully marched east toward Waverly Place.

Gustav, Diana, and I were bunched up three-abreast now, with me in the middle and Woon behind. It was easy to forget the bulky detective was there at all, though, and I certainly didn't feel like a prisoner being herded off to the hoosegow.

"Woon," I said, "I think I'd feel better about this if you had us in handcuffs or something. A bull ain't supposed to just mosey into the slaughterhouse without at least a prod, know what I mean?"

"Oh, Mr. Woon doesn't want to put us in handcuffs, Otto," Diana said. "If he did that, how could we escape?"

"Excuse me?"

"Think about it," Old Red said. "Woon can't turn us over to Mahoney."

"Whyever not?"

"Because we know Woon kept the real 'suicide note,' remember?" Diana said. "So now he's just waiting for us to . . . 'make a break for it' is the term, I think."

Gustav nodded. "He's probably hopin' we'll skedaddle right on out of Chinatown. But that ain't gonna happen, Woon."

The detective said nothing.

I shook my weary head. "You know, it's gettin' awful damn lonely back here."

"Whadaya mean 'back here'?" my brother asked.

"Two steps behind you two."

Old Red and Diana leaned forward to glance at each other around my big chest.

The lady smiled. My brother cleared his throat and looked away.

"Tell me, Woon," Old Red said, "what did that note really say? You may as well cough it up, cuz I'm just gonna . . . hel-lo."

"You mean good-bye," Diana said.

They were both glancing back over their shoulders, so I did the same. Woon was gone.

"Guess he got tired of waitin' for us to escape," I said.

"Didn't wanna get asked any questions, that's what." Gustav cursed and kicked at a warped sidewalk plank. "Ain't nothin' to do now but go and collect Charlie."

Our agreed-upon rendezvous point was less than two blocks away: Portsmouth Square, or simply "the Plaza" as most folks call it. A charming little park on the edge of Chinatown, it sports trees and flowers and strips of immaculately manicured grass—and, by night, street strumpets, foot-pads, and maculately manicured tramps.

"There," Old Red said as we walked into the park.

He pointed at the Plaza's southeast corner. A thin man in dark clothes was stretched out on a bench there, his hands resting on his stomach. My brother's Boss of the Plains covered his face.

We started toward him.

"So," Diana said, "what next?"

"We oughta consult with Charlie on that." Gustav looked up, blinked at the sun a second, and frowned. "Whatever we do, we best get to it quick. It's already mid-afternoon. Half a damn day we spent chasin' our tails, and what do we got to show for it?"

"A beef-jerky scorpion and the face off a busted doll," I offered help-fully.

Well, alright—not so helpfully.

"Oh, that face didn't come off no doll," Old Red said. "Didn't you see? Back in the cathouse? When you . . . don't stop walkin'."

"What?" Diana said.

"*Don't stop*," Gustav hissed at her. "That ain't Charlie."

The bench—and the prone figure lying motionless upon it—was now no more than thirty paces away.

"Ain't Charlie?" I said. "How many other Chinamen you see around here wearin' Stetsons?"

"Look at his head, goddammit."

I looked. I saw. I just about soiled myself.

The man's head was pointed toward us, so even with my brother's big hat over his face I could see the way his hair was pulled tight and tied off.

Into a queue.

Now that I'd noticed that, certain other things came to my attention, too. Certain other *people*. The black-clad ones scattered two-by-two along the benches lining the path ahead, for instance. The ones watching our approach the way a pack of wolves eyes a lost lamb.

"Uhhh, Brother," I said, my voice low. "Why ain't we runnin'?"

"Cuz I don't recognize these fellers . . . and maybe they ain't gonna recognize *us* if we don't stop."

"A good-lookin' lady, a man-mountain, and a feller dressed like a drover who's lost his lid—and they ain't gonna know who we are?"

Old Red shrugged miserably. "I'm hopin' we all look alike to them."

Then we entered into the Valley of the Shadow of Death—hatchet men on benches to both sides of us.

"Smile, gentlemen, smile," Diana whispered, linking her arms to ours. "We're just three carefree friends out for an afternoon stroll."

As we drew even with "Charlie," I dared a little peep over at him. The queue was the only thing that would've given him away as a fraud, for not only was he as tall and slender as the real deal, I saw to my horror that he was actually wearing Chinatown Charlie's clothes.

"Did you see—?" I said, a bogus smile pasted to my face.

"Yup," Gustav grated through his own phony grin.

"That must mean—"

"Yup."

"Why, those goddamn murderin'—"

"Stop," someone said behind us.

"Now?" Diana asked.

"Not yet," Old Red answered, not bothering with the smile anymore. "*Stop.*"

"Now?" Diana asked again.

"Not yet," Gustav said. "*Stop!*"

Footsteps crunched on gravel—a lot of footsteps, from big feet.

"Now now now!" my brother hollered. Not that it mattered. We were all running already.

Still, it helped me feel better, him shouting like that. Like we had a plan . . . and a chance.

The feeling didn't last long.

26

HIGH RISK

Or, Our Hopes of Escape Plummet—As Does One of Us

"Never look back," some folks will tell you. They're speaking symbolical-like, of course, warning against fixating on things past, letting a preoccupation with what's behind you keep you from seeing what's ahead.

But if you're running for your life—from a band of bloodthirsty highbinders, let's say—I have very different advice.

Go ahead. Look back. Look good and hard. Because nothing sets the feet to flying faster than the sight of the Reaper on your heels.

Or, as was the case for us there in the Plaza, six scowling *boo how doy*.

"Whoaaaoaaaoaaa," I said when I saw those highbinders dashing after us. Or maybe it was more of a "Wahhhhahhhh." Or perhaps an "Eeeeeeeeeeah!" In any event, you won't find it in any dictionary, unless you can find one written by terror-stricken monkeys.

A fence of wrought-iron bars runs around the Plaza, with only four gaps through which you can go in or out—one at each corner. The nearest one was less than forty feet away, and Old Red, Diana, and I should have been through it in five seconds flat, fast as we were fleeing. Unfortunately, somewhere around the four-second mark, three hatchet men swung in from Kearny Street to block our escape.

Assuming more highbinders were guarding the other corners, we had more than a dozen men after us.

This wasn't a tong we were up against. It was the goddamn Army of the Potomac.

"Follow me!"

I swerved off the path, tearing through a very surprised-looking couple's picnic spread in the process. My left foot came down in something soft and slippery—an apple pie by the feel of it—but I managed to stay upright and on the move.

I glanced back again to make sure Gustav and Diana had followed me. And they had—as had enough hatchet men to field a baseball team.

I led the whole herd up an incline toward the park's southwest corner.

"Dammit, Brother . . . they'll be on us 'fore we can shimmy over them bars," Gustav puffed out as we scrambled up the slope to the fence along Clay street. "You just went and got us tra-*ahhhhhh*!"

The "*ahhhhhh*!" part was pretty much unavoidable. Most people'll "*ahhhhhh*!" if someone grabs them by the collar and the seat of the pants and hurls them over a six-foot fence—which is exactly what I'd just done to my brother. I swung him up hay bale-style, and by the time he was halfway through his arc I was already turning to Diana.

"My apologies, miss," I said as I laid hands on her in places that would've got me slapped just a few minutes before. "I know I should've sent you first, but I wasn't entirely sure I could actually *do* this."

"Look, Otto, I don't th-*ahhhhhh*!"

I paused just long enough to make sure she didn't land on her head (she didn't—she landed on my brother) and then I leapt up, grabbed hold of the bars and hauled myself over.

Only "over" didn't come as quick I'd hoped. As I swung my legs up above the bars, thinking I'd simply drop down to the sidewalk on the other side, I jerked to a sudden stop, and a crushing pressure enveloped my . . . now how do I put this delicately?

My delicates.

I cut loose with more monkey-words—"Ah-oof!" or "Ee-aff!" or something along those lines—then just dangled there, afraid to struggle too mightily lest I do permanent damage not just to myself but to my future prospects of fatherhood. After a moment, a shredding/splitting sound ripped out from behind me, and I finally fell.

I hit the sidewalk, rolled over in pain . . . and saw my tattered trousers flying from the fence like a flag.

I thanked God I'd put on fresh underdrawers that morning. Then I asked Him why he was so pissed at me.

Hands appeared next to my snagged britches, and a hatchet man came sailing over them. He landed next to me as graceful as a cat, crouched, his legs apart.

Diana stepped up and did to him with one dainty foot what an iron bar had just done to me.

I still don't know much Chinese, but I can tell you what a Chinaman says if you kick him in the delicates: "Eyii!" Then he clamps both hands to his freshly scrambled huevos and topples over sideways.

"Up up up!" Gustav barked, grabbing me by the arm. More *boo how doy* were clambering over the fence as he pulled me to my feet. By the time he and Diana had me hobbling away across Clay, it was raining highbinders back behind us.

Once we were on the other side of the street, we turned east—and saw another gaggle of black-clad Chinaman bearing down on us. We whipped around to the west and saw more of the same.

There was only one direction left to go—south, into one of the buildings facing the Plaza. Diana led the way, charging toward what looked like a ramshackle tenement.

We reached the doorway the same moment as a bent-backed old woman carrying a mesh bag filled with vegetables.

"Pardon, ma'am!" I said as we pushed our way past into the building.

Whether it was the hatchet men on our trail or the sight of a de-pants *fan kwei* that set her off, I'll never know. What I do know, though: That old crone sure could scream.

Inside, it was as dark and dank as a cavern, or perhaps I should say as a sewer, since that's what it smelled like. I have no idea what the residents called the place, but "The Cesspool Arms" or "Septic Manor" or simply "The Big Privy" would suit it to a T. Folks popped their heads out of their apartments to see what the fuss was about—then promptly slammed the doors shut when they caught sight of us. Whoever we were, we were obviously trouble.

"This way!"

Diana ducked into the building's narrow, shadowy stairwell.

"Shouldn't we be lookin' for the back door?" I asked even as Gustav and I hurried after her up the steps.

"This . . . could be . . . better," the lady panted, the climb (and her heavy skirts) quickly slowing her.

"*Could* . . . be?" Old Red huffed.

"Save . . . your breath . . . for runnin'," I told him.

We were up past the second landing when a low rumble arose all around us, and the stairwell started to shake. We weren't the only ones pounding up those steps anymore—not by a long shot.

"Wherever . . . we're goin' . . . we'd best . . . get there," I said between gasps.

When we hit the third floor, the stairwell narrowed even more, turning into a tubelike set of steps up one more flight.

"This is it! We made it!"

Diana went springing up the last stairs two at a time. There was a door at the top, and one-two-three we burst through into blinding white light.

We'd reached the roof.

I slammed the door shut and pressed my broad back up against it. There was no lock.

"*This* . . . is . . . *it?*" Old Red wheezed.

I understood his disappointment. Unless the next part of Diana's plan was to sprout wings and fly off, I didn't see how being on a rooftop worked in our favor. Quite the opposite, in fact: The highbinders could now keep their hatchets clean by simply *tossing* us to our deaths.

Diana began scurrying around the roof, eyes down.

"One of my Pinkerton friends once told me about a tong trick," she said, disappearing behind the little shacklike structure that covered the top of the stairs. "The highbinders keep . . . *a-ha!*"

She returned cradling a thick-cut beam of wood about three feet long.

"For the door," she said just as the sound of footsteps thumped up from the last stretch of stairwell behind me.

I grabbed the timber and jammed it in place, one end down on the roof, the other propped against the door. It made the perfect brace—and if there was any doubt, the door didn't budge when someone tried the knob mere seconds later.

"That buys us a little time, but what—?" my brother began.

Diana held up one finger, then hurried back around the corner again. When she came back this time, she was dragging a longer but thinner cut of wood—a plank that, placed upright, would've been twice as tall as me.

"The *boo how doy* leave these on rooftops all over Chinatown," Diana said. "Just in case."

"Just in case *what?*" I asked. "They need to build themselves an emergency pigeon coop?"

"Oh, use your head for more than a damn hat rack, would you?" Old Red grumbled. Then he moved toward the lady with a mumbled, "Lemme help you with that."

Seconds later, that plank was no longer a plank: It was a *bridge* stretching to the roof of one of the tenements next door. Once we'd crossed over, we could cross again to either the east or south, for all the buildings thereabouts were of a like height, and they were jammed up tight. No matter how many hatchet men might be after us, there was no way they could keep an eye on every rooftop and doorway we'd soon be able to reach just by walking the plank.

"Alrighty then!" I said. "Looks like we're in business long as—"

A fist came through the door behind me.

Let me repeat that.

A fist came through the door behind me.

Remember: This is a *closed* door I'm talking about. One crafted, as one might expect, from solid wood. Yet someone had punched his hand clean through it like it was made of paper.

The fist unclenched into waggling fingers that groped around for the beam holding the door shut.

"Y'all get! *Now!*" I hollered at Old Red and Diana. Then I grabbed that hand and yanked as hard as I could.

There was a thud from the other side of the door, followed by a grunt and a groan. Whoever'd managed to get his fist through, he'd had less luck repeating the feat with his face.

I turned and dashed to the edge of the roof, where my brother was hunched over holding the plank steady for Diana. She was already halfway to the next building, her skirts aswirl in the wind as she scampered across with small but quick steps. I spared a glance down at the trash-strewn alley below her, then quickly brought my eyes up again, vowing not to repeat the mistake when my turn came.

Looking back when you're being chased might give you a little extra speed, but looking down when you're over a forty-foot drop gives you nothing but the collywobbles.

The second Diana reached the other side, she crouched down and grabbed hold of the other end of the plank.

"Next!" she shouted.

"You go," Old Red said to me.

I shook my head. "You."

"You'd do better protectin' the lady."

"Probably. But that worm-eaten ol' wood might not even hold my weight."

"There's no time to draw straws, dammit!" Diana yelled at us. "One of you just *go*!"

There was a splintering sound from behind us.

A slipper-covered *foot* was now sticking through the door.

Gustav clapped me on the shoulder—then hopped up onto the plank. "I hate to admit it, but you got yourself a point about this here wood." He took a deep breath. "See ya on the other side. And . . . be careful."

"If I was careful, I wouldn't even be here, would I?"

"Heh," Old Red grunted. "I reckon not."

Then he charged across the plank so fast I couldn't bear to watch. By the time he was three steps into his dash my eyes were squeezed tight.

The clatter of wood hitting the rooftop popped my eyes back open and jerked me around toward the door.

Our little barricade had been tipped over. The door was swinging open.

"Otto!" Gustav hollered. "Come on!"

"Come on, come on, come on!" Diana added in case I didn't get the point.

I stepped onto the end of the board. It was less than a foot across, and the other rooftop was more than a dozen feet away. There'd be little room for error and a *lot* of room for death.

My blood ran cold—and I mean that literally. You ever try a high-wire act, I suggest you do it with some pants on, because it gets mighty cold up there with the breeze blowing over your BVDs.

I managed to get my feet moving just as I heard someone else's hurrying up behind me.

Step one, all was well.

Step two, ditto.

Step three, I noticed a little more play in the plank than I would've liked.

Step four, "play" turned into a definite "sag."

Step five, "sag" turned into "Damn my fat ass—this bastard's gonna snap like a twig!"

Step six, I was halfway home.

Steps seven and eight, the wood seemed to firm up under me, and I felt myself begin a grin I never quite finished.

Step nine, I noticed Diana and Otto staring past me, wide-eyed, horrified.

Step ten, I looked back.

There was no step eleven.

Behind me, at the other end of the plank, stood a short, wiry *boo how doy* with a bloody nose. He was bringing his foot up high while his compadres crowded in around him, leering and laughing.

When the little hatchet man knew for sure I'd seen him, he smiled, nodded—and brought his heel down hard.

The last foot of the plank snapped off clean. The rest of the plank fell.

And me, I did the only thing a man could do at such a moment. I fell, too.

Now, there's a certain skill you pick up when you've been thrown from enough horses. It's the Not-My-Head Twist. Because when you come off the back of a bucking bronc, you want to land on your butt, your back, your feet, even your shoulder or your knees—anything but the top of your skull.

So doing a little midair curl is nothing new to me. I can wriggle like a fish on the line if need be. And need *was* when I felt that plank give out from under.

With the last bit of purchase I had, I sent myself twirling around toward Gustav and Diana, arms outstretched. They both leaned out to make a grab at me—and they both missed.

Cold air rushed over me. The alley below grew larger. Someone screamed. Me, most likely.

Then my palms slapped down on something solid, and my fingers instinctively curled into hooks.

I swung down and slammed face-first into the side of the building. It was like being smacked by a whale's tail—a stunning slap to the entire front-side of my body.

I lost my grip.

Fortunately, other grips quickly came into play. Hands wrapped around my wrists, locking on tight before I could slip over the rooftop lip I'd been clawing at.

I looked up and saw Diana and my brother peering down at me, one to each arm. They were gritting their teeth, gasping and flushed from the strain of the battle: the two of them versus the earth's gravity (and my girth).

I wanted to say, "Drop me! The highbinders'll be on you in no time 'less you run for it *now*!" Truth to tell, though, I'm not that selfless. In fact, I've got plenty of self—enough that I desperately wanted onto that roof even if the *boo how doy* were just going to chuck me right off again.

I kicked at the bricks, trying to find a foothold. But there was no extra leverage to be had, and Old Red finally hissed at me, "For chrissakes, stop it! This is hard enough without you down there doin' the goddamn Texas two-step!"

I forced myself to go limp, and a moment later Gustav and Diana hauled me up onto the roof. We ended up collapsed side by side by side, panting for breath.

"You know, I . . . ain't never said this . . . to you before," Old Red wheezed at me. "But I reckon . . . now's the time."

"Yeah?"

He put a hand on my shoulder.

"You could stand to lose a little weight."

"A joke? At a time like this?" I said—and I laughed with what little breath I had in me. "Brother, I do believe I'm finally startin' to have a good influence on you."

Then I heard the creak of an opening door and the clomp of footsteps, and the laughter stopped.

A man was stepping out onto the roof—the runty, bloody-beaked highbinder with the iron fists and feet. A half dozen hatchet men spread out behind him.

"You," he said to us, shaking his head.

He brought up one finger and waggled it back and forth.

Tsk-tsk.

"Such big trouble."

I was inclined to agree.

27

YANG

Or, Chinatown's Number One Crook Gives Us the Third Degree

"We're in big trouble?"

I pushed myself to my feet and laughed my best booming nothing-scares-me laugh (which I only use, of course, when I'm scared shitless).

"There's only seven of you up against one Big Red Amlingmeyer! Please! *You're* the ones in big trouble."

A trickle of blood was still flowing from the little hatchet man's nose, and he flashed me a smile that was smeared dark red.

"No," he said. "Big mistake."

"You keep talkin' big, mister," I said. "But I'm gonna *show* you big."

Gustav and Diana had stood by now, too, and I took off my jacket and handed it to the lady.

"Get ready to run," I whispered.

"Run *where*?" Old Red asked. "Case you haven't noticed, there's only one door offa this roof, and there's seven Chinamen between it and us."

"Maybe we should see what they have to say," Diana suggested.

" 'Die, *fan kwei!*' seems to be the gist of it," I said. "Nope—this here's the only way."

I turned back to the highbinders and began rolling up my shirtsleeves.

It was awful cold up there with no jacket, no *pants,* and now nothing over my arms. But I was aiming to make a spectacle of myself—a distraction, to put a finer point on it—and a little showmanship was called for.

"Oh, boy . . . this is gonna be fun." I brought up my dukes and got to pinwheeling them pugilist-style. "I haven't whipped seven men at once in *months.*"

The assorted *boo how doy* looked about as intimidated as a cougar in a standoff with a cornered chipmunk.

"No, no," their little leader said, shaking his head. "Mistake. You not *in* big trouble. You *are* big trouble. Someone wanna talk to you, that all. No need for run. No need for fight."

"Otto," my brother said.

"Oh, yeah?" I snarled at the hatchet man, moving toward him fists a-spinning. "Breakin' that board out from under me—that the kinda innocent little chat you're talkin' about?"

The highbinder grinned again, but his eyes were bored, sleepy, scornful.

"I know you make it," he said.

There was something about his smirky smile that seemed familiar, but I shook the feeling off. How many Chinamen had I seen wearing black hats and baggy black clothes the past day? Of course he'd seem familiar.

"*Otto,*" Old Red said again.

But I was already lunging forward, right arm whipping out to throw my best punch—into empty air.

The hatchet man stepped under the swing, popping up just to my right. He could've driven a fist into my belly, broken my jaw, tripped me, knocked off my cap, pulled down my underpants, whatever he wanted. The same with his buddies.

They didn't touch me, though, which I found damned irritating.

I'd hoped the gang would try rushing me in a bunch, open up a hole Diana and Gustav could dash through to the door. But the other highbinders didn't budge.

"Last chance," their boss said. "You come on feet or you come on back. But you come."

I threw another jab, but I may as well have been the tortoise trying to

193

cold-clock the hare. The hatchet man pivoted, putting his side to me, and my fist whizzed right past his face.

Then he did something strange, or so it seemed to me for the next quarter-second. He leaned back so far on one foot I thought his head might actually touch the roof.

But it wasn't his head I should've been watching. It was his free foot—the one that came flying up into the side of my skull.

Nothingness came on me as quick as the snuffing of a candle.

Somethingness returned a lot more slowly. First as a dull awareness of light and sound. Then as a much sharper awareness of pain.

I put my hands to my head and was surprised to find it didn't have the consistency of oatmeal.

"Easy, Otto," Diana said gently.

I pried my eyelids apart and found her and my brother peering down at me anxiously. The lady placed a reassuring hand on my shoulder.

"You took quite a nasty blow to the head."

"Good thing, too," Gustav grumbled. "At least he took that kick where he has the most fat to pad it."

"That must mean I'm gonna live," I croaked at Diana. "If it looked like I was gonna die, he wouldn't be givin' me guff."

"I wouldn't be so sure about that," Old Red said. "You deserve guff and plenty of it."

"Why?"

"Why don't you sit up and see?"

I struggled to push myself up, noticing for the first time that it was soft cushions beneath me, not hard roof. I was properly attired again, too—or I had something over my underwear, at least. Whether the pants I was wearing could be called "proper" would be a matter for debate. They were black trousers of the type the highbinders wear, only this pair fit me so snug it looked like I'd been stuffed into a little boy's knicker-bockers.

"Don't belly-ache," Old Red said when he saw my look of vexation. "The feller who had to donate them drawers to you, now *he* had reason to complain."

"What are you talkin' about?"

"One of the *boo how doy* had to give you his pants," Diana explained. "So the others could bring you here."

"'Here' bein' *where*?" I said, and I finally got myself propped up enough to get my bearings.

I was stretched out on a divan in a room that was equal parts hotel lobby and museum. The floor was plushly carpeted, the ceiling high, and comfy-cozy settees and armchairs were bunched together in little knots here and there. Windows lined one wall, a large bookcase another, while an array of glass cases formed an L around the rest of the room. The dark mahogany shelves behind the glass were empty but for one item: an age-browned folding fan propped up on a little stand. The fan was spread out to full flower, and painted upon the brittle-looking paper was the faded image of a snarling dragon.

You couldn't ask for a jail with more class. Yet a jail it was, for the burly highbinder loitering by the only door was clearly there to keep us from going through it.

Upon noticing me noticing *him,* he opened the door and walked out, speaking in Chinese as he went. He shut the door behind him, but it didn't stay closed long. Two other Chinamen joined us in the room a moment later. The second I saw them, I knew where I was—and why the Artful Dodger, the nimble hatchet man with the feet of steel, had seemed familiar. The day before, I'd spotted him out for a bite with his boss.

The first man to enter was the Dodger himself, his face wiped clean but his nose still bulbous and red. Following him was his employer—a lean, stiff-necked fellow attired in silken robes so blinding bright they'd make a bouquet of posies look like a bucket of coal. The flashy man had a regal bearing (or you could call it just plain haughty) and a long-striding yet slow-stepping gait that carried him through the doorway with all the painstaking pageantry of a bride coming down the aisle.

It was Little Pete, Chinatown's crime king, and he'd brought us a gift: my brother's Boss of the Plains.

"A-ha! The cowboy!" he exclaimed upon laying eyes on my brother. His stern expression gave way to a beaming, boyish grin. "I hear so much about you! Here, here!" He rushed over to Old Red with the Stetson held out before him. "Every cowboy must have his big hat!"

Gustav accepted the hat back gingerly, as if taking a vial of nitroglycerine from a baby.

"Yes, yes?" Little Pete said, his smile wavering as his gaze moved from Gustav's head to the Stetson and back again.

Old Red got the idea—and put on the hat.

"Ah! Perfect!" Little Pete proclaimed, giving his hands three quick claps. "I never meet a cowboy before. Howdy, partner! Yeeeha! Giddyup!"

The tong boss looked back at the Dodger, who laughed on cue, but I didn't get the feeling Little Pete was trying to humiliate my brother (though he most assuredly had). He seemed genuinely excited to be in the presence of a bona fide cowpoke, and he was still chuckling as he bowed deeply to Diana and acknowledged me with a little nod.

Maybe that's why folks call him "Little Pete," I thought—his childlike enthusiasm. He was actually rather tall for a Chinaman, and there was certainly nothing undersized about his personality.

"Please, sit," he said, lowering himself into a throne-ishly overstuffed chair that I had a hunch only his underpadded rump ever rested upon.

Head swimming, I pulled myself up from a sprawl to a slump so Diana could join me on the divan. The Dodger stayed on his feet, drifting over to stand behind Little Pete.

And Old Red—he didn't move an inch.

"Where's Chinatown Charlie?" he said.

"Chinatown Charlie?"

Little Pete turned his head to one side, and the Dodger bent down and whispered in his ear.

"Oh. The guide." Little Pete gave a little wave of the hand, and the Dodger stepped back, dismissed. "Don't worry. He is fine."

"And why should we believe you?" Diana asked.

Little Pete looked at the lady approvingly, as if admiring a particularly well-crafted piece of art.

"Because I give you a reason," he said. "He owe me."

"And dead men don't pay off their debts, is that it?" Gustav said.

"Lots living men don't!" Little Pete laughed. "But yes. You are right. Dead never do. And I am a businessman. Debts to me I want paid."

He glanced away, turning a wistful gaze on the empty cases along the walls. When he looked back at my brother again, a sly smile was curling up the corners of his thin lips.

"Like I must pay debts *I* owe."

Old Red nodded. "I understand . . . Mr. Toy."

"Mr. *Fung*," the Dodger barked.

Little Pete said a few quiet words to him in Chinese—something along the lines of, "Now, now . . . the poor, ignorant heathens don't know any better," I'm guessing.

"Family name come first," Little Pete explained to Gustav. "Family *always* first."

"Toy . . . Fung?" I said. The sounds seemed like something I'd heard before—not long ago, neither—yet I still couldn't place them as a name.

"Fung Jing Toy," Diana corrected me. She looked at Old Red and offered him the kind of congratulatory nod you give someone who's just beaten you at checkers. "The collector who loaned Dr. Chan all the Chinese art for the Exposition."

"Not all . . . just best," said Little Pete, a.k.a. Fung Jing Toy. "Vases, jars, cups, bowls, all Tang Dynasty. One thousand years old. Gee Woo Chan want to show Americans beautiful things Chinese make so long ago. He think, 'Now maybe they see. Now maybe they respect.' "

The Chinaman sighed.

"So foolish of me to listen."

"But you would've lost it all, anyway, right?" Old Red pointed at the rows of empty shelves lining one side of the room. "You didn't send all *that* to Chicago. You sold the rest off cuz you got skinned in the Panic."

Little Pete nodded. "Advice to you. Gambling, drinking . . ." He paused, eyeing Diana as he searched for the right words. ". . . entertainment for lonely men. These are all good investments. But a *bank*?" He gave his head a rueful shake. "Big risk."

"So you had to pay your creditors, and Doc Chan had to pay you," Gustav said. "And Chan *still* owed you."

"Oh, yes. Owed lots. And it is like you say. Dead men cannot pay."

"Is this why you had us chased down and dragged here?" Diana said sharply. "So you could tell us that Chan's debt to you is the very reason you *wouldn't* have had him killed?"

Little Pete showed no sign that the lady's razor tongue had sliced him in the slightest.

"I want you to know that, yes," he said pleasantly. "It was important that Gee Woo Chan think I am displeased, that he might be . . . made uncomfortable by my *boo how doy*. Otherwise, maybe he forget what he owe me. But I would never have really harmed him."

Little Pete dismissed the subject with a limp, regal wave of his right hand.

"That is past. More important to me now is to meet you. I hear about you all day. Cowboy, lady, and . . ."—he groped for the words that'd sum me up—". . . *big man* looking for Hok Gup and Fat Choy. Going to opium dens. Fighting Big Queue. Meeting Chun Ti Chu." He paused again, though this time it was merely a buildup to the punchline. "Taking brass band into Madam Fong's!"

He burst into hysterical cackles, clapping his hands like a delighted child. The Dodger joined in with some halfhearted chortles of his own, glowering at us all the while. I got the distinct impression we weren't kowtowing enough for his tastes.

"Oh, such a day," Little Pete sighed, wiping laughter-tears from his almond eyes. "I could not let anything happen to you until I see you for myself."

"Uhhh . . . and now that you *have* seen us?" I was about to ask, but Old Red jumped in first.

"You sure know a lot about what we been up to."

"This is Chinatown," Little Pete said. "I know more about what you know than you know."

While I was still puzzling over that, Gustav dug a hand into his pocket and took a step toward Little Pete's throne.

"Stop," the Dodger barked, practically hurling himself in front of my brother.

"No need to fret," Old Red said. "I just wanted to put what your boss said to the test."

He stretched out his right hand. In it was the little china face we'd found in Chan's flat.

The Dodger snatched it away. "What is this?"

My brother looked around him at Little Pete. "I was hopin' you could tell me."

Pete held out a hand and snapped his fingers, and the Dodger turned and gave him the shard of porcelain.

"Oh. This is nothing," Little Pete said after giving the small, white face a quick once-over. He sounded sincerely disappointed. "From statue of Kuan Yin. Chinese goddess. Very cheap. Hundreds like it all over Chinatown."

He handed the face to the Dodger, who threw it to my brother with a contemptuous flick of the wrist.

"I figured it ain't valuable, but it *is* important," Old Red said, pocketing the china chip again. "The statue it came off was used to kill Doc Chan . . . or knock him cold so he could be gassed, anyway."

"The statue from Gee Woo Chan's own altar?" Little Pete asked.

Gustav nodded.

"Ha! And this is how she repay him!" Little Pete crowed. He turned to the Dodger. "His offerings must been very stingy!"

The Dodger laughed for real this time.

"Kuan Yin is goddess of mercy," Little Pete explained to us between chuckles. "Fat Choy must appreciate . . . ."

He spun his hands in the air again, his eyes rolling back in his head.

"Ah, yes. *Irony.*"

"Seein' as you know so much," Gustav snapped, looking like he wanted to stomp over and wipe the man's grin away with a greasy rag, "surely you know what this is."

He pulled out the scorpion and tossed it into Little Pete's lap.

The first thing Pete made from it, of course, was a cringe, a gasp, and a (Chinese) curse. The Dodger, meanwhile, made a beeline for my brother.

I pushed myself off my saddle warmer and stumbled to Gustav's side. But by the time I got my feet planted (and my head to stop swimming), he didn't need me there. The hatchet man's charge was called off by a fresh peel of laughter from his master.

"Oh, I like this cowboy! He is crazy!" Little Pete giggled, playfully wagging a finger at Old Red. "I just wonder"—his tone suddenly sharpened, and he turned a look on his henchman that could've made a gelding out of a stallion—"how he is allowed so close to me without his pockets searched?"

The Dodger went skulking back to his place beside Pete's throne, while I hobbled to the divan and slumped next to Diana again.

"So?" my brother said. "That mean anything to you?"

"Mean? It is a scorpion." Little Pete pitched the dried husk back to my brother. "What does it mean to *you*?"

"Not all I'd like it to . . . yet." Gustav stuffed the brittle little critter back in his pocket. "But this much I do know now: Doc Chan wasn't done in cuz some hophead hatchet man was jealous. This whole thing with the gal—the Black Dove, Hok Gup, whatever you wanna call her. It runs a lot deeper than her and Chan and Fat Choy. Which is the real reason I'm here talkin' to you, ain't it? A feller like you don't bother with the likes of me just to amuse himself, no matter how you might play-act it. You got some kinda stake in this, and I'm wonderin' what it is."

Little Pete nodded, still looking plenty amused, play-acting or not.

"In Chinatown, I have a stake in everything."

"Including Hok Gup?" Diana asked.

"Of course. What the stake is, though . . . ?" Little Pete gave the lady a head-shaking shrug. "I don't even know. But Madam Fong and Kwong Ducks want the girl. *Chun Ti Chu* want the girl. So *I* must have the girl. If Six Companies say she is worth one thousand dollar, then maybe she is worth two thousand, or five thousand, or ten thousand."

He looked away for a moment, his gaze moving to the empty showcases that once housed ancient treasures of the Orient.

"Maybe she is priceless," he said, his tone turning strangely melancholy.

Then he brought his eyes back to my brother, and there was no emotion in his voice whatsoever—just the cold sound of a businessman talking trade.

"But two thousand dollar is what I offer *you,* cowboy. You are crazy, but you are clever, too. Maybe you find Hok Gup. You do, you bring here. I give you two . . . thousand . . . dollar."

Now, two thousand dollars wasn't just twice what the Six Companies was offering. It was twice the money my brother and I had earned in five years of drovering—and about two thousand times what we had left of it.

So did I think about what that kind of cash could do for us? I'm proud to say I did not.

Which isn't to say I thought Gustav shouldn't accept the man's offer. A yes would get us out of there. A no, though—that would get us nothing but trouble.

You might assume a wily fellow like my brother would know that—and he probably did, down deep. Up top, though, he was pissed, and it was his up top that did the talking.

"You go to hell."

"Probably," Little Pete said, looking unperturbed—perhaps even pleased—by Old Red's answer. "Only you go first, you are not careful."

He turned then, saying something to the Dodger in Chinese, and the highbinder moved toward us.

"My friend Scientific will show you the way out," Little Pete said, nodding at the Dodger.

" 'Scientific'?" I asked.

" 'The way out'?" asked Gustav.

"You're letting us go?" asked Diana.

"Yes," Little Pete said, answering all our questions at once. "Go. And good luck. Or perhaps I should say . . . *fat choy*."

He started to smile at his own little funny, but his lips never made it to full curl. They froze halfway up, then drooped downward into a frown.

Then I heard it, too. A muffled thumping coming through the door. It had a rhythmic quality to it—one-*two*, one-*two*, one-*two*—like men driving railroad spikes or chopping together at a big tree.

Little Pete muttered something under his breath, and the Dodger (a.k.a. Scientific) nodded brusquely and slipped a hand under his tunic. It was my fervent hope that he was just scratching at a sudden itch.

Here was a man who could bust through doors with a fist and snuff out my lights with a foot. What he could do with an actual *weapon* I did not want to see.

And I didn't. The thumping gave way to a splintering sound, then shouts, then screams, then pounding feet.

A moment later, the men with axes rushed in.

28

FACE

Or, An Old Acquaintance Returns with a New Axe to Grind

The axe men were an entirely different breed from the hatchet men with whom we'd been tangling that day. To a man, they wore cheap suits and bowlers and bushy black mustaches.

Oh, and they were white, to boot.

A pair came bursting into Little Pete's parlor, axes at the ready, and past them we could see more swarming up the stairs.

"We found 'em," one of the men said. "Get Mahoney."

His partner lumbered back out shouting, "Sarge! Hey, Sarge!"

"You're with the Chinatown Squad?" Diana asked the fellow who'd stayed behind.

"Lady . . . ," he said.

His eyes drifted over to me—and the black knee-pants straining at the seams to contain my manliness—and all the wind went out of his lungs.

"It's a long story," I said. "You were sayin'?"

"Lady," he began again. "We *are* the Chinatown Squad. All of us. You don't raid Little Pete's place without bringing every man Jack."

"You no raid Little Pete at all, Wood-a-gate!" Scientific snapped.

The copper—"Woodgate" I took his name to be—jerked his head at the doorway.

"Try telling that to *him*."

Then he took a step toward the nearest glass case—the one that held the dragon-bedecked fan, the only item left from Little Pete's collection of ancient Chinese bric-a-brac.

"Alright, we gotta make this look good . . . ."

He hefted his axe up high.

"Don't you dare!" Little Pete roared.

And that's when Woodgate did something truly shocking, something my brother and I have just about never seen a lawman do.

He listened.

"Fine," he said, lowering his axe. "But you know how it is. I've gotta use this on *something*."

He started toward the divan Diana and I were sitting upon.

"Hold on there, now!" I protested. "You can't bust up the glass, so you gotta give *us* the chop?"

"Get up," Woodgate barked, already bringing the axe up again.

Our butts were barely clear of the cushion when the blade came swinging down to give the back of the divan a whack.

Within half a minute, the settee was nothing but kindling and scraps of fabric. Little Pete and Scientific just stood by and watched Woodgate work, obviously disgusted but making no move to interfere. In between lops, I heard more hacking and crashing out in the hallway—as well as the softer thuds of axe handles on flesh and the piercing cries of men in pain.

"Shouldn't we take to our heels while we can?" I whispered to Old Red and Diana. I nodded at Woodgate as he knocked over an end table and began stomping it to pieces—but only after getting a curt nod of approval from Little Pete. "I don't mind dangerous, but now things are gettin' downright bee-zarre."

"We stay," Gustav said. "Or *I'm* stayin', at least. If you two wanna get out while you can, you just—"

"You were right the first time," Diana cut in. "*We* stay. After all, we can't leave before we've talked to—"

"Well, howdy howdy howdy . . . if it's not my favorite railroad dicks and dickette!"

Sgt. Cathal Mahoney came strutting into the room, a grin slicing into his big, pink, baked ham of a face.

"Mahoney," Old Red grated out by way of greeting.

Diana opted for honey over vinegar.

"Ah, our knight in shining armor—or tweed, anyway."

Mahoney gave her a bogus-bashful shrug. "Just doing our job. You folks alright? Cuz I heard . . . ."

He finally noticed there was something a mite irregular about yours truly south of the border.

"Say, Tex . . . what happened to your pants?"

"Nothin'. I'm just goin' through a growth spurt."

"And we ain't from Texas," my brother added sourly.

Mahoney looked at Gustav as if he'd just announced that iced cream gives him gas and his favorite song is "Yankee Doodle."

"Do I give a damn?" he said.

And then Little Pete was on him, striding over to shake a long finger an inch from the cop's bulbous nose.

"You go too far, Mahoney! You may have one, two supervisors back you! You may have money back you! But I got City Hall! I got the machine!"

The sergeant slapped Little Pete's hand away, snarling out a three-word phrase of which I will only transcribe one, as no printer would dare set the other two to paper anyhow.

"—*you*—"

The insult brought Scientific charging in, but Mahoney never so much as glanced in his direction. The highbinder stopped short, clenching his fists in impotent rage.

"You're the one who went too far," Mahoney said to Little Pete. "Chasing *white people* around the Plaza in broad daylight? Even the cops in your pocket couldn't ignore that."

He shot a glare at Woodgate, who'd been lingering silently near the showcases as if he wished he could climb inside and join Pete's collection.

"The Panic woke people up again, Petey," Mahoney went on. "All the bribes in the world won't save you and your kind this time."

"Ha!" Little Pete spat. "*You* talk about bribes? How you like your new boat, Mahoney? How your wife like her new—?"

Mahoney hit him so hard the Chinaman's queue whipped around and bopped the side of the sergeant's face.

Before Little Pete even hit the floor, Scientific was on Mahoney, delivering a kick across the chest that sent him stutter-stepping backwards. The cop tripped into Little Pete's throne-chair and flew back into the seat, his eyes wide with surprise.

Scientific moved up fast, spun himself sideways, and leaned back on one foot, just as he had before delivering the kick that had cleaned my clock so thoroughly. He was going to flatten Mahoney's nose—or crush his throat.

"Stop," Woodgate said. Calmly, coolly, not shouting.

Which is maybe what turned the highbinder around. A man that collected at such a moment must have good reason to be. And Woodgate had excellent reason indeed: He'd traded his axe for a short-barreled Webley Bulldog pulled from a shoulder-holster.

Scientific planted his kicking foot back on the carpet.

"He didn't have a choice, Sarge," Woodgate said as Mahoney pushed himself out of Pete's seat. "You popped his boss right in front of him. Big loss of face. He *had* to do something."

"Sure. I get it." Mahoney took a step closer to Scientific. "Honor."

And he gave the *boo how doy* such a wallop to the stomach I almost expected to see his fist pop out the other side clenching the Chinaman's spine.

The fleet-footed highbinder could have easily sidestepped Mahoney's gut-punch. Yet he just stood there and took it—though the standing part didn't actually last long. The hatchet man grunted and doubled up and hit the floor beside Little Pete.

But even that wasn't enough for Mahoney.

"Well . . . what . . . about . . . *our* . . . honor . . . you . . . yellow . . . bastards?" he huffed out, getting in a savage kick with each word. Scientific took the first four. Little Pete the second quadruple set.

"Sweet Jesus, Mahoney . . . ," I said hoarsely. I couldn't rate Pete too high as a host, and my brain was still bouncing around inside my skull on account of Scientific, yet it gave me no pleasure to see the two of them stomped like grapes.

Beside me, Diana flinched with each kick.

Old Red looked disgusted, too, but there was more to it than that. His face had that intent, squint-eyed look he turns on folks at times—the one that suggests a man's merely gauze or fog he might see right through if only he finds the right angle on him.

Mahoney was oblivious to it all. He was enjoying himself too much.

When he was done, he squatted down over Scientific, and for a second I thought he was actually going to spit on him.

"How's your 'face' now, asshole?"

The only answer he got was groans.

Mahoney turned toward Diana and straightened his necktie. "I'm sorry you had to see that, miss."

"I am, too," the lady said.

"Come on." Mahoney held a hand out toward the door. "Let's get you folks out of here."

Diana, Gustav, and I started trudging out slowly, still stunned, and the sergeant moved in to hustle us along like a cowboy rounding up strays.

"What about them?" Woodgate said, nodding at the moaning men curled up on the carpet.

"What do you mean, 'What about 'em?'" Mahoney snapped back. "Haul 'em in."

"You know Little Pete's got the sharpest shysters in town. They'll have him out in an hour."

Mahoney whipped around and stalked back toward the other cop.

"Dammit, Woodgate! Who do you take your orders from?" He shook a thick finger at the lumpy pile of bloodied silk that was Little Pete. "Him or me?"

"You, Sarge," Woodgate answered quietly.

But his eyes had a different reply—a question that flared there, unspoken yet so obvious even I could hear it loud as thunder. I glanced at my brother, and the piercing way he was still peering at Mahoney told me it was echoing through his mind, too.

Who do you take your *orders from, Sarge?*

29

QUESTIONS

Or, Once Again, We Sow Data and Reap Nada

As Mahoney herded us from the room, Diana turned for a last look back at Pete and his little lackey. They were still on the floor in twin heaps, but at least said heaps seemed to be breathing.

Mahoney took the lady firmly by the arm and steered her toward a wide, red-carpeted staircase just outside the door.

"Don't shed a tear for the likes of them," the copper said, practically dragging her down the steps. "Believe me—they wouldn't think twice about selling your pretty, pampered self into white slavery, if they thought they could get away with it."

"Well, thank goodness 'the Coolietown Crusader' was here to protect the virtue of the white race," Diana replied tartly, and she yanked her arm from his grasp.

Mahoney glared at her with pucker-faced fury, but he said nothing. He just glanced back to make sure Gustav and I were following and kept on stomping down the stairs.

As we left, I got to set eyes for the first time (consciously, anyway) on the rest of Little Pete's H.Q. It looked like it had been a mighty impressive place . . . before the cyclone hit. The ornate lamps and wall hangings and stained glass that hadn't yet been busted would be soon enough, for the Chinatown Squad was laying into everything—including several *boo how doy*.

When we were halfway down the stairs, a particularly unlucky hatchet man went tumbling past us. He rolled to a stop at the feet of a cameraman setting up a portrait: two grinning coppers brandishing their axes, a cringing, bloody-nosed highbinder in handcuffs between them.

"Hey, watch it, would you?" one of the policemen shouted up the steps. "You almost knocked over the man from the *Morning Call*!"

"Oopsy daisy!" someone called out from behind us, and another Chinaman came thumping down the stairs.

The lawmen all laughed.

Outside, it was raining wood—chairs, tables, idols, and even axe-smashed desks were being pushed out second- and third-story windows. Blue-suited street bulls patrolled the edges of an onlooking mob, but they didn't have to work too hard to keep the gawkers back. Wrong place at the wrong time, and you'd end up with a two-by-four through the brainpan.

As we stepped outside, a ripple of titters spread through the crowd—and sudden chills ran through *me*. Night was falling, and those little britches I was squeezed into didn't do a thing to keep out the cold.

"Over here," Mahoney said.

He led us toward one of three boxy wagons lined up along the street. Each had windows cut into the sides over the words S.F. POLICE PATROL. Two of the wagons were packed peapod full of grim-faced *boo how doy*. The third was empty—until Mahoney waved us inside.

Once we'd climbed in, the sergeant rapped his knuckles on the low ceiling. A uniformed policeman up top roared out "Coming through!" and gave the reins a snap without even waiting for the crowd to clear.

Clear it did, though, and we managed to roll away from the curb without crushing anyone under hoof or wheel. Which struck me as sheer luck. The cobblestones clattering away beneath us could have been Chinamen's breaking bones for all Mahoney or his driver seemed to care.

"Cute little soapbox ya got here, Sarge," I said, leaning over sideways to keep my head from bouncing up through the roof. "Whose idea was it to put wheels on it?"

Old Red saved Mahoney the trouble of ignoring me by changing the subject himself.

"Where you takin' us?"

Mahoney rolled his eyes. "Unbelievable. No thank you? From any of you? After the Chinatown Squad just saved your skins?"

"They were letting us go," Diana said.

"Please. If they told you that, it was only because they wanted you to let your guard down."

"Guard down or up, it would've made no nevermind," I said. "They coulda killed us any ol' time . . . but they didn't."

Mahoney gave me an "awww, pshaw" swipe of the hand. "That just means Little Pete thought you could be of use to him somehow."

"*Sergeant,*" my brother said, "*where are you takin' us?*"

Mahoney glowered at Gustav like he couldn't decide which eye to poke out first.

"Look," he growled.

Then he took a deep breath, and when he blew it out he seemed to have blown out the flame burning inside him, as well. His tone softened so much he actually sounded civil for once.

"I just needed to talk to you, that's all. Alone. You three have been pretty busy today, don't think I haven't heard. I need to know what you've dug up."

"Dug up about what?" Diana asked dryly.

The big cop sighed, defeated. "Chan's murder."

"Murder?" Diana said, all wide-eyed innocence. "Not suicide?"

"Yeah, yeah—*murder,*" Mahoney said. "The autopsy won't be official for days, but it didn't take the coroner ten seconds to find a wound on the back of Chan's head. Somebody clobbered him and turned on the gas."

"Do tell." I gave my chin a thoughtful rub. "Seems like I've heard that theory somewheres before."

"Alright, Brother. The man's had his fill of crow," Old Red said. "Tell you what, Mahoney—I'll answer your questions, provided you'll answer mine."

"Fair enough." Mahoney took hold of his lapel and pulled, revealing a dull-gold seven-pronged star pinned to the lining of his suit coat. "But this means I go first."

Gustav eyed the man warily (while Diana, I noticed, eyed *him*). Then he nodded.

Mahoney let go of his lapel, and his badge dropped out of sight. "I'll make it easy for you. No questions. Just tell me everything that happened after you left Chan's place this morning. And I mean *everything*."

"That's makin' it easy?" Gustav said.

"Alright, maybe not easy." Mahoney leaned back (as much one could in that little rolling cabbage crate) and put on the air of a fellow settling in to hear a yarn. "But it's simple, anyway. Just tell me what happened."

"Fine." Gustav gave me a little sidelong nod. "But I'm gonna let Otto here spin it out. If you're lookin' for 'simple,' he's the one to turn to."

"You don't know what a favor he just done you," I said to Mahoney. "My brother tells a story like a tadpole rides a—"

"Just get on with it," Mahoney said.

So I did, laying it all out while our wagon rumbled slowly through the darkening streets of the city: how we'd met Chan on the Pacific Express; our encounter with him (and Little Pete and the old man, Yee Lock) the day before; our close call at Madam Fong's; Ah Gum's escape from the cathouse to tell us about Fat Choy, the hophead/hatchet man; Chinatown Charlie's tour of the quarter's opium dens; our attempt to pull the wool over Chun Ti Chu's eyes only to have him fleece-up our peepers instead; the chase through the Plaza and up over the rooftops; our audience with Little Pete; and finally our rescue by the valiant officers of the San Francisco Police Department's legendary Chinatown Squad.

Of course, thorough as my report might have been, it wasn't wholly unexpurgated. I didn't volunteer that we no longer worked for the Southern Pacific, for instance, nor did I bring up the items we'd burgled from Chan's place after we'd sneaked back inside.

Mahoney listened intently, the occasional puzzled grimace or surprised grunt his only commentary. My brother remained mum, as well. In fact, he didn't jump in to correct me or scold me for overembroidering even once—quite the uncommon show of restraint on his part.

As for Diana, she seemed less concerned with what I had to say than how Mahoney and Gustav heard it. She kept her gaze on them as much as on me.

"And that's about it," I said as I wound my account down.

I looked over at Old Red, inviting him to "remind" me about the scorpion—or the things we'd heard about Mahoney himself. But he just stared back at me, tight-lipped, so I forged on.

"Seems to us the Black Dove is the key to the whole caboodle. That Hok Gup—she saw something, heard something, knows something . . . *something*. Cuz if it was just one love-crazy hatchet man killin' Chan, you wouldn't see all these other characters in such a rush to grab the poor gal. So we been tryin' to get to her before she gets herself got."

Mahoney nodded silently a moment, then turned to my brother. "And that's everything?"

"More than everything," Gustav said.

"Hey, I told it quick as I could," I protested. "This is what you call 'a tangled web' we got a-woven here. Most folks couldn't have unraveled it in less than—"

"It's our turn now," Diana said to the sergeant, cutting me off. "Would you mind if *I* asked the first question?"

Mahoney sat up straight, his expression souring with a contempt too intense to have just come over him. It must have been there all along, shackled out of sight. And now it was being unleashed.

"You're through asking questions. All of you."

He rapped on the ceiling again, and the driver angled the wagon in toward the sidewalk.

"Well, hell," Gustav sighed, looking vexed but surprisingly unsurprised.

"You ain't gonna keep your word?" I said to Mahoney.

"I didn't give my word. I just lied," the cop replied. "Now, if you want my word on something, here it is: If I catch you back in Chinatown, I'll throw you in a cell with those tong Chinks we just dragged out of Little Pete's. And believe you me, they won't need their hatchets to make mincemeat out of you."

The wagon came to a stop.

"And just in case you're so thick-headed you need *another* reason to stay away, here you go," Mahoney went on. "The Kwong Ducks just put up a *chun hung* on all of you. You know what that means?"

"There's a bounty out for us?" I asked.

"A *big* bounty. Five hundred dollars a head." Mahoney's broad face contorted into a sneer so extreme he looked like he was about to sneeze. "More than you ass-pains are worth alive, that's for sure." He leaned over and opened the wagon's back door. "Now get out. And just be glad I'm too busy to waste any more time on you."

I climbed out first. It was full-on dark now, and there was little light to go by outside. I had no trouble recognizing where I was, though.

The wind whipping in off the Bay, the clanging of buoy bells in the darkness, the howls of the debauched, the mad/merry music spilling out of the melodeons. We could only be one place—the eastern edge of the Barbary Coast. Mahoney may as well have dropped us into a snake pit.

I helped Diana climb down to the filth-soiled sidewalk, but Old Red showed no sign of budging from the wagon.

"Just promise me one thing," he said to Mahoney. "No matter what it is you're really up to, you'll do what you can to help Hok Gup."

"Here's a promise for you."

Mahoney slipped a hand into one of his pockets. When he drew it out again, there was a dull shine along one side, as if he was wearing a gold ring on every finger.

His fist was wrapped around a pair of brass knuckles.

"Understand me?" he said.

Gustav nodded. "I'm startin' to."

My brother hopped from the wagon.

"This is your last warning." Mahoney pulled the door shut and gave the ceiling a knock. "Butt out."

The driver sent his team into the street. The first chance he got, he whipped the wagon around and went clattering back toward Chinatown. Getting there—for him or us—meant passing through a neighborhood so dodgy a policeman wouldn't walk it alone in the daytime—and this was darkest night.

In more ways than one, we were further from the Black Dove than we'd been since we'd begun our search for her.

30

GRIT IN THE INSTRUMENT

Or, My Brother Opens Up His Heart . . . and an Old Wound

After the sun went down, it seemed, the city of San Francisco no longer even pretended the Barbary Coast was anything but its own kingdom, separate and lawless—except for the law of the jungle. There were no cable cars running, no coppers on patrol, and of the gas lamps along the street, only one in ten were working. Most of the light to see by came in little streams spilling out of dancehall doorways and bawdy house windows (from which also spilled raucous music, rowdy laughter, pie-eyed men, and half-clothed women). In between these pockets of light and life were long stretches of gloom where dark figures lurched or lurked or merely lay in a heap, moaning . . . or not.

If the Coast was no place for a lady during the day, by night it was hardly fit for anyone but Vikings.

"Funny-lookin' hack you took here," cracked a war-painted harlot as Mahoney's police wagon rolled away.

"Yeah," added a swaggering little man with the dandified pugnacious-ness peculiar to pimps. "That's the first time I've seen one of them wagons drop anyone off 'round here. Usually they're pickin' people up."

"In the morning," the strumpet snickered.

Her mack laughed. "From the gutter!"

We ignored them—just as we ignored their colleague attending to a customer in an alleyway and the retching soldier bent over on the corner and the trio of young swells whistling at Diana's shapely figure (or perhaps mine, given my form-fitting britches).

"One question . . . that's all I was hopin' to get in," Gustav mumbled. "One lousy question . . . ."

"You're going back, aren't you?" Diana asked him. "To Chinatown."

He said what I knew he'd say.

"Of course I am."

"Well, then," Diana replied, "I—"

Again, I knew what was coming from my brother's mouth before his lips even parted.

"No, you're not."

But then Old Red ran a hand over his mustache and looked the lady in the eye, and for the next few minutes everything I thought I knew about my brother was dead wrong.

"Not unless we settle something first" is how he started it all off.

The light was dim and Diana recovered fast, but for a split second her eyes seemed to go as perfectly round as a doll's.

"So you're willing to let me come along . . . even with the bounty on us?"

"Don't see as I can stop you. And leavin' you here"—Gustav waved a hand at the squalor around us—"that'd be just as bad as takin' you back to Chinatown. And it ain't like I could get my mule-headed brother to drag you off somewheres safe."

"No way you're goin' back to Chinatown without *me*," I said.

"See?" Old Red said to Diana.

"What do *we* have to settle, Gustav?" she asked him. But the asking was mere formality. She knew.

My brother just tilted his head to one side, his sour expression saying he knew she knew, and the time for game-playing was past.

"Alright, I'll make you an offer," Diana said. "The same one as Mahoney: You can ask one question . . . if you answer one question first."

Old Red nodded curtly. "Agreed, but let's do this quick, huh? We've wasted enough time already."

The lady gave him a grim smile that didn't waver even as a gaggle of peacoated (and most likely pee-coated) sailors staggered past hooting lewdly.

"I'm glad you trust me to honor an arrangement like this, given what Mahoney just did."

"Miss, it remains to be seen whether I trust you or not. Now *ask*."

"Alright. Tell me—"

Diana took in a deep breath, obviously struggling to find the right words. When she had them, she exhaled slowly with an air of satisfaction, like a man blowing out the smoke of his first cigarette in too long a spell.

"What's bothering you, Gustav?"

"That's your question?" Old Red said. "After all that's happened to-day?"

"Yes. That's my question," Diana said. "Don't forget—I saw you on the Pacific Express. Those were hardly ideal circumstances for you, yet it made no difference. Yes, you lost your temper once or twice, but you were always thinking, always looking, always seeing what no one else saw. Always . . . inspired."

Gustav didn't blush or look bashful. Instead, he seemed abashed, almost embarrassed.

"And today?" he said.

"Something's been distracting you. Getting in the way."

"Oh, this is ridiculous!" I spluttered. "A friend is dead and we're bein' hunted by fellers with *hatchets,* and you wanna know why the man's a tad distracted?"

I may as well have been yet another stumbling, muttering drunk—Diana and Old Red paid me no mind.

"I ain't been at my best, I know it," my brother said so quietly it was hard to know if he was speaking to the lady or himself.

"You don't got nothing to apologize for," I told him.

"I reckon there *is* something that's been draggin' on me," he went on.

"You don't have to say another word, Brother."

Gustav finally seemed to hear me. "Yeah, I do. To you as much as her."

Sweet Jesus, I thought. *Here it comes.*

I'd tried to head him off, but it was too late now. The cat was about to come bounding out of the bag, and that little bastard had him some claws—sharp enough to cut my brother deep.

It was plain enough to me what the extra weight on Gustav had been the past day. And I wouldn't have minded (much) hearing my brother admit it over a beer later, just him and me. But not here, not now, not like this.

The truth hadn't hit me all of a sudden. It had just kept creeping up and creeping up and creeping up behind me until I could feel it there without even turning to look: Gustav was in love with Diana Corvus.

It was why he'd felt so betrayed when she'd disappeared on us a month before. Why he was so oversensitive about her motives in tracking us down again now. Why his already short fuse had been snipped down clean to the nub.

Old Red Amlingmeyer had finally opened his heart to a woman. And what could a beautiful, brilliant, witty, wonderful lady like Diana do but slam it shut again?

I mean, I'd have a hard enough time wooing her myself, and I'm . . . well, *me*. A crotchety, skirt-shy runt like my brother wouldn't stand a chance.

"Back when we was on the Pacific Express, I told you I was through keepin' secrets from you," Gustav said to me. "Remember?"

His eyes were on me in that unblinking way that blocks out everyone else, every*thing* else—whittles the universe down to just the two of you.

All I could do was nod.

"Well, I meant that, Brother. So what I'm about to speak of . . . I wasn't holdin' it back from you. It's just . . . the subject didn't come up."

"Until today," Diana cut in. Her voice was soft, though, almost remorseful, like she already regretted what she'd pushed Gustav to.

"That's right. It come up today—come up and got me riled up. Got me *stupid*." Old Red snorted and glanced into the shadows nearby, at the pimp and his pathetic little harem. " 'Grit in the instrument.' 'A crack in the lens.' "

For once, he wasn't quoting Holmes directly. These were words from John Watson *about* Holmes.

Or, to be more specific, about Holmes's attitude on a certain subject—one Gustav himself had never discussed with me at any length beyond a grunt and a glower. And as I placed both those quotes ("A Scandal in Bohemia," page one), I felt my gut curl up tight as a diamond hitch knot.

"Grit in a sensitive instrument," "a crack in one of his own high-power lenses"—according to Watson, that's how Sherlock Holmes viewed love.

"Brother . . . ," I said, trying one last time to save his heart from a hiding.

"Just let me finish it quick," Old Red said. He locked eyes on the lady. "I'm gonna be plainspoken here, miss."

Don't laugh, Diana, I silently prayed. *Be kind. Don't laugh.*

"Me and my brother," Gustav began, "we ain't whorin' men."

I stopped my praying, I was so stunned. As professions of devotion go, "We ain't whorin' men" leaves a lot to be desired.

"But there was a time," Old Red went on, "back before Otto come out on the trail with me, when I did as every other drover does. Even got to be a real regular at a seedy little place down to San Marcos, Texas. Started goin' there cuz it was cheap, kept goin' back cuz . . . well . . . I had me a favorite. And, with time, she come to be more than that. She was . . ."

He choked off into silence, and it took a hacking cough to get himself going again.

"She was my *only*. My only ever. And it wasn't what you might think. I ain't one of them men gets crazy ideas about a gal just cuz she . . . you know. She and me—we talked. A lot. Bet you can't believe that, can you, Brother? Me and a woman talkin', jokin' . . . *dreamin'* together?"

"I believe it," I said, the words catching in my throat, coming out as whispers.

Gustav nodded, then sucked in a quick breath. The rest of the story he spewed out fast, like it was acid he had to spit out before it burned a hole clean through him.

"Well, one day, somebody up and did to her as is done to so many of them gals, sooner or later. Did it to her mean, crazylike. Did it to her til she was dead. A customer, folks said. Some sick son of a bitch just passin' through. By the time I heard of it, she'd already been plowed under. And of course there was no talk of a posse, of *justice* for the likes of her. Other than me and the other chippies, nobody gave a shit except maybe her bastard pimps, and they was just put out about the lost income. Ever since, I ain't had no use for macks or madams nor any of it."

He paused again, his eyes a-glistening in the dim light.

"So this business with the Black Dove, I reckon it just . . . grits me up a little."

I put a hand on his shoulder.

"I'm sorry," I said. And I swear to you, at that moment at least, there was not the smallest part of me, not the most minute jot of selfishness or small-mindedness, that begrudged my brother keeping this to himself all those years.

"I'm sorry, too," Diana said, and to her credit, she truly looked it. "If I'd known—"

If you'd known? I thought, actually angry with the lady for the first time since I'd met her. *What is it you were* expecting *him to say?*

"You asked your question, you got your answer," Gustav said, his eyes suddenly cold and hard as ice. He gave me a little nod, and I took my hand away. "Now it's my turn."

"Yes, it is," Diana said. "What is it you want to ask?"

"Same thing I hoped to ask of Mahoney: Who do you really work for?"

There was no pause for thought or drama. Just a flat answer that landed at our feet with a thud.

"Colonel C. Kermit Crowe."

The Southern Pacific's head detective in Ogden, Utah. The man who'd once hired *us*.

"Oh, Miss Corvus," I moaned. "You mean you still work for the S.P.?"

"No, Otto—please, believe me," Diana said, her voice taking on an edge of desperation I'd never heard from her before. "It's like I told you yesterday: Colonel Crowe was fired by the railroad, as was I. Since then, the colonel's started his *own* detective agency in Ogden, and I'm working for him again." She looked over at Gustav. "He's looking to hire other operatives, as well, and, of course, I recommended you. Raved about you."

The lady's gaze lingered on my brother in a way my pride didn't like. It was entirely unclear whether her "you" referred to one Amlingmeyer or two.

"But given how things ended with the railroad, your role in the Pacific Express disaster . . ." Diana shrugged. "The colonel needs a lot of persuading."

"So he sent you to spy on us," Old Red said. "Test us a little, maybe."

"No—I sent myself," Diana insisted. "I was hoping Otto's letter from *Harper's* might provide new ammunition I could use on the colonel. After all, an operative writing for *Harper's Weekly*—it would have been quite the promotional coup for a new detective agency."

" 'Would have been,' " I said glumly.

"Yes. That was quite a disappointment—for both of us," Diana said. "But then you told me about Dr. Chan's troubles, and I thought *that* might be the opportunity I was looking for. If I could go back to the colonel and tell him you'd stood up to a tong lord like Little Pete to protect a friend . . . well, he couldn't help but be impressed."

"Only things got a mite more complicated than that, didn't they?" Gustav said.

"Yes. A *lot* more complicated."

The lady looked down, her lips pressed into a tight, thin line. For just a moment, she looked as buffaloed as Old Red trying to work up the nerve to talk to *her*.

"I hate to say it, but Chan's death doesn't change the situation as far as the colonel's concerned," she said. "If anything, it makes this an even better opportunity to prove yourselves to him."

"You mean all this could still land us jobs detectivin'?" I asked her.

She watched Old Red warily as she nodded.

"That ain't what we got into this for," he snipped. "It ain't no 'opportunity.' "

"I know, I know, of course," she said, holding up her hands. "But wouldn't it be better if *something* good could come of all this?"

"The only good I'm thinkin' of is catchin' a killer and maybe savin' a young gal's life," my brother said.

But then his expression brightened a smidge, and his gaze drifted off to the shadows ahead of us.

"Still . . . whatever comes about *after* we get the job done, that don't do no dishonor to the Doc, does it?"

Neither Diana nor I answered. He obviously wasn't asking us. He was asking himself.

He didn't let himself debate on it long.

"Anyway, what are we standin' around here for?" Old Red rumbled.

It was yet another rhetorical question, and yet again I didn't give voice to the obvious answer.

Cuz the longer we stand around here, the longer we're likely to stay alive.

Such gloomy truth would only slow us down, and we had to move quick.

Chinatown was six blocks of hell away.

31

BARBARIANS

Or, The Worst the Coast Has to Offer Brings Out the Best in Me

Between Davis Street and Montgomery, Diana was propositioned, insulted, or otherwise disrespected a dozen times. I would've felt bad for her if my own tally hadn't topped *two* dozen. Those skin-tight short-pants I was in may as well have been a bull's-eye on my back, and every drunk and bawd felt compelled to comment on them.

The final straw came when a passing seaman slapped me on the ass. I returned the favor—though with a pointed toe rather than an open palm. After Old Red got the two of us pulled apart, Diana found a way to keep me out of the sights of every passing sot: The first time we encountered a candidate of ample enough proportions, she offered the man twenty dollars for his checked trousers. He happily accepted, and the trade was made.

While I was changing in an alley, a pair of lurking footpads tried to mug me, and I had to flee with my new trousers down around my knees.

Welcome to the Barbary Coast.

"Can't even hitch up your drawers in peace in this hellhole," I groused as we set off toward Chinatown again.

"Well, remember—the Coast's entire economy revolves around getting a man's pants *off*," Diana pointed out.

I forced out a feeble chuckle—the lady's blue streak could still throw me—and changed the subject with the question I'd been too busy dodging abuse to ask up till then.

"So what exactly are we gonna *do* when we get back to Chinatown?"

"I been tryin' to cogitate on that," Gustav grumbled. At the time, we were passing a concert saloon in which the house band was either falling down the stairs or being trampled by buffalo, to judge by the din. "Mr. Holmes himself couldn't put two and two together amidst all this commotion."

"Which is another way of sayin' you don't know," I said.

"No, I don't know, but I'm a-workin' on it. What have *you* been doin' besides makin' eyes at sailors?"

He glanced over at Diana, and his glower shifted, its sour edge softening. The lady wasn't giving my brother the jitters anymore, but for some reason I didn't feel as pleased for him as I once might've thought.

"I don't guess the colonel would be much impressed with what we done so far," he said. "We been at it all day and we still ain't even laid eyes on that poor gal."

"Hmmm," Diana said.

"Hmmm?" Old Red said back, making it a question.

"Well . . . I'm just noticing how you keep thinking of Hok Gup as 'that poor gal.' A helpless victim. But there is the possibility that she went along with Fat Choy willingly. She might have even helped—"

Gustav shook his head gruffly. "Nope, uh-uh. She was happy when Chan bought her away from Madam Fong, remember? Ah Gum told us that. And the doc, he may have hit him some hard times, but he wasn't no opium-eatin' crook. He was a good man. After all Hok Gup had been through, she'd wanna stick with him over some no-account like Fat Choy."

"We *think* Chan was a good man," Diana replied. "But we only knew him a few days. Can you really see into a man's heart in so short a time?"

"A few days?" I said. "Hell, you can know a feller your whole life and still be surprised by what he's got locked up inside him."

The words came out sharper than I'd intended somehow. They had enough sting to make Old Red wince.

"Or so I've been told," I added lamely.

"Look . . . ," my brother began. But then something ahead caught his eye, and soon enough it had mine and Diana's, too.

A half-block up, four hoodlums were circling a tall, lanky man like a bunch of low-flying buzzards. They were taunting him, tormenting him with swats and kicks that teetered on the brink of an outright beating. Yet their victim never even tried to block their blows. He seemed afraid he'd just make matters worse, and as we drew closer we saw why.

It was Chinatown Charlie.

"We caught a Chink! We caught a Chink!" one of the hoodlums crowed. He had a spare cap in his hand—snatched off Charlie's head, most likely—and he swiped at the Chinaman with it like it was a whip.

"Trying to pass for a white man, huh?" another of the ruffians spat. He was a squat, toadlike little SOB with a puffed-out chest and eyes that burned with the yearning to hurt. "What for? So you can screw a white whore?"

"N-no, I j-just—" Charlie stammered.

The Toad rammed a fist into his stomach.

The hooligans around Charlie were too busy cackling to notice me come striding up. Not a one of them even looked my way until I had the Toad by the back of the pants and a fistful of hair.

"Johnny Clay!" I roared, marching him toward the nearest building. "I oughta tear you limb from limb for what you did to that little girl!"

And I launched him headfirst into the wall. It was clapboard, not brick, so the man's brains remained inside his thick skull. But that was really just a lucky break for him.

The element of surprise—and befuddlement—worked in my favor. As their little compadre hit the ground with a splat, the other thugs could only gape at me, each of them trying to splutter out some variation on, "Wait! His name's not Clay!" Perhaps they thought I might pause and listen.

I did not. I moved and swung.

The hoodlum holding Charlie's hat instinctively brought the soft cap up before his face. As armor, of course, it was sorely lacking, and my fist drove the tweed into his teeth.

"Musgrave, you son of a bitch!" I bellowed as he toppled backward into the gutter. "For what happened to your sweet ol' granny alone, you oughta swing!"

I whipped around to face the last two hoods.

"Stark! Roylott! You two monsters are the worst of all! A baby? A *baby*? How could you?"

"Stark" and "Roylott" looked at each other, holding a silent powwow with nothing more than wide eyes and slack jaws. In less than a second, they came to a consensus and put their agreed-upon plan into action.

They turned tail and ran.

"Yeah, you'd better skedaddle!" I shouted after them. "And don't let me catch you on Pacific Street again or you'll get a lot worse than your pals here!"

An amused crowd had gathered around by now, and a few of the nightcrawlers actually applauded. They were the self-same people who would've stood around guffawing as Charlie got his guts kicked out, I'm sure. But make it a fight between some white men, and they'd be happy to cheer for whoever won.

"Thank you, thank you," I said. "Boy, can you believe the nerve of some people?"

And I dusted off my hands and set off toward Chinatown again.

Old Red and Diana were waiting for me the next block up—along with Charlie, of course. As I'd hoped, they'd quietly collected him while I made a spectacle of myself. I'd tried much the same trick when facing Scientific and his highbinders earlier in the day, and I was pleased to see I could come up with a plan that worked at least *half* the time.

"Thanks," Charlie said as I walked up.

"My pleasure. I'm just surprised you're still alive to almost die. What happened to you, anyway?"

"I was just about to tell the others—"

And Charlie spun his yarn.

He'd been waiting for us in the Plaza when Scientific (so named for the Edison-like ingenuity with which he dispatched enemies) showed up with his boys. The *boo how doy* dragged him away for an audience with Little Pete, during which he convinced the tong lord we were folks he should talk to, not do in. Charlie was held prisoner in the basement until

Scientific had us in hand, then he was kicked out on the street—and told he should be grateful to be alive.

He'd lurked around outside, not sure what to do, until the Chinatown Squad showed up. When he saw Mahoney cart us away, he tried to follow on foot, hoping he could bluff his way through the Coast.

"It was dark, I'm tall, I don't have a queue, I wear American-style clothes, I'd bought a new hat to pull down over my eyes." Charlie shrugged, chagrined. "I thought I could pull it off."

"Yeah, well, I was wearin' a highbinder's trousers for a couple hours, but nobody mistook me for a Chinaman," I said.

"I know where we need to go," Gustav announced out of the blue. "*Now.*"

"Excuse me?" I said.

"I know where Fat Choy spent the whole damn day—only I bet he's cleared out already." Old Red clenched his fists and grimaced, looking like he wanted to sock himself upside the head that had so miserably failed him. "Goddammit! Why didn't I see it before?"

"Gustav," Diana said gently. "Just *go.*"

My brother nodded, his anger simmering down to grim determination.

"Right."

Ten minutes later, we were back in Dr. Chan's shop. And Old Red, we quickly learned, had been right on both counts.

We found Fat Choy's hiding place—and it was empty.

32

OUR DARKEST (HALF) HOUR

Or, Gustav Sheds Some Light on the Case . . . but It Doesn't Last Long

We didn't even have to climb through a window to get into Chan's store this time. The back door was wide open.

"That was a big ol' clue right there," Gustav said when he saw it.

"Big ol' clue as to what?" I asked.

"Just think about it," Old Red said, then he lit up a lucifer and crept inside.

I tried to do as he suggested as Diana, Charlie, and I followed him into the darkened pharmacy. Yet all I could think about was whether Fat Choy was going to jump out of the shadows with a hatchet in his hand.

Even in the puny little light of my brother's match, I could see that the storeroom was a wreck. Every drawer, crate, and bag had been opened and upended, and the floor was aclutter with the tools of Chan's trade: roots, leaves, nuts, powders, and assorted unidentifiable blobs that either crackled beneath my shoes or stuck to the soles.

"Should be right over . . . hel-lo," my brother muttered.

He squatted down and brought the lucifer toward the floor. Or where the floor used to be, more like. The flickering little flame revealed a square-cut hole in the floorboards—a trap door.

"Shit," Gustav hissed as the fire reached his fingers. He shook out the match, plunging us into a blackness so thick you could bottle it and sell it as ink.

A moment later, another lucifer flared to life.

"Why don't you just hand matches around to everybody?" I asked.

"Cuz this is my last one," my brother said. "Now shut up so I can make the most of it."

While I gritted my teeth and murmured curses, Gustav stuck his head and shoulders down through the trap door.

"What's down there?" Charlie asked. "A cellar?"

"Yup. A small one." Old Red pushed himself to his feet. "And that's all, thank God."

"What's He done for us lately?" I said.

"Enough . . . for the moment. I can only think of one thing Fat Choy might have left behind."

Diana nodded slowly. "A body."

Gustav gave me a look that asked why *I* couldn't be so swift on the uptake.

"Did you see any sign Hok Gup was ever down there at all?" Diana asked.

"All there is to see is a hole in the ground not much bigger than a *ow- shit*!"

Old Red jerked his right hand down, and the world around us winked out.

For the next few seconds, all was black silence as total as the dead must know.

"So, Brother," I finally said, "what's an owshit?"

"Har har," Gustav grumbled. "None of y'all's got a light?"

"Don't look at me," Charlie said.

"We can't," I pointed out. "That's the whole problem."

"Why don't *you* have any matches?" Charlie asked me.

"Oh, I got a bundle of 'em . . . in my other pants."

Though I couldn't see Diana beside me, somehow I could still sense the warmth of her presence, and I moved toward it.

"What about you, miss? Got any matches tucked away in your purse?"

"I'm afraid not."

"Too bad," I said. "How 'bout a torch?"

"Sorry, no. And no lantern, either."

I heard the lady's skirts rustle as she turned away from me. Funny how we feel drawn to face people even when we're talking to them in utter darkness.

"Gustav," Diana said, "how did you know about—?"

Old Red cut her off with a shush.

"You hear something, Brother?" I whispered.

"Yeah, unfortunately. *You*," he groused. "All day long we been out in them crowds, in all that noise, runnin' runnin' runnin'. This is the first peace I've had all day. The first chance to just think."

"Make use of it, then," Diana said. "Think. We won't disturb you . . . right, gentlemen?"

"Yeah. Sure," Charlie said, sounding dubious.

"Think away," I added.

So there we stood, saying nothing, seeing nothing, but smelling plenty—the rotten-egg stink of gas still hung all around us.

I pinched my nose. What else did I have to do?

"Look, I'm sorry," Charlie said after maybe a half minute of silence. "This is just too weird."

"Oh, you'll get used to it," I told him. "My brother keeps *me* in the dark all the time."

Old Red sighed, defeated. "Miss, I believe you had a question. May as well go on and ask it."

"Alright, Gustav," Diana said. "I was wondering—how did you know about the cellar?"

"Well, I didn't *know* about it. I just deducified it."

"How?"

"Oh, it wasn't much. I feel like a danged fool for not seein' it sooner," Old Red said, and there was no false modesty about it. He truly was pissed with himself.

"We been lookin' for Hok Gup and Fat Choy pretty much all day," he explained. "And not only ain't we come across 'em, we ain't found a single soul that's seen 'em. It's like they walked in here and just disappeared. And those two—they're known 'round these parts, and Chinatown ain't that big a place. Hell, Little Pete hears of every step we take, but even *he* can't find Fat Choy and the gal? It put me in mind of something Mr. Holmes once said."

"I figured it would," I said. No way my brother could talk this long about a deduction without roping Holmes into it somehow.

Gustav didn't even slow down to growl at me.

" 'When you have excluded the impossible, whatever remains, however improbable, must be the truth. ' "

"Which could mean Fat Choy stuffed the Dove in a basket and flew off the roof in a hot-air balloon," I said.

My brother *did* growl now.

"Hey, I'm just sayin'—that has got to be the dumbest pronouncement ol' Holmes ever made."

"It got us here, didn't it?" Old Red snapped.

"But how?" Diana asked. "I still don't see it."

And she did dearly want to see. I could hear it in her voice. She wanted to learn, and she thought my brother, of all people, could be the teacher.

He seemed inclined to agree.

"First off, you gotta think back to this morning," he lectured in a pontifical sort of way. "We was told both the front and back doors of this place was left open when Chan killed himself. Now, as suicides by stinky-gas go, that makes no sense on the face of it. It was almost as if someone *wanted* the gas to be noticed. Wanted someone to come inside, find the body, and get the gas shut off. Well . . . why?"

"Because he'd still be hiding inside," Diana dutifully said, the star pupil finishing the schoolmarm's thoughts.

"Exactly. Then there was the willy-nilly way all the boxes was stacked up back here. Upstairs, the place was packed solid, but neat. The doc was an orderly man. So why would his storage room be like a damn corn maze? Could be there was something bein' hid. But I didn't put it all together till Charlie said he hoped he could pass for white at night. Got me to thinkin' maybe Fat Choy was waitin' for nightfall, too. He'd have Dr. Chan's clothes to pick through. And remember—"

"Chan's spectacles were missing," Diana said.

"Yes, indeed. From here on in, we gotta figure Fat Choy's in disguise."

"He's more than that," I said. "Doc Chan's chest armor and gun was gone, too. The man's ready for trouble."

"And he's gonna get it," my brother said.

"But, Gustav . . . ."

Diana sounded hesitant, and I knew what was coming next—the student was about to question the teacher's sums in front of the whole class.

"Doesn't all this strike you as a rather sophisticated plan for an opium-addicted street thug?"

"Low-born don't mean no-brain," Old Red replied, giving the lady a taste of the vinegar he usually bottles up just for me.

"No, she's right," Charlie threw in. "Fat Choy's no moron, but to come up with something this tricky . . . ? I mean, it seems so—"

"*Scientific*," I finished for him.

"Actually, I was going to say 'clever,'" Charlie said.

But it was my answer that hung in the air for a long, silent moment, dangling like the proverbial other shoe. I couldn't help thinking it was going to drop sooner rather than later—on us. And maybe squash us like bugs.

"Is there a *reason* we're still standing here in the dark?" Charlie finally said.

"Sure," I told him. "We don't have the slightest inkling where we oughta go from here. Am I right, Brother?"

"That's what I was tryin' to ponder on a minute ago!" Old Red protested. "But nooooo. You two had to start jabberin' and—"

"You don't have to 'deducify' anything," Charlie cut in. "I can tell you where Fat Choy's gone."

"Oh?" Gustav, Diana, and I said in chorus. We were even in tune.

"Yeah. He's out looking for opium. That's why he turned this place upside down before he left."

"Hold on," Old Red said. "Why would he think Doc Chan would have opium lyin' around?"

"Because half the pharmacies in Chinatown sell it. More than half. It's just another herbal remedy, right?" Charlie grunted out a sour chuckle. "But Chan wouldn't have any. He was too respectable for that kind of thing."

"Oh, Lord," I groaned. "Don't tell me we're off to the damn opium dens again. Only thing that finally got the stink of 'em outta my nose was comin' back in *here*."

"No—no more opium dens," my brother said. "Fat Choy's movin' now. Runnin'. He ain't gonna lay low all day just to let himself get cornered in one of them pits tonight."

"I agree," Charlie said. "He'll want to buy his supply—or steal it—and take it with him. So the thing to do now is—"

"Yeeeeee Lock!" Old Red called out like a "Yeeeeeha!" "The old man! He's a doctor, too. Only on the seamy side, am I right, Charlie?"

"He's not just on the seamy side—he's *all* seamy. And yeah . . . he sells opium, if that's what you're thinking. Keeps the sing-song girls supplied when he does his rounds. Perk of the job."

"That settles it, then," Gustav announced. "We lost Yee Lock's trail way back. About damn time we picked it up again. He got him a shop, like Chan?"

"Yeah," Charlie said. "Over near Waverly Place."

"Well, lead on."

"Wait," I said before anyone could start groping their way toward the door. "We were lucky to get *here*, what with that chunk-hunk the Ducks put on us. If we're gonna do more runnin' around Chinatown, shouldn't we oughta make like Fat Choy and try masqueradin' ourselves up somehow?"

"What are you talking about?" Charlie asked. "The Kwong Ducks haven't posted a *chun hung* on you. They wouldn't dare. Madam Fong and Big Queue wouldn't mind seeing you dead, sure. But no tong's going to admit to that on paper. Not with whites. Something like that could bring the axe down on all of Chinatown."

"That's not what Sgt. Mahoney told us," Diana said. Not like she was challenging Charlie—more like she was inviting him to challenge her. Which is exactly what he did.

"Mahoney?" he sneered. "You haven't seen through him yet?"

"Not all the way," Gustav said. "What's there to see?"

"The Anti-Coolie League."

Charlie said the words the way a farmer says "banker," an old rebel says "Yankee," or a cat, I imagine, says "dog."

"The Panic's the best thing that ever happened to those . . . those . . ."

"Assholes?" Diana suggested.

Charlie cleared his throat. "Ummm . . . yeah. I was trying to think of a polite way to say it."

"I don't think there is a polite way," I said.

"What *about* those assholes, Charlie?" Old Red prompted.

"It's just that you whites look to the League every time the economy takes a turn," Charlie fumed. "'Oh, it's the heathen Chinee! They're the reason we're broke!' Like *we've* got anything to do with the price of silver."

"Nobody in this room ever said you did," my brother said, his voice low.

Charlie took a deep, calming breath.

"Yeah, right, anyway . . . the League's got enough money now to buy a couple city supervisors, and that was enough to get their man put in charge of the Chinatown Squad. And believe me—the 'Coolietown Crusader' isn't there to crusade against crime. He's there to crusade against the Chinese."

"I do believe you," Diana said. "We've seen what Sgt. Mahoney's crusading can look like. It's not a pretty sight."

There was a sudden, sharp clap—Gustav slapping his hands together.

"Alright, we done gabbed enough," he said. "The hare's on the run. This is our last chance to bag him."

"Oh, that's a good one, Brother. Practically poetry," I cracked, but my heart wasn't in it. *Chun hung* or not, I didn't relish a return to the streets of Chinatown—not with Mahoney, Scientific, Big Queue, and who knew how many other hatchet men out there on them already.

Once we'd stumbled outside into the murky light of the moon, Charlie led us up the alley. The closer we drew to the street, the more I found I actually missed the oblivion of Chan's darkened shop. There was a comfort in not seeing—and, more so, in not being seen. The second we were back on the sidewalk, I felt a thousand eyeballs on me. Never mind that the streets were nearly deserted.

There was a streetlamp maybe once to a block, and a working one more rare even than that. Yet still it felt like we were walking in the *look-at-me!*

glare of a music hall spotlight. It took us five minutes to get to Yee Lock's place, and by the end of it I feared folks would have to start calling me "Big Ivory," for surely my hair had gone chalk-white from fright.

"There. That's it," Charlie finally said, pointing ahead at a dingy little shop much akin to Chan's. There was even the same big, stringy tuber in the window.

Flickering somewhere beyond it was the low glow of a lit candle.

Somebody was home.

"That place got a back door?" Old Red asked.

"Of course," Charlie said.

"Alrighty, then. You and me, we're gonna circle around and go in the back." Gustav looked at me, then the lady. "You two stay out front. But well away from the window. Don't want you gettin' spotted."

"Are you trying to keep me out of harm's way?" Diana asked. "Because if you are—"

"What I'm doin' is settin' me up some pickets in case whoever's in there tries to hightail it," my brother said. "Does that plan meet with your approval?"

"Yes. Of course," Diana replied, abashed.

"Good. Now, come on, Charlie."

The street was lined with businesses that had closed for the night, and when Old Red and Charlie turned the corner, Diana and I were alone at last.

"Just when I think I've won your brother over . . . ," the lady sighed, still staring off after Gustav though he'd disappeared from view.

"Oh, he's won over, miss. He just don't know how to show it." I stuffed my hands in my pockets, slumped my shoulders, and did my best to affect a heart-melting pout. "It's me you oughta be worried about."

"Oh?" Diana said without even turning to look at me.

"Sure. You been doin' so much droolin' over my brother's big ol' brain, it's got me wonderin' if I'm even included in this detectivin' deal you're workin' on."

At last, the lady turned and offered me a reassuring smile.

"Of course, you're included, Otto. You're a very brave and resourceful young man."

I'd been fishing for a compliment, but this wasn't quite the kind I'd hoped to land. "A resourceful young man"? It sounded like something an old maiden aunt would say about you. Diana may as well have patted me on the head.

"And anyway," she went on, "I can't imagine your brother doing anything without you. For all your bickering, you two seem very close."

"We do?"

I couldn't help but think of that chippy down in Texas Old Red had never gotten around to telling me about. I'd been on the drift with my brother five years, and only today had I learned he'd once been in love . . . and the girl had been *murdered*? Sure, he and I were close—as in never able to escape each other's company—but were we *close*?

For a moment, I was too lost in these thoughts to even attempt more flirting. Then my brother returned, and the time for flirting was through.

"Get in here," Gustav said, leaning out the front door of Yee Lock's store. "Come on. Quick."

We hustled into a shop that was Chan's reflected in a fun-house mirror: the same but more squat, dense, and grimy.

"So," I said as Old Red closed the door behind us, "the old man here?"

"Yup. Right back there by them bushels."

I turned—and saw no one but Charlie looking grim in the dim light of a candle set on a countertop nearby.

"Awww, hell. Are you kiddin' me?"

Four more steps toward the back of the store—that's all I needed to peer around the bushels and see what I knew I'd see.

A man on the floor, his long beard soaking in the blood that pooled all around him.

33

FACE OFF

Or, We Make a Gruesome Discovery—and Are Discovered Making It

Diana moved up behind me.

"I ain't tellin' you not to look," I said, "but I can't say as I'd advise it. Not if you ever wanna sleep again."

"You wouldn't believe the things I've seen, Otto." The lady stepped around me. "And I sleep just fine."

Then she saw the body.

"Oh."

She turned away. Slowly, though. In control. But admitting that she hadn't been quite ready for *that*.

The body, that wasn't so bad. Just curled up, knees drawn in, spindly arms clutching across the stomach.

It was the face that made it a nightmare—the fact that there wasn't one anymore. The old man's nose, eyes, teeth, and jaw had been crushed back into his skull, mashed into one gaping, red maw. It would've looked like nothing so much as sausage if not for the whiskers trailing out from the fresh-ground flesh.

I looked at Charlie, grateful to have anything to fix my eyes on other than that mess on the pharmacy floor.

"You sure that's Yee Lock?"

"Oh, yeah. I must've passed the old man in the street a million times.

235

That's him, alright." Charlie allowed himself a brief, sneering, almost gloating glance down at the body. "I always figured he'd end up like this."

The store had blinds over the front door and windows, and Gustav drew them down.

"Well, if it was Fat Choy killed the geezer, he surely got him his opium," he said.

"What makes you say that?" I asked.

My brother turned and waved a hand at the room around us. I tried to take it all in quick, as I knew I'd be racing Diana to the right deduction—and, to be honest, I was growing a little weary of her always winning.

There was a sort of corridor up the middle of the store leading to a counter and, beyond that, a back door. On either side of the center aisle were tables laden with the same strange assortment of "medicines" Chan had stocked: nuts and pods and roots, most of it in faded shades of yellow and brown. The shop was dingy, dusty, and stuffed wall to peeling-papered wall with merchandise, but you couldn't call it cluttered, exactly. The little trays of herbs and whatnot were arranged just so, with no space wasted, and the floor was clear of—

I had my answer.

"The place ain't been messed with—not like Doc Chan's was," I said. "Ain't been no searchin' *here*."

Old Red nodded—while Diana didn't so much nod as dip her head, conceding that I'd reached the finish line first, for once.

"Yee Lock would've kept his opium stashed away somewhere," Charlie said. "Fat Choy must've beaten the hiding place out of him."

"Well, *somebody* beat *something* out of him, that's for damned sure," Gustav said, stepping away from the window. "But that don't—"

He froze mid-stride.

"You hearin' or thinkin'?" I asked him.

"*Hush*," he shot back—which answered my question well enough.

I would've had my answer without asking had I waited just a moment longer. The sidewalks thereabouts were lined with planks of rotten wood that squeaked like mice when you trod on them. And just then someone was stepping on a mighty big mouse with what sounded like mighty big feet.

More mice got squished with each passing second. Rats, they could've been, they screeched so. And then the sound stopped—right outside the door to Yee Lock's shop.

There was a rap on the glass.

"*Hide,*" my brother whispered.

He needn't have bothered. Charlie, Diana, and I were already ducking for cover—ducking slow, though, lest we kick up any telltale squeals from the floorboards. Charlie ended up behind the counter, while the rest of us wormed our way under one of the long display tables.

There was another knock—a quick, hard *tap-tap* that rattled both the glass and my nerves.

"Who do you think it is?" I whispered into the bottoms of Old Red's boots.

"All I know is it ain't Yee Lock or Doc Chan," my brother answered, voice low. "Other than that, it could be just about—"

The door rattled again, but different this time, not from more knocks. Whoever was outside was trying the doorknob. Trying and succeeding, of course, since the thing wasn't locked.

The door swung open.

Diana was squished behind me, on her side, back to the wall. I could feel her go stiff, hear her breathing stop. It was only then that I noticed *I'd* stopped breathing.

I didn't give myself good odds for ever starting up again, either.

If I saw baggy black pant legs and dark slippers moving past my nose, I'd know Scientific or Big Queue or some other hatchet man had tracked us down—and we were getting the chop at last. If it was tweed trousers and brown brogans, on the other hand, that meant Mahoney was about to catch us in the company of a freshly murdered man, and it was just a question of whether he'd wait for us to be hung or speed things up and shoot us on the spot.

The footsteps started up again—inside now. The door creaked closed.

And then there they were: plump legs in wrinkled white seersucker moving with a shuffling, worn-out waddle.

It was either Wong Woon or an overweight bear that had borrowed his suit. My money was on the former.

"Yee Lock?" he said as he lumbered down the aisle. "Yee—?"

Woon took in a sharp breath and stopped just a few feet into the store. He'd either spied the old man's battered body or one of *us*.

He muttered something in Chinese then started moving again, faster now, hurrying past us.

"*Stop him,*" Gustav hissed.

So I did the only thing I could—stretched out a leg and tripped the Chinaman as he toddled by.

Woon hit the floorboards so hard some of them splintered under his big belly. Before he could catch his breath, I rolled out from under the table and hopped atop him, a knee in his back. If I'd had any rope on me I could've hog-tied him in seconds, rodeo-style, but I had to settle for pinning his arms behind him by hand.

"Don't bother tryin' to buck me, Detective," I said. "I used to bust broncs for a livin'."

Woon roared and writhed beneath me anyway. He didn't have more than a few seconds of fight in him, though. Then his whole body went slack, sagging, and he seemed to spread out over the floor like a puddle.

Still, I wasn't about to take any chances.

"Miss . . . my necktie . . . get it offa me."

To her credit, Diana didn't question. She just wriggled her way out into the aisle, pushed herself to her knees, and got to work. Within seconds, she had the necktie in her hands.

Old Red crawled out to join us. "I'll take it from here, miss."

"Oh, no—that's alright."

And she proceeded to bind Woon's hands with a perfectly serviceable diamond hitch.

I whistled. "Miss, by any chance have you ever worked a cattle drive?"

Diana just smiled.

"Kill me," Woon muttered.

Diana's smile vanished.

Woon's face was smooshed into the floor on its side, rolls of billowing fat smothering his words, and I figured I must have misheard him.

I leaned in closer.

"Pardon?"

"Kill me," Woon said again. "You learn nothing from me. Only waste time. So kill me. Quick. And go."

"He thinks *we* killed the old man," Charlie scoffed, stepping out from behind the counter. "Some 'detective.'"

Woon snarled at Charlie in Chinese, his normally soft voice going guttural, ferocious.

Charlie sneered something back at him that didn't sound any more neighborly.

"Now just hold on a minute . . . ."

Old Red stepped between them and crouched down to look Woon in the eye.

"It look like I just beat a man to death?" he asked, holding up his hands. "Otto, Diana, Charlie—show the man."

I climbed off Woon's broad back and waggled my gore-free fingers before his eyes. Diana showed off her dainty digits, too.

Charlie needed another prod from my brother, but eventually he trudged over and grudgingly held up his hands for Woon. He had to step over Yee Lock's blood to do it.

"As I'm sure you noticed, *Detective,*" Gustav said, "the old-timer there died recentlike . . . and died *messy.* If we was the ones what done him in, either you'd see proof of it splattered all over us or you wouldn't see us at all—cuz we wouldn't still be lollygaggin' 'round here just a-baskin' in our handiwork."

Woon's one upward-turned eye squinted at us dubiously. Yet the Chinaman nodded and grunted, acknowledging my brother's logic.

"Alright, then," Old Red said, settling himself on the floor Indian-fashion, "now that we got that out of the way, I think this'd be a fine time for us to have a little chat."

Woon tried to shake his head but just managed to mash his nose into the floorboards. "Do what you want. You get nothing from me."

Gustav rolled his eyes and sighed. "Don't you get it, Woon? We ain't goin' to torture you. We just wanna know what the hell's been goin' on around here. You got a side to tell, lay it out for us. If you're in the right, we'll let you go. Hell, we'll help you do whatever it is you're doin'. But if you don't tell us . . . ."

Old Red gave Woon a reluctant "What's a man to do?" shrug.

". . . then you stay trussed up like a Christmas turkey till somebody stumbles on you here. And who knows how long that might be?"

Woon eyed my brother a moment, then shifted his cyclopean stare to me, Diana, and, finally, Charlie.

"What you want to know?"

Gustav's eyes lit up so hungrily I almost expected him to lick his lips.

"That 'suicide note' you took from Chan's pocket . . . what was it, really?"

"It *was* suicide note."

Old Red's excitement instantly turned to irritation.

"Oh, come on, Woon! Remember, now—I saw you switch the note on Mahoney, and we *know* Chan didn't kill himself. There ain't no use lyin' about it no more. For chrissake, just tell us what was on that paper!"

Woon turned his head so he was staring straight down into the floor. He looked like he wanted to dig his way back to China.

"It was receipt for Black Dove," he said softly.

"A receipt?" I marveled. "For a gal?"

"'One slave girl, slightly used,'" Charlie said, quoting one of my weaker wisecracks from earlier in the day. "Sure. That really is how it's done around here."

Diana knelt down next to my brother.

"What did you give Sgt. Mahoney?" she asked Woon.

The Chinaman peeked up again. There might have been a little smile tucked into the folds of blubber around his face, it was hard to tell.

"Laundry ticket." He struggled to lift his hands from the small of his back. "Now . . . untie, please."

No one made a move to unstring him.

"Why would you wanna swipe that receipt?" Old Red asked.

But before Woon could reply—and it didn't look like he was in any hurry to do so—my brother nodded dreamily and offered up an answer himself.

"The money Chan got to buy Hok Gup . . . Chun Ti Chu gave it to him, didn't he? *That's* why you wanted the receipt. I mean, here the doc owes a pile to Little Pete, of all people, yet he's gonna shell out two thousand dollars for a 'wife'? That's gonna set people to wonderin'."

Woon just gaped up at Gustav round-eyed and limp as a dead fish. So my brother pushed on.

"Chun Ti Chu himself told us Chan came to see him yesterday. Seein' how news travels 'round these parts, it's a good bet half the Chinamen in town know about it. Feller breaks wind on Dupont and they're pinchin' their noses from Pine to Pacific 'fore he's even finished. So I reckon it wouldn't take long for folks to figure out how Chan come up with that cash."

Still Woon said nothing, and Old Red cocked his head to one side and leaned back as a man might when considering a pretty picture from a new angle.

"I notice you ain't denyin' any of this, Woon. Good. So that just leaves the question of *why*. Why would Chun Ti Chu bankroll the buyin' of a prostitute? You wanna walk outta here anytime soon, you'd best answer me that."

Woon turned his head again so he was looking straight down. After a moment just polishing the floor with his face, he spoke.

"Chun Ti Chu, Gee Woo Chan . . . friends. Chan very unhappy. Face so much trouble alone. Chun Ti Chu want to help. He can't pay debt to Little Pete. Big loss of *mien tzu* for Six Companies. Maybe quiet he can help Chan, though. Make so not lonely, at least. But if other men know . . . trouble. Everyone want money to buy pretty wife. Chinatown—lots men. Women, no."

Woon said all this so whisper-quiet Charlie had to come crouch down beside us just to hear him. When Woon was through, I looked over at our native guide.

"That sound square to you?"

"Well, he's telling the truth about that last part, at least," Charlie said. "Men come over here to make a buck, and that's it. Most of them either don't have wives yet or leave them back in China, so you've got a lot of lonely sojourners around here. If word got around that Chun Ti Chu was buying sing-song girls for his pals—buying *the Black Dove*. Yeah. Like he said. Trouble. The rest of it, though . . ." He shrugged. "It *could* be true."

"What about the girl, Mr. Woon?" Diana asked. "The Six Companies is offering a reward for her. Why?"

Woon twisted his neck, trying to look at her full on, with both eyes. He couldn't quite make it.

"Why you think? No suicide. Hok Gup and Fat Choy murder Gee Woo Chan."

"That does it!" Gustav slapped his knees and pushed himself to his feet. "You had your chance, Woon. Now you're gonna spend the night watchin' a dead man go stiff."

"But—," Woon began.

That was as far as he got.

"Bullshit!"

My brother turned, hopped over Yee Lock's body and stomped to the counter at the back of the store.

"The gal ain't got no reason to kill Chan," he fumed, scrounging angrily behind the counter. "No money to steal, with Chan broke the way he was. And that Fat Choy ain't exactly prime husband material for a woman tryin' to get *away* from whorehouses and the like. Naw. You just wanna get your hands on her so you can keep her quiet, am I right? *Am I right?*"

Woon didn't bother answering. He just took to staring down into the floorboards again. Throw a sheet over him, and he'd have served nicely as a sofa. He sure wasn't going to do any more talking.

"What are you huntin' for back there?" I asked as Old Red pulled out boxes and bags and dumped their contents on the countertop.

"Rope, of course. Or twine or straps or a strop. Anything we can use to . . ."

My brother turned into a statue. "Pop-Eyed Man with Box in Hand" the artist might call it.

He was staring down at the counter, at the contents of the container he'd just upended.

"Hel-lo" he'd usually say when greeting some new clue. But that just didn't quite capture the moment.

"Ho-lee shhhhit," he said instead.

I stood and took a step closer to get a better look. Then I took an involuntary step back.

Heaped on the counter was a pile of black scorpions.

34

SCORPION TEA

Or, We Visit Another Healer but Develop a Whole New Pain in the Ass

There were six scorpions in all. They landed in a pyramid, the one on top on its back.

None of them moved.

It seemed plain enough that they were dead. Yet we still gave them plenty of time to prove otherwise, staring for at least half a minute before my brother finally dared picking up the topmost by the tail.

"Like the one from Dr. Chan's flat?" Diana asked. "Desiccated?"

"It's all dried out, if that's what you mean."

Gustav pulled out the small black husk he'd had in his pocket most of the day. It had crumbled down to just the abdomen and one pincer, with the tail dangling by a single scrap of papery skin.

He held the two scorpions up side by side.

I squinted at them from a safe distance away. "Look enough alike to be kin."

"Yeah," Charlie said. "Brothers, maybe."

Old Red put the scorpions down amidst the jumbled whatnot he'd spread across the countertop.

"You know . . ." He looked up and gazed around the room, taking in the assorted bins and bowls lining the little shop's one aisle. ". . . I think I finally got a handle on what this little critter is."

"Seeing them in a pile like that, it's obvious," Charlie said.

"It is?"

I stared at the pile of scorpions and saw . . . a pile of scorpions.

Unfortunately for my pride, Diana nodded and said, "Yes, I see it now, too."

So the only (live) people in the room who couldn't figure it out were me and Wong Woon, and the big detective wasn't even trying. In fact, he'd gone so still down there on the floor beside the old man it almost seemed like *neither* of them was breathing anymore.

Gustav picked up a dark blob that had tumbled from one of the other boxes he'd spilled out on the counter.

"Beetles."

He pointed at a bowl near where I stood. It was abrim with yellow-brown sticks sporting fuzz on both sides. It looked like someone's mustache collection.

"Centipedes."

He swung his finger to a bowl on the other side of the aisle.

"And I don't even know the name for them things. But they used to be alive, whatever they are."

Diana peered down into the bowl. "They're seahorses. And I see dried shrimp and lizards, too."

"Sweet Jesus," I said, finally making the leap—and finding that it landed me somewhere pretty unpleasant. "So them scorpions are medicine? Folks . . . eat 'em?"

"Grind them up and drink them, actually," Charlie corrected. "As a tea."

"Eat, drink, either way . . . ." I put a hand to my stomach to keep it from doing cartwheels. "I don't like the idea of a scorpion on the outside of me, let alone the inside."

"I'm sure you've had cod liver oil," Diana said. "And prairie oysters and fried brains. Why not scorpion tea?"

"I don't know. Cuz it's disgustin'?"

"So, Charlie," Old Red said, "you got any idea what boiled scorpions would be a remedy for?"

"I didn't know they were a remedy for *anything* till just now."

Diana knelt down next to our prisoner. "What about you, Mr. Woon? Do you know?"

The detective finally lifted his flabby face up off the floor. It was covered with dust.

"I am not a doctor."

"That ain't what the lady asked you!" Gustav snarled. "Now I'm givin' you one last chance to get yourself back on your feet." He snatched up one of the scorpions and shook it so hard a pincer flew off. "What would Doc Chan or Yee Lock use these little black bastards for?"

"Ask him," Woon said, nodding at the body curled up half a dozen feet from where he lay. Then he put down his head and went back to playing possum—or, in his case, dozing walrus.

"Yeah, well, maybe him I can't ask, but that don't mean there ain't others," Old Red said. "Charlie—there gonna be any more of these herbal-type pharmacies open this hour?"

"None of the respectable ones. But there are a couple that stay open all night." Charlie glanced over at Diana. "For the right kind of customer."

The lady opened her handbag and fished out her bankroll—only it wasn't much of a *roll* anymore. It was more like a cracker.

"I hope nine dollars can make me the right kind of customer," Diana said after a quick count.

"It'll have to," Gustav said. "Now come on, all of you—help me find something to tether Woon proper. I ain't gonna leave the job to no necktie."

After a couple minutes searching, Charlie came up with some twine that would do the trick. We used it to bind Woon's wrists and ankles, while my tie we wound round his face for a gag.

Woon didn't fight us, but he didn't help us either. Tying him was like trying to put a bathing suit on a bag of wet cement. Old Red wanted to leave him behind the counter, but after one back-breaking attempt to lift him, we gave up and left him where he was.

He didn't say a word through the whole sweaty ordeal.

Not five minutes after we left Yee Lock's, we were in an identical shop a few blocks away. The only things missing were the bodies on the floor.

Everything else—the narrow center aisle, the crowded bins of dried "medicine," the flickering light of a single candle—was exactly the same.

The proprietor was a short, surprisingly cheerful Chinaman Charlie referred to as "Lee Kan." At first, he'd peeked out through a barely cracked door, looking drowsy and distrustful. But the second his sleepy eyes opened wide enough to take in who we were, he smiled and ushered us inside. He and Charlie chatted casually in Chinese as we filed in, but the bantering turned to bartering quick enough.

Considering the late hour, Charlie told us, a consultation would cost ten dollars.

"Highway robbery!" Old Red huffed, and he started to stamp out—exactly as we'd planned if a little extra leverage was needed. (It was agreed by all that my brother was the natural choice for a show of pique.)

As Diana and I turned to follow, Lee Kan blurted something out in Chinese

"*Wait,*" Charlie said to us.

The two Chinamen wrangled for a minute, at the end of which Charlie nodded brusquely and handed over five dollars.

Lee Kan grinned and waved us further into his shop.

"Alright—the folderol's out of the way," Gustav said to Charlie. "Get to askin'."

Charlie spoke to the healer for a moment, then turned back to my brother.

"Alright. Show him."

Old Red pulled out one of the scorpions from Yee Lock's store.

Lee Kan's grin turned into a grimace.

It took the man a moment to find his tongue again, and when he did his voice was a strangled whisper. It was as if he feared not just the thing the words represented but the very words themselves. They were hoodoo words—cursed.

He pointed at the scorpion as he talked, then held the finger aloft, plainly saying "one" or "only." When he was done, Charlie repeated back the last two words to leave the healer's lips: "*Mah fung.*"

Lee Kan nodded. "*Mah fung.*"

"*Mah fung?*" Gustav said.

"Yeah, *mah fung*?" I threw in. I glanced over at Diana, but she didn't seem tempted to join our quartet.

"Old Joe," Charlie told us. "The pox."

"A-ha," said Old Red.

"Oh-ho," said I.

I started to translate Charlie's translation for the lady, but it wasn't necessary.

"Scorpion tea is a treatment for *syphilis*?" she said.

Charlie nodded.

Lee Kan gaped at our guide, then unleashed a gush of gibbering Chinese. Charlie tried to turn back the flood with a shake of the head and a curt, one-word answer.

"He's asking a lot of questions," Charlie said.

"Well, bully for him. But he's gonna have to wait till *we're* done." Old Red gave his scorpion a little waggle. "Ask if he stocks these things hisself."

Charlie dutifully converted the question into Chinese.

"No," he reported after hearing through Lee Kan's answer. "The black scorpions are special. They have to be shipped over from China. He doesn't have any."

Lee Kan spoke again, unprompted. He pointed at Old Red, Diana, and me as he jabbered, his strangely sunny smile returning.

"In case he's wonderin'," I said, "*no*, the scorpion tea ain't for me."

"He's saying he's heard about you," Charlie said, beginning his translation before Lee Kan was even through talking. "That's the only reason he let us in so cheap. He's got information he thinks you'll pay big money for. He knows—"

Charlie broke back into Chinese, his voice rising, excited.

As Lee Kan answered, his grin stretched so wide I could see every tooth in his head.

"What? *What*?" my brother said.

"He knows where Fat Choy is."

So at last, at least one mystery was solved: I now knew what Lee Kan had to be so chipper about.

"I don't think four bucks quite qualifies as 'big money,'" I said. "And that's all we got left, remember? How we gonna get Lee here to spill the beans?"

"I'll get him to talk," Charlie said, his tone turning tough. He brought himself up to his full height and clenched his long, bony fingers into fists.

It was funny seeing scrawny Chinatown Charlie trying to act hard. To me, he looked about as menacing as an understuffed scarecrow.

Yet little Lee Kan picked up on the change in Charlie, and his big grin changed, too. The lips lost some of their rubbery stretch, and the eyes widened, turning wary.

"Actually, we've still got plenty of cash," Diana said. "Charlie—what about the fifty dollars I gave you this morning?"

"What about it?" Charlie growled back, clearly not caring for the direction the conversation was taking.

"Why not loan it back to us?" she suggested. "At, say . . . one-hundred percent interest? Compounded daily?"

Charlie snorted. "I'm not a bank."

"Oh, come on, Charlie," my brother snapped. "We ain't got time for this. Offer the man twenty bucks outta your stash. You know the lady's good for it."

Charlie glared at him a moment, then slowly unclenched his fists and pulled out his folding money. He peeled off a ten note, held it up in front of Lee Kan and spoke in Chinese.

The healer nodded and snatched the bill away, looking relieved. Then he started talking.

Fat Choy had been standing right there in his store not half an hour before, he told us (via Charlie). The hatchet man had been dressed in an American-style suit that seemed a touch tight on him, and his queue was tucked under the collar of his jacket. He bought opium—a lot of it—and asked about herbal remedies for seasickness. While Lee Kan mixed up a batch of his own secret recipe, he'd slyly (or so he said) inquired as to Fat Choy's need for the stuff. Fat Choy had laughed.

"You know why I can't stay here," he'd (supposedly) replied. "I have an uncle in Honolulu. I'll go live with him until everyone's forgotten about Gee Woo Chan."

"He really came right out and mentioned Doc Chan by name?" I asked when Lee Kan was through.

Charlie passed the question along, and Lee Kan nodded.

"Well, I reckon there ain't no question about it now," I said to Old Red. "Fat Choy done in the doc for sure."

My brother didn't even look at me.

"Fat Choy said '*I* can't stay here'? '*I'll* go live in Honolulu'?" he was saying to Charlie. "No 'we'? No mention of the gal at all?"

Once again, Charlie Chineseified the question. This time, Lee Kan answered with a burst of words and a shake of the head.

"No," Charlie told Gustav a moment later. "Fat Choy didn't say anything about Hok Gup, and Lee Kan sure wasn't going to bring the subject up." He rolled his hands in the air like the paddlewheel of a steamboat pulling away from the dock. "So are we through here? Because it seems to me we've heard everything we need to know."

"I gotta agree with Charlie," I said. "We finally got a real bead on where Fat Choy's gonna be. All we gotta do now is grab us a paper and check the shippin' listings. Can't be more than one boat bound for Hawaii tonight. We hightail it over to the right pier, maybe we can catch Fat Choy 'fore his ship sets sail."

"If it hasn't already," Diana said.

Charlie wasn't waiting for more debate. He spun away from Lee Kan and pushed past us toward the door.

"Not yet, Charlie!" Old Red barked.

Charlie stopped and whirled around. "More questions?" he asked through gritted teeth.

"Just two." Gustav looked up at Lee Kan. "Does that seasickness cure of yours cost a lot? And how much of it did Fat Choy buy?"

Charlie did his translating from behind us, near the door. Though he surely knew Old Red couldn't understand a word, Lee Kan gave his answer directly to my brother, looking him in the eye the whole time.

"Yeah, the seasickness powder's expensive," Charlie said. "Twenty bucks a bag. Hard-to-find ingredients, Lee Kan says—which just means he had a customer who didn't have time to haggle. Fat Choy only bought enough for a couple nights."

"Well, then . . . ." Gustav turned to face the rest of us. "He ain't goin' to Hawaii."

I held up a finger. "Uhhh, if I may interject." I cleared my throat. "*Huh?*"

"*Fat . . . Choy . . . is . . . not . . . going . . . to—*"

"Oh, would you stop it? I ain't goin' deaf. I just don't get it. You're sayin' Fat Choy blew forty bucks on a remedy for seasickness so he could turn around and go to *Idaho?*"

"Could be."

"You think it's too simple," Diana said to Old Red. "Too obvious."

"But simple is good!" I protested. "*Obvious* is good! We ain't had enough of neither today."

Old Red chided me with a quote from Holmes: "There is nothing more deceptive than an obvious fact."

"You know, that one makes about as much sense as that claptrap about the truth bein' whatever ain't impossible."

Gustav rolled his eyes. "Just think about it, would you? Fat Choy's spooked enough to spend the whole day down in that hidey-hole, but when he finally climbs out he comes here, to *him*—"

He waggled his thumb back at Lee Kan, who stood stiffly behind his counter watching us with an even stiffer smile.

"—a man Charlie tells us is three miles to the left of respectable. And he up and lays out exactly where he's goin' next?"

Old Red shook his head.

"That don't sit right. Not unless he *wanted* to spread around that fairy tale about an uncle in Hawaii. And use your noodle on *this*: Fat Choy buys him a big mess of opium but goes stingy on the stomach soother? When it takes a ship . . . what? Two, three weeks to get out to them islands? Naw."

"If he was lying, why buy the seasickness remedy at all?" Charlie asked from his spot by the door. He looked so anxious to get going he may as well have been tapping his foot. "Fat Choy's a hoppie. He's not going to throw away forty dollars he could spend chasing the dragon."

"Wellllllll . . . ," Gustav said, stretching the word out like taffy while he did some quick figuring. "Maybe he really did need some of that potion. Only not for a long trip. For a short one."

"Los Angeles and Portland ain't but a few days away by boat," I suggested.

"Or," Diana said.

Just that. "Or." And she cocked an eyebrow at my brother.

"Oh, yes . . . oh, yes, yes, *yes*," Old Red said, giving her a nod that started small but kept growing until his head was doing such a bobble he could've been bobbing for apples.

I nodded, too. "Of course! Why, it ain't just elementary, it's kindergarten!"

"What is?" Charlie demanded.

I shrugged. "You got me."

Diana took mercy on the two of us and provided an actual answer.

"If you want to get as far away from San Francisco as quickly as possible, a train's the best choice. But you can't catch any of the major lines from the city itself. For that, you have to go to Oakland."

"Of course," I said. And I meant it this time. "On the ferry."

"Last one leaves at nine o'clock—right, Brother?" Old Red said. "So that means we probably got no more than . . . hey, hold on, Charlie!"

I turned toward our guide only to find him blowing out the door. He threw a glance back at us as he stepped outside, the expression on his face a strange gumbo of opposing emotion. I saw contempt there, and fear, and regret.

Then he bolted.

I ran after him, but by the time I reached the sidewalk, his long, lean legs had already carried him across the street to yet another alleyway. He disappeared into the shadows without another look back.

"He's gone." I stumbled back inside, stunned. "He just . . . run off."

"Of course, he has," Diana said, less like it was something she'd been expecting than something she'd been dreading. "He's gone to tell his boss what we know. We're in a race for sure now, gentlemen."

"A race with who?" I asked.

"His boss?" asked Old Red.

The lady was able to answer us both with the same two words.

"Little Pete."

35

SHIPPING NEWS

Or, We Race the Clock to Make the Ferry, but the Clock Up and Cheats

I t took a few seconds for Diana's pronouncement to sink in. By the time it had, my hopes were sinking, too.

"So Charlie was a spy?"

"More than a spy," Diana said. "He's been guiding us, using us all along." She looked over at Gustav, her expression turning sorrowful. "We ended up working for Little Pete, after all."

My brother gave her the slow, somber nod of a man accepting the fact of his own failure. "How'd you deducify it?"

Diana gestured back at the ever-smiling Lee Kan, who'd gone so still he could've been a grinning gargoyle propped up on the shop counter.

"Charlie still had money to pay *him*, for one thing. If he'd really been captured by Little Pete's hatchet men this afternoon, like he said, would they have let him keep the fifty dollars I paid him to help us?"

She answered her own question with a shake of the head.

"I already had my suspicions before then, though. The men we spoke to in the opium dens this afternoon didn't help us much, but they didn't throw us out, either. That's more than I would've expected, given that we were just some nosy *fan kwei* and a lowly *ki di*. It makes a lot more sense if they knew Charlie was working for Little Pete. That way, any questions they were answering for us, they were really answering for *him*."

"Explains why Little Pete wasn't pissed when I said no to him, too. That bounty he offered us for the gal—that was just some kinda test." Old Red drove a fist into an open palm. "Dammit, I should've seen it all along."

"You're a natural-born detective, Gustav, but you're not naturally devious." Diana offered him a small, sympathetic smile. "We'll have to work on that."

"Why didn't you say something about Charlie sooner?" I said to her.

"Until a minute ago, it was no more than a vague inkling. And anyway, where were we going to find another interpreter? We needed him."

As she spoke, I noticed movement in the dim candlelight behind her. Lee Kan was edging toward a bead-draped doorway at the back of the shop.

"You goin' somewhere?" I asked him.

He stopped, still grinning, and gave me a confused shrug.

I had an inkling of my own.

"No sabe Englee, huh?" I said.

Lee Kan nodded.

"Uh-huh. Right." I turned to my brother and dropped my voice. "You know, just to be safe, I think we oughta wrap a rope around this little feller like we did—"

Lee Kan darted through the doorway.

I started after him, but Gustav hooked me by the arm before I'd taken two steps.

"Lemme go! We can't have him tattlin' to who knows who!"

"We ain't got time to chase after him now," my brother said. "Fat Choy gets on that ferry without us—or gets hisself bagged by Little Pete—and we'll never find Hok Gup or know what really happened to Doc Chan."

He steered me toward the door, and Diana fell into step behind us.

"Folks," my brother said, "we got us a boat to catch."

Once outside, we proceeded east at a canter. A full-on gallop wouldn't do—not with nearly a mile between us and the Ferry House. We'd over-bake ourselves before we were halfway there.

It's at times like these a cowboy truly misses his horse.

We could've headed down to Market, eight or nine blocks south, and probably hopped a trolley or hack from there. But Old Red pointed out that we likely had a war party of *boo how doy* on our trail, and the best place to shake them would be the Barbary Coast. So into the breach—and the debauchery—we headed yet again.

On our way out of Chinatown, we passed the Anti-Coolie League sandwich man, who was busy abusing any Chinese within earshot. I "accidentally" knocked him into the gutter as we whipped by.

"*Entschuldigung, Arschloch!*" I called back apologetically as we hustled away.

"You mean 'Pardon me, sir'!" the stupid *"Arschloch"* bellowed. "You're in America now, dammit!"

Mere seconds later, we were weaving through hoodlums, harlots, sailors, and toffs—many of whom were weaving themselves. Or staggering, anyway. In the hour or so that had passed since we'd last left the Coast, the number of drunken revelers had doubled, and the sidewalks were overflowing with people (not to mention—and perhaps I shouldn't—puke and piss).

Our jog slowed to a walk, then a shuffle.

It was hard to gauge whether our slowed progress should have us worried, panicked, or downright suicidal without knowing the hour. Maybe we had half an hour to catch the ferry . . . or maybe it was already cruising past Alcatraz Island. So we tried asking folks the time. We were told, "Not late enough," "Who cares?" and "Ask that bastard in the slouch hat—he just stole my watch," before someone graced us with a straight answer.

It was eight-fifty. We had ten minutes to travel ten blocks.

"We ain't gonna make it."

"Thank you for statin' the obvious," my brother grumbled.

"Oh, I do what I can."

"Which ain't much."

"You want me to do more? How 'bout if I was to pick you up and *throw* you to the—?"

"Look," Diana cut in, pointing up at one of the wooden poles running along Pacific Avenue. "Some of these buildings have been wired for telephone service. Maybe we could get inside somewhere and find a phone. Ring up the Ferry House and have them hold the boat."

"That's a mighty big 'maybe,' " I said.

"Too big," said Old Red.

"Well, squabbling's certainly not going to get us to the Ferry House any faster."

"Don't underestimate the power of squabblin'," I said. "It's served me and my brother well enough so far."

Gustav stepped sideways into the throng, headed for the street. "What we need to find is a . . . hel-lo."

I heard what he was hel-loing before I saw it. It was loud enough to cut through even the din of dance-hall bands, crib girl come-ons, and cackled laughter.

The clattering whir of wheels. The heavy *clop-clop* of hooves on a city street.

A wagon was coming.

Diana and I wormed our way out to the gutter with my brother. He was looking west down Pacific, back the way we'd just come. There were no cable cars or carriages in sight—none would risk a trip through the Coast after nightfall. But the Coast being the Coast, there was money to be made if a man was willing to brave the chaos. And men being men, there were takers.

The buckboard rolling toward us was toting a dozen kegs. Some concert saloon or melodeon had raised the alarm, so here they came like the fire brigade: the beer men, making an emergency run.

Appropriately enough for beer men, they were barrel-chested. And loaded, too—as in with bullets. The fellow holding the reins was wearing a gunbelt, and his shotgun rider lived up to the name.

They were a block away, moving at a pace just shy of brisk. We had all of thirty seconds to come up with a plan.

Gustav took a stab first.

"We'll stop 'em, then—"

"Ho! Hold on there, Brother!" I said. "You can't move on to 'then' that easy. Stop 'em how? Them fellers probably got drunks flaggin' 'em down all night. They ain't gonna . . . Miss?"

Diana was walking out into the street.

"Stay back," she said without turning to look at us. "Don't let them know we're together."

She planted herself in the wagon's path and waved her arms over her head.

I started toward her, but Old Red held me back.

"They won't run down a lady . . . I hope."

"You'd *better* hope," I said. "Cuz if she gets hurt, I'm gonna—"

"Don't worry. She gets hurt, I'll do it myself."

The driver had spotted Diana by now, and he jerked his reins to the right, trying to steer around her.

Diana put herself in front of his horses again. If he didn't rein up, and hard, she'd be rolled out like a pie crust in five seconds flat.

The driver called out "Whoa!" and jerked back on the reins with such force I could hear the leather creaking over the rumble of the wheels. The horses whinnied and skidded over the cobblestones, and the whole kit and caboodle—ponies, harness gear, the wagon—seemed to squeeze up like a concertina.

When it all came to a stop, Diana was practically nose to muzzle with the lead horse.

"Gentlemen," she said coolly, "thank you for stopping."

The driver immediately launched into a tirade so larded with profanity I'm sure even the passing sailors picked up a phrase or two. The gist: The lady had just done a darned foolish thing. Why?

"I'm sorry, but it was an emergency." Diana walked around to the left side of the buckboard—pulling the beer men's eyes with her, away from us. "I'm in desperate need of transportation. Would it be possible to hire out your wagon? Just for a little while?"

The driver uncorked another torrent of vulgarities.

"Hold on, Aldo," the shotgun man said. He leaned toward Diana, his scattergun resting on his lap. "How much for how long?"

"Four dollars for ten minutes."

Once again, Mt. Aldo erupted with expletives.

"Look, lady," the shotgun man said, "they need this beer at the Bella

Union *now* or, trust me, we wouldn't be out here at all. We don't have time for charity cases."

"Ten dollars for five minutes," Diana said.

There was no cussing this time. The haggling had begun.

As had the skulking. While the lady distracted the beer men, my brother and I crept up alongside the wagon, Gustav on the driver's side, I on the other. I was mere steps from the shotgun guard's back when he whipped around to glare at a gaggle of guffawing passersby that had slowed to take in the show.

"What are you laughing at?" he snapped.

"At the big son of a bitch trying to steal your wagon!" a hoodlum in the crowd crowed. And he pointed right at me.

And he was calling *me* an SOB?

I lunged and grabbed the barrel of the guard's scattergun before he could turn around. But the beer man, alerted, had tightened his grip. I couldn't pry the shotgun away.

The guard and I wound up playing tug of war, me trying to wrench the scattergun out of his hands, him trying to work both barrels up even with my face.

"Heeeyaaah!" someone hollered, and I heard the reins snap.

The wagon lurched forward, and the guard vaulted *upward,* launched into the air as his seat jerked out from under him. He flew over my head, landing on his back with a grunting thud—and with the shotgun still in his hands.

"Otto, hurry! Get in!" Diana called back from the buckboard as it rumbled up the street. Old Red was hunched over beside her, clutching the reins.

I sprinted after the wagon. It hadn't worked up to much of a lick yet, and after a few long strides I was able to grab hold of the side and vault up into the bed.

"Y'all get the gun off the driver?" I was about to ask when the *pop* of a single shot offered the answer.

I felt something warm and wet down run down my ankle.

"Sweet Jesus!" I cried. "I been—"

But I hadn't. When I looked down, I saw that it wasn't blood soaking my foot. It was beer.

"You alright back there, Brother?"

There was another *pop*, and one of the other kegs sprung a leak.

I peeked back at the street.

"I'm fine," I said. "But you might wanna ask again in a second or two."

Aldo was little more than thirty feet behind us, giving chase at an awkward side-turned lope, a smoking Colt at the end of his outstretched hand. In addition to the occasional potshot, he was firing off obscenities Gatling-gun fast.

The guard was on his feet now, too, and he scampered after us, shotgun up. He couldn't fire with Aldo still in front of him—not without peppering his pal with buckshot. But the second the two men drew even, he'd let loose.

"Can't you get them nags goin' any faster?"

"Not with all that dead weight back there!" Gustav hollered.

"Hey, who you callin'—?"

Pop.

The barrel next to my head sprung a leak, and beer gushed down onto my shoulder and chest, quickly drenching me. I wriggled around to escape the cascade, ending up pressed against the back gate of the wagon bed. It felt loose, and I noticed it was held in place only by a three-inch peg on a short length of twine. The little bolt danced around in its hole, every bounce over the cobblestones threatening to pop it out altogether.

Well, isn't that just dandy? I thought. *If I'm not shot in the next minute, I'm gonna roll off the back of this buckboard like a . . .*

Hel-lo, as my brother likes to say.

I pushed myself up onto my knees and pulled the peg all the way out. The back gate dropped open.

"Don't do it, asshole!" Aldo screeched. "Don't you *dare* do it!"

I dared anyway: I rolled out the barrels.

The first took a bullet from Aldo's Peacemaker as I pushed it out. The little spout of beer that poured forth was nothing compared to the geyser when it hit the street.

The barrel disappeared in an explosion of wooden planks and foam.

The second keg actually survived its drop to the cobblestones, and it bore down on Aldo and his buddy fast, a giant skittle ball about to take out a pair of pins. As the beer men threw themselves from its path, I shouted the magic words that would ensure their pursuit was over.

"*Free beer! Free beer! Free beer!*"

Cheering rowdies rushed into the street, only to be mowed down by the barrels that didn't bust when they hit. By the time the last keg had been shoved out, Aldo and the shotgun man had disappeared into the waves of hooligans and beer like the Pharaoh's army being swallowed by the Red Sea.

With the wagon's load lightened so, we were able to tear over to the waterfront in mere minutes. Of course, mere minutes were all we had, and after abandoning our chariot on East Street, we took the last stretch at a sprint. There was just enough light from the streetlamps out front to espy the time on the Ferry House's squat clock tower: five till nine.

The usually bustling building was nearly deserted, and we came racing up to the ticket windows inside just as the last clerk was closing up for the night. We all started jabbering at him at once.

"Hold on!"

"Don't go!"

"Hey! Wait!"

The clerk's sleepy, half-lidded eyes didn't open a hair wider.

"Closed," he said, and he snapped down his window shade.

"This is an emergency!" Old Red shouted. "Matter of life and death!"

The shade stayed drawn.

"We're detectives!" I tried. "We think you got a killer on the Oakland ferry!"

The shade stayed drawn.

"Four dollars for three tickets," Diana said.

The shade went up.

The ride to Oakland costs seventy-five cents.

"You see any Chinamen tonight?" Gustav asked as the clerk handed over our tickets.

"I see Chinamen every night," the clerk said, and once again he vanished behind the black cloth of his window shade.

259

Diana pointed at an oversized clock hanging from the east wall. "*Gentlemen.*"

"Well, of all the goddamned luck," Old Red spit, while I opted for the blunter but no-less appropriate "Shit!"

It was five *after* nine. The tower clock was slow.

Another dash took us around to the building's back doors. Then we were outside again, the cutting breeze off the bay giving me chills as it blew over my beer-soaked clothes.

But my blood suddenly running cold the way it did—that had nothing to do with the temperature. It was the sight of our ferry that did that.

There were no ropes or gangplank to link it to the pier any longer. Just a stripe of foamy water churned up by the turning of the paddle-wheel.

The ferry was already a hundred yards out.

We'd missed the boat.

36

MANDARIN STANDOFF

Or, Old Red Goes to the Edge—and We Wind Up in the Middle of a Mess

I waited for the explosion. It was going to be big, I knew. Blow-out-your-eardrums loud.

Gustav took in a deep breath . . . and I fought the urge to put my fingers in my ears.

But then he let the breath go, and there was no scream of rage, no glass-shattering obscenities. He didn't throw down his hat, stomp his feet or look for something to break. Why, he didn't even try to take it out on *me*. He just walked to the edge of the pier as the boat to Oakland chugged off into the darkness of the night.

It almost looked like he was going to follow the ferry, try to walk across the waters after it. Or just drop off the pier like he was walking the plank.

I hustled up next to him. Diana did the same on the other side.

Old Red stopped one step from plummeting into the bay. It would've been a long fall: twenty feet down to water as cold and black as oblivion.

"We can still check for Hawaii-bound ships," Diana said softly. "Maybe we were wrong about—"

"No," Old Red said.

"We could head back to Chinatown," I suggested. "Try to find—"

"No."

Diana leaned forward to look my brother in the face, putting herself out over the void in a way that made me sweat even as I shivered in the frigid night air.

"You're not giving up, are you?"

Gustav refused to meet her gaze. But it wasn't out of shyness anymore. It was more like she was a mirror he couldn't stand looking into.

"It ain't a matter of givin' up. We just plain failed," he said. "Failed the doc. Failed the gal."

"You don't know that, Brother. Could be Hok Gup's still stashed away someplace. A prisoner. So many folks after her, who's to say where she ended up?"

Old Red shook his head. "If she's on that boat, she needs our help. And if she's still back there"—he jerked his head to the west, toward Chinatown—"she's beyond our help."

"So," Diana said, "you *are* giving up."

Gustav finally looked over at her. "Miss, you can dig in your spurs much as you want, but it don't change facts. We . . . have . . . failed."

Then he looked away again, back out at the ferry as it dwindled to a hazy blob of light that shimmered in the gloom like a lonely star. The lady stayed there beside him, following his gaze, and I did the same. It seemed like the first time we'd actually stood still together all day, just the three of us, with nowhere to run to and nothing to run *from*. Woebegone and weary though I was, I kind of liked it.

Nearby, a buoy bell clanged in time to the lapping of the water against the pillars of the pier. Further out, a boat horn blew mournfully, sounding remarkably like the lowing of herd-cattle bedded for the night. Below us, something stirred in the brine—a big fish or sea lion. Maybe even a shark.

And then another sound blew in on the wind off the water.

Voices. *Angry* voices.

Gustav and Diana's heads turned at the exact moment mine did, like we were three ponies in the same bridle.

The pier stretched out into the bay another seventy-five feet, at least, and there were crates and coils of thick rope and what looked like a shack further down, to our right. That's where the voices were coming from: the very end of the pier. The very end of San Francisco and California and the United States, too, if you angled yourself right. It may as well have been the end of everything. One more step dropped you into the abyss. It was as far as you could walk without drowning.

And somebody was out there—a few somebodies who didn't care much for each other, from the sound of things. I didn't recognize words or even voices so much as tones: a man barking orders, a woman wheedling, another man jeering, and all of them speaking over each other, as if they were competing to be heard.

Old Red, Diana, and I moved toward the sound, walking slowly, wordlessly. Our pace picked up once we were close enough to make out actual words. Not that we understood half of them.

They were Chinese.

"Stop gibbering that monkey talk!" a man snapped. "English only when I'm around!"

It had to be the Coolietown Crusader himself—Sgt. Cathal Mahoney.

"Oh, Charlie just say, 'Look at *fan kwei* son of bitch. He still think badge is crown.'"

It sure sounded like Scientific.

So that gave us three names on the guest list. The rest we filled in when we peeked around the corner of the shed near the end of the pier. A big, red-tinted lantern hung out over the water from a post, and by its crimson light we could see Mahoney squared off against Scientific and Chinatown Charlie—and Madam Fong and Big Queue, to boot.

The latter held a familiar-looking gun in one massive hand: Doc Chan's derringer. It was easy to see how the hatchet man had come to have it. All you had to do was look where he was pointing it—or, to be more precise, look at who he was pointing it at.

Facing the others, their backs to the bay, were two Chinamen in dark business suits and bowlers. One was tallish, sunken-eyed, pale, with the saggy-prune look of a man who'd recently lost more weight than was good for him. Fat Choy, I had little doubt. His left hand was wrapped around his right wrist, seemingly nursing a fresh sprain—like the kind you get when a bigger man twists a gun from your grip.

The other fellow was the highbinder's opposite in every respect—short, bespectacled, dark-skinned, bulky, with cheeks as round and smooth as a pair of peaches. His neck and hands were surprisingly slender, though, giving the man an altogether feminine air that made a lot more sense once I realized he was, indeed, altogether feminine.

He was a *she*. We'd found the Black Dove at last.

I stared at her hard, studying her, searching beneath the eyeglasses and bowler and bulging men's clothes for the great beauty men had killed for. I couldn't see it. The Black Dove looked more like the Overstuffed Turkey, and all I found in her face was fear.

She was cowering half-behind Fat Choy, peering around at Mahoney and the others with the same look of bewildered desperation a treed coon gives the baying bloodhounds below it. Fat Choy was keeping his left elbow jutted out over her chest, but it was impossible to say if he was trying to protect her or fixing to knock her backwards off the dock.

Madam Fong turned toward the girl and said something in Chinese, her voice as smooth and cool as fresh-churned butter.

"I said *English,* dammit!"

The madam looked over at Mahoney—as did Big Queue beside her. She smiled. The hatchet man scowled.

"I just told her not to worry, that's all. If she comes home, everything will be OK. We can fix whatever needs fixing."

"Hok Gup has no 'home' with you," Scientific said.

"She still belongs to the Kwong Ducks."

"Not anymore, she doesn't," Charlie said. "You sold her."

Madam Fong flicked a sneer at Charlie, her smile disappearing for the one second she bothered looking at him.

"Show me a receipt."

Then she looked back at Scientific, her smile returning. She obviously considered the man an equal—or at least a worthy adversary.

"What claim do *you* have on the girl?"

"She belong to Gee Woo Chan. He owe Little Pete." Scientific shrugged. "Now I collect."

"Shut up, the both of you," Mahoney spat. "I'm the law here. She's coming with *me*."

Scientific held his hands out toward Hok Gup and Fat Choy, palms up. "Why you not take, then? Why stand here for this talk talk talk?"

"Like I told you when I first got here," Mahoney said, "before I do anything with those two, I want the rest of you to clear the hell out."

"Why? So you do what you want to *him*?" Scientific jerked his head at Fat Choy—then ran a hand lightly over his stomach, which was no doubt bruised grapeskin-purple from the punts Mahoney had put to him earlier. "Or because you afraid we don't let you leave?"

Mahoney looked as though he'd upchuck if he could actually believe his own ears.

"Afraid that *you* won't let *me* leave?"

Scientific nodded, smirking like he'd just told the pope the one about the priest, the monk, and the nun with the naughty habit.

"Very foolish, you come here alone. Or . . . you have reason?"

Mahoney's face glowed as red as the lantern overhead, and he snarled out the Curse of Curses. (I've heard said curse a million times but have never seen it written anywhere but outhouse walls, so I won't besmear these pages with it now.)

"The girl's coming with me," he went on, and he slipped a hand inside his jacket.

"*Stop him.*"

That was all my brother needed to say. I knew who he was talking to. And I was more than happy to oblige.

I charged out of the shadows and slapped a bear hug around Mahoney from behind before he could draw his iron from its shoulder-holster.

"Surprise," I whispered in his ear.

Mahoney knew just what to do, I'll give him that. He tried to elbow my ribs and stomp my toes and bring his heel up into my balls. I just squeezed him tighter.

"I'll let you go if you promise to play nice," I said to him.

He dropped his head forward—another classic tactic, given the circumstances. Before he could throw his head back, smashing my nose with his thick skull, I lifted him off his feet and threw him down to the planks onto his tailbone.

He instinctively grabbed his ass and wailed. Which was all the opportunity I needed to bend down and relieve him of his equalizer.

"Oh, ho!" I crowed, enjoying the heft of Mahoney's stubby Colt Lightning. "I been waitin' all day to get my hands on a—"

Quick as that, my hand wasn't on anything. A blur, a jabbing, stabbing pain to my wrist, and the gun was gone.

"You clodhopper shithead!" Mahoney hollered up at me. "You've screwed us all!"

Scientific had the cop's Colt.

I saw now why the little *boo how doy* had goaded Mahoney so. He'd planned on doing to the detective what he'd just done to me, though probably a hell of a lot rougher. I'd spoiled his fun—and his chance to win back some *mien tzu*.

He glared at me like I'd just stepped on his marbles.

"Sorry," I said with a shrug. I looked over at his lackey. "Hey, Charlie. Miss me?"

"Not particularly." Charlie's gaze strayed to my left—to Gustav and Diana, who'd followed me out into the open. "You should've given up when you had the chance."

Old Red threw Diana a rueful, sidelong glance.

"I tried," he said.

That's when Fat Choy started blathering in high-pitched Chinese. I turned to find the hoppie pointing at us with a long, skeletal finger—and Big Queue pointing at us with Chan's gun.

"Fat Choy wants to know who you are," Charlie said, translating for us out of force of habit, perhaps.

"I will tell him," Madam Fong said, and she hocked out a wad of harsh, guttural sounds. Whatever she was calling us, I assumed it'd make "foreign devil" seem like a compliment.

Her words didn't calm Fat Choy. If anything, his eyes went even wider with fear.

Behind him, though, Hok Gup seemed to take some strength from what the madam said. She uncurled out of her cower, revealing herself to be taller than I'd first reckoned, and I saw what might have been a glimmer of hope upon her face—a hope that was directed at *us*. It brought out the beauty in her, and for the first time I noticed how her large eyes were both black and gleaming, dark yet flashing with life.

"What'd that pimp-mistress just say?" Old Red asked Charlie.

Charlie looked over at Scientific.

The highbinder answered the unasked question with an indifferent shrug. From the way he was holding Mahoney's gun, it was hard to tell if it was pointed at us or at Big Queue beyond us.

"That you're just a bunch of meddling fools," Charlie said. "Friends of Gee Woo Chan who don't know what they're trifling with."

"You put it too nice," Madam Fong sniffed. "But it doesn't matter. What matters is what we do with the *fan kwei*."

"Which 'we' are you referring to, exactly?" Diana asked. "Because it seems to me that you and Mr. Scientific here aren't necessarily a 'we.'"

"We are until you are dealt with," the madam replied.

Scientific said something to her in Chinese, and her cool went straight to a boil. She snapped something back fast, and within seconds they were yapping at each other at the same time, hands flapping at Hok Gup and Fat Choy and all us white folks.

"Care to translate?" I asked Charlie.

"Not this time."

"It's not hard to guess," Diana said. "They're debating. Haggling. Who gets who—"

"And who does what *to* who," I finished for her. "Miss, I am truly sorry we got you into this mess."

"Think back, Otto," the lady said. "Who talked you and your brother into helping Dr. Chan?"

I rubbed my chin. "Oh, yeah. I reckon you owe *us* an apology."

Then I had to back up and brace myself for more trouble—as if we could *be* in more trouble.

Mahoney was pushing himself to his feet.

"Just go ahead and shoot it out, why don't you?" he shouted at

Scientific. He whipped around to jeer at Big Queue, too. "You! You're no coward! Go on—drill the little bastard! You know he'll plug you the first chance he gets!"

The highbinders ignored him. Charlie didn't.

"That's what you'd really love, isn't it? If we'd all just kill each other."

"Save decent people a lot of bother," Mahoney sneered.

Gustav stepped past him, out toward the end of the pier. When he was between Scientific and Madam Fong, he stopped.

"Before you two come to some agreement or do each other in, either one, there's something you oughta know," he said to them. "It's *you* who don't know what you're triflin' with."

The hatchet man and the madam just kept talking around him.

Big Queue grunted and waggled the derringer at the rest of us, his meaning plain.

Get back. Over there.

My brother didn't budge.

"We know everything," he said. "What it's all about."

Big Queue took a step toward him.

"*Mah fung,*" Old Red said.

Madam Fong and Scientific finally shut up.

Big Queue froze.

Fat Choy frowned.

Hok Gup closed her eyes.

Mahoney blinked.

And me and Diana, we just gaped.

The only one who didn't act like he'd just been hit upside the head was Chinatown Charlie.

"What's syphilis got to do with anything?" he asked.

"Syphilis? Nothing," Old Red said. "I'm talkin' about *mah fung.*"

"But—," Charlie began.

Gustav stopped him with a raised hand. "Please, Charlie. It was plain as day you were lyin' about that medicine Fat Choy bought. I mean, Lee Kan doesn't exactly cater to high society fat cats, does he? Highbinders, hopheads, and chippies—that'd be his clee-on-tell. Yet he ain't gonna stock a remedy for Old Joe?"

My brother shook his head.

"Naw. We got the truth out of him after you cleared out. Then Miss Corvus here, she went straight to a telly-phone and rang up her friends at the *Examiner*. And whoo-eee, were they ever wound up. Front page stuff, they said. Am I right?"

Old Red looked back at Diana, one eyebrow arched.

How's that *for devious?* he was saying.

The lady nodded her approval. "The morning edition's probably on the presses even as we speak."

"Well, there you have it," Mahoney said. He turned a gloating grin on Scientific. "Within a few hours, the whole town's gonna know. The whole country. And if anything happens to us tonight, it's gonna go all the worse for your kind all the quicker."

Gustav spun around to face the copper. "Sounds like you know about the *mah fung,* too."

"Well, I didn't know the Chink word for it till just now . . . not that I care. But yeah. Sure." Mahoney looked over Old Red's shoulder, toward the end of the dock, his face contorting with disgust. "I know all about it."

He was staring at Hok Gup.

As was Fat Choy now. And funny thing—he looked every bit as revolted as Mahoney.

"*M-m-mah fung?*" he said with a stammer that built up into a screech. "*Mah fung!*"

Hok Gup opened her eyes—and seemingly opened the flood gates, too. In an instant, her face was wet with tears.

"*Mah fung?*" Fat Choy screamed again. When he didn't get an answer other than silent crying, he started to walk away, leaving the girl alone on the edge of the pier.

Hok Gup grabbed hold of his arm, babbling hysterically, her words quickly breaking down into wracking sobs. When he couldn't tug himself free, Fat Choy lifted up a hand and slapped the girl hard across the face.

She crumpled to the planks in a wailing heap.

The highbinder stalked away from her.

Scientific, Big Queue, Madam Fong, Mahoney—they all stood there staring down at Hok Gup with cold contempt, like she was some mewling, filthy animal that ought to be put out of its misery. Charlie at least had the decency to look more saddened than sickened. Yet, like the others, he made no move to help her. Which left it to us.

Old Red reached her first, squatting down and awkwardly patting her on the back. Diana came up next, whispering words of comfort Hok Gup probably couldn't even understand. Together, we helped her to her feet.

It was like lifting an anvil, and a closer look at the creases and bumps in the girl's bulky clothes told me why: Underneath the suit, I now saw, she was wearing Doc Chan's bulletproof chain-mail vest.

"You lie," Scientific said as we got Hok Gup upright. "You not know *mah fung*."

"What makes you say that, Sci?" I asked.

"It's obvious, you dumb son of a bitch." Mahoney jutted his chin out at the weeping, wobbly-kneed girl we were still holding up. "Nobody wants to touch a *leper*."

37

THE ISLAND OF DEATH

Or, the Last Pieces of the Puzzle Come Together, and It Isn't a Pretty Picture

There are certain words your body just reacts to, no brain work required. "Look out," for instance. Someone shouts it, you up and *look*. Same with "Fire!" or, if you're a drover, "Stampede!"

"Leper," I learned, is one of those words, too. The moment Mahoney said it, I found myself flinching back from Hok Gup, shoving away the slender arm I'd been supporting with such chivalry just a second before. Gustav and Diana had the same reaction—letting go, jerking back. Even after the shock wore off, we didn't stop moving away, shuffling back warily like Hok Gup was a puma crouched for a pounce instead of a sniveling girl alone and forlorn under the lantern at the end of the pier.

"I see it now," my brother muttered. "I see it . . . ."

We stopped next to Mahoney and Fat Choy. It certainly wasn't the most welcome company, but we couldn't have sought out better had we tried. Not with Scientific and Big Queue—and their guns—blocking our way back to the Ferry House.

"Yee Lock must've found out first . . . or suspected it, anyhow," Old Red said, his voice low and slow, like he was mumbling for his own ears only. "He'd have noticed the signs when he was inspectin' the gals over to Madam Fong's. But leprosy . . . that'd be a damn sight more serious than what the old man was used to. Crabs and the clap and what-have-you. So he brought in another doctor, just to be sure. One of the most respected healers in Chinatown. Did it right in front of my eyes, too."

"When he fetched Doc Chan yesterday," I said.

Gustav nodded. "Chan, he would've seen the danger straight off. And not just sickness-wise. That's why he went to Chun Ti Chu for money . . . and got it. Hok Gup"—he looked over at Mahoney—"she's the bomb that could blow up all of Chinatown, ain't she?"

The copper puffed out his chest and curled his lips into a haughty sneer. He may have been a prisoner, but he wasn't about to admit he was powerless. Even a chained dog can still bite.

"Not just Chinatown, Tex. A Chink whore *leper*? Spreading her filthy disease to white men? When word gets out—and it will, mark my words—they'll never let another slant eye into this country again."

"And that's so important to you?" Old Red asked, looking both perplexed and strangely saddened, as if what went on in Cathal Mahoney's mind wasn't just *a* mystery but *the* great mystery of mankind. "Worth killin' for?"

"What the hell are you talking about?" Mahoney snarled.

Scientific jumped in with his own "What do you say?" While Madam Fong contributed a "What?" I, for once, was the soul of brevity: All I said was "Huh?"

"Yee Lock is dead," Gustav said, turning first to the hatchet man, then the madam. "The sergeant here beat him to death."

"Why, you crazy little hick . . . ."

Mahoney took a step toward my brother. I took a step toward *him*. We stopped with our chests a hair's width apart.

"How'd you find out about the gal's leprosy if not from thrashin' the old man . . . huh, Sarge?" Old Red said. "I can't imagine anyone in Chinatown racin' to *you* with news like that. And don't forget—I seen how you work when we was at Little Pete's place. You're a feller likes to kick a man when he's down. Double him up holding his gut while you put your toe in—just like we found the old-timer. And his face?"

Gustav grimaced at the memory.

"Only thing could do that would be a brick or brass knuckles. I doubt if you got a brick on you, but I *know* you carry knucks . . . cuz you waved 'em under my nose not two hours ago."

Mahoney swung an arm out toward Scientific and Big Queue.

"Oh, like *they* don't have brass knuckles? Like they don't kick people? Open your eyes! Some Chinaman killed another Chinaman, that's all. It happens all the time—and nobody gives a damn. The real issue here is that girl. She's living, breathing poison! How many men are going to die because of *her*?"

For a moment, no one spoke, which spoke volumes in itself. Mahoney's pathetic attempt to change the subject, his obvious desperation— that said it all. We didn't have enough people out there to make a proper jury, but it was clear enough we'd reached a verdict: guilty.

Old Red broke the hush.

"I don't know about any other men dyin'. I've just been tryin' to work out what happened to *one*." He turned toward Hok Gup. "Gee Woo Chan."

The girl stared back at him, utterly still but for the wisps of dark hair that fluttered in the biting-cold breeze off the bay. She'd lost her bowler when Fat Choy hit her, letting the long, straight tresses pinned up inside cascade over her shoulders and down her back. Doc Chan's spectacles she'd taken off so as to better wipe the tears from eyes.

She had nothing to hide behind anymore, and even knowing there was something unclean, diseased inside her, I saw her true beauty at last. I saw the Black Dove.

Then, for the first time, I heard her, too. She started haltingly, stammering, but she picked up speed as she went along. Her voice had a musical quality to it, rising and falling so that it almost sounded like a melancholy song.

I didn't understand a word.

"Tell us what she's sayin', Charlie," Old Red said.

Charlie's eyes darted over to Scientific.

"For god's sake, Charlie," Diana snapped, "*speak for her!*"

"Alright, alright. I'll try," Charlie said. "But her Hoisanese . . . it's pretty bad."

"You mean she don't even speak Chinese?" I said.

"Barely. Just look at her—she's not from the mainland. She was probably grabbed off some little island in the South Seas. I bet she doesn't even know its name."

Charlie said something to the girl then, putting out both hands palms up and curling the fingers in twice. Coaxing.

Keep going.

She did.

"She says she liked him," Charlie said. "Gee Woo Chan. He was kind. Gentle."

The girl looked at Madam Fong, and I knew her words had turned bitter even before Charlie turned them into English.

"The madam treats her girls like caged animals, and she knew the heartless . . . uhhh . . ."

"Bitch?" Diana suggested.

"Yeah," Charlie said, avoiding Madam Fong's venom-spitting glare. "She knew the heartless bitch would toss her in the gutter when she was used up. So when Gee Woo Chan bought her, she was glad. Landing a husband like him—"

Fat Choy suddenly took an angry stomp toward the girl, eyes ablaze. Whatever she'd just said, he didn't like it. "—that was luck she hadn't even dared hope for," Charlie finished.

The gaunt highbinder spat something at Hok Gup, shaking his fist. I grabbed his bony, upraised wrist and jerked him back hard.

"Charlie, be so kind as to translate *this*," I said. " 'Leave the girl be or I'll snap you in two like a dried twig.' "

Charlie obliged, and Fat Choy backed away muttering.

Hok Gup watched the hophead shuffle away with an expression that seemed half-hateful, half-tender. Then she started talking again, and she was just plain misery through and through.

"After Gee Woo Chan brought her home, he told her the reason he'd bought her," Charlie said. "The numbness in her hands and feet, the bumps she'd started to notice on her face. They were the first signs of *mah fung*. Leprosy. She wasn't to be Gee Woo Chan's wife. She was to be sent to Molokai."

The girl stifled a sob as that last word left her lips, and even Charlie couldn't say it without a shudder. I'd read enough about the place in magazines and newspapers to feel a little chill myself.

"Leper colony out in the Hawaiian islands," I explained to my brother. I thought it best not to add what its nickname was: the Island of Death. I reckoned we were all feeling plenty morbid as it was.

Hok Gup choked back tears, fighting to finish her tale.

"Gee Woo Chan said he was sorry," Charlie said. "But it was the only place she could go. She couldn't stay in Chinatown. She couldn't stay with people. Not *normal* people. And when she heard that, she was so heartbroken, so frightened, so angry, she went wild. She kicked him, slapped him, threw things. She . . ."

Charlie gaped at the girl a moment, speechless. Yet I knew exactly which words were stuck in his throat. I'd felt them coming for a long time now.

I looked over at Gustav and saw that he'd been bracing for them, too. His mouth was puckered shut, his jaw clenched, as if there was something he was trying to keep from crawling up out of his gut.

Then he opened his mouth, and out it came.

"She killed him."

38

THE END

Or, The Black Dove Brings Her Tale of Woe to a Close

Hok Gup put her hands together as if praying, and as she continued with her story, fresh teardrops trickled from her dark eyes. It had grown so cold out there over the water I wouldn't have been surprised to see the tears freeze into icicles dangling from her apple cheeks.

"She wants you to know it was an accident," Charlie said, his voice husky, strained. "A statue she threw—it hit Gee Woo Chan in the back of the head. When she realized what she'd done, she was going to just run out the door, keep going for as long as she could. She didn't know what else to do. But then Fat Choy showed up looking for her, and she thought maybe she had a chance after all."

The girl turned toward Fat Choy, her palms still pressed together in a plea for understanding.

"Fat Choy was the only person who could help her," Charlie said. "So she told him what he wanted to hear. She loved him and she'd said as much to Gee Woo Chan and he'd flown into a rage—that's why she'd killed him. All lies. But she had no choice."

Fat Choy snorted scornfully, unmoved. I got the feeling he would have actually spit in her face if he hadn't been afraid I'd put a fist to his.

Hok Gup gave up on him and told the rest of her story straight to me and Gustav and Diana, the friends of the man she'd killed. Scientific, Madam Fong, Big Queue, even Charlie, her voice for the *fan kwei*—them she ignored.

"They faked the suicide," Charlie said, not just translating but condensing now, too. This part of the story we already knew. "They hid in Gee Woo Chan's basement. They tried to leave on the ferry to Oakland. They were caught."

"Yeah," I said under my breath. "Thanks to you."

"No. Thanks to *him*."

Charlie jerked his head at my brother, trying to dump all his guilt that way in the process.

"There's just one last thing I need to know," Old Red said, sounding weary. He'd already accepted the burden Charlie was loading him with—the *blame*—and I could see it weighing on him so clear it could have been a pack saddle strapped to his back. "Doc Chan didn't die of a blow to the head. He died from the gas. Did she know that? Did she *know* she and Fat Choy was killin' him when they left him up there on that bed?"

Charlie didn't even get through the asking. The look of shock on Hok Gup's face, the way she sobbed so hard it nearly bent her over double, that gave us our answer. If we needed any further proof, Fat Choy jumped in with panicky blabbing and finger pointing that needed no translation.

He didn't know. Hok Gup said Gee Woo Chan was dead. It was all her fault.

Mahoney whistled. "A leper *and* a murderer . . . two for the price of one . . . ."

There was a gleam in his eye, a hunger, almost as if he was a customer ogling the girl back at Madam Fong's. But it wasn't what he could do to her he was thinking of. It was what he could do *with* her. She was a bludgeon he still longed to have in his own hand.

"She ain't no murderer and she ain't your damn toy, neither," Gustav growled at him. "Charlie . . . tell her we'll help her. Tell her we'll . . . we'll . . . do *something*."

Charlie opened his mouth to speak.

"*Charlie*," Scientific snapped, and what followed we couldn't understand, though the gist was easy enough to guess. Charlie nodded, eyes down, shame-faced.

He'd been told it was time to shut up.

"You 'help' no one," Scientific said to us, and he gave Mahoney's Colt a little "Remember this?" waggle. "This is not for *fan kwei* to decide."

Who would decide, apparently, were the tongs: Scientific turned to Madam Fong, and the two of them got back to the angry wrangling they'd left off a few minutes before. The jury had been reduced to two, and we were all on trial this time—most likely for our lives.

"Listen," Mahoney hissed at us, turning his back to Charlie. "I don't like you, and you don't like me. But we're all in a jam now, and we need to work together."

He slipped his right hand into his jacket pocket, and I could picture the fingers coiling around brass stained with an old man's blood.

"Tiny," he whispered to me, "you take Little Pete's man. Your brother and I can rush the big one and the bitch. You . . . ." His eyes flicked over to Diana. "We need a distraction. Faint or go hysterical or something."

"Just so I understand," Diana replied, voice low and even and anything but hysterical, "you'll take reinforcements to go after the clumsy oaf with the derringer, while Otto—by himself—takes on the expert fighter holding *your* revolver?"

Mahoney leaned in closer, looming over the lady. "We don't have time to argue about this."

"Sure we do. We got the rest of our lives." I turned to Gustav. "What do you say?"

But he said not a word. Not then. He didn't even look at me. He was staring at Hok Gup.

She was utterly alone. No one beside her, only the black bay behind her. We couldn't understand the debate raging over our fates, but she surely could—and she didn't like what she heard. Her wracking sobs had quieted, but the tears kept coming. She watched first Madam Fong, then Scientific, and from the way she shook her head and widened her eyes, it was clear neither one was suggesting she be packed off to a cushy sanitarium to be looked after by the best and brightest. The worst and darkest . . . that's what awaited her.

Eventually, she couldn't take any more. She turned her back to the rest of us, facing the bay.

"Snap out of it, would you?" Mahoney murmured at my brother. "We've got to do something. Now. It's our last—"

"No!" Old Red cried out.

He rushed for the girl. She was walking away from us, back straight, steps quick and steady.

The only problem was she had nowhere to walk *to* except the end of the pier. And that's where she went . . . and beyond.

She dropped out of sight so fast it was as if God Himself reached down and plucked her right out of existence between eye blinks. We heard the splash, but by the time we reached the edge of the dock, the only sign of her in the water below was a little cloud of churned-up foam. And then even that was gone, washed under the pier by the ceaseless pushing of the tide.

My brother started to shrug off his jacket, but I grabbed him by the shirt-front with both hands.

"*No*. The current's too strong, the water's too cold. You'd drown for sure."

"You couldn't reach her anyway, Gustav," Diana said. "Dr. Chan's chain mail—it pulled her straight down. She's already on the bottom by now."

"But she's still alive down there!" Old Red wailed, trying to worm his way out of my grip. "She's still alive!"

"Not for long," Diana said softly. "Then she's free."

Gustav stopped his squirming, yet I didn't let him go. We were right on the edge, where one step—one second's desperation and despair—meant death.

There was a thud somewhere behind us, then another splash. When we whirled around toward the sound, we found Scientific leaning out over the water about twenty-five feet back.

"Very brave. Very foolish," he said gravely. "Sgt. Mahoney . . . he jump in to save girl. Long way down." The hatchet man shook his head and shrugged. "I think he land on his head."

By the time we'd scrambled over to where Scientific was standing, there was no sign of the Coolietown Crusader in the roiling waters below. We didn't hear anyone thrashing around in the water or crying out for help, either—nor did we expect to.

Needless to say, I didn't have to worry about Old Red attempting a rescue this time. Mahoney was beyond our saving even if we'd wanted to save him.

Dark as it was out there, the body'd have to stay right where it'd landed for us to have the slightest chance of spotting it, and that wasn't likely with the bay's unpredictable currents. The waves had probably already pushed it underneath the pier, and from there the S.S. *Mahoney* could sail just about anywhere. Come morning, it might be spotted bobbing off the Union Street Wharf . . . or it might be halfway to Monterey. There was no way to say.

As we stood there peering over the side of the dock, Scientific, Charlie, Madam Fong, and Big Queue formed a sort of ring around us. Fat Choy lingered behind them, either too rattled or too opium-addled to slip away when he had the chance.

"So," Scientific said, "what to do?"

I looked at Old Red.

Diana looked at Old Red.

Old Red looked at nothing. He just kept staring down into the darkness, lost in thought. And I mean truly *lost*—like he didn't know where he was or how he'd got there.

I put a firm hand on his shoulder. Not so much to anchor him to the dock. More to anchor him to *me*.

"There's nothing *to* do," Diana said to Scientific. "Hok Gup is dead, and Sgt. Mahoney is . . . lost. That's the end of it."

"You don't go to police?" Scientific asked, looking skeptical.

Diana shook her head. "The sergeant was no friend of ours, as I'm sure you saw. And even if we did go to the police, they wouldn't thank us for it. Zealots aren't good for business. The S.F.P.D. won't be sad to see Mahoney gone. And as for what happens amongst the Chinese . . . well, you know as well as I do, the police don't want to be bothered with that. And it's certainly no concern of our employers."

The hatchet man nodded thoughtfully. "Yes. Southern Pacific?"

"That's right," I said, praying Scientific hadn't made the same telephone call as Chun Ti Chu.

If it wasn't just me and Gustav and Diana out there by our lonesome— if there was some big unseen *we* backing us—the three of us might just have a chance. Mahoney wouldn't be missed, but Scientific would have to figure we might be.

"All done, then?" he said. "On honor?"

Diana nodded. "On our honor."

She turned to me.

"Absolutely," I said. "On every shred I got."

We both looked at Old Red, dreading what he might say.

Which turned out to be nothing. He simply nodded glumly, mute.

Scientific spoke to Charlie in Chinese, and our former guide replied with a nod of his own.

"Just so you know, I'm vouching for you," Charlie told us. "You may be *fan kwei*, but . . . I'd trust you."

Madam Fong shook a finger at us and piped up with what sounded like an objection. I'm guessing *fan kwei* were *fan kwei* in her book, and we weren't to be trusted no matter who vouched for us.

Scientific sighed, stepped toward her talking softly—then lightning-quick whipped to the side, stripped the derringer from Big Queue's hand and sent a foot up into the highbinder's broad face, all in one smooth motion. The burly *boo how doy* slowly toppled backwards like a felled tree while Madam Fong shrieked with rage.

"You much lucky my boss like you," Scientific chided us lightly, not winded in the slightest. He paused just long enough to throw both the derringer and Mahoney's Colt into the bay. "Now go . . . and never come back to Chinatown. I told don't kill you unless have to." He shrugged. "Next time, maybe have to."

"If he doesn't do it, we will!" Madam Fong screeched as Diana and I dragged Gustav away. "Set foot in Chinatown and we'll hack it off! Kwong Ducks never forget!"

"I thought that was elephants," I muttered under my breath.

As we drew closer to the Ferry House, Old Red found his footing and shrugged free of us.

"We can grab us a hack out on East Street or Market," he said, his voice gaining strength with each word. "Don't know how we'll pay for it, but we ain't got no choice if we're gonna beat the rest of 'em back."

"Beat the rest of 'em back *where*, exactly?"

"To Chinatown, of course. We got one last thing to take care of there."

"What about your word of honor?" Diana asked.

"A nod ain't a word," Gustav said. "Anyway, what good's a feller's honor if it gets folks killed?"

He glanced back at the end of the pier. All we could see there now were dim shapes shifting in the red-tinged lantern light.

"What good's the truth if it's just gonna lead to *that*?"

39

A WEE SPOT OF UNTIDINESS

Or, Loose Ends Are Tied Up Even as Old Red Comes Unraveled

Our last errand in Chinatown was a return trip to Yee Lock's pharmacy. Wong Woon was mightily surprised to see us—and downright stupefied when we cut him loose.

"The girl's gone for good, that's all you need to know," Old Red said as the portly detective sat up and rubbed his wrists. "Yee Lock's killer, too. That part of things is done."

"And . . . the rest?" Woon asked warily.

"Chun Ti Chu will hear from us about that tomorrow," Diana said, just as we'd agreed during the hansom-ride over. "I suggest you help him accept our perspective on the matter."

"We could've just left you here hog-tied next to *him*." I jerked my head at Yee Lock's bloodied body without looking at it. I'd had enough of that kind of thing for one day. "So we're savin' you big *mien tzu* lettin' you go like this. Don't you forget it."

Woon ruminated a moment, eyeing us each in turn, then gave a jowl-shaking nod.

"Alrighty, then," I said. "Let's get the hell out of here."

Our hack was waiting around the corner, and Old Red, Diana, and I hurried out to it, climbed inside, and made our way to our last stop of the night: Diana's hotel, the Occidental on Montgomery Street. It's not the fanciest digs in Frisco, but it's close, and I expected a doorman to hustle me and my brother out the service entrance any minute. Diana seemed to feel right at home, though, and as long as we stuck close to her we were spared the bum's rush.

After a brief chat with the wax mustache who ran the place, Diana collected enough cash from the hotel safe to pay off our cab and secure a room for me and Gustav. My brother didn't cotton much to bunking on Diana's bill—or borrowing money for tickets to Oakland, as we also did—but we had no choice, broke as we were. Talk about a loss of *mien tzu*.

We said our good nights in the lobby, agreeing to meet there again the next morning to wrap everything up. We'd done some planning since leaving the pier, but what had actually happened out there we'd avoided like the . . . well, like something one avoids. Diana came closest to speaking of it as we parted for the night.

"Please . . . *sleep well*," she said to Old Red, and she reached out, took his hands in hers, and gave them a squeeze.

Gustav pretended he didn't know what she meant, grunting out a "You, too" as he pulled back and headed for the stairs.

"Pleasant dreams," I said to the lady before hurrying after him.

She just smiled grimly, looking like she was thinking, "Not likely."

She stayed behind as Old Red and I trudged upstairs—she had an urgent call to make on the manager's private telephone.

Although we'd asked for the smallest, cheapest accommodations the hotel had available, Gustav and I soon found ourselves in a room with almost as much floor space as the farmhouse in which we'd both been born. The bed alone seemed as big as our entire kitchen growing up, and it was so cushy-soft it could've been stuffed with cotton candy.

After undressing and turning down the gas-lit wall lamps, I stretched out on one side of the bed, my brother on the other.

"Just so you know . . . I don't wanna talk about it," Old Red said. He was flat on his back, face pointed upward, and I imagined him there searching the blackness above us for answers that weren't there.

"I understand."

I let a moment slide by in silence.

"Of course, if you change your mind, you can always—"

"I said I don't wanna talk about it."

"Sure. Fine. We'll just let it lie, then."

"*Good.*"

"But, you know," I added a minute later, "it can really help a man unburden himself if he's willing to—"

The bed creaked, linens rustled, and I felt something spongy and thick thump across my face.

"Alright, I'll shut up," I said, voice muffled by linen and feathers. "But just for that, you ain't gettin' your pillow back."

And he didn't. When I awoke the next morning, Gustav was still lying there on his back staring straight up at the ceiling.

"Sweet Jesus, Brother," I said through a yawn. "Did you catch yourself a single wink?"

Old Red rolled out of bed and got to dressing himself. "I don't want to talk about it."

He couldn't avoid talking forever, though. At the appointed hour, we found Diana awaiting us, and it was decided we should hash out the final particulars in the Occidental's dining room.

Having not eaten since noonish of the day before, when I'd snagged myself a handful of pork buns while on the run down Dupont, I was hungry enough to eat not only a horse but its saddle, bridle, and probably rider, too. Sadly, the hotel offered only a "continental breakfast," which (to my considerable disappointment) translates as "no taters, no grits, no eggs, no meat." Still, I managed to fill my plate, and as Diana gave us her report, I had to peer at her around a pile of pastries that reached nearly to the ceiling.

"I was able to reach Col. Crowe's friend Dr. Battles last night. He didn't know much about leprosy himself, but he consulted with a colleague and called me back early this morning. I was told the disease *is* communicable, but it's not highly contagious. You may have heard of Father Damien? The famous leper priest of Molokai?"

I nodded.

Old Red just stared. He had no heap of sweets before him to peek around, just a cup of coffee and an unbuttered—and untasted—slice of bread.

"Well . . . he was on the island for years working with lepers every day before he finally contracted the disease. You almost have to try to catch it."

"So Hok Gup didn't pose no real threat to nobody?" I asked.

"Probably not, if you're just talking about the leprosy. But the stigma attached to it, the uses it could be put to—"

"We talked all that through last night," Gustav cut in irritably. "If the gal wasn't infectin' folks, we'd keep our mouths shut. That's what Doc Chan died for—so this wouldn't get out to foamy-mouthed SOBs like Mahoney. The thing to do now is telly-phone Chun Ti Chu and—"

It was Diana's turn to interrupt now, and it looked like she enjoyed taking it.

"Already done. I spoke to Chun Ti Chu this morning and offered the terms for our silence. He said he needed some time to think on it . . . then rang back two minutes later and accepted."

"My, oh my," I marveled through a mouthful of Danish. "You *are* persuasive, ain't you?"

"When and where?" was all Old Red said.

"Portsmouth Square. Ten o'clock."

Gustav snatched his hat off the seat next to him and hopped to his feet.

"Well, what are we sittin' around here for?"

"Cuz I'm starvin' and we don't need to leave for another half hour?" I suggested.

"I ain't gonna chance this just so's you can pack yourself fulla strudel," Old Red snapped, and he whipped around and stalked off.

"Sorry, Otto," Diana said as she got up to follow him out.

A moment later, I was on the fly behind her—with an entire cruller in my mouth and pockets abulge with cinnamon buns.

I finished my breakfast on a bench in the Plaza. Diana sat beside me. Gustav paced.

And then there they were at the southwest corner of the square, one big and round, the other small and scraggy as a stick. They lingered there a moment, coming no closer. That was the deal. We just wanted to see them together: Wong Woon and Hok Gup's brave little friend from Madam Fong's. Ah Gum.

But then the girl spotted us, and the deal didn't matter. She bolted toward us.

"I really don't wanna have this conversation," my brother muttered.

"I don't think you got much choice."

Ah Gum was making a beeline straight for him.

"You find her? You find her?" she panted as she drew up close. She jerked her head back at Woon, who was clumping up the path after her. "Fat one tell me nothing."

She stopped directly in front of Old Red, eyes on him alone.

"Ummm . . . you see . . . the thing is, miss . . . Hok Gup's . . ."

Gustav looked away, as if the girl's hopeful gaze was the noonday sun—something so bright it pained a man to face it.

"Hok Gup's gone," he said. He forced himself to look at her again. "That's all I can say. That . . . and I'm sorry."

Ah Gum's slight shoulders went into such a slump it took a full inch off her height—and she didn't have much height to spare, teeny thing that she was.

She blinked up at my brother, brow knit in confusion.

"And now *you* buy *me*?"

"Oh, no no no no no," Old Red stammered. "We . . . uhhh, well . . . we kinda talked this acquaintance of ours into buyin' you off Madam Fong. Not for hisself, you understand. For *you*."

"Ol' Woon here's gonna take you to the Presbyterian Mission House," I said, giving the detective a slap on his broad back as he lumbered up to join us. "Over there, you can learn you a trade, pick up some more English. Maybe even scrape up enough money to get back to your family in China."

Ah Gum finally spared me a glance—or a glare, more like. To her, it seemed, I was just something that dragged along after my brother, a glob of muck stuck to his heel.

"Thank you," she said. To Gustav, of course.

Woon shrugged my hand off his shoulder and said something to the girl in Chinese. "Time to get a move on," apparently, for she nodded and started toward him. After a couple steps, though, she whirled around, dashed back to my brother, and planted another kiss on him, just as she had the day before. She even whispered in his ear again.

The blushes Diana had slapped across Old Red's face the past few days had nothing on the one he was wearing now. Ah Gum may as well have slathered his cheeks with strawberry jam.

"Yeah, alright . . . uh-hum . . . that's mighty sweet of you," he croaked hoarsely as the girl backed away. "Good-bye, now, miss. And *fat choy* to you."

Ah Gum gave him a little curtsy—and a little smile—before turning and walking off with Wong Woon. Needless to say, I didn't get so much as a wave or even a "Good riddance."

I turned toward Gustav set to needle him about his newfound way with the ladies, but the expression on his face stopped me cold. I was expecting embarrassment, relief, chagrin, maybe even satisfaction, for once—just about anything other than the bitter disappointment I saw.

Old Red didn't just look like his dog had died. He looked like he'd just lost his favorite *horse*. And that's about as glum as a cowboy can get.

"That's it, then," he said. "It's over."

It wasn't over for him, though. I could see that. It wouldn't be for a long while.

Diana sensed it, too.

"Gustav . . . ," she began.

"So what're you gonna tell your boss, Col. Crowe?" he asked. "We solved us a mystery but got a girl killed in the process? An old man and the cop that done him in, too? But it all balances out fine in the end . . . cuz we got one little chippy out of the whorin' business?"

"I'll tell the colonel what I always tell him," Diana said. "The truth. And I don't think he'll see it as a failure. He knows these sorts of things rarely work themselves out neatly."

"Oh, is that what you'd call what happened last night?" Old Red snipped. "A lack of 'neatness'? A wee spot of untidiness?"

"Solving mysteries and solving problems are two very different things. You can't blame yourself because—"

"Well, who *should* I blame, then? Last three 'cases' I've stuck my nose in, I've got myself shot, a train wrecked, and a woman drowned. I may as well go back to punchin' cattle for all the good I done!"

"You've done a lot of good with your deducifyin', Brother. If not for you—"

"Feh!" Gustav said.

Then he waved his hands over his head and barked it out again. Not just to me, but to Diana, to the Plaza, to the world, to creation. It was a declaration, that one little sound. A regular manifesto.

"*Feh!*"

He was done.

My brother spun on his heel and stomped off toward the southeast corner of the square—and most likely the Ferry House a ways beyond it.

"I'm sorry. I gotta go after him," I said to Diana. "My brother, he's . . . well, he's just . . . ."

"I understand."

I surprised her—and myself—with a smile.

"You know," I said, "I truly believe you do. That's one of the things I love about you, Diana Corvus."

The lady flushed so pink she could've passed for a flamingo.

"Otto," she said as I turned to go. "If I can't find you again . . . find *me.*"

"Miss, you got yourself a deal."

As I hustled after my brother, I spotted another familiar figure up ahead of him. The Anti-Coolie League sandwich-board man was planted just outside the Plaza handing out pamphlets.

"Well, if it isn't my Kraut friends!" he called out when he saw us. "Do me a favor, Fritz—don't run me down this time, huh?"

He laughed at his own funny, then stepped into Old Red's path.

"Thought I spotted you back there in the square socializing with a couple Chinks."

He shook his head reproachfully, and when he spoke again he did it in the slow, overenunciated manner folks use when addressing the village idiot.

"Remember, boys: No . . . mixee . . . with . . . Chinee . . . ja?"

"Otto," Gustav said as he sidestepped the man. He hadn't even looked back to see if I was behind him. "Would you mind?"

"Not at all, Brother."

"Hey," the sandwich man said, "you two speak—"

That was as far as he got.

I did him the favor he asked: I didn't run him down.

I just flattened his damn nose.

40

THE BEGINNING

Or, Gustav and I Turn Chicken, and a Long-Lost Bird Comes Home to Roost

My brother and I said nary another word to each other all the way back to Oakland. Gustav didn't even want to hear a Holmes tale to help him get across the bay without barfing. Nor did he ask me to read him anything that night or the next day or the day after. I didn't ask him why.

Old Red's feelings are like a rabbit in its hole. You don't draw either out with prodding or coaxing. You just have to wait. They'll come out in their own good time.

Eventually, we got our hands on a new *Harper's,* and the lure of Doc Watson's latest story—"The Greek Interpreter"—was more than Old Red could resist. I was immensely amused to discover that ol' Sherlock had a brother . . . who was *smarter* than him, but I resisted the urge to guy Gustav about it. Even weeks after Gee Woo Chan's death, my brother was still mopey and morose—and damned tired, too, for the only times I actually saw him sleeping he was twitching like a Mexican jumping bean.

"Very neat. Very tidy," he said when I finished the new story for the first time (though the tale actually struck me as neither).

Neat, tidy endings were much on both our minds by then. This very manuscript was well under way, and I knew I couldn't carry it through to its conclusion without cooking up some kind of bunkum. We had Hok Gup's leprosy—not to mention a small handful of murders—to keep mum about. I couldn't very well go blabbing it all out in the pages of some dime novel . . . assuming someone published the thing in the first place.

"Just put it down like it happened," Old Red said when he saw me struggling over my pencil and paper one day. "You can tack on some bull-shit happy ending later."

"Yeah, I suppose. That's the big advantage of writin' it rather than livin' it, ain't it? You can always go back and change the ending."

My brother just grunted and wandered away.

Despite his advice, I couldn't push my way through to the end of the book. When our last pennies left our pockets, we drifted up to Sonoma County hoping to hire on as hands at one of the cattle spreads thataway. Unfortunately, it was autumn by then, and the ranches were letting men go for the season, not filling the bunkhouse with more. So the only work we could find was sexing chicks and sweeping floors in a factory-scale hatchery. It was a chickenshit job, literally, and I ended each day with eyes and back athrob. We'd always thought cowboying was tough, but it turned out birdboying wasn't any easier.

I didn't have much extra time or pep for the hard work of writing, and our only day off I always spent the same way: taking the train down to Oakland to check for messages at our old haunt, the Cosmopolitan House. (I didn't trust the management there to hold mail for us more than a few days, let alone forward it.)

In the first month after our move, my weekly pilgrimage paid off twice. The first time it was with a package: my first stab at a book, returned (at my expense) from the offices of Harper & Brothers Publishers in New York City. The second time it was a telegram, short and not altogether sweet.

HELLO BOYS STOP COLONEL NOT BITING STOP BEING MY MOST QUOTE PERSUASIVE UNQUOTE STOP HOPE YOU ARE STILL INTERESTED IN DETECTIVE WORK STOP WILL HAVE GOOD NEWS ONE DAY STOP DIANA C FULL STOP

Full stop indeed. That's what it seemed like things had come to—until the day I found a letter awaiting me at the Cosmo.

"Pack up your war bags," I told Gustav when I got back to our little boarding house room that night. "Tomorrow mornin', we are on our way east."

My brother looked up from the issue of *Old Sleuth Library* he'd been flipping through on the bed. He had nothing but disgust for Holmes's detecting rivals, yet he had to admit their picture-packed magazines were easier "reading" for an unlettered man like himself.

"What are you talkin' about?"

I pulled the letter from my pocket and opened it with a crisp snap of the wrist.

"Dear Mr. Amlingmeyer," I read out. "Thank you for sending us your book, *On the Wrong Track, or Lockhart's Last Stand, An Adventure of the Rails*. We would like to publish it *immediately*, and stand ready to wire to your bank the sum of two hundred dollars for the right to do so. Please contact us via telegram as soon as possible if you find this acceptable. Enclosed is a contract, which we will need you to sign and return to us without delay. In your book, you mention other works that you have written about yourself and your brother, and we request that you send any and all such material to us for possible publication. Everyone here at Smythe House feels as though we have made a great discovery in you, and we have high hopes for a long and mutually beneficial partnership. Sincerely yours, Urias Smythe, Proprietor, Smythe & Associates Publishing Ltd."

My brother blinked at me a moment, so stunned the magazine he was holding actually slipped from his hands.

"You're pullin' my leg," he finally managed to say.

"I'm nowhere near your leg, Brother. This is the real thing. You are about to become an honest-to-goodness dime novel hero."

Old Red scowled at that.

"I ain't no hero."

"You are in my book."

I glanced over at the teeny writing desk crammed into one corner of our cramped room. Atop it was my unfinished opus, *The Black Dove*— which wouldn't remain unfinished much longer, I knew then.

"Correction. You are in my book*s*."

"Yeah, well . . . things in books ain't always what they seem," Gustav muttered. "So what was that you said about us headin' east?"

"Don't you see?" I waved Urias Smythe's letter over my head like a rallying flag. "This works out, we finally got options for once in our lives. We could go to Ogden and stick this under Col. Crowe's nose, see if it changes his mind about hirin' us. Or we could go to Denver or Dallas, whatever town we like, and do what we never even thought about doin' before: start our *own* detective agency. Hell, we could even go to Kansas, buy back the family farm, and just get to sodbustin' again, if that's what you really want."

"Well, which'll it be? It's your money."

"Feh, as you like to say. It's *our* money. And there's no way I'm decidin' what to do with it solo. I choose the wrong way, you'll never let me hear the end of it. Naw. I'm leavin' it up to you."

I headed for my writing table and took a seat. I hadn't done any work there in days, but a fresh pencil was waiting for me, I found. It had been sharpened to a needle's point, no doubt by my brother's pocketknife.

"You can't decide right now, fine," I said as I picked the pencil up. "Sleep on it."

I found where I'd last left off—Chapter thirty-three, our gruesome discovery in Yee Lock's shop—and put pencil to paper. The words came easily, perhaps because I'd found a sort of happy ending at last, and I only paused to resharpen the pencil or relieve my bladder.

Every time I turned around, I saw Old Red stretched out on the bed, eyes wide open. He didn't say a word for hours, not until sometime in the middle of the night.

"Brother?"

"Yeah," I said without turning around.

"Congratulations. I'm . . . I'm proud of you, you know."

"I didn't know that, actually. So thank you for sayin' it."

"Yeah, alright. Just don't get all swell-headed about it."

I grunted out a chuckle and shook my (swollen) head. Then I got back to work.

Just as I find myself reaching the end here, the light of a new day has started streaming in the window. A minute ago, I put down my pencil—it's little more than a stub now—and stood up for a stretch before tackling the last lines of this book. Gustav, I saw, had finally fallen asleep.

It was a silent slumber, with no tossing or turning. The most peaceful sleep my brother's had in ages.

When he wakes up, I'll ask him what he dreamed of.

ACKNOWLEDGMENTS

The author wishes to thank:

Dashiell Hammett and Robert Towne—for inspiration.

Crafty Keith Kahla, editor, poodle rancher (retired)—for picking up the ball and running with it.

Elyse Cheney, agent, butt kicker (still active)—for getting the ball rolling (and not letting it stop).

Sally Richardson, Andy Martin, Matthew Shear, and everyone else at St. Martin's—for keeping the faith.

Ben Sevier, Big Red's Posse (especially Don Collins, "Hungry Bob" Bartlett, Joan Gallo, Lee Ann Nelson, and Matthew Szewczyk), and more booksellers than I can list here (and I'm afraid I'd leave someone out if I tried)—for giving us something to keep faith in.

The Mystery Writers of America, the Independent Mystery Book-sellers Association, the Private Eye Writers of America, and the always-fabulous folks of Bouchercon—for noticing.

Herbert Asbury, author of *The Barbary Coast*; Richard H. Dillon, au-thor of *The Hatchet Men*; Evelyn Wells, author of *Champagne Days of San Francisco*; and last but not least (*most*, in fact, because she's willing to an-swer incredibly strange questions from total strangers), Judy Yung, author of *Unbound Feet: A Social History of Chinese Women in San Francisco*—for lighting the way.

(Additional light was shed by Tom Carey of the San Francisco Public Library's San Francisco History Center, Doris Tseng of the San Francisco Public Library's Chinese Center, Robert Crowe of the Telephone EXchange Name Project, Linda Lee of All About Chinatown Tours, and Fisher L. Forrest of . . . well, he's just a guy, but he sure knows a lot about guns.)

Helen Chin and Cecily Hunt—for helping me look good (no easy feat).

Mark and Alyssa Nickell—for helping me stay sane.

Billie Bloebaum, Aldo Calcagno, "Cap'n Bob" Napier, and Matt Nigro—for getting me there.

Kate and Mojo and Mar—for being there.